No End To The Lies

A JOHN MORGAN NOVEL

Trish
thank you for keeping John
Morgan alive.

D.

PubliBook IRELAND

ISBN: 978-0-9574252-7-9

Published in 2013 by **PubliBook Ireland**
an imprint of **CUE | Design, Media & Marketing Solutions**
Bective Villa – Bective Street – Kells, Co. Meath, Ireland

A CIP Catalogue record for this book is available from
The British Library and the Irish Copyright Libraries.

Designed, typeset, printed and bound in Ireland by **PubliBook Ireland**

www.publibookireland.com

No End To The Lies

A JOHN MORGAN NOVEL

DARREN DARKER

For

ADAM

ACKNOWLEDGMENTS

This is the second novel in the John Morgan series which in its own way was both harder and easier to write. Easier in the sense that I didn't need to create the character and his environment but harder as I knew that he needed to grow in both depth and personality. I worked hard to make sure that it was a worthy successor to 'Under An Irish Sky', hopefully once you read it you will all agree!

I need to thank my sister for enduring rough draft after rough draft without complaint. As before, I also owe a lot to the wonderful Deirdre Handy for her wonderful and often brutal editing of the original draft. Two of the readers of 'Under An Irish Sky' allowed themselves to be guinea pigs for this novel and I want to take this opportunity to thank them as well – Ramona P. & Catherine K. Their opinions helped give the novel a more rounded feel.

For support, love and advice, I wish to thank my mother, Catherine & Ryan S, The extended Winter's family; Ciara L. and the entire Doyle Family; Derek L, Rob M, Olivia M, Paul O'S, Frank O'G, Keith G. and Rachel along with all the lads at A Plus Service Centre in Bray.

I also want to acknowledge the hard work and effort of my publisher, PubliBook Ireland, without them this book would have taken a lot longer to get published and not look half as well. Not to forget Trevor Chow for the cool Double D logo. Thanks guys!

Thanks, See you all again in the next John Morgan novel – 'Fighting Back'.

DD

Darren Darker

Darren Darker was born in Dublin in 1971. He is the proud father of one son, Adam and lives in Bray Co. Wicklow.

He is an avid reader since a young age, when he would devour books by Sven Hassell, Agatha Christie and anything else that he could get his hands on.

Now a successful businessman he previously worked part time as a Doorman in various bars and niteclubs in Dublin and Bray, a role that helped him to understand the human condition and gave him an insight into the seedy underbelly of Irish society. A perfect nurturing ground for his writing !

Details of Darren Darker's Under The Irih Sky – the first installement of the John Morgan Novel series – are available at the end of this volume. You may also see www.darrendarker.ie for more information on 'John Morgan' and other characters.

Prologue

The tall man stood back into the shadow of the deep doorway of the office building. He did it not just because he did not want to be noticed but because of the heavy rain shower that had come out of nowhere. Deep in the shadows, he could hardly be seen except by the most observant passer-by, as he was dressed in black from head to toe, including a black hoodie, which he was wearing up to help hide his face. As he stood there damp and shivering, he looked up into the dark dreary wet night, wishing that he had brought a heavier overcoat with him, but the earlier weather report hadn't forecast rain.

The doorway in which he was standing was at the junction of three Dublin city streets, just off the busy premium shopping area around Grafton Street. His position gave him a great view of all three approaches so that nobody could follow him without being spotted. He knew from the one-way layout of the streets, which way the car he was waiting for would be coming from, but was wary of being seen so he shrank into the shadows and kept a close eye on everyone coming and going from each of the three directions.

He had never met his employer in circumstances like these before. In the six months that he had been working for him, they had met twice, both times outside of the city in a secluded spot well away from prying eyes and accidental encounters. Their meetings were normally meticulously planned and unhurried. But the murders of two members of the gang in less than seven days and the subsequent rapid disintegration of a very lucrative business empire required that drastic measures be taken. His phone call to his foreign based employer was outside of their normal routine and had not gone down well, but events beyond his control were influencing his reactions. Risks had to be taken, but were always minimised. Unfortunately, this high stakes visit during a time of heightened Garda surveillance of gangland members couldn't be avoided.

It was six o'clock on a dark December evening and although it was raining, it had turned bitterly cold. Every time he exhaled, the vapour could be seen hanging in the air before dissipating along with the other moisture streaming down from the heavens. The sudden heavy rain was helping to keep people off the streets even though the normally busy streets of the capital were relatively quiet that night anyway. At this time of year there was a lull in the otherwise hectic pedestrian traffic as all of the offices were closed for the Christmas holidays and although the department stores premature January sales had already started they hadn't as yet picked up any momentum. Recession or no recession, it was the calm before the shopping storm.

At one point an unmarked Garda car had cruised up along the narrow road. From the distance it looked like any other 2002 registered Ford Mondeo but the man skulking in the doorway instinctively knew what it was.

And he immediately tensed.

If he had been a dog his hackles would have risen. From both the streetlights and the light pouring out from the shop fronts, he could make out the shape of two men sitting in the front seats as the car rolled towards him. There was no doubt about it they were Gardaí all right, he thought. Only the Gardaí would wear their uniforms as they cruised around in an unmarked car. It was like they got half of the idea but the full concept of being inconspicuous hadn't quite clicked with them yet. As they neared his hiding spot, the man in the shadows pressed himself back as far as he could in the darkened doorway, flattening his back up against it. He unconsciously held his breath as he tilted his head to the ground, his hood completely hiding his face from the passing vehicle. The Gardaí either didn't see him or feel that he warranted any attention as the unmarked patrol car glided by without stopping, its occupants oblivious to the very dangerous man standing only feet from them. Relieved the man hiding in the shadows watched the car as it disappeared up the narrow street around a corner and out of sight.

Of the variety of different people passing him by, one man walking towards him grabbed his attention. He was on his own and talking aloud to himself while moving his arms very animatedly, oblivious to the pelting rain that was soaking him to the skin. Even though from his clothes he did not look like an escaped mental patient, the man in the shadows thought that he was obviously touched in the head until he passed him by. It was only then that he saw that the man had one of those Bluetooth earpieces hanging off the side of his head.

He continued waiting huddled in the doorway, watching the passers-by. He was disgusted to see one young woman carrying an armful of expensive brand name shopping bags, ignorantly forcing an old woman in a tattered raincoat off the path and into the narrow road where she was almost knocked down by an oncoming car. The once mighty Celtic tiger, the economic pride of Europe, seemed to have reared some very bad cubs. As far as he was concerned, they were all losers.

He was better than them, they didn't know it yet but they soon would.

All of Ireland would know of him soon.

He glanced at his wrist watch, the illuminated face of his expensive Tag Hauer watch told him it had just gone five past six. His normally prompt employer was unusually late for their meeting. He imagined that the sudden arrangements probably had a big part to play. But just as he was wondering if he should call him to check if everything was all right, a pristine black Range Rover with tinted windows cruised slowly up to the junction and stopped, its rear brake lights flashing vivid red momentarily in the drizzling rain.

The man in the shadows stepped out of the doorway and jumped in. The interior courtesy light in the jeep had been turned off so that when one of the doors opened, no light illuminated the secretive occupants within. All that was visible was a large dark shape sitting brooding in the back, his hardened face occasionally illuminated by the glow from a large cigar. While he couldn't be sure, the man from the shadows thought that he looked angry. This was a very bad sign. You didn't make a man like this mad. It was tantamount to letting a dog suffering from rabies into a crèche full of crying children.

It would get very bloody, very quickly.

The big vehicle moved off even before the door had been shut properly. To anyone but the closest and most observant of onlookers the jeep had never even stopped.

"How was your flight?" the man from the shadows asked the older heavy-set man in an attempt to lighten the mood as he pulled down his damp hood and wiped the few drops of rain from his face.

John Connolly was in his early fifties, his face scarred from being in several brutal fights back in the day where guns were unheard of. In those days if you wanted someone dead, you did it yourself.

Up close and personal.

You got your hands dirty or nobody respected you.

But now with his new home in the Costa del Sol in Spain he, unlike many of his counterparts, kept well away from any known gangsters. He was eager to build a new life, to separate himself from his inglorious past and adopt the persona of the successful businessman abroad. In Spain, he was a model citizen, paid his taxes and donated to charity all while wearing exceedingly expensive suits in an attempt to hide the vicious animal within.

"Rough and fucking ready", was the terse reply the man from the shadows got. "The customer service was terrible. Nobody wants to fucking work at this time of year. Everybody just seems so miserable, going around with long faces and bad attitudes. Let me tell you my young friend that the Christmas spirit is long fucking dead".

"It's gone much too commercial", the man from the shadows cautiously agreed, knowing that he should side with him whatever the statement.

"You can say that again".

"Are you going to be in the country long?" the Shadowman quizzed politely.

"Not long, just for a few hours. I fly back early in the morning. I only came over here to try and sort this mess out, but while I am here, I have some old friends to meet. Now enough of this pointless chit chat", he said twisting around in his seat to face the Shadowman square on, the leather of the seat creaking as he moved. "Who killed that nobody O'Dwyer and where are my fucking drugs?"

"I don't know yet. I am looking into it but it is more difficult with the Garda investigation poking its nose into everything".

"You are supposed to fucking know. That's what I pay you for".

"Well of course it is and you can rest assured that I will find out but it seems that we should have acted quicker after Murray was killed".

"Who was to know that they would try and move so fast after killing Murray last week?" the older man said shaking his head in disbelief. "It would have taken an Irish gang weeks to organise another hit. Fucking Poles".

"We were not to know. The way I look at it, the more important question that we should ask ourselves is who else knew that O'Dwyer was regularly holding drugs for us? He was a nobody who had sourced from outside the normal groups and deliberately kept out of the loop so that he couldn't be found. There cannot be that many people who knew he existed".

"Did Johnson let his existence slip to someone? Could he be double crossing me and setting himself up?"

"That's what I thought at first but I don't think he is remotely clever enough", the Shadowman agreed, obviously having thought this through earlier. In fact he had thought of nothing else for the last few days. The various options and possibilities were still confusing. While a major setback for the group it opened huge possibilities for him personally.

"He probably knew the writing was on the wall for him after Murray was killed. Where is Johnson now?" Connolly asked.

"Hiding, but I know where he is," the Shadowman answered confidently as he had tracked him down earlier that day.

"Hiding? What the fuck is he hiding from? He should be sorting this fucking mess out. You should be sorting this mess out for me".

"I am trying to. As far as Johnson is concerned, I'm guessing that he thinks he is next on the list", suggested the Shadowman defensively.

"Look it's Christmas and I want to start the New Year with a clean slate. I have a container of the horse tranquiliser Ketamine legally coming into the country next week and after O'Dwyer was killed, I don't trust that even if we can get Johnson back into the game that he is up to the task of taking over the running of the operation from Murray. The Ketamine has to be broken down s soon as possible and sold off to the main dealers to mix with the coke", the older man turned to face him, "So it is probably no surprise to you, that I want you to take over".

"Thank you. That's quite an honour and an awful lot of responsibility".

"Yes, it is. But a man with your... connections, you should be up to the job".

"I won't let you down", the Shadowman said with an air of confidence. This is what he had hoped and worked for.

"You had better not because you're going to learn exactly what it means to fuck with me. Now before you deal with that fuckup Johnson, you will have to meet each of the main dealers that he deals through. They will have to be kept in line. I don't want any of them thinking that I am weak and getting delusions of grandeur about setting up on their own. There are eight of them spread throughout the city and county".

"That could be a problem as I don't know all of them".

"Neither do I. I have been out of the loop a bit since I moved abroad, a mistake on my part. One that I won't make again. You will have to get Johnson to arrange meetings with them".

"Me? But I can't risk being seen by them. You know that..." the Shadowman said horrified by the suggestion.

"This is a hands on job. I don't care how you do it but this has to be done", the older man snapped back tersely. "I have no time for excuses. We have to get back on top now. If you want this job then make this happen. If you don't, I will get someone who does".

And with that an awkward silence descended in the car. The Shadowman stared at the back of the head of the driver, as the car cruised aimlessly through the tight narrow streets. Outside there was a kaleidoscope of changing colours as the rain on the windows distorted the bright shop fronts as they drove past. The man from the shadows loved the city and its frantic pace. There was always a buzz in the air that he thrived on. It fed his very being. He wouldn't live anywhere else, except maybe a bigger city like London or New York. But right now, he would have preferred to be in any other city as the silence in the car was oppressive. The only noise in the luxury vehicle was the deep rumble from the huge tyres on the tarmac and the metallic pinging sound of the rain hitting the roof. He glanced back around only to find that the older man was staring at him, his eyes drilling into the side of the Shadowman's head.

"And what about the stock that this O'Dwyer character was holding?

"Unfortunately, the drugs are still missing", the Shadowman reluctantly replied.

"Does that Polish bastard The Wolf have them?" the older man asked in a tired voice.

"I am not sure yet but I don't think so. The Gardaí National Drugs Unit investigators questioned him about his gangland activities only the other day but nobody has interviewed him in connection with these murders yet. Interdepartmental communication in the Gardaí isn't great but I suppose that they will get there eventually".

The conversation dried up again as the older man contemplated their next move. The Shadowman returned to look out of the window as they drove around. It was difficult to see properly as the world outside was a mass of blurring colours as the rain twisted and contorted shop front lights and lights from other cars together. He could see people striding quickly underneath their hard-working umbrellas as they made their way home.

"Okay. This is how I want it. Firstly, I want you to get a message out around town that I am back and I will kill anyone that crosses me. Then get me back my missing drugs and when all of that is covered, I want Johnson and that Polish bastard out of our hair for good. And I want it all done yesterday. Do you understand me?"

"That is a lot of things to do in a short time. I will have to hire some help from outside the country to get it done. It might be expensive in such a short time frame".

"Monies will be made available to you through the normal accounts".

"And my money..."

"Get this right and you will never have to worry about money again. Get it wrong and you will never have to worry about money again either. Do I make myself clear?"

"Crystal".

And with that John Connolly leaned forward and tapped the driver on the back of the shoulder. Without saying a word the driver slid the big vehicle over to the kerb and stopped. The implication was obvious. The meeting had ended.

"Keep me informed on what is happening", ordered Connolly as he dismissed him.

"I will", said the Shadowman as he opened the door.

"Before you go..."

"Yes…"

"A lot of people had better die over the next few days. Just make sure that you're not one of them".

"I have no intention of being one of them," the Shadowman stated defensively.

"Good. Now shut the fucking door, you're letting all of the cold in".

And with that the driver smashed his foot down onto the accelerator pedal and the massive four-litre petrol engine roared as the Range Rover sped away and disappeared amongst the other traffic up around St Stephen's Green. The Shadowman pulled up his hood and hugging the high green fence of the green, slipped unseen back towards his car.

His blood was boiling after his encounter. How could Connolly not have believed in him? He was the best thing that could happen to that gang. He was a born leader and would revitalise it. He would make it a force to be reckoned with again. Connolly should see that just by looking at him, and it pissed him off that he had to prove himself. He wanted to scream in anger, let the rage build up and release it violently into the air. But he had to wait until he was in a more private part of the city.

Angry or not, he had to remain discreet.

He walked through the streets to his car parked in a late night multi storey car park, coat collar up and shoulders hunched against the rain. He took a short cut down a narrow side street and was half way down the deserted street, when he spotted a homeless man sleeping in a doorway, similar to the one he himself had been standing in only fifteen minutes earlier.

But that was where the similarity ended. There was a world of difference between the two men.

While the Shadowman was successful and groomed to perfection, the vagrant who was of undeterminable age was down on his luck, filthy and ragged. He was propped up in the corner of the doorway, wrapped in a dirty sleeping bag and covered with flattened cardboard boxes for warmth. There was a brown and white mutt, resembling a Jack Russell sticking his head out from under the makeshift bed, eyeing the Shadowman suspiciously.

Stupid fucking dog, the Shadowman thought.

He had nearly walked past them when he stopped mid step. Despite the rain, the Shadowman stood motionless staring down at the man and his dog. The homeless man in turn, watched him closely but didn't say anything. He had seen this type before, out to pick a fight, but he wasn't going to get it with him. After years on the streets and living in shelters, the vagrant knew better than that.

"What are you looking at you piece of shit?" the Shadowman demanded. He received no answer. He was about to deliver a kick; after all nobody cared for this man and hurting him would be a victimless crime, but he thought better of it. Instead of physically hurting the man, he could take away the only thing that was probably important to him.

"I said what are you staring at you piece of shit". But he still got no answer, just the noise of the rain pelting down. The heavy rain drops bouncing off the cobbled ground as he stood there.

"Fucking answer me", the Shadowman roared, as he lashed out a foot at the dog which cowered away deeper under the cardboard layers just in time. The homeless man was right, the man in front of him did want a fight and the fact that he didn't want to make it easy for him by rising to his challenge only seemed to infuriate him more. Before he could react, the Shadowman had bent down and grabbed the dog by the scruff of the neck.

"Whiskey..." called out the homeless man to the dog, his voice filled with terror. "No... please... "

"Shut the fuck up, you little prick", the Shadowman sneered. He turned the dog around so that he could look straight into its eyes, which was a bit of a struggle as the dog was growling and snapping at him while struggling to get out of his grasp. Fucking dog, he thought before he flung the dog against the far wall. The little terrier's head splattered against the wall with a dull thud, crushing its skull. The dog yelped briefly in pain and then slid down the wall, its body twitching as it lay on the cold wet ground. As the dog lay there, he felt a rush through his body akin to an orgasm. His body shuddered and he momentarily closed his eyes in ecstasy.

The homeless man was scrambling with difficulty to his feet, screaming in anguish as he looked at his dog, lying on its side and whimpering pitifully.

"Why? Why would you do that? You bastard, Whiskey never did anything to you".

The Shadowman laughed at the two pathetic figures in front of him, when another man came around the corner and headed straight for them. The man wasn't paying any attention to them;

in fact he was so hidden under his big golfing umbrella that he didn't even see them until he was right on top of them. The pedestrian was shocked when he saw the scene in front of him. It didn't take him long to figure out that something bad was going on. He didn't say anything but the look on his face said it all. The Shadowman glared at him.

Not wanting to get directly involved, the passer by continued quickly on down the street but the Shadowman could see him taking his mobile phone from his pocket as he disappeared around the corner. Then the Shadowman, his anger now sated with the unprovoked attack on the dog, decided that discretion was the best approach. The last thing he needed now was to be seen by the Gardaí.

So, straightening his coat he composed himself and with a final disgusted look at the homeless man weeping while gently holding the body of his little friend, he slipped away into the night.

Chapter One

Later that same night outside a busy pub in Bayview, County Wexford John Morgan or Morgan as he was known to everyone wasn't having it all his own way either.

"Look, I have already told you. You have too much drink on board and you are not coming in here tonight", said Morgan clearly and distinctly. It was the third time that he had to repeat himself to the very drunken man and his rather sober and quite embarrassed girlfriend standing in front of him. Experience told him that he would have to be as clear as possible to avoid any chance of confusion and the need to repeat himself a fourth or fifth time. The man swaying drunkenly before him wasn't getting in here tonight in that state and Morgan knew that he would be fired on the spot if he let anyone in, in that condition. In fact as far as he was concerned, he wouldn't be getting in ever if he kept this crap up for much longer.

"Ah, fuck off it's Christmas", slurred the drunken man throwing his arms up into the air in frustration.

"I know it is and you would normally be more than welcome, but you have consumed more than enough drink already. So not tonight, alright?" Morgan calmly replied.

"I don't want a drink, I only want to go in and get a packet of cigarettes".

"Well you are still not going in, but your friend here can go in. She seems fine", Morgan said looking at the drunken man's companion who was doing her best to pretend that she wasn't there at all.

"My friend?" the drunken man said accusingly as if Morgan had insulted both of them, their family history and the very fabric of Irish society all by this single remark.

"Yes, your friend".

"How dare you call her my friend", the drunken man slurred, repeatedly pointing a finger threateningly at him.

"I didn't mean anything by it"; Morgan said trying not to sound too defensive. Doing a job as a pub doorman meant he couldn't sound weak or appear like he was backtracking in any way, but he was getting tired of this game and just wanted it to end. This was exactly the sort of thing that he didn't miss about this job, drunken idiots who wouldn't go away, shut up or listen to reason. However, on the greater scale of potential problems facing any doorman, this was near the bottom of the list. Over his eight year career in various pubs and clubs around Dublin, he had been confronted by hammer-wielding maniacs, faced down ten angry men by himself, dragged apart feuding men and women and countless numbers who were determined to end each other with broken bottles and so on. There had been so many incidents over the past eight years that he had forgotten most of them. He was always proud of the fact that he could talk himself out of most situations but he occasionally had to put his game face on. While he had eventually always come out on top, he had ended up with various cuts and bruises and even had broken a bone in his arm once. So all things considered this was nothing but hassle and hassle like this was something he just didn't miss. He had gotten soft and used to his quiet secluded life.

"My friend?" the drunken man repeated, determined not to let it go, as if Morgan had issued the worst possible insult, his voice rising up a few notches for emphasis. Perhaps he was trying to use this as a reason to cajole him into letting him in? Fat chance, Morgan thought. While he was facing outwards towards the street, Morgan was conscious of the din of the small crowd in the smoking area behind him dropping slightly as the voice of the man rose. He knew that there was nothing that a crowd liked more than a bit of trouble to watch. It was the equivalent of going out for a drink and getting some colourful entertainment thrown in for free. He could imagine them, cigarettes and drinks in hand nodding to each other to draw the attention of their friends, their ears straining to listen to what was being said. Morgan did his best not to turn around and look at them. Like it or not, he needed to give the man in front of him his complete attention.

"I called her your friend, sir as you are clearly wearing a wedding ring and she isn't. I wasn't sure what to call her. I thought your friend was a good discreet compromise", Morgan replied confidently with just the tiniest hint of sarcasm. It worked though. It did shut the drunken man up. His mouth opened and closed again several times without a word coming out. It was like watching a goldfish. Morgan could hear Keith beside him holding in a snigger.

"I'm not going to stand here and waste my time speaking to the likes of you. Now let me in to get the cigarettes".

"No, I said", Morgan repeated for the fifth time. He broadened his chest and squared his shoulders as a final non-verbal warning. Move on or I will move you on, it said in no uncertain terms.

"Can I go in there and get them then?" the man's friend said speaking for the first time as she tried to do something to resolve the situation.

"Yes, no problem", Morgan said positively. He was happy there was some hope of a peaceful resolution. He stood aside slightly. Keith on his right did so as well, giving the sober woman a clear unobstructed path towards the bar door. Realising that this was the best result that he was going to get, the drunken man put his hand into his pocket and dragged out a fistful of change before dumping it unceremoniously into hers. Some of the coins fell to the street but she didn't bend to pick them up. She left them there and walked straight between the two men acting as sentries and disappeared inside the bar. The noise from inside flooded out as she swung the door open only to dim again to its normal muffled level as the heavy door closed behind her.

Once she vanished inside, the demeanour of the drunken man changed considerably. Gone was the pleading and out came his nasty vindictive self. "You think you're fucking hard do you? Standing there all dressed in black. Chests stuck out. Well you know what - you're fucking not. I'm going to have you done you bastards. I know people in this town that will tear you both apart".

Neither Morgan nor Keith said anything.

They knew better than to encourage him. So they just stood there impassively as he got it out of his system.

But Morgan relaxed considerably.

He had very little to fear from a person who threatened to get someone else to hurt him. At the very least the man should have threatened them himself. But getting someone else to do it? That was just pathetic. It was school kids' stuff; my dad is bigger than your dad. But then things got a bit more sinister. It might have been false bravado on the part of the man but it was a bit disquieting. He had taken out his mobile and despite the drunken state that he was in managed to dial a number. Deliberately speaking loudly so that the two doormen could hear him he spoke to the person at the other end.

"Yeah...Yeah, there is these two cunt's here...yeah...you still got the shotgun...yeah..... look I'm coming over...no now...ok", he hung up the mobile with a satisfied flourish just as the woman reappeared.

She walked by the two doormen and her boyfriend and continued up the street without saying anything, flashing the packet of cigarettes at her drunken companion as she went past as a signal for him to follow her. She wasn't stopping to listen to any more of his ranting. The man called after her and realising that she wasn't going to stop hurried after her. As he stumbled up the road, he took one final opportunity to shout a bullying obscenity and run his hand across his throat in a slashing motion, his meaning crystal clear.

"Fucking idiot, the state of him trying to get in anywhere. You were too nice to him, I would have dragged him around the side lane and kicked the living shit out of him", Keith said as they watched the man disappear up the road. He couldn't walk straight and was literally bouncing off the parked cars and back against the shop fronts as he made his way along the path.

"Why bother, whatever we could have done to him, that girlfriend of his is going to do ten times worse and she'll keep it up for days. No, I wasn't going to give him any reason to get sympathy from her", Morgan said thoughtfully, enjoying the cool night breeze.

"Ha, you're a cruel fucker", Keith laughed as he imagined the telling off the man would get tomorrow morning. If she were anything like his Rachel, it would be weeks before he would be in the good books again.

Morgan had quit door work over two years ago but had recently agreed to do a few nights leading up to Christmas for a guy he knew who had been let down by one of his regular lads and was badly stuck. Initially he wasn't eager to do it but apart from some odd jobs around the Bayswater Hotel as their handyman, he wasn't working these days he could do with some extra money. What amazed him was how fast he fell back into the flow of it. He didn't even have to put on his old black suit as it wasn't that kind of bar. He just wore his old pair of black jeans and a black shirt.

Donned his big heavy overcoat and put his radio earpiece in and all of a sudden he was there. In the eight years that he had worked as a doorman, he had never covered this door. In fact he had never worked in this county, never mind this town. But ten minutes after he started his shift and even before he had drunk his first steaming mug of tea, it was like he had never left. Apparently working as a bouncer was akin to riding a bike.

Morgan had in him an innate ability to size people up, to cut through the bullshit to the very heart of the person standing in front of him. Other men he had worked alongside for years, still couldn't judge a person as accurately or as quickly as he could. He would ignore the clothes, ignore the walk and look into their eyes. Would they be good customers or would they kick off some sort of trouble later? It was his gift and he brought it to his job dispassionately. So professional was he in his approach that he had automatically taken the position of head doorman within an hour or so of arriving the previous night. The other two doormen who had worked in the bar for over two years conceded the position to him without batting an eyelid. He was just better at it than they were. He was a born leader, a man who inspired confidence. He had his colleague's backs. They knew it and reacted accordingly.

At times, since he had retired, he did miss some aspects of the job. The camaraderie of the men he worked with, he missed most. Like him most of the men he worked with were simply men working a second job. They were doing a hard job earning a few extra pounds that hopefully the taxman would never find out about, to help make ends meet. While he had worked with some right bastards over the years, men who got off on the flimsy temporary power that they held, Morgan generally got these weekend warriors off his doors as soon as possible.

John Morgan or Morgan as he had been known since he was in secondary school, stood a good six-foot tall with a solid build developed from years of working on building sites to pay for his college fees, playing college rugby and punishing gym workouts. But now at thirty-three and still recovering from a badly torn Achilles tendon, which refused to heal properly, he had to admit that he was getting a little soft around the edges. Although he had no tattoos, he did have a long scar on his right hand, a souvenir from being slashed with a broken bottle as he had tried to break up a drunken fight. He never thought of himself as attractive but he had been told that he was handsome in a mischievous sort of way.

The looks of a bad boy come good. Apparently, he had a smile that could melt the heart of even the coldest woman.

It had been a lovely mild day for the time of year, clear and bright and you would hardly have figured it for late December. But that had changed. The night was really cold and there was a strong wind blowing adding to the chill. The bar was near the Bayswater harbour and was quite exposed, but the breeze wasn't bothering Morgan and on the whole, he was enjoying his stint back on the door. He particularly loved being outside on nights like these. He stood there admiring a particularly attractive woman walking down the street with her boyfriend when an old silver 5 series BMW with tinted out windows pulled up outside the bar. With its engine still running, the driver's window powered down and the drunken man from earlier leaned out, focusing on the two doormen. The small crowd of smokers gathered outside turned and watched silently as this new turn of events unfolded.

"You're both fucking dead", the drunken man slurred. "Who the fuck do you think you are refusing to let me in ? I'm going to enjoy fucking you up".

"Come on, you are making a fool of yourself", his girlfriend could be heard scolding him from inside the luxury saloon. The drunken man threw her a worse look than he was giving Morgan and Keith. How dare she embarrass him during his big moment - fucking bitch.

"And what the fuck are you all looking at?" he shouted threateningly at the watching crowd, which hushed immediately and took an involuntary group step backwards. The crowd wanted to look on but didn't want to be drawn into it directly. They were only there as spectators for the show, not to be abused, either verbally or physically. That was supposed to be the sole privilege of the doormen.

"Just come on, will you", his girlfriend pleaded once again, tugging at his arm. He glared at her one more time before slurring his parting gesture. "I'll be back and next time I'll have a gun", he threatened as he powered the window up and gunned the big three-litre diesel engine. It roared away sending a cloud of hot exhaust air up into the freezing night air before disappearing off around the corner and out of sight.

"I'll be back. Did you hear him? Who does he think he is? Arnie?" Keith jeered in a mock German accent, breaking the tension that hung heavily in the air. Someone in the crowd laughed and then the collective chatter started up once again. It was strange. The crowd turned away from the street, as though the last few minutes had never happened.

"Idiot. How can he possibly think that he was capable of driving? He mustn't be able to see the end of the dashboard he's that drunk", Morgan said shaking his head in disbelief at the foolishness of the man behind the wheel. He didn't care if he killed himself but the problem was that he'd probably take someone else with him, if no one else then his saintly girlfriend.

With that bit of excitement over and the night starting to wind down, their conversation turned to more normal everyday matters. Women and what they were or more importantly weren't wearing even on that cold and chilly night. As always, the girls with the shortest skirts or lowest tops garnered most of the attention but not for the reason they might think. While admiring their female attributes, Morgan wondered why any woman standing shivering in the cold, her body covered in goose bumps would consider that sexy. Of course, maybe he was just getting old.

The bar was busy and there was a constant flow of people through the doors. Morgan and Keith were busy constantly checking the crowd to make sure everything was all right. Every now and then, Morgan would send Keith in to have a walk through the pub to check up on things there.

It was nearing eleven o'clock and almost an hour since the drunken man had disturbed an otherwise peaceful night when Morgan spotted the silver BMW cruising slowly up the street towards them. The light from the street lamps reflecting off the immaculately polished paintwork. Although it was a popular model and looked like every other BMW 5-series in the town and could have been anyone's, Morgan instinctively knew it belonged to the drunken man from earlier.

But was it actually him driving it?

From the state he was in earlier, Morgan imagined that by this time he would be snoring loudly face down in his bed and possibly in his own vomit. But yet here was the big car, crawling suspiciously towards him.

Keith, following Morgan's gaze also recognised the car. "Is that yer man from earlier? He asked, stepping off the path to get a better look up the road.

"I think so..."

"What the hell does he think he is up to?" asked Keith in a quizzical tone as he moved back to Morgan's side.

"God only knows...."

"You don't suppose he got that gun he was mouthing on about earlier, do you?" Keith joked but there was a flash of concern in his eyes as he looked at Morgan. This was the countryside after all. There was easy access to guns of all sizes and types now that hand-guns were legally allowed in Ireland.

"God only knows", Morgan repeated, the words trailing off slightly as he stared at the approaching vehicle. He was trying in vain to see anything through the heavily tinted windows. He had no idea who or what was inside but his gut told him that it could-n't be good. You didn't drive like that and not expect it to be intimidating.

When the car was about twenty feet away, the semi-permanent crowd out smoking behind the two expectant doormen also spot-ted the silver BMW. The chattering noise in the background picked up slightly as the car's approach was pointed out from friend to friend, then with a collective hush the crowd fell silent as they eagerly awaited the latest developments.

Despite its slow speed the brakes on the heavy vehicle squealed gently as they stopped the car. Then nothing happened for a sec-ond.

The driver's side front window started slowly to descend.

Everyone, doormen and customers alike held their breath. Keith, standing shoulder to shoulder with Morgan took an invol-untary step back.

Morgan now found himself standing alone facing the driver's tinted side window. Feeling detached and quite vulnerable stand-ing there, he did all he felt that he could do under the circumstances. He didn't run for cover or even take a step back like Keith; instead he squared his shoulders and put his game face on. Apart from the muffled noise seeping through the closed doors and windows of the bar behind him, he was surrounded by com-plete silence. There was a palpable tension in the air similar to that before a storm. It was like a dam was going to burst. Something was going to happen and of that there was no doubt.

As the window finally descended, one of the women behind him let out a muted scream, but Morgan refused to look around at her. Instead he stood motionless and undeterred by the possibili-ties facing him. Now, with the window half open, the drunken man could be seen sitting in the driver's seat, smiling out menacingly at him. Morgan just stood there casually, hands in his pockets and smiled back at him. Fuck you, he thought, you are not going to scare me so easily. I'm not made that way.

When the window was fully down, Morgan half expected a large gun to appear, followed by a loud bang, swallowed hard. But no gun barrel slid out; there was no flash of a gunshot, no searing pain ripping his stomach apart.

Nothing.

The drunken idiot just stuck his hand out and made a gun shape before pulling the imaginary trigger. Morgan breathed a silent sigh of relief and his shoulders slumped as the tension flooded out of them. All that for nothing, he laughed out loud, shaking his head in disgust. Within seconds the smoking crowd and Keith had joined in, mocking the would be gunman. They roared with laughter at the drunk driver who was left bewildered that his trick hadn't had a better effect.

"Well fuck all of you", the man roared in anger before driving off, his tail between his legs. The taillights of the car flashing bright red before it disappeared around the corner, hopefully never to be seen again.

Keith returned to his place at Morgan's side and slapped him on the back. "I thought that you were a goner there, my friend".

"Me too. Thanks for backing me up there".

"I had your back", Keith answered grinning broadly.

"My back?"

"Did you get attacked from behind?"

"No..." said a sceptical Morgan doing his best not to laugh.

"See I told you I had your back", he said smiling.

"And what about my front ? No chance of you taking a bullet for me".

"I couldn't, I have to go my mums for dinner tomorrow and if I got killed and couldn't go, she'd be very unhappy", Keith joked. Morgan just laughed at that.

"Yeah, I could see how that would upset her alright".

"What are we going to do about him?" Keith asked, nodding in the direction of the vanishing BMW.

Morgan just shook his head. "I have his registration number from the first time. I wasn't going to do anything about it but now I think I will call the Gardaí and see if they can catch him drink driving".

"They won't be arsed. Even though it's only up the road, it's cold out here and nice and warm inside their station"

"Maybe, maybe not, but it might give him a scare if nothing else."

"The Gardaí? The Gardaí are lazy and self-serving. If work was in bed, they would sleep on the floor".

"You don't have a very high opinion of our boys in blue do you? Maybe in the old days they might have simply waved him on after a telling off but the Gardaí take drink driving very seriously these days", Morgan said as he dialled the number of the local station on his mobile. A light gust of wind cleared the sheen of sweat from his brow. He looked up into the night sky as the phone started to ring in his ear. The weather was changing.

It was going to rain.

Chapter Two

It was nearly nine o'clock that night when the man walked out of the bookies and lit a cigarette. He took a long deep exaggerated drag from it and tilting his head back, he expelled a plume of smoke high into the frosty night air. The smoking man then sighed forlornly and kicked at an empty beer can lying near the doorway sending it rolling and rattling noisily out onto the quiet street where it waited to be crushed by a passing car.

With no moon visible through the thick clouds the sky was pitch black and the only light came from inside the bookies, creating an eerie glow around the doorway. It made the doorway look like an entrance to another world, a gateway from one dimension to another. But the smoking man wasn't bothered by anything so philosophical or insightful. He lived in a much more basic realm. The here and now were the only things important to him and so far the here and now weren't going well for him. The big football match of the night between Manchester United and Liverpool hadn't gone his way. He had bet heavily on United to win but it had been a draw and then to make matters worse, all four dogs running at Shelbourne Park that he had bet on had lost. He had only been at the betting office forty-five minutes but he was already down nearly two thousand euro. And it was money that he couldn't afford to lose. Not now anyway. A few weeks ago, he would have shrugged his shoulders, walked away and not given it another thought but times had changed dramatically and not for the better.

He was feeling very deflated as he had been convinced that he was going to win the last bet, he had been so sure. He had roared at his dog on the television as it went into a slight lead from the traps, but it had got bumped on the last corner and hadn't been able to recover. It had ended up coming in a dismal fourth.

Fucking useless dog, he had screamed at the television set placed high on the bookies wall. If he saw it in the street, he'd run his car over its worthless mangy head, he thought as he threw the now useless crumpled betting slip onto the litter-covered ground.

A few more deep pulls from the cigarette and he flicked it away into the corner where it rolled under a large metal bin on wheels. He was about to walk back inside when he realised that someone had been standing in the darkened corner all along watching him. He stopped and stared into the dark corner but even as his eyes adjusted he couldn't see who it was due to the deep shadow.

"You're an idiot Johnson", came a voice out of the dark corner, startling him.

"What the fuck?" replied the surprised man recoiling in horror. Terrified and shaken he stumbled backwards until he came up against the wall of the adjoining building where, unable to retreat any further he stopped, glued to the spot. He looked furtively around him to see who was there to close the trap on him. He could just about make out a man standing in the shadows. Although he couldn't be sure, the man appeared to be on his own. But who was he and how did this man know his name? But more importantly how had he found him? Johnson was about to turn and bolt away when, the shadow realising what he was planning to do said, "It is no good running Johnson. I'll only find you again. You leave a trail behind you that a blind man in a wheel chair could follow".

"Who are you?" Johnson asked a barely detectable tremble audible in his voice. His hands were clenched into fists as if to defend himself but the man in the shadows knew that he had no fight left in him. He was a bully in a world that wasn't afraid of him anymore.

Powerless and pathetic.

"It's me", the voice replied and a man stepped out of the shadows. He was tall and dressed all in black. He wore a baseball cap and had a scarf pulled up covering his mouth. Not to shield his face against the biting cold but to hide his features. All that Johnson could see were the man's eyes. They were deep and penetrating and flickered with a quick intelligence. They reminded him of the eyes of a rattlesnake just before it strikes. He knew those eyes. He knew the man from the shadows. He didn't know his name but he would recognise those burning eyes anywhere. Johnson breathed a sigh of relief.

"Don't fucking do that to me." I almost had a heart attack there", Johnson complained as he wiped the thin bead of sweat from his brow. His shoulders slumped and his potbelly reappeared as the tension left him.

"You're lucky it is me. If it was the Wolf or one of his men you'd be dead right now".

"Don't fucking remind me", Johnson replied shaking his head and looking around just in case one of the Wolf's men was there as well.

The stillness of the night was broken by shouts of delight coming from inside the bookies. Somebody on a premiership team must have scored a goal or a heavily favoured horse had just won its race. Whatever climax had been reached, it seemed that the punters had come out the right side of the bet for once. The Shadowman knew that it wouldn't be long before someone came out and disturbed them.

And he needed privacy right now.

"Come on, let's go somewhere more private to talk...," the Shadowman said looking around. The betting shop was the last in a row of shops, which were all closed for the night on a quiet road just off the main street of Naas in County Kildare. There was a car park at the other end of the street behind the local bar, The Horse and Carriage, "...my car is up the street".

Johnson didn't immediately move to follow him though. Despite knowing the man he was unsure of what was going to happen when he left the comparative security of the front of the bookies and went around to the deserted car park at the rear. He stood riveted to the spot, wondering what to do next.

Should he trust this man?

They both worked for Connolly but that was no guarantee. Not after the events of the last few days anyway. There was no honour amongst thieves, especially where money was involved.

"Come on. If I wanted you dead, I would have done it when you were walking up the lane earlier", the Shadowman said mockingly as he turned and walked away. Johnson realising, that he really had no choice, meekly followed a few steps behind.

The car park was pitch black. Vandals had smashed most of the lighting except the few nearest the pub itself. Johnson noticed that these were now out as well. He was sure that these were working earlier? Broken glass crunched underneath his feet as he passed by. The work of this guy no doubt, Johnson imagined, having to walk faster to keep up. The Shadowman led Johnson down to the very back towards an old wreck of a Toyota Avensis.

"You have to be kidding me. This is your car? It's a piece of shit", Johnson couldn't help it and scoffed loudly when he realised that this was the man's car.

"Shut the fuck up and keep your voice down. Do you want to attract everybody's attention?"

"Ah, but you can't blame me. Look at it", Johnson said defending himself.

"Do you think that I would drive out here and meet you in any car that could be traced to me? Do you think I am that fucking stupid? Well, do you?"

"Err. No", a cowed Johnson replied.

"Good. Now shut up and get in", the Shadowman ordered as he unlocked the car door, which issued a loud sharp metallic creaking noise as the door opened as if anyone need confirmation of its poor condition. Inside the car wasn't much better. Although it was spotlessly clean, the interior light showed that the fabric seats were badly worn and the lustre had long since disappeared from the cracked plastic and rubber dashboard. The car was about ten years past its sell by date. God only knew how many times the engine had been around the clock.

They sat in silence for a second before the Shadowman, still with the scarf up around his mouth, turned to Johnson. "Well, you fucked up royally didn't you?"

"How did I fuck up?" Johnson retorted in mock disgust. But it was only a put on and they both knew it. Johnson had messed up and now he was in real danger of getting killed, either by the Wolf or by his own people. He was on very thin ice. Both gangs had their reasons to kill him and now members of his own gang had the opportunity.

"Well, let me see first Murray was killed and then O'Dwyer and what have you done since then but hide out like the little cowardly shit that you are", the Shadowman said aggressively. He practically spat the words out so hard that he had to adjust the scarf, which had begun to fall down.

"You're forgetting that I was nearly killed outside that nightclub too. They were after me as well. Those bullets passed a fucking inch from my head, man".

"It's a pity that they didn't kill you. It would have saved us all a lot of trouble".

"Fuck you", Johnson spat back. "I worked hard to get this gang to where it is now".

"Where is the gang now? I will tell you where it is. It is dead in the water that is where it is now. You have no men left to call on. They all literally abandoned you overnight. You have no drugs left as they went missing and your customers are leaving you like rats leaving a sinking ship. So much for your professed leadership skills".

"Hey, I did what I was told. Murray was always the boss...." Johnson said back, disputing his level of responsibility in the whole affair.

"Yes, but after he was killed, you were. And what did you do? Let that week's consignment of Coke get taken. And you didn't do anything. You didn't contact anyone for help. You didn't kill anyone in retaliation. You just upped and disappeared".

"I was giving it a couple of days. Till the heat died down, you know. There were pigs everywhere. Then I was going to contact Spain."

"Why didn't you call them straight away?"

"I didn't know what to do. I had to get away. The Wolf he is a fucking animal..."

But before he could finish, the Shadowman slapped him back handed viciously across the face. "He is nothing compared to me. Nothing! You hear you fucking useless little prick? I will eat you alive," he spat. Then after a second's pause, he hit Johnson again and again. It was like a dam burst within the Shadowman and he couldn't stop himself. Johnson screamed and brought his hands up to protect himself and lashed back in a half-hearted attempt to defend himself. It descended in to a minor scuffle inside the cramped confines of the old car. During the melee the Shadowman's scarf was torn away from his face. Although Johnson got a good close look at the man he didn't recognise him. When the Shadowman realised that his temporary disguise had come undone, he pulled the scarf back across his face and sat back fully in his own seat. His heart was still racing and his blood was still up but his bubbling anger was somewhat sated.

To anyone watching outside the car, the commotion inside it was barely noticeable, as the windows had all steamed up. Unlike the Range Rover from earlier, this car didn't have air conditioning to keep the windows demisted. It was so old it was lucky to even have a radio. There were just a few brief muffled yells, the car rocked once or twice on its creaking suspension. Then...nothing.

It was all over as soon as it had begun.

"You didn't know what to do? I can't believe that. You're supposed to hit them back. Wipe them out". The sheer frustration returning to the voice of the Shadowman, he wiped the sweat from his forehead. Johnson opened his mouth as if to answer but closed it again. He didn't say anything for fear of enraging the man once again. He just sat there wondering what was going to happen next.

After a couple of seconds of silence, the man from the shadows fully regained his composure. "You might still have your uses. I don't know why but I have been told that all will be forgiven as long as you get the drugs back and help me deal with the Wolf and secure the services of the other dealers. Help fix this fucking mess and Connolly will let you live. He'll even help put you up in Alicante in Spain until all of this blows over".

"He will?" Johnson responded to the offer enthusiastically. After all that had happened, it was more than he could have hoped for. The pain in his face and his hurt pride were immediately forgotten. He had a chance after all.

But the Shadowman meant none of it. As soon as he had all of his assigned tasks completed, Johnson was going to wind up dead in a lime filled grave in some obscure part of the Dublin Mountains, where with any luck he wouldn't be found for years. It wasn't part of his orders but he was going to do it anyway especially now that Johnson had seen his face. But mostly because he would enjoy doing it, the useless prick had it coming to him. He couldn't let him live but right now he was needed. There was too much to do and very little time to do it in.

"Yes, but mark my word, if this goes wrong and we don't get the drugs back and secure the dealers, I am going to kill you very slowly and I am going to enjoy every second of it. Do you hear me?"

"Yes..." Johnson stammered.

"Now, where are the drugs that O'Dwyer was holding?"

"I don't know".

"Well do you have any ideas?"

"I know that the Gardaí don't have them because they kept asking me the same questions and I don't think that the Wolf has them so I don't know".

"Do you know where O'Dwyer kept them?"

"No".

"Do you know anything? Well, lucky for you, I have been thinking about that and I an idea. But it's something that you can look after yourself alright".

"Sure, no problem, anything that you want".

"Good. To get the dealer network back up and running I am going to contact each of the main dealers that you supply directly to. But because of the policy of keeping all of the dealers separated so that one doesn't know the other, it seems that you are the only person left who knows them all. So, I want you to write down the names of everyone that I need to speak to. Include any of the dealers that they supply to as well. Give me as much detail as possible". He opened his coat and took out an envelope and a pen. Stuffing the contents of the envelope back into his pocket he passed Johnson the paper and pen.

Johnson quickly scribbled the list of names on the piece of paper and passed it back over.

"I only recognise a few of these names. Who is the most important here?" the Shadowman asked.

"This one", Johnson answered, pointing to the first name on the page, "Shane McNevin".

"Right, I'll start with him then".

Chapter Three

John Morgan stood watching, his clenched fists thrust deep into his heavy coat pockets, as his friend's coffin was lowered into the freshly dug grave. Four gravediggers, carefully feeding ropes slowly through their gloved hands, lowered the coffin into the ground, swallowing it up. The dark brown of the wooden coffin blended in perfectly with the rich brown colour of the freshly dug earth. In stark contrast green wreaths and colourful bunches of flowers had been placed on top of the mound piled up neatly to the left of the gaping hole.

The gravediggers lowered the coffin in with the narrow end holding the feet towards the missing headstone, the head towards the footpath. East to west. According to Christian theology, the coffin faced east so that the deceased would be ready to face God on judgement day. As they lowered it down, the bright winter morning sun reflected brightly off the brass engraved nameplate. The coffin sank slowly and evenly below the surface until a gentle thud could be heard as it ended its final journey. Then after pulling the ropes free, their work still not completed, the workmen walked solemnly over to one side, hands clasped respectfully together as they waited for the funeral to end.

The rainstorms of the last few days had mercifully let up, giving the mourners a brief respite from the driving deluge. Even the sun had decided to make a welcome appearance for the occasion. It helped to dispel some of the grey dreariness from the landscape but offered little or no heat. And while the wind was not as strong as the gale force winds that had battered the country for the last week, they were still hardy and the trees lining the walls of the cemetery did little to shelter the mourners. The bitterly cold wind cut through those standing there, making them all shiver and huddle deeper into their heavy coats. With the coffin lowered,

Morgan noticed that the parish priest had started to drone on again, but the combination of the strong gusts of wind blowing across the exposed cemetery and the restrained sobs of anguish from both Rob's mother and his children, drowned out the priest's sombre voice even with the battery-powered microphone that had been set up.

".... faith in the mercy and the love of God...he was a loving husband and a loving father... those of us who mourn here today, be re-united one day with Robert..."

It wouldn't have mattered what he said though, his words were entirely lost on Morgan. There was no celestial or spiritual plan, God had nothing to do with this, he thought bitterly. He had had no part to play. There had been no divine act on his part; drug dealers had killed Rob.

Plain and simple.

Yet, when it came to the prayers, Morgan still mouthed them silently along with the rest of the mourners. Disillusioned with his belief in God since the death of his fiancée the previous year, he had fallen out of the habit of praying. But he prayed now for Rob because it was all he could do for him now and with Rob's chequered past, he knew he would need every bit of help that he could get if he was to be let through those pearly gates.

Morgan recalled listening to news on the radio as he drove out to Rob's house on the morning that Rob had been killed. There was a standard radio sound bite lasting less than twenty seconds on it that would turn out to be his obituary. "A man in his 30's, who is as yet unnamed, was gunned down in his house in Greystones, Co. Wicklow last night. His family including three children were asleep upstairs. Gardaí are appealing for witnesses." Then they said the magic words, that the victim was "known to the Gardaí". At that point, Morgan would have stopped caring, "Fuck him", he would have thought, as he had thought, after that phrase in countless other news bulletins about gang related deaths that he had heard over the last few years. If you were involved in that crap, then you had gotten what you deserved.

Except he did care about what happened to Rob.

This big-hearted but flawed man had been one of his best friends.

The announcement had been short and sweet, compartmentalised into a news bulletin but it said nothing about the good there had been in the man. It never mentioned the fact that he was a loving husband and the devoted father of three children or the fact that he had been a coach for the under twelve-soccer team. Why hadn't any of that been mentioned?

Morgan knew that Rob didn't deserve what had happened to him. He had been monumentally stupid but he had only got into the periphery of dealing drugs due to his financial problems. Since his murder, everyone he had talked to was shocked to learn of the drug connection to Rob's death. They had no idea that he had been involved in anything like that. In life Rob had been very popular and Morgan knew that if he had died in a road accident or if some sudden tragic illness had taken him, then things would have been very different. The local church would have been filled to capacity. There would have been a long funeral cortège down to the cemetery and the Gardaí would have had to close the roads. The radio stations would have had to alert motorists of traffic diversions. Now most of those whom he would have expected to attend wouldn't consider going to Rob's funeral after they heard on the radio that it was a yet another gang related killing and being honest, Morgan could not blame them.

So instead of the traffic-stopping multitude, only a tiny fraction had turned up, standing scattered around the graveside. The few who had made it, probably about twenty-five or thirty in all, were family members and close friends who knew the real Rob. For them, he was the good-looking blond guy with three kids, who always looked out for his friends before himself.

John Morgan stood on his own off to one side of the group of other mourners, his long black coat wrapped tightly around him in an effort to ward off the bitter January chill. He was concentrating on recalling Rob, as he should have been remembered. He still couldn't believe that it had happened. He had known Rob for nearly twenty years. They had even gone to school together. He couldn't and shouldn't be dead. And even though Rob had been shot a few days ago, Morgan still couldn't reach a decision on his emotions. His mood swung from disbelief and shock to anger and guilt and it was tearing him apart. His murder hadn't sunk in yet.

Maybe it never would.

The wind came up and shook both the branches on the nearby trees and him out of his daze. He stared around, looking at the faces of each of the mourners in turn. There were precious few. There was Rob's family, his widow Sinead and their three children. He corrected himself they were her three children now. They weren't Robs' anymore, just Sinead's, and they stood in a line, the eldest beside her mother getting smaller as they went along, like a row of living Russian nesting dolls. Linda who was born with Down Syndrome was twenty one, Ian was ten and little Niamh was only five. There was an older couple whom he hadn't seen in years but recognised as Rob's parents, along with his mother-in-law, Pauline. Robs father in law wasn't there as he had passed away a few years previously.

Standing close beside them was the owner of the garage that Rob worked in. Morgan assumed that the two other men standing beside him were the other mechanics who worked there as well.

The big man standing on the right near the narrow access road close to where the hearse was parked was John Smith. Smith ran the private security company that supplied bouncers to the local bars and clubs that both Morgan and Rob had worked in part-time for the past six years. Standing with him were a couple of the other doormen and a few of the staff from the pub. One of the bar-maids, Helen, seemed particularly upset and stood there crying, she was so upset that she was shaking. Another one of the girls had her arm around her, trying to comfort her. That made up the bulk of the mourners. Apart from that there were a couple of faces that Morgan didn't recognise. They were probably just distant relatives that came out of the woodwork for the day.

Off to the far right of the mourners stood the two senior investigating detectives whom he had met over the course of the last few days. The older man in his mid-fifties, who was thin and wiry, was DI Higgins. The tall attractive woman in her late twenties or early thirties standing beside him was Garda Callaghan. Earlier back at the church, both detectives had seemed much more interested in who was at the funeral than in the proceedings themselves. Now they looked like they wanted it to end as soon as possible so that they could get off.

Turning back to the service, he watched as the priest directed both Sinead and Rob's parents to throw a handful of soil onto the coffin lid. Sinead was a pillar of strength as she walked over to the grave's edge. She stood tall and proud and performed her solemn task with a dignity that any reigning monarch would be proud of. Breathing in deeply she leaned down and grabbed a handful of the soft clay before mouthing a final private farewell to her murdered husband. She closed her eyes and let the earth fall from her open hand. The clay making a hollow sound as it bounced off the lid of the coffin.

Rob's mother, who was usually confined to bed with a hip problem, needed help to get over to the edge. Rob's father linked her as they walked over to the rim where he picked up two lumps of soil for them. Unable to check her emotions, she started to cry once again, only regaining her composure at the last minute. Clinging to each other his parents paid their final respects to their son.

"....almighty and ever living God, remember the mercy that you granted your servant Robert in this life. We pray that you receive him into the mansions of the saints. As we make ready our brother's final resting place, look also in mercy at those who mourn and comfort them in their loss".

Then as the wind stepped up yet another notch, the priest gave a final blessing and after shaking the principal mourners' hands, he quite literally made his escape. He rushed out of the cold January air and into his waiting car, dragging his microphone equipment behind him.

Morgan waited patiently until each of the mourners had said their goodbyes and the various travel arrangements had been made to get back to the house for the customary drink, before he walked over to Sinead. She gave him a sad smile as he held both of her hands and looked deep into her eyes, before hugging her tightly.

"I am so sorry about everything," he said as he let her go.

"I know".

"It's over now. Everything is going to be alright".

"Is it?" She said tearfully. She reached up and gently touched his face before walking away to catch up with her mother. Morgan watched as she walked away, following the little throng of people back to their parked cars. He shivered but he hardly felt the cold biting breeze, the cold was coming from deep inside him.

"Are you coming back to the house?" She called back over to him.

"Yes. But I will follow you there. There is something that I have to do first".

He turned away and as he stood looking into the grave, he remembered the other graves he had stood beside so recently. First there was Eimear's, his fiancée which was just over a year ago. He tried not to think about her now...their life together had been filled with moments too beautiful to forget and far too painful to remember. Then only six months previously he had watched as old Karl Muller was lowered down into the ground in his adopted Wexford.

Back when Eimear had died and Morgan had returned from Canada feeling completely lost and aimless, Rob had been his friend and he could not have done enough for him. As Morgan stood there, he might have cried except that he had vowed never to do that again.

Chapter Four

Morgan sat on the back of the headstone opposite Rob's plot, staring solemnly over at his friend's last resting place. There was no headstone on Rob's grave yet, as Morgan had only finalised the wording with Sinead the other day. She had wanted to put on it that Rob had been murdered or something about being cut down in his prime. But Morgan had argued otherwise, asserting that it would only cause more pain and anguish in the years ahead. Luckily she had eventually conceded so the waist high plain black marble headstone with gold engraving would simply read, "Here lies Rob O'Dwyer, beloved husband and father". Morgan sat there now imagining reading it over and over again in his mind, tormenting himself, until he forced himself to look away from the plot altogether.

The funeral had ended over fifteen minutes ago and the priest and all of the other mourners had long since gone but Morgan still did not want to go yet. It felt like this moment was the last link to his friend, the last important occasion that they would share together. Yes of course he would be back here on anniversaries and occasionally just to visit, after all his father was buried across the other side of the cemetery and he visited his grave as often as he could, but it would never be the same. After today, he would be just visiting a cold, hard and lifeless headstone. Like his father's grave, there would be no Rob left there. He was gone, never to return. This was the last chance to be alone with Rob, to tell him that he was sorry for letting him down.

As Morgan sat there he could not help but stare at the wreath that dominated the burial mound with its bright yellow and white flowers woven to form the word DAD. He kept thinking of Rob's children as they had placed the wreath on his coffin earlier at the church.

So now he sat there, his hands stuffed deep into the pockets of his long dark coat and his collar up as he tried to shield himself against the cold January wind mercilessly cutting through the open cemetery.

Although Morgan knew in his heart that he was not to blame for Rob's death, that the man who shot him was fully responsible, he could not escape the feeling that he had let him down badly. He had known that Rob had got himself into money problems and had considered getting involved with a known drug dealer. He had tried to reason with Rob, to warn him of the dangers to both him and his family and thought that he had convinced him when Rob said he would find another way to get the money. Morgan, distracted by his own personal issues, had been relieved and had chosen to believe that everything would be okay. But obviously Rob hadn't. And everything was not okay. Rob had lied to him, told him what he wanted to hear and gone along and done it anyway. And he now lay dead in a coffin, six feet under good Irish earth. A life wasted.

Morgan felt that he could have, no should have, done more. He should have done whatever it took to help his friend. But he hadn't. He had left it up to Rob to sort his own life out even though he knew that Rob had made bad choices before. He should have known that he would make them again. The alarm bells should have rung loud and clear in his head especially when completely out of the blue Rob had asked him to take care of his family if something were to happen to him. Morgan had asked him what he meant but Rob had just brushed it off. Even back then, Rob must have known that he was getting in over his head. He had tried to tell him but Morgan hadn't listened.

The gravediggers had been waiting for him "to have a moment" as their foreman had put it, but when they saw that he was not moving on anytime soon, they eventually just went ahead and started filling the grave. They reversed a battered yellow JCB out from a nearby compound and backed up to the plot and scooped muck unceremoniously from the pile near the pathway.

Morgan looked on with thinly veiled disgust. There was no respect in the way they were doing their job. There was a person down there. Down there was his friend and they were just dumping soil on top of him. Separating them forever. He understood that it was just their job, but it did not help quell the huge sense of anger and frustration that he felt. His feelings had nothing to do with the gravediggers yet for some reason he had decided to focus his ire on the hapless workers. With every shuffle from the big bucket, he was that bit more removed from Rob. After only a few minutes they finished and smoothed the top down with shovels. Before they left, they placed all the wreaths neatly on the new mound and walked off with the JCB rattling along after them, happy to be away from Morgan's cutting glares.

Sitting on the headstone he felt as if he was outside of time. It didn't seem to matter as he sat there. He stayed at the graveside because he did not know where to go. He knew that he had to show up at Sinead's mothers for the afters and eventually he had to go home but right now he felt adrift in a sea of remorse. Completely lost. It felt like his body weighed ten times its normal sixteen stone.

The wind howled and the trees nearby swayed and creaked with the strong gusts. Morgan knew he could not put it off any longer. He struggled to stand up, stiff from the cold wind and sitting on the hard marble. It was time to go.

"I'll look after them for you buddy," he said out loud as he strode away from his friend's final resting place. "I promise".

Chapter Five

Detective Inspector Tom Higgins walked through the door into the cramped room in Dun Laoghaire Garda station that was operating as the briefing room for the duration of the murder investigation. Looking around, it seemed that all of the investigation team were already there, crowded into the cluttered room at and on the various desks and spare chairs brought in from other offices especially for the update.

The room was a buzz of conversation but everyone took time to acknowledge their senior officer with a mixture of hellos and nods as he took his place at the head of the room. Higgins paused as he stood in front of them looking each one over in turn. The men and women all looked so young, fresh faced and naïve. Shaking his head imperceptibly, he thought that they seemed like they had come straight off the beat and that there was hardly an experienced detective amongst them. It wasn't their fault though. Between the soaring crime rate and a Government policy of reducing Garda numbers through non replacement, experienced detectives were spread very thinly, with rookies brought in to fill the spaces before they were ready. Even task forces set up like this one, to probe gangland related killings, suffered chronic shortages in terms of experienced staff, skills and resources. Not to mention that it was a nightmare trying to get the labs to do anything in a hurry. He was still waiting on toxicology reports that should have been done days ago. How was he supposed to lead an investigation under conditions like this? Sighing audibly he opened his tattered briefcase before turning to the large white boards behind him, which had the various crime scene information reports, timelines and suspect photographs that they had gathered so far stuck to them.

"Alright, everybody settle down", Higgins said, trying to create some order. The room slowly descended into muffled whispers as the man in charge of the investigation asserted his position at the head of the room. Like a professor giving a lecture, he said in an authoritative voice, "As you are aware, I attended the funeral this morning of Rob O'Dwyer. As you can imagine it was a very hard time for his widow, her children and the wider family. It is very worrying but not completely unexpected that this drugs war has escalated to murdering peripheral targets. I had a lengthy conversation with the superintendent last night and we both agree that we have to get these bastards and soon before somebody else gets killed. We especially do not want another Michael Brown incident".

The DI was referring to Michael Brown, a twenty year old home carer who was shot through the front door of a house, just as he was about to go out shopping for the invalid man for whom he was caring. Despite a lengthy investigation, they could not figure out a motive for the slaying until it was later discovered that the hit man had simply got the address wrong. He got the right house number but he had gone to The Crescent instead of The Grove. The hit man had made a simple stupid mistake that destroyed an innocent life.

At this moment, the door creaked slowly open as a female detective in her late twenties slipped into the room.

"Garda Callaghan....."

"I was just on the phone chasing up on the ballistics".

"No problem. Please take a seat", he said nodding towards the last available spot over by the window.

Callaghan was the best that the training college in Templemore was putting out, scoring maximum points in both psychology and law and rating highly in physical training. She had served briefly, but with distinction, as a Garda on the beat before transferring over to the detective division. She had been working under Higgins for over a year now and what had really impressed him was how she had discovered new breakthrough information on a previous extremely complicated murder case. The information that she had pieced together resulted in his solving the case after only one week. The Chief Superintendent had congratulated and awarded him a citation and Higgins in turn admired her even more. Being gracious in his final case report, Higgins stated that

Callaghan was a credit to all Gardaí and even went as far as to proclaim her the future of the force.

"Okay, now that we are all here, let's review what we know", Higgins said before opening the briefing notes. "So, we now know that Rob O'Dwyer was a low level employee of Dave Murray, who was himself shot and killed outside a nightclub last week", Higgins stated, indicating a gruesome picture of a man lying dead on the ground in a pool of blood, with several large bullet wounds to his chest and head.

"O'Dwyer was apparently sleeping in an armchair in the front room of his house at 12:15am when the murderer got into the back garden through the unlocked side gate and entered the house through the back door. His wife and three children were asleep upstairs. There was no sign of a forced entry but Mrs O'Dwyer cannot remember if she locked the back door before she went to bed. Considering the murder of Dave Murray last week, we are currently working on the basis that this man..." Higgins said, indicating a picture of a large man wearing a tracksuit walking an un-muzzled bulldog "...Brian Johnson is our main suspect. He was Dave Murray's right hand man and our initial investigations seem to indicate tensions between them in how to run the business. The working theory is that there has been a coup in the gang, led by Johnson. We have tried to locate him, with no luck. Some of you are involved in staking out his house to see if he shows up. However, as he probably knows that we are looking for him, he won't come back there until the heat dies down. So I want him found and quickly. Start to ask around. We now have a sketchy list of his contacts in the drugs world, I don't know if there is much point but I need these questioned to see if anyone has seen anything of him. I want one of you to see if he has any other properties registered anywhere. Start with the banks. Check credit cards and withdrawals. I will be meeting with the Criminal Assets Bureau later to discuss immediately seizing all properties belonging to both Johnson and Murray."

After a long morning at both the funeral and the cemetery, DI Higgins was already getting tired standing and paused briefly to take a sip of water.

As he drank he looked around, scanning the room for any reaction to his initial comments. But there was none, just blank faces staring back at him. They made no comments, had no queries and God forbid anyone should offer any suggestions. They just want to be spoon-fed this investigation, to be told what to think, Higgins thought. They should be asking questions. That's what makes good detectives.

"Right, that brings us back to the physical evidence", Higgins said continuing once more. "The crime scene investigators could not get any prints from either the front or back doors but have so far found a staggering twenty two different prints from inside the house. Where are we on that?"

"I have gotten a list of the people known to be in the house in the last two weeks and we are in the process of getting their prints into the lab so that they can be ruled out", Callaghan volunteered.

"Good. How long will that take?"

"With any luck, we will get all the prints today and then it is up to the lab sir".

"Put all of their names through the Pulse database and see if anything turns up as well."

"I already did that, but nothing of interest so far. But then again the Pulse system is so out of touch that Jack the Ripper isn't on it", she answered sarcastically.

"Fine...Okay. Moving on. The pathologists report has come in," Higgins said waving a brown manila file in the air. "She has confirmed that O'Dwyer was shot with a 9mm pistol, probably silenced. There were two shots, one to the chest and the other to the head. This pattern indicates a professional hit."

He paused to allow this new bit of information sink in, before continuing. "The markings on the shell casings indicate that they were fired from a Heckler & Koch P2000SK, which as you all are aware was the same type of gun used to kill Murray only last week".

At this point he turned back to DG Callaghan, "Are the ballistics results confirming this back in yet? Have they matched the guns?"

"No, that's what I was doing earlier but apparently there is a backlog. They promised to have it later on today".

"A backlog?" he said in disbelief, throwing the manila file down onto the table with a resounding smack, "This is a murder investigation. Did you tell them that?"

"Of course, I did, several times in fact. And they said that it would be done as soon as possible", Callaghan replied. She had used more colourful language than that to the ballistics technician but that was the gist of it.

"Alright, that will have to do", he sighed, looking at Callaghan somewhat annoyed as if the delays were her fault entirely. Higgins recognised the fact that he was placing too much pressure on her but he had no choice. Callaghan was the only one in his team whom he trusted. He had requested other more experienced staff but his request had been refused. He knew that this case was not being treated with a high level of priority by other sections of the Gardaí hierarchy. The prevailing feeling amongst the force was why stop the drug dealers killing each other? Wasn't it one less scumbag to deal with? Both the media and the Minister for Justice had other ideas though. Maybe now that two murders were linked he could get better resources.

"Okay", Higgins said through gritted teeth as he turned back to face the room. "It appears that we are still awaiting the ballistics report on whether it was the same weapon that was used to kill Murray a week ago. However at this moment in time I think that we can safely assume it was the same gun".

This finally created a bit of a stir, as everybody in the room knew that as soon as the report came back matching the ballistics the case would be upgraded. Two murders by the same gun in la week was big news by anyone's standards.

"So let's go over the basics once again. The killer comes in the back door, shoots O'Dwyer and then makes his escape through the front door. A man walking his dog had seen a large man running in the direction of the local park before riding off on a waiting motorbike. We have a composite of the motorbike's tyre. How is that going Griffith?" Higgins asked while looking around him for the young officer whom he had placed in charge of following up that lead. Griffith was sitting over by the water cooler and he stood as he read awkwardly from his notes.

"It appears that it is a very common tyre on a racing motorbike," Griffith answered, consulting his notes. "The thread identifies it as a Michelin Pilot Sport back tyre apparently. I was told, it comes as standard on a few different bikes. A Yamaha R1 and a Suzuki GSXR 1000 to name two examples "

"So there is nothing special about it? Any strange cuts or markings in the thread that could identify it?"

"No, but the forensics people put me onto a Garda in the motor pool who is involved in building and repairing racing bikes and he said that from the depth of the threads, that the tyre appeared brand new. They were hardly worn."

"Well that's something. Right...get the list of all the tyres sold in the greater Dublin region in the last six months and see if any of the names ring a bell."

"I have already started on it. There are twelve bike shops in Dublin and another ten in the Wicklow, Kildare and Meath commuter belt. I have contacted most of them. I will get to the rest of them today".

"Excellent work", DI Higgins said smiling. "Now yet another mystery remains, the drugs that O'Dwyer was apparently holding for Murray are missing. We are still unsure exactly how much he was holding, but according to our sources, it was a significant amount, worth somewhere in the region of three quarters of a million Euro. There is also the possibility that O'Dwyer was holding a weapon as well. However, the man seen near the scene was not carrying anything and a detailed search of the house has turned up nothing. By all accounts the killer did not have time to search the house himself, so where are they?"

"Maybe O'Dwyer had already passed them back to Murray last week before they both were killed?" one young fresh faced Garda ventured half-heartedly.

"Probably not, as there were no big quantities of drugs found at either Johnson's or Murray's premises. And anyway, if he had then why was he killed? No, we are getting reports from our colleagues in the National Drugs Unit that what's left of Murray's gang are currently searching for them as well. So everybody get out there and start asking around. Somebody has got to know something".

The room went silent as everybody thought of who they could lean on, when Callaghan suggested a different approach for the investigation, "What about this Morgan character sir? He seemed very close to the widow on the morning of the killing. And as far as I am aware he was one of the first people that Sinead O'Dwyer called".

"Yes he was. Apparently he is a close family friend. He has no history of drug or gang involvement. What are you driving at?"

"At the initial interview I just got the impression from her that he might have been something more than just a family friend. And I don't know if you had noticed the way that she looked at him when he walked into the room. It seemed to be more than just friendship. I know that look sir".

"What look?"

"The look a women gives to a man that she is in love with".

"Are you saying that they were having an affair"?

"Maybe, anything's possible, but there is more to it than meets the eye".

"What you're saying is that this might not be a drugs murder at all, that it could be in fact a crime of passion?" Higgins questioned, contemplating her suggestion. "And what about Murray being murdered? Was he involved with her as well?"

"That probably was a gangland hit. The MO is different after all. Murray was gunned down outside a nightclub. It was a very public execution. It was designed to be seen. The gunman didn't care if anyone else was hurt as there were several other people injured and considering the panic the first shots caused the gunman was lucky to have killed his target. O'Dwyer's murder on the other hand was a much more professional affair. The killer was in and out silently, with no witnesses and no doubt about the outcome. It must have been two different killers either working for the same person or it was someone else taking advantage of the situation. Maybe they used it as an opportunity?"

"They...?"

"Yes, they. I think that O'Dwyer could have been set up by his wife and this Morgan character".

"You are saying that she had some sort of involvement in it?"

Callaghan now had a chance to explain her theory, which she had begun to work on when she had seen John Morgan and Sinead O'Dwyer after the questioning at the station. Taking a deep breath she began, "Well, the gunman got into the house quietly which as you said previously probably meant he had at the least a good sense of familiarity with the place. There were no signs of resistance from the deceased, which could indicate that the deceased knew his murderer. And the witness said he saw a well-built man running away from the scene. Morgan would fit that description."

That was a pretty good theory DI Higgins thought to himself. But with every fibre in his body he still felt that it was gang related, but then thought about it for a few seconds longer. Early interviews with family and friends of the family had suggested that it wasn't the happiest of marriages but that there was no one else involved so it seemed a highly unlikely scenario but maybe it was not completely far-fetched. He knew that each lead or possibility, however vague, must be followed up.

"Alright everybody, that's it for today. There will be another meeting tomorrow morning at ten o'clock. I will be giving each of you your individual assignments for today in the next thirty minutes." Higgins called towards everyone in the room before turning to face his protégé. "Fiona can you come over here?"

"Yes, boss".

"I want you to do a background check on this John Morgan fellow. See what he's about and if he could be a player in all this".

Although the briefing had gone on for some time there was an air of electricity in the room. After the quietness forced upon them in the meeting, the room was now a hive of activity. Detectives and Gardaí talked loudly on phones and clicked noisily away on keyboards as they continued on yesterday's list of tasks.

Chapter Six

Ten miles away from the cemetery and at about the same time as the Garda briefing was ending, an urgent knock came to the door of a nondescript rented semi-detached house. The house was in the middle of a sprawling development near the Lucan and M50 motorway turn-off in west Dublin. When nobody immediately answered, the anxious visitor who was constantly looking over his shoulder to see if anyone was watching knocked again. It took a few moments but the door eventually swung open.

"You're late. Where have you been? I have been trying to get you on the phone since this morning", asked a man in a rough eastern European dialect, as he opened the door. The visitor didn't answer instead he disappeared straight into the front sitting room.

"I am sorry but I had to dispose of my phone", came the respectful reply from the visitor as the homes occupant caught up to him in the living room.

Krupski was a deeply superstitious man and was insulted that his visitor had walked straight into the house. Piasecki should have remembered that he met and shook every visitor's hand outside the house as the old Polish custom dictated. It was one of the many traditions that he had brought with him from Poland to this country. For instance, he would not live in a house or stay in a hotel room with the number thirteen in it. He tied red ribbons to items associated with his family or business for luck. But Piasecki knew this, thought Krupski and it was not like him to forget. Something must have happened to upset him and he was not a man easily upset.

Piasecki had the edge of the net curtains pulled to one side and was glancing furtively up and down the road.

"So what has happened, my friend?" Krupski asked.

Piasecki turned around to face him and said somewhat sheepishly, "I went there last night to the house where that man had been shot as you ordered. There was a policeman on duty outside, so I waited for a while until he fell asleep and then crept through the back of the house. I searched it for nearly an hour but found nothing".

"Nothing? So who the fuck has them then?" Krupski demanded, raising his voice, "We still need them". He had his own delivery of cocaine coming in next week but it wasn't going to be enough. Not for the plans he had. He was intent on flooding the Dublin drugs market so quickly that it would entice every dealer in the city to come over to him. It would be a grand show of style to amaze the lowlifes crawling around in the darkness, drawing them to him. But he needed those drugs and time was running out. Not to mention, he needed to know, who had gotten to them before he did. Things were happening that he did not fully understand and that was dangerous.

"That is not all. I went up to the forest this morning as you wanted to, where we buried our weapons, but there were, how would you say...loggers, cutting down the trees?"

"Loggers? What do you mean loggers? This isn't Poland; there are no big forests like Bialowieza here for logging".

"Well they were cutting down the trees nearby, whoever they were so I had to leave it. I was going to go back later but when I drove back down I noticed that a black car was following me".

"Who was it?"

"It wasn't marked but I am sure that it was the police", answered Piasecki still checking the road outside for movement.

"What did they want?" asked Krupski, very concerned at this new development.

"I don't know. They didn't stop me, just followed me for a while. Then they pulled away and that was that. I kept an eye out for them but I didn't spot them or anyone else following so I stopped off and bought us new disposable mobile phones and drove around for an hour to make sure that I wasn't followed before coming over here". Piasecki took two phones and chargers out of his coat pocket.

Krupski thought about this for a moment. He was worried. Why were the police watching them now? A development like this meant he had a lot of unanswered questions. Did they know about the consignment of drugs that he had coming in next week? No, they couldn't. They had been very careful...hadn't they?"

Very discreet.

They had done all of their business so far through intermediaries. There was nothing tangible to lead anybody to them yet. And anyway if the Irish police did suspect them both as drug dealers and murderers then they would be down in some police station being interrogated right now. No, they were just trawling to see what would come up.

But why now just as they were ready to make their move into the big time? He didn't like these turn of events.

Didn't like them one bit.

"First things first, did you go back to get the guns?" Krupski who was also known as the Wolf asked. He had quickly taken to the nickname 'The Wolf' since first being described as one by an overly eloquent military prosecuting solicitor a number of years ago. Krupski encouraged people to call him this, as he was flattered to be linked to an animal renowned for its hunting and predatory skills.

"No, I didn't want to collect them, only to be picked up with them a few minutes later".

"Are you sure you weren't just being paranoid?"

Piasecki looked at him in mild disbelief. "Yes, I am sure. I know when I am being followed".

"Okay, relax, I did not mean anything by it".

"There, there it is," Piasecki said excitedly as a black Ford Mondeo pulled up to the kerb about a hundred yards down the road on the far side. The Wolf went over to the window and looked out but his angle looking out the window was bad, so with the reflection on the car windscreen he couldn't see how many people were inside the car, but as he watched nobody got out. The car just sat there with its engine running. Exhaust fumes coming out of the rear. Shit. As usual Piasecki was right.

There was a pregnant pause in the room as both men thought about their next move. Just then, the sitting room door opened and a young blond woman, around eighteen or nineteen, walked in wearing only a man's white t-shirt. It was large on her and looked more like a dress, but it was obvious to anyone looking at her that she was wearing no underwear beneath it. Her firm full breasts swelled under the flimsy top and her nipples were clearly defined.

So that's what he was busy with, thought Piasecki.

The girl came over and put her arms around the Wolf and snuggled her head into his broad chest while giving Piasecki a suggestive look. The act told a story even without saying a word. She looked even younger standing next to the hard faced bald man, who was at least fifteen years' her senior. The two men gave each other a knowing smile.

"So, what are we going to do?" asked Piasecki.

"What can we do? They cannot know anything but we are being watched, so we must find out why and by whom before we make another move."

"But tonight..."

"Tonight will have to wait," Krupski said shrugging his shoulders. "We can collect the guns another night. They are not going anywhere and anyway we have our own consignment of merchandise coming in in the next few days. It will give me an opportunity to think about where we will look for Murray's missing stock". And with that he kissed the girl on the head and gently pushed her away. "Go make us some breakfast", he said to her, slapping her on the bottom as she turned to leave. She giggled as she left the room.

The Wolf stomped back up the stairs and retrieved his mobile from the bedside locker. He looked up the number he wanted and then typed it into the new phone. He sent a message "Call me now" to the number, before he went back down to eat his breakfast.

Chapter Seven

On the day of the funeral, the Gardaí still had Rob and Sinead's house closed off as a crime scene. As the front lawn was open with no fence delineating it, a blue and white striped tape labelled 'Garda' went from the bushes in the neighbours' garden to several metal bars stuck in the grass on the inside of the pathway to help cordon off the area. And if that hadn't been enough to keep unwanted visitors out, up until yesterday the Gardaí had a patrol car stationed outside on the road.

The Garda tape stopped any chance the neighbours had of trying to forget the whole thing. It kept them focused on the murder and delayed life in the quiet suburb from getting back to normal for a few more days. Cars slowed down and drivers and their passengers rubbernecked as they crawled past wondering what had happened. Neighbours still gathered in small clusters in doorways and looked anxiously towards the house, wondering how such a thing could happen in their nice picturesque neighbourhood. The women gossiped, telling and retelling rumours until everything was distorted like a real life game of Chinese whispers. The neighbourhood men already fretting about faltering house prices in a worsening economy could only imagine what it would do to their own homes' l values. But Sinead didn't care about any of that. Let them stand there gossiping. What did it matter to her? Her husband and the father of her children was dead.

Nothing else mattered after that.

Nothing.

The Garda scene tape and the continuing Garda presence was there to help maintain the integrity of the scene, just in case the investigating team needed to go over anything again, Detective Inspector Higgins had told Sinead. With the technical team finishing up the morning after the shooting, what he really meant was that the tape was there to stop press photographers from breaking in and taking illicit pictures, not to mention stealing souvenirs from the scene. It would not be the first time that a photographer had gotten pictures of a supposedly sealed room in which somebody had been killed. Blood stained floors or stairs in dishevelled rooms with tabloid style headlines helped sell papers. Lots of them. An editor in one of the larger Irish tabloid newspapers was famous for saying "if it bleeds, it leads". Even the bigger traditional dailies were not against such shock tactics if they thought that they could get away with it.

In an otherwise quiet news period, the information hungry journalists were searching for any new angle to keep the story fresh and interesting and would talk to any neighbours who wanted to share the limelight, and there usually were a few around. In this case they all would say the same thing, that they were a nice quiet family and that their children played together. However no parent interviewed added that none of their children would be allowed to play together again if the O'Dwyer family ever came back to live in the house. The story going to print along with eye-catching pictures didn't even need to be factually correct; people summed it all up from the picture. The details were secondary.

After all a picture says more than a thousand words.

When Sinead and the children had gone to stay in her mother's house, the reporters had simply upped stakes and followed them. It was like a macabre show travelling around the county. In a vain attempt to get rid of the pack of information and quote hungry reporters massing outside, Morgan had volunteered to issue a statement on the family's behalf. While he wasn't expecting the statement to bring about the end of the siege on its own, he hoped that this trickle of quotable material coupled with a continuation of the current solid silence would help the reporters reach the conclusion that there was nothing to be gained in hanging around. Not really knowing what to say, Morgan had kept the statement short and to the point. He had fussed over it for nearly an hour before eventually just going with his first version.

"I wish to make a statement on behalf of the O'Dwyer family. Rob O'Dwyer's widow and children have suffered an appalling loss in terrible circumstances that they are still trying to come to terms with. They had no knowledge of any of the gang related dealings currently being speculated upon by the press. I appeal to all of you to respect the

privacy of the family at this very difficult time. There will be no further comment on this matter".

It did have the desired effect, at least initially. The number of reporters and correspondents camped outside dropped dramatically from that point on. Everyone in the house was relieved to be out of the media's glare, although they all expected the reporters to reappear if and when the Gardaí investigating the murder arrested anyone for it. That was until one of the more enterprising reporters realised who Morgan was and tied him to the death of a neo Nazi and the recovery of World War II counterfeit money the previous year. Then the whole thing seemed to kick off again. Their saving grace came when the news broke of a well-known married politician getting caught in a homosexual act in the Phoenix Park. Morgan couldn't have been happier to hear that the sanctimonious bastard had been caught, quite literally with his trousers down.

The O'Dwyer family house being sealed off brought an unexpected problem as it meant that the gathering after the funeral could not be held in Rob & Sinead's house, as the case would normally have been. So the reception was held at Sinead's mother's house in Foxrock instead. This was where Sinead and the children were all staying for the time being so it made some sense. Morgan was going to ask Sinead why she hadn't simply booked a hotel, he would have given her the money. But when he saw the state that she was in, he knew why. It was only a few miles further away and having the family around in a familiar and safe atmosphere was more comforting than being in a hotel. She was doing her best to hold it together for the children. Their need was the greater now; they had lost their father in a truly horrible way and it would stay with them all for the rest of their lives. Morgan thought that he should probably have taken over and made these arrangements himself but Sinead's mother had been adamant that it would be held at her house and the last thing that he wanted to do now was fight with her.

The detectives did allow Sinead to return to the house two days after the killing to take some clothes and toys for the children. Especially Linda, who was having real difficulty getting to sleep without her pink teddy bear, called Giggles. Rob had made it for her in the teddy bear factory in Dundrum Shopping Centre that very Christmas. It was her favourite toy now. She clung to it and kept telling people that her daddy had made it for her and that he had promised to get her another one on her birthday. To listen to her it was like her father would come back through the door at any minute. It was very upsetting for everyone to hear her talk like that. Even Morgan could feel his eyes welling up. Neither Sinead nor anybody else could seem to convince her otherwise, although they probably did not try that hard, preferring instead to let her mind cling on to the hope that one day he might. At least for now anyway.

When Morgan walked into Sinead's family house, he hardly believed that he was there with the same group of people that had stood so solemnly alongside him in a cemetery an hour or so earlier. In fact, you wouldn't have had an idea of where they had all come from except that everybody was dressed formally in black. A group of about twenty friends and relations had gone back to the house and formed small groups where they talked about anything and everything except what had happened.

They were all laughing out loud and joking amongst themselves as if they were at a happy family get together like a birthday party or an anniversary party. He knew that in private though, they talked of nothing else. What would happen now? Where would Sinead and the kids live? How would she manage now? Wasn't it awful what happened, but what about the drugs or drug dealers or how Rob had come to be involved with them? And the poor children, the poor innocent children, what chance did they have now? Wouldn't they be scarred for life by his horrible death and reputation as a drug dealer of all things? They didn't stand a chance was the general consensus.

Morgan made his way through the various small groups and headed for the kitchen at the back of the house to find Sinead, only to be told that she was upstairs with Niamh and Ian and would not be down for a while. Linda, the oldest girl had gone out with friends. Sinead's mother, Pauline was busy making tea and cutting sandwiches for the mourners. A few bottles of beer and some spirits were on the kitchen counter still unopened.

There were obviously no takers yet.

Morgan offered to help and ended up carrying plates of sandwiches out to the front room, depositing them prominently on a side table before taking a handful for himself.

Morgan was somewhat surprised to see Smith there. He hadn't seen him in nearly two years and now twice in one day. He had known Smith well but had never taken him to be someone who would come back to the house. Although, Rob had worked for Smith for the last few years, as far as Morgan knew, Smith had never been to their house or met Sinead before. He was standing alone, somewhat awkwardly over to one side of the front room by the fireplace, surrounded by little groups of people chatting. With his big hulking frame, he looked out of place standing there. A couple of the older visitors gave him the odd quizzical look as they stood chatting. For his part, he seemed to be just waiting out his time before he could politely slip away, which made his presence there seem even stranger. Why did he bother to come at all if he didn't want to be there? However when he saw Morgan coming in, he smiled and walked over to him.

"So, how are you?" Smith asked eager not to be left alone again.

"Grand, I suppose, it's still a lot to take in. But I suppose it was as good a turn out as possible considering the circumstances", Morgan mumbled, his mouth still full of cheese sandwich.

"Yeah, I hope as many turn up to mine when I kick the bucket", Smith joked, taking a mouthful of tea.

"The church would be packed but not because we care about you. We'll all turn up just to make sure that you're really dead," Morgan answered grinning.

"That will be more like it", Smith smiled back. Then his mood darkened slightly and he spoke softly. "Not a nice way to go, being shot in the head".

"I can think of better ways alright", Morgan agreed, but he didn't comment on it further as he really didn't want to think about it. Changing the subject, Morgan commented, "I wasn't expecting to see you back here."

"No? Well I just had to talk to Sinead for a few minutes", Smith said in way of explanation.

"Oh yeah? About what?" Morgan said curiously, wondering what the big man was up to.

"No, nothing like that", Smith replied quickly. "I just wanted to see if she needed anything.

Maybe give a bit of money to help her out?"

"Give her a bit of money? You? That's surprisingly nice of you. Are you sick?" Morgan was amazed by the generosity of the man who made the stereotypical Jewish moneylender seem overly extravagant and complacent about his cash.

"Fuck off, I can be nice when I want to be", Smith retorted, putting his hand across his broad chest, feigning hurt.

"Most of the time, you just normally choose not to be, is that it?" Morgan couldn't help but laugh.

"You all seem to have a very low opinion of me. So changing the subject, have the Gardaí been to see you?"

"Yes. I gave a statement to a DI Higgins and some female detective. I can't remember what her name was. I did it that morning as I was with Sinead and the family. They took my prints too so that they could eliminate me from their enquiries," Morgan said imitating a thick country accent. "Could you believe that they wanted an alibi for my movements? I wasn't able to give him one though as I had been watching a DVD at home in Wexford on my own."

Morgan drifted off slightly as he recalled giving his own statement down at the station a few days earlier and it hadn't been a pleasant experience. It had been held in a small interview room just off the reception of the local Garda station. The table and the chair that he was directed towards had both been secured to the floor and there had been a security camera positioned high up on the wall angled down to cover his side of the room. He did not know who, if anyone, had been watching him. The plastic chair which was bolted to the floor was hard and uncomfortable and he had found himself squirming on the seat after only a few minutes. The two other chairs in the room, which the two detectives sat on, could be moved. These chairs had made a scratching, screeching noise on the tiled floor as they sat down.

Morgan had been interviewed by the senior Gardaí investigating the murder, DI Walsh and Callaghan, who was sitting in and was mostly silent. She spent most of her time just watching Morgan's reactions and occasionally glancing at the manila folder in front of her. The interview had been easy enough considering the circumstances. Morgan had been asked what he assumed were all the usual questions. Did he know anything about the murder? Did he own a motorbike? Who could have done such a thing? Did he know anything about Rob's business problems?

But as routine as the questions were, Morgan had a suspicion that the interview could have turned against him in the blink of an eye. The tension in the room visibly increased when the Garda asked the inevitable question: where was he at the time of the murder? He was watching a DVD at home. Could anyone vouch for that? When he said no, Morgan caught the two detectives giving each other a quick glance.

It was at this point, about thirty minutes into the interview that the female detective had asked him about his relationship with the deceased's wife. Morgan had turned on her, surprising himself with the level of venom in his voice.

"My relationship with Sinead? What relationship? She was my best friend's wife for God's sake. That was my relationship with her. That was my *only* relationship with her."

Callaghan had struck home but the DI had not followed up. Instead he decided to change tack and refer back to the time when Morgan and Rob had worked together as bouncers. Could Rob have refused someone who had a grudge? Did any known dealers come into the bar? Morgan composing himself deliberately took his time to answer each question. He had made sure that he did not allow the Gardaí the pleasure of seeing him getting ruffled again. Eventually after nearly two hours of having asked a lot and having learned precious little, they had given up. Both detectives had walked him to the door and asked him to contact them if he remembered anything. "Yeah right", he had thought. "Don't hold your breath."

Realising that he had zoned out, he snapped back to the present. "What about you? Have you been interviewed yet?"

"Yeah, yesterday by some thick fucking detective straight out of the Garda school down in Tipperary. You know they should sit them down and make them watch The Bill or CSI or something to get some technique. He had me waiting for over an hour for him and then kept me for another two hours asking stupid questions. And not just about Rob but about my business as well. This is all I need right now. Things are bad enough without them poking their noses into that. They took my prints then as well even though I told them that they had them on file already after that incident at the chip shop a few years back. You know it took me ten washes to get that crap off my hands", he said holding his hands up in the air as if to show Morgan exactly how clean that they were now.

"What do you mean about the business as well?" Morgan enquired, but Smith didn't answer- instead he just stared over his shoulder, causing Morgan to turn to see what he was looking at. Sinead had come down the stairs holding the smallest child in her arms she went past them into the kitchen. Both Morgan and

Smith stopped talking and watched as she walked by the door. Sinead looked up and when she saw them both staring at her, she seemed to walk faster, staring coldly in front of her. She glanced in their direction, her eyes skimming them both. She seemed afraid to look at them properly as if they were strangers to be wary of and she couldn't get away from their gaze quick enough. Morgan thought that it was as if seeing him had somehow made her feel worse, if such a thing were possible. He felt a sudden rush of blood to the face when she turned away so quickly to get away from him. He was going to comment on her state to Smith, but stopped when he saw the way the other man was looking at her. Was that desire in his expression or something else? Smith amazed him by admitting it.

"She is a good looking woman and she's got great tits," he whispered, as Sinead disappeared up the hallway. Morgan was surprised because although Sinead was a very attractive woman, Smith usually went for them much younger.

"Jesus but you're not thinking of making a move on her while her husband's body is not even cold in the ground?" Morgan said, half joking, half serious. He actually surprised himself how quickly he came to her defence, but he realised that he would need to protect her from circling predators like Smith. Smith never had a chance to reply because at that point Sinead's mother came over carrying a pot of tea asking them if they needed a fresh cup. Smith politely refused and seemed to take the interruption as his cue to leave.

"Look, I got to go. I'll catch you later alright?"

"Yeah, no problem" Morgan nodded. He watched Smith leave and walk up the drive with some curiosity. He continued to stare long after he had disappeared out of sight.

Morgan had planned to wait till the guests were gone, so he could get Sinead on her own, but as he waited Pauline cornered him saying that Sinead needed to go to bed and rest. Morgan reluctantly agreed, as he knew that Pauline could be very stubborn over such things. "Okay," he said grudgingly, "Just let her know I will call her tomorrow or she can call me anytime if she needs to talk."

"Of course, I will", came the reply and with that Morgan left to go home.

Chapter Eight

It was after nine o'clock, and apart from the flickering light from the open fire it was dark in the room. Morgan turned on the small antique table lamp in the living room of his mother's house casting the corner of the room in a soft warm glow.

Even though the central heating was on, he had lit the fire about an hour ago, just after his mother and he had finished eating dinner. They had an informal arrangement between them that on the rare occasions that he visited and stayed over, that after dinner, she would do the dishes and he would light the fire. Morgan always thought that there was nothing like a real fire. It was a lot of work, cleaning out the grate, getting the coal and the logs together and nurturing it so it would burn properly. But once lit, the way the flames jumped and the colours constantly changed was mesmerising. He loved watching the reflection of the flames on the walls and ceiling as they lit up the room. The flames were a living thing and could not be replicated no matter how good a modern electric or gas fire was. A modern heater could warm the body but a real fire could warm the soul, his mother always said. And she was right.

With the two Labrador dogs lying lazily on their expensive dog beds at their feet, Morgan and his mother sat in the darkened room. They talked about the past, about this person and that and how good things were in those days. Simpler. Not like nowadays, where everything was rushed and nobody had time for anyone else. Of course those days weren't any easier, but nostalgia and rose tinted glasses had a big part to play in the conversation. There were times when the lively banter would fade and they would simply sit in silence. The only noise was the wind and rain beating down outside or the creaking of the leather couch inside. The combination of the soft light and the silence made the living room a very peaceful and tranquil place to be in. It was exactly what Morgan needed.

The room had slipped into silence once more as Morgan and his mother drank the hot tea that his mother had just made. Morgan began to drift off and reminisce about a time when Rob, Sinead and himself were much younger and back in school, when their biggest concern was their looming Intermediate Certificate exams. Looking back, everything had seemed much easier then. People were right when they claimed that your school years were your best. God, how long ago was that? Morgan thought that it must be nearly twenty years ago. Back then if their teachers were to be believed, they all had had a bright future in front of them. Life seemed to offer so much more than it had delivered.

Of all of his classmates, Rob definitely seemed to have the brightest future ahead of him. Back then he was one of the cool kids in school. The girls all loved him. They would swarm around him during breaks in class, hanging on his every word, giggling away loudly, as only teenage girls can. Rob always seemed to wear the trendiest clothes, listen to the coolest music and was the typical iconic class rebel with his blond hair and good looks rounding out the perfect package. In school, Morgan had looked up to him with a certain level of awe. There were times when he would have sold his soul to the devil to have what Rob appeared to have. He would have liked to say that he was a good friend with him back in those days, but he wasn't. At that time in his life, Rob was out of his league, socially speaking. The closest he ever got to him was sitting beside him in Geography class, where he would bask in the glow of his presence.

And as for Sinead, she and Rob made the perfect couple. She was something that teenage boy's fantasies were made of. She was about five foot seven or eight and had a great figure. Slim, toned, well-proportioned and a chest to die for. Morgan always remembered one particular day in school when he had seen her coming back from playing hockey in the gym. She was wearing tight gym shorts and a clinging t-shirt, with her face covered in sweat and her chest heaving from the exertion. She looked fantastic. It was enough to make Morgan run to the toilets straight away. Unlike Rob, when Morgan had been in school, he had been shy and lacked confidence and was more than a bit awkward around girls.

Sinead hadn't changed much even after all these years and three children. Physically she was still slim, just not as well toned.

Her long dyed blond hair had been allowed to return to its natural brown colour and had been cut back into a more manageable bob. But while she looked similar, Morgan thought that she had seemed tired compared to the girl of old. Her eyes didn't sparkle as once they had. Life's hard knocks had taken their toll on her. But there was still something about her. Something that made you look twice when she walked by. That quality she had not lost.

It was shortly after Christmas 1987, when Rob had announced to everyone that he had got Sinead pregnant. Morgan remembered that school day clearly, as being a single Mum was a big deal back then. Probably still was to a certain degree, but it was definitely an issue back in the eighties. Sinead also had the distinction of being the first girl in the school to have become pregnant. The school head master had wanted her to leave immediately as in those days a teenage mother was still considered a black mark against the schools image. Especially in the Catholic run school that they were in. After all, she could become a bad influence on the other girls. The school management had wanted her to join a special school for girls in her situation, but in fairness to Sinead's parents, they had insisted that she go as far in her education as she could, hoping that she could return to it in later years.

The school authorities had eventually relented and she stayed on and did her Intermediate Certificate exams that summer. By then, Sinead's bump was looming large. She waddled around looking a bit out of place. She loved the attention that she was getting from the other girls and from the teachers trying to make sure she was comfortable wherever she went. But Morgan always thought that she looked a little sad, especially when she thought nobody was looking. As far as Morgan could remember, both Sinead and Rob passed their exams, but she did much better than him. Then they left school, she to become a full time mum, he to become an apprentice mechanic in his Uncle's garage.

But things were to take an unexpected twist. They had a little girl and named her Linda after her grandmother who had only recently passed away. Linda was born 9lbs 13ounces. She was born at five minutes past one in the afternoon after only three hours of labour, a relatively easy labour by all accounts. She was born healthy but she wasn't the baby they had expected. Not that they wanted a boy instead. They hadn't bothered about the child's sex; in fact they had fun creating lists of names for both, waiting to see the little face staring back up at them before settling on one.

Five minutes after the birth while, Rob and Sinead were still coming to terms with the arrival of a new little person into the world, the nurse left the birthing room with little Linda and returned with a doctor a few minutes later. These comings and goings unsettled Rob more than a little. The doctor approached the new parents with a solemn expression and informed them in muted tones that their new baby had been born with an additional chromosome, twenty-one instead of the usual twenty.

Linda had been born with Down Syndrome. She was the one in every thousand babies born with Down Syndrome in Ireland every year. Not a statistic to aspire to. Morgan wasn't a parent and probably never would be but he could only imagine the initial shock and distress felt by parents on finding out that their child was born with such an affliction. Initially the couple mourned the loss of the ideal of their perfect little girl but they came to love Linda's infectious smile and quickly got over their disappointment. To this day, there was little doubt about the love and devotion both parents showed their daughter.

Later that day, the doctor told Rob and Sinead that Linda would have a number of developmental issues. Macroglassia or a large protruding tongue would dominate Linda's appearance, coupled with an unusually round face and almond shaped eyes. She would be a late walker and need physiotherapy to aid in her physical development. Mentally she would develop as normal until she reached approximately eight years of age. The doctor went on to warn them about possible congenital heart defects, ear infections and thyroid dysfunctions. The doctor was trying to be kind but came across as cold and it was all too much for Rob and Sinead to take in.

Over the next few months they came into contact with many parents groups which proved invaluable for advice and support to the young couple. They came to terms with what had happened and got on with normal day-to-day parenting. It did however bring along a whole extra list of challenges and worries.

But this didn't put off Sinead, as she used to come into school every now and again at lunchtime, proudly pushing the pram to show her off to all her old classmates. All the other girls would ooh and aah at the sight of the baby. To them it was like a living doll all ready to play dress up with. But Sinead's visits to school grew less and less frequent until eventually they stopped altogether. The last time Morgan had seen her she looked well but it was to be another fifteen years before he would meet Rob and Sinead again.

When he did meet Rob again, he didn't initially recognise him. It had been about four or five years ago and Rob had cut his hair razor tight and had put on a lot of weight. Morgan's boss, John Smith had phoned him up earlier that night and told him that Ian, Morgan's usual Friday night colleague was sick and there was a new man working with him later. His name was Rob and he had never worked on the door before but he was a big enough lad and John Smith was sure that he would work out. Morgan never thought for an instant that it would be the same Rob from all those years before. They had joked about it later, but Morgan had always thought that it was strange how things had worked out. Nobody's life ever went the way that they thought it would.

As usual Morgan had been about ten minutes late to work that night. When he arrived, he found an out of shape guy who looked in his early forties standing by the door looking more than a little out of place and very self-conscious.

"Hiya. How are you doing?" Morgan said as he hurried up through the car park, offering his hand to the new guy. "Are you Rob?"

"Yes. I am", Rob said smiling, relieved that he wasn't on his own anymore. "I wasn't sure what to do, so I was just waiting here".

"Yeah, Sorry I'm late. I was watching the end of Dr. Who. Did you clock in?"

"No, I didn't know that you had too".

"No problem. This place is pretty handy; we get very little trouble here. Come on in, I will show you around", Morgan said, gesturing for the new guy to follow. The evening continued pretty much like any other. Being a doorman in a suburban pub can be quite boring. You get to know most of the regulars by name. You see the same faces, week in and week out. You could set the time on your watch by most of them. They sat in the same places in the bar and ordered the same drinks. Some were chatty, some weren't. It was all quite predictable. Morgan and Rob checked the odd young looking person for age, which if truth were known, some-times made Morgan feel old. Occasionally, you took someone out for being too drunk or a bit rowdy, but that was pretty much it. Most of the time, it was what Morgan would call handbags at ten paces, where lads would posture and stick their chests out in front of you eager to save face in whatever situation they found themselves in. Over the years, Morgan found that the best policy was just to stand there and ignore them while they got it out of their system. To respond would only encourage them. All the while he would be sneaking looks at their girlfriends as they stood beside them. You could go for months without having to do much to earn your money.

Those moments when you did end up earning your nightly money could be very intense and quite violent but were mostly over as soon as they had begun. Mostly doormen just drank tea, ate chocolate and flirted with all the female customers. The women could be young or old, good looking or plain, it didn't matter, as it was expected of them.

It had been a warm summer evening that first time Rob had worked. It was night time really as it was after nine o'clock, but as it was still so warm and bright out, you could be excused for think-ing it was the afternoon. The glorious summer day refused to end. Morgan was glad he was outside, even if he was working. He would hate being stuck inside on a night like this. In a few months, as the days got colder, he would be crying out for days like this. Best to enjoy every chance to get out that he could. Occasionally as they stood there, the sharp call of a bird singing happily could be heard over the bar's background noise. It was the height of sum-mer and everywhere was buzzing with life. Morgan thought that if he were not working that it would be a perfect night to drive out to Bray or Greystones in County Wicklow and go for a stroll along the beach or maybe just have a quiet pint in one of the many bars along the seafront.

Morgan had stood in his usual place on the right hand side of the doorway, leaning his shoulder casually against the doorframe and watched the throng of people in the patio area beside him. They were sitting there under the patio heaters, as the night air grew that bit colder, laughing, telling stories and catching up on the day's gossip. Who did what, where and when? "Look at the state of her", "What did she ever see in him anyway" or "Do you remember yer man?" they could be heard saying. At that point Rob had returned carrying two cups of piping hot tea. Getting tea was part of serving your time on the door, Morgan had joked with him.

"Here you go," Rob said, taking sachets of sugar and a spoon out of his pocket. "I couldn't remember how many sugars you said you take, so I brought some out".

"Fair play to you. It is two sugars. I am supposed to be on a diet, but to hell with it", Morgan joked, patting his small belly. "I am not going to give up sugar in my tea"

"Well in that case", Rob said with a mischievous grim, "You'll be wanting one of these" as he held up two Club Milk chocolate bars. Ah yes, Morgan thought, the cornerstone to all doormen's diet, chocolate.

"I can see that you are going to get on very well here." He had laughed heartily and a bond had been formed immediately between them.

The conversation faltered at that point as they both ate the chocolate and sipped, almost contemplatively on the tea. It was about then that a lounge girl came up to them and told them that they were needed upstairs. A customer was arguing violently with his friends and needed to be put out immediately.

"Come on", Morgan said to Rob as he went for the stairs. "It's time to put the game face on".

With Rob nervously following, they went up the stairs to the other bar. Once up there, they found nothing that needed their attention. It was usually an older crowd that went upstairs and tonight was no exception. The music piping through the speakers was a little bit softer and a little bit mellower. It was just couples and small groups sitting around chatting amongst themselves. They walked the room, pushing by the small tables until they got to the bar. There, the barman who was busy serving customers, nodded in the direction of the fire exit.

As Morgan pushed the double doors open, it was obvious that they were in the right place. They were confronted with a very large man in his late twenties, wearing a red shirt and arguing with two much older men, who by all accounts were just trying to calm him down.

"Are we alright here lads?" Morgan asked the men. The red shirted man turned and told him to fuck off and mind his own business while the other two looked on embarrassed.

"Look lads. I think it is time that you finished up," Morgan stated.

"Yeah. Well I don't, so why don't you fuck off".

"Now come on Derek there is no need for all of this. You have had too much to drink so come on home with us", said one of the older men in a conciliatory tone. But when he went to take the younger man's arm, he was rewarded with a push that nearly sent him flying backwards down the stairs. Only the quick reaction of the other man saved him at the last possible moment.

"That's it. Come on time to go", ordered Morgan and went to grab the red shirted man. The big guy lunged at him knocking him violently to one side but Morgan wasn't letting him get away with that too easily. With just his fingertips, Morgan managed to snag the man's arm, spinning him around. Morgan was a pretty big man but he was conceding at least two stone to this guy. Not only that, but this guy, Derek, or whatever his name was, had a manic expression on his face. His eyes were on fire. Years of experience told Morgan that this was not going to be easy.

But he had to take the man down. Fast.

The now snared Derek turned to face all his unbridled rage towards the man who dared to hold on to him. He bunched a large fist and drove it straight for Morgan's head. But it was a clumsy attempt and Morgan easily dodged it. As Derek's fist whizzed past him, Morgan ducked down and Derek's fist slammed painfully into the wall. Morgan twisted around behind Derek, grabbing both his arms and tried to pull him backwards but he was very strong and no matter how hard Morgan struggled he couldn't hold him. Derek flung his body left, then to the right in an attempt to shake Morgan off, but Morgan maintained a tight grip on him. His fingers digging into the soft flesh under the big mans' biceps. As they fought for control over each other, his muscles strained with the effort and sweat ran down his face. As he struggled with Derek, he could hear the large man's older companions begging him to calm down, but Derek wasn't listening to them. Instead he tried to reverse head-butt Morgan before pushing backwards and crushing him up against the wall. Morgan gasped as the air was forced out of him but through sheer effort and determination he still somehow managed to hold onto the man.

Over the big man's shoulder, Morgan could see Rob standing there stunned and motionless just inside the doors. Rooted to the spot and unsure of what he was supposed to do, he had a terrified look on his face.

"Come on Rob. Give me a hand here", Morgan yelled, breaking Rob out of his stupor. But Rob made a disastrous rookie error and stepped straight in front of the aggressive drunk, who simply head butted him, splitting open his nose and making his eyes water. To Rob's credit he stood his ground. As the three men fought they collapsed into a heap of flailing arms and legs onto the cold hard floor. Elbows were flung this way and that; kicks were made at impossible angles as Derek tried to cause as much damage to the two doormen as possible. Morgan ended up taking a glancing blow to the side of his face. This rough and tumble continued in the narrow fire exit for another five minutes but soon after the intensity started to fizzle out along with the men's adrenalin. It still took another good minute or two to wrestle Derek into submission. Only then did Morgan realise that a group of people including the red shirted man's older acquaintances surrounded them, some watching in real concern others just stretching up and looking over one another's shoulders and enjoying the impromptu show that they were putting on.

"You alright?" Morgan asked Rob as they lay there panting from their effort on top of Derek. Their combined weight of thirty stone keeping him pinned down.

"Yeah, I'm fine", Rob replied gasping with the effort.

"Your face is very familiar. Do I know you from somewhere?" Morgan asked Rob as he struggled to keep the big man on the ground. He asked it so casually like they were sitting around drinking tea and not lying on the ground pinning a drink-fuelled maniac down.

"Don't think so? Where are you from?" Rob answered, blood from his nose running into the corner of his mouth.

"Just down the road."

"Me too." At this point both men began to stare at each other more intently. An observer could imagine seeing the cogs in their brains turning as they searched their memories. They both seemed to be ticking off a list of similarities and differences from old mental images.

"Are you Rob O'Dwyer?"

"Yeah, I am". Rob replied, still none the wiser.

"I'm John Morgan. We were in school together"

"Of course John. It's been such a long time since I've seen you. How are you?"

Morgan laughed at the relaxed comment considering the situation. Gesturing towards the incapacitated man on the ground, he laughed, "I'm grand! And you can drop the John bit. People just call me Morgan now".

A few minutes later, the earlier rush of adrenalin used up and the fight gone completely out of him, the man was dragged down the back stairs to the fire exit at the bottom. There he was marched unceremoniously down to the car park gate and let go. But first, he was told in no uncertain terms what would happen to him if he ever returned. He stumbled off into the night, followed closely by the two older men who had now been joined by two women.

Their wives probably, thought Morgan.

When the panic was all over and Morgan had filled out the bars incident book, he did what all doormen did. While Rob went off to clean himself up, Morgan went back to his side of the door and his mug of tea, which was now cold and waited for the next bit of excitement.

Years before, Morgan had always wondered why the Gardaí always seemed to have a 'them and us' attitude to dealing with people. But after working on the doors for so long, he knew why. When a small group of people depended upon each other in sometimes very stressful and dangerous situations then they became close.

Very close.

For Rob and Morgan, their friendship was formed for a different reason. Rob had lost a lot of his friends over the years because of his ill thought out plans and get rich quick schemes which always ended in him borrowing money and then moving away. Morgan thought back fondly to their school years and just wanted to catch up with everything that had happened to his role model since the last time that they had seen each other. Whatever it was, they just seemed to click as friends. Most nights after working on the door, they would stay back for a pint before going home, telling stories of what happened on such or such a night. Like the time that six lads had squared up to fight them for refusing them entry or when Morgan hit one lad over the head with his walkie-talkie radio when he had been attacked with a broken bottle. Over the years, there were always plenty of stories to tell.

It was on one of those nights, that Rob had opened up and told Morgan everything that had happened to both himself and Sinead in the intervening years since school. Rob had gone to FAS, Ireland's main training agency to become a mechanic. As soon as he qualified he worked full time in his uncle's workshop. Initially everything was going reasonably well but with two more children to feed, he found himself in ever deepening financial problems trying to keep a roof over their heads. After a few more pints Rob admitted that he got involved in changing number plates and engraving different serial numbers on stolen cars for a local criminal after-hours in the workshop.

But the whole operation was badly run and it was not long before the Gardaí were on to them. Rob was inevitably caught red handed working on a stolen Jaguar. It wasn't his fault of course but the last car they stole had a tracking system on it and it led the Gardaí directly to it and him. It turned out that the gang was responsible for the theft of over ten million euro worth of high performance luxury cars. Through lack of evidence on the rest of the gang, Rob was the only one convicted. But he managed through the combination of having a clever solicitor, giving information on the car scam and his lack of any previous convictions, to get only two years in prison with the last eighteen months suspended. He was lucky with his timing, if you could call it luck. It was 2002 and the jails were all full to the brim. So he only spent a week in Mountjoy jail before being released under the controversial revolving door policy.

Needless to say, Rob did lose his job. You couldn't blame his father for that. According to Rob, it had been years before his father even talked to him again. It had only been in the last two years when Rob's mother had been diagnosed with Parkinson's disease that they had become close again.

So out of prison and with no money but not having any other trade, Rob tried to start his own little business. With the help of Sinead's parents, he and his family moved away from the area and into a rented house in Kilcoole in County Wicklow. Rob then took a lease on a large lockup in an old industrial park in Bray, where he opened his own workshop. They settled down in their new home and things went well for a couple of years. Rob built up a respectable business but financial problems crept up once again. The business was struggling and he needed some extra income to make ends meet. And that's how he had ended up working on the door. But even that hadn't helped and he had found himself being forced to give up his little workshop and working for a local garage instead. Rob had hated it, giving up the control over his own life. It had made him feel that he had failed yet again. Tom, his new employer on the other hand, couldn't have been happier as Rob brought in a lot of new business.

Over the months they were working together on the door, Morgan had tried his best to comfort and support Rob, telling him that it was all just a setback, that he would be back on his feet in no time and that he would make it in the long run. But as it turned out, he never had the chance. Rob saw to that himself.

Chapter Nine

Morgan had been up having a shower when the knock came on the bathroom door. At first he wasn't sure he heard it properly over the noise of the powerful electric shower. But there it was, his mother knocking on the bathroom door and calling out to him that he had a visitor. It was the Gardaí, she said loudly. A female detective no less, she added with a funny disapproving tone. So, cutting his shower short, Morgan dressed in the set of spare clothes that he kept in his old bedroom and went down the stairs. There he found Garda Callaghan alone in the brightly lit living room, his mother having made herself scarce in the kitchen. The detective did not hear him come up behind her, as she was busy searching through the myriad of photographs of both him and his sister that his mother proudly displayed on top of the piano and the surrounding walls.

"Can I help you?" Morgan asked, causing Callaghan to spin around, half shocked to see him standing there, towel in his hand as he continued to dry his hair. He recognised her immediately as she had been the lead detective that had interviewed him after the death of Rob. He hadn't liked her line of questioning then and wondered what she was doing here at this hour of the night?

"I am sorry for disturbing you so late in the evening. I just have some questions for you", she said by way of explanation.

"Okay. But couldn't this have waited until the morning?" Morgan asked, still drying his hair.

"Sometimes, these things can't wait", she replied curtly, gesturing for him to sit down.

"Fine". Why should he mind? He had nothing to hide after all. "But I have already gone over everything with yourself and DI Higgins the other day."

"I know. These are just some follow up questions. They help us get a better picture of the situation".

"Alright, ask away", Morgan said, moving one of the dogs off the couch before sitting down. The seat was warm where the big dog had been lying. He dropped the wet towel onto the ground beside him.

For a second Detective Callaghan looked like she was going to sit down as well before thinking better of it and standing near the fireplace opposite him.

"You were friends with both Rob and Sinead back in your school days. Isn't that right?" Callaghan asked.

"Yes, I knew them both".

"Were you not friends back then?"

"No, not really. They were the cool kids. I was not in their league in those days".

"Are you now?"

"Now...?" Morgan paused. "Yes. Now, we are friends".

"Did you see them much?"

"I used to but not in the last year since I moved down the country".

"Since the last time that we talked, I've had the opportunity to do some background checks on you. It seems that I am in the presence of a bit of a hero". Callaghan said referring to his recent run in with a group of German Neo-Nazi's in his new home in Wexford.

"I don't know what you have read but I'm no hero", Morgan said dismissing her remark immediately. He had never liked the hero label that the newspapers had labelled him with. He had just done what anyone in his situation would have.

"That's not true according to the reports that I have read. You rescued a woman and child from international kidnappers and blackmailers, all while recovering stolen Nazi treasure. Not bad for a weekend's work".

"It sounds much more exotic and exciting than it really was. I was just helping some friends out of a bad situation".

"It said that one of the kidnappers was never found".

"One drowned. It wasn't my fault. His body was never recovered". What was she driving at? Morgan wondered.

The detective paused and stared him straight in the eye. "Would you kill again to save a friend?"

"What do you mean, would I kill again? I haven't killed anyone yet!" Morgan shouted unable to contain his growing frustration any longer and jumped up onto his feet.

"Okay. Calm down. I believe you".

"Look if you have something to ask, just ask it", Morgan snapped. He was extremely annoyed as he could imagine where she was going with this and was wary of any trap she might be laying for him. But he forced himself to calm down before sitting back down, albeit on the edge of the chair.

"Fair enough", Detective Callaghan replied. Deciding to change to a more direct approach, she asked, "Where were you the night Rob O'Dwyer was murdered?"

"I have already told you this. I had been painting and decorating one of the mobile homes in the hotel grounds that I live in. I was tired and went to bed early to watch a DVD. I have already given you the number of Albert Muller at the Bayswater Hotel for you to check".

"Oh, I checked that. But he only accounts for your whereabouts up until six o'clock when he saw you packing up your tools. Nothing after. There was plenty of time to drive up to Rob's house and kill him. But you said that you went to bed early. Can anyone confirm that?

"No. I was in bed alone. Okay?"

"Do you have a steady girlfriend? You're a bit old to be still playing the field aren't you?"

"No. I don't have a girlfriend at the moment. And anyway my love life is none of your business. What is this all about?" Morgan said firmly.

She ignored him and pressed on. "What about Sinead? Did you ever go out with her?"

"I told you, she was out of my league back in school."

"She's not now though is she? Married to a convicted criminal, always stuck for money. She turned out to be a real loser. Still pretty enough though, isn't she? And then there you are, all confident and flash, successful. You are good with women now as well. You turned out better than him. She made a bad choice back then. You could have taken her away from all that."

"I lost my fiancée just over a year ago. I have no time for any woman at the moment, especially not the wife of one of my best friends".

"Ah, so you still fancy her then? You still have a long held teenage crush on her," Callaghan quickly retorted. "Were you jealous of Rob? Did you want him out of the way?"

"Fuck off", Morgan snapped. He was getting sick of this.

"Were you sleeping with her?" the detective asked as she pressed home her attack.

"No, I wasn't" Morgan said, angrily jumping to his feet again. "Now I have a lot to do. If you have any more questions to ask you can do so in the presence of my solicitor", he indicated towards the hall door. He wasn't going to talk to her anymore.

Detective Callaghan stood, knowing that she had hit a nerve. She was on to something and she wasn't about to let go now. "There is something going on between you isn't there? Or at least there was? Did Rob find out? Is that why you killed him?"

"I killed him?" Morgan said in disbelief. "Why are you here harassing innocent people when there is a real murderer out there...." he shouted, pointing towards the front door... "walking around. I hadn't seen either of them in nearly a year. There is nothing going on between Sinead and myself".

"Don't you worry, we will get the murderer. But one last question if you don't mind. Her phone records tell us that on the night Rob was murdered, straight after she called the ambulance, she called you next. You before her own mother or his parents. Why do you think that was?"

"I don't know. Have you asked her?" Morgan shouted at her and throwing his arms up into the air.

"We did. She said you were a family friend."

"Well there you go. I am a family friend".

"You must have been a very close family friend, yet you admit that you hadn't seen them in nearly a year. Yet she still calls you up out of the blue to tell you that her husband has just been murdered".

Morgan refused to comment. Normally he always managed to maintain a cool and calm exterior but this woman instinctively knew which buttons to push and read his reactions. Although she was a mile off the mark as regards his participation in Rob's murder, she was closer than he liked her to be in regard to his relationship with Sinead. Although he had never slept with her, when he was younger he had always wanted to. But it was just never meant to be. Now after Eimear's death, he no longer thought of her like that. No one could replace his Eimear and he was sure that she felt the same about Rob.

"Were you a shoulder to cry on?" Callaghan persisted. "Did you comfort her in her hour of need? After all she is alone and vulnerable right now."

"That's it. I told you I am not answering any more of your ridiculous questions unless my solicitor is present. I am not answering anymore of your questions. In fact, I am going to contact my solicitor to complain about you coming here on the night that I buried my best friend accusing me of having an affair with his wife. This is a form of harassment." Morgan marched out of the room and flung open the front door with a crash. Cold air rushed into the warm house.

Realising that there was nothing to be gained by staying, Detective Callaghan walked out the hall door and turned to face him. "You seem to have forgotten that two men have been murdered. We have to ask questions Morgan."

"Not ones like that you don't. Now get the hell out of my house", and with that he slammed the door in her face.

Chapter Ten

Later that night despite the biting cold Sinead was sitting on a bench in her mother's back garden. The light coming from the kitchen window lit up that half of the garden. All of the relatives and friends who had come to the house after the funeral had finally left. As far as Sinead was concerned, they could not have gone quick enough. The effort required to deal with their pleasantries and condolences was simply too much to bear. People had been coming up to her ever since she had walked down the stairs to discover her husband murdered on the sofa and telling her that everything would be alright, but she could not see that.

Everything was not all right.

Everything was all wrong and she could see no light at the end of the tunnel.

Her marriage to Rob hadn't been good for a long time. She had imagined leaving him on numerous occasions only to stay because she feared the effect that it would have on their children. She wanted to be single again, to be away from him but not like this. Now it was the first time in nearly twenty years that Rob wasn't with her and she felt totally and absolutely alone without him. At night she lay in bed unable to sleep and called out his name to the darkness, hoping that he would answer. She still could not believe all this was happening. She did not want to believe it. It was like a bad B movie script and she was just waiting, praying for some unseen director to shout, "CUT" and end her misery, and let her life return to normal. Why had this happened to them? To her? She was a good person; she raised her kid's right, sent them to school and helped them with their homework, looked after them as any mother would. What had she done so wrong to end up like this?

The more she thought about it, the more her anger boiled over that the man she loved most in this world had let her and the kids down. He had gone off on some crazy scheme and had gotten himself killed for it. She thought that Rob was lucky he was dead because if she had ever found out that he had gotten himself involved with drugs then she would have killed him herself.

She had kept wondering if what instead of him, that Robs involvement had got one of the kids killed? She would never have forgiven him. But she still missed him; she missed him so much that it tore her heart apart. But she could not stay mad for long. She never could with him. She remembered his smile and the way that he used to put his arms around her, for a few minutes making her feel like a carefree teenage girl again. With him, she felt both beautiful and loved.

"I miss you, Rob" Sinead said out loud and began to cry gently, her laboured breathing visible in the cold night air.

After her nap and with the children either asleep or camped in front of the television, she had helped her mother do the cleaning up even though her mother had insisted that she would do it herself. She had no desire to do dishes but it was more to keep herself busy after the guests had left. She could lose herself in the routine and monotony. She had come to dread the quiet points throughout the day because they gave her time to think. And she had nothing good to think about. She tried to get on with things; anything that kept her busy and her mind active was good, regardless of what it was.

Even washing the dishes.

Sinead's mother, Pauline, for her part was hopelessly lost as to what to do or say to calm her daughter, but what could any mother do in these circumstances? Only try and support her child. Little did she know that Sinead was having panic attacks as she lay in her bed at night, when everything rushed through her mind at a relentless speed over and over again. Pauline fretted about everything. What if she had done this or that differently? She was an intelligent woman and knew it made no sense to think this way but she could not stop herself.

Sinead lit another cigarette as she sat there on the wrought iron bench, her hands trembling slightly as she did. She had no jacket on but did not feel the cold January air. She was numb to it. She was pretty much numb to everything. She had quit smoking five years ago and had taken it up again that dreadful morning nearly a week ago as she sat in the Garda crime scene truck. It had just seemed so natural to accept one when the detective had innocently offered it to her. She had lit it and inhaled like she had never stopped. It was like riding a bike. What was the point of not smoking? What good would it do her? God knows how many she had smoked that day or in the past week but they were helping to steady her nerves, so she was not about to stop now. She'd give them up again in a few weeks or maybe she wouldn't.

Nothing mattered now.

Painful as it was the funeral today had brought her a measure of relief. With Rob buried at least there would be a degree of closure. Contrary to what the detective said, she believed the Gardaí would probably never catch the man who did this. What were detection rates in murders these days, something like one in four; she thought that she read somewhere? Probably less where gang crime was concerned, as witnesses would feel too intimidated to willingly come forward. They would be too afraid of retribution. Detective Higgins said that they would allow her back into the house in a couple of days, but she didn't want to go back.

Not now.

Not ever.

As she sat there, smoking her cigarette and biting what was left of the nail polish off her nails she had reached a decision. She needed a fresh start, a new beginning to build a life of her own. Whatever happened, she could never sleep in that house again. She would always be afraid to walk back down those stairs. Her mind couldn't cope with seeing images like that twice. No, she had made up her mind. Now that she had a death certificate, she would ask Morgan or her mother to go to the solicitor tomorrow and get the house transferred into her name and then she would sell it. She'd probably have to sell it for a lot less then it was worth but she didn't care. She just wanted out; it was not her home anymore. She'd move away with the kids and start again and leave all this pain behind. Maybe she would move to Kilkenny as she'd always enjoyed her weekends away there. It would take her and the kid's years to come back from this, but at least the worst was over now. It was time to rebuild, if not for her sake then for the kids. Poor Linda was fretting terribly. Despite being twenty one, her mind could not understand what was happening and Sinead knew that she had to normalise things as soon as possible.

So for the first time in a week, she saw a chink of light in her bleak future and felt a bit better for it. At least she had a rough plan on how to move forward and that was enough to take a little of the load off. She stubbed the end of the cigarette out in a flower pot beside her and stood up, smoothing down her dress and was ready to go back inside to face her mother and her endless cups of tea when all of a sudden a dirty gloved hand was placed roughly over her mouth and her body dragged backwards towards the unlit side of the house. She tried to scream but the hand was so firmly clamped over her mouth nothing more than a muffled yelp came out. Nearly suffocating she could taste the dirt and grime of the glove. Her attacker said nothing as she was being dragged backwards, losing one of her shoes in the process.

Terrified that she was going to be dragged into the corner and raped, Sinead tried to grab onto something, anything to stop herself being taken. At one point she managed to catch hold of a drainpipe running down the side of the house, but her attacker jerked her sideways so violently that she let go. Scraping her knuckles on the pebbledash as she did so.

When they were down the side pathway of the house, well away from prying eyes, she was twisted around and slammed against the wall of the house, her head slamming violently against the pebble dashed wall. She could imagine a trickle of warm blood running down the back of her head, matting her hair. Her attacker was pressing his body tightly against hers to stop her moving while using one hand to cover her mouth. His face right up against hers, like they were lovers about to kiss. His breath stank. It was foul. It was so bad it nearly made her gag.

"Right, Bitch. Shut the fuck up and listen", snarled a rough Dublin accent.

Sinead tried to scream again and was looking around wildly for someone to save her. Her attacker loosened his hold on her just long enough to punch her hard in the stomach, Sinead gasped in a mixture of pain and shock. She wanted to vomit but somehow held it in.

"Stay still, you fucking cow" He spat at her, before violently pressing against her again. "And listen". Sinead stood trembling, her eyes wild with terror, unable to do anything. Fear had completely taken over.

"Your husband had something very valuable belonging to me. It is a package about the size of a suitcase and I want it. Now we know that the Gardaí don't have it, so it must still be hidden somewhere here."

Sinead tried to protest. To tell the man that she didn't know where this package was, that she never knew what her husband had been up to. But her attacker wasn't having any of it. He just pressed his body against her harder forcing her cruelly back up against the pebble dashed wall. Despite the pain, his squalid smell overwhelmed her. He mustn't have showered in days.

"You have three days from now to find it", her attacker said. "I will contact you to arrange collecting it. If you don't find it or if I even smell a fucking pig, I will come after your kids starting with that mongoloid bitch and working my way through them until I get to you. Do you understand? Well do you bitch?"

Sinead nodded as best she could with his hand clamped over her mouth. The fear in her eyes saying more than words ever could. She got it, find the drugs or her children would be hurt. No Gardaí.

"Three days and I'll be back and you better have it. I will be watching. If you contact the pigs I will fucking know about it. I will make you wish that you'd never been born".

And with that he ran off, banging the side gate loudly behind him as he went but Sinead didn't take the opportunity to run away in the opposite direction. Instead she just stood petrified, fixed in the same spot as if he was still holding her and started to cry. As her tears mounted she slid down to the ground before sobbing loudly. She then stifled her own cries, afraid that her attacker might take it into his head to come back and beat her for making noise. She must have been there ten minutes, the side gate banging gently in the wind, so terrified that she could not catch her breath properly never mind move. Not until the security light in the back garden came on and she heard her mother's voice calling out to her.

"Are you alright out there Sinead? Come on in before you catch your death of cold."

Another couple of seconds passed before she heard her again. "Where are you? Come in please, its freezing out here."

Sinead looked up and saw her mother staring at her from the corner of the house. She looked shocked and had her hands over her mouth. She seemed to be saying something but Sinead couldn't hear her as she had started to roar uncontrollably. Through her tears Sinead heard her mother call out in a panicked voice, "Oh, my God. What is after happening to you?

Chapter Eleven

It was a beautiful winter morning and after the previous night's storms, the sea air was crisp and fresh. The sky was bright blue and completely devoid of the heavy black clouds that had covered the east coast of the country all week. And the high winds that had flung the rain violently against his old bedroom window were gone; only to be replaced by a gentle breeze, which brushed softly across Morgan's face as he went for a run.

When he had awoken that morning, he had still been annoyed about the unexpected interview with Garda Callaghan, especially her line of questioning the night before. Deciding that he wasn't going to let her get to him, Morgan sent an email to his solicitor outlining the events of the impromptu questioning. Then he decided to go for a run to clear his head before he got on with his day. It had just gone nine o'clock in the morning and apart from the odd walker, Morgan was largely alone on the promenade in Bray. He had parked his classic Mercedes in the small car park down near the harbour and was heading the mile or so towards Bray head with its tall white cross on top, which dominated the small coastal town.

When he was younger and training hard, Morgan regularly came out to Bray to run the seafront and then challenge himself on a timed run up the head. In his prime, he could reach the top in less than twenty minutes. He knew that today would be a much different affair. Morgan had started out slowly to get the feel for it again. His leg muscles were stiff and tight because he had not run much over the last few months due to his earlier ankle injury but he knew that they would stretch quickly enough due to the fact that he had recently started to train on the treadmill in the gym. As far as Morgan was concerned this was the perfect opportunity to measure himself against his old benchmarks. To help focus on where he was and where he needed to be.

His ankle, which had never fully recovered from the injury received in his fall at a lighthouse six months earlier, was already aching with every stride that he took. His physiotherapist had warned Morgan to stay off his feet for a few months after the fall but he hadn't been able to. Even without a full time job there were always things that needed doing. Not to mention that Morgan had nobody to wait hand and foot on him, to help him with getting dinners, shopping and washing. Not that he would have anyone looking after him anyway. He hated being dependent on anyone for anything. It wasn't his style.

By his watch, it took him just over two minutes to reach the aquarium which was midway along the old Victorian era promenade. Another three minutes saw him nearing the end. With a spurt he raced by the amusement arcades and the old Bray Head Hotel at the end and up along the path leading to the initial slopes. Unlike in his younger days, Morgan was already noticeably panting a little as he crossed Fiddlers Railway Bridge and turned right through a set of gates. He left the cliff walk to Greystones, six miles away, and ran up to the start of the hill climb.

Being winter, most of the bushes and trees covering this part of the head had no leaves. Bare branches whipped Morgan's face and bare legs mercilessly as he passed. But focusing on getting up the hill as quickly as possible, he hardly noticed them. The official concrete path had finished some distance back and had become a rough track through the trees, ground into the earth by thousands of walkers and hikers over the years.

Feeling more alive and free than he had in days, Morgan ran as fast as he could up the incline, which seemed to get steeper with every step that he took. The ground was very rough in places and sometimes he had to scramble using his hands to pull him up the slippery parts. Although there were still wet muddy patches, the woodland was remarkably dry, considering it had rained so hard the previous day. The high winds from the sea on the exposed slopes had cleared the excess water away.

Morgan's legs had stopped aching long ago. They were now infused with a burning pain. His leg muscles were so tight; he felt he could tear a muscle at any second. But he didn't care because as his legs and body grew heavier and heavier, his mood lightened. Although the hill seemed to keep going higher and higher, with no end in sight, Morgan knew the summit was up there. Each step he took brought him closer to it and to the point of his collapse.

By now his clothes were plastered to his body with sweat even though it must have been only one or two degrees above freezing. Morgan was exhausted but determined to make it. He was nearly there, so he kept pushing himself on through the fatigue. He could sense the top as much as see it. A few more minutes were all it would take. Keep going, keep going, a few more agonising steps would do it, he kept repeating to himself like it was some sort of mantra. He was nearly at the top when he was startled by two deer, which were grazing lazily on tufts of grass along the edges of the muddy pathway. The deer grunted loudly in surprise before hopping off quickly into the underbrush. He had not noticed them as he approached, as he was only interested in the ground immediately in front of him. Anything more was beyond his oxygen-starved mind. With only the slightest pause to watch them disappear, Morgan continued on upwards.

All in all, it took him twenty-six minutes to run the seafront and up to the cross. Only about six or seven minutes off his best. Not too bad considering he was nearly ten years older and training with an injury. But there was no excited jumping like Rocky at the top of the flight of steps. Instead Morgan collapsed onto the concrete base with a sense of immense satisfaction, leaning his tired back against the high cross, his leg muscles shaking uncontrollably as they were filled with lactic acid. His throat was dry and he wished he had brought a bottle of water with him. As he rested and caught his breath, he looked down at the seaside town as it hibernated for the winter. From this commanding view, the sea far below was dark blue and calm as it lapped up to the stone covered beach. A lone fishing boat could be seen heading out to sea with a small flock of seagulls shadowing it, waiting for the inevitable scraps.

Far below him, slightly to his left was Bray town itself. It was a picturesque scene with the mixture of Victorian style houses and hotels on and near the seafront. As you looked further back into the town they disappeared into the more modern yet slightly decaying town behind them. When he looked left, he could see the various tree covered hills surrounding Bray, with the grey shale capped Sugar Loaf Mountain in the distance.

Morgan didn't know why but as he sat there he suddenly thought that he should check his phone. But when he looked at his mobile he saw that there was no signal. Not even one bar was showing on the screen. It had always amazed him. Here he was up the top of the highest hill in the area with a clear view of everywhere around and still could not get a signal. It was the same when he ran up to the top of Three Rock Mountain in South Dublin. It didn't make any sense to him.

He was not sure how long he sat there, but as he was cooling down his sweat-drenched top was getting cold. Morgan did not have much planned for the rest of the day. He intended to go home to his mother's and shower before paying a visit to his own house in the suburbs to check on his tenants. He had rented it out, when he had moved down to Wexford in an attempt to restart his life after the death of Eimear, his fiancée. It was nearly a year ago now and the lease was almost up. The current tenants wanted to sign up for another year and Morgan was only too happy to accommodate them. There were too many memories in the house and he didn't want to go back. He had been lucky in getting such a lovely couple that looked after the house as if it was their own. But since he was up here, it would be no harm to drop in to see if everything was alright. Then he had planned to meet his mum for a quick lunch and head into a music shop in Dublin to pick up a new set of Gary Moore guitar music sheets before heading home to his retreat down in County Wexford.

It was nearly ten thirty when Morgan decided to head back down the hill. Not an easy task with his tired legs feeling like rubber. He made his way slowly, putting one foot cautiously in front of the other on the steep slippery slope. After a number of wild slides and other scares he decided to cut off from the normal steep track and go sideways through the trees and bushes, eventually coming out near the ruins of a thirteenth century church in the field overlooking the upper car park. It was a longer route down but not nearly as steep and fifteen minutes later Morgan made it to the main seafront path. He was exhausted, his earlier energy and determination had all but gone. Now all that was left was an overwhelming desire to lie down and close his eyes. But he felt great inside. Completely relaxed after the stress and tension of the last few days. Ready to go back home to his simple life.

By the time Morgan got down, a few dark clouds had appeared in the sky and the wind was starting to come up again and it was turning very cold. Morgan wished that he had not parked the car at the other end of the seafront. The thought of running the last mile was disheartening. As he started to jog once again, the exercise warmed him and helped ease out his sore legs so he felt more comfortable, but he knew that he would be in pain tomorrow.

Finally arriving back at the car park, Morgan opened the car door and sat in heavily. He was delighted to be out of the cold. Gulping down water from a bottle, he turned on the engine but sat there for a few minutes as the car heated up. Just as he was about to drive off, his mobile rang. It was dragging him back into the real world. He sighed and looked at the screen. Sinead's mobile number showed up. What now? He wondered.

"Hiya," Morgan said cautiously. He had had two calls from her in the last week and not one of them brought good news. Hopefully it would be third time lucky.

As always these days when they spoke she was upset. But this was different. There was panic in her voice. "Can you come over...?"

"Of course I can. Why what's happened?"

"Last night. I was attacked".

"What!" Morgan exclaimed. "Are you alright? Are the kids okay?"

"We're fine. But I need to talk to you", Sinead said. Now that she reached him her voice was calming down. "I tried to call you earlier but I could not get you. I left messages."

"I was somewhere with no signal. Sorry." And he was but not about the signal. "I am on my way. I won't be long".

Sinead started crying. Morgan's heart went out to her. She was having an incredibly hard time. He had promised that she would be okay, that everything would be all right. But clearly it wasn't.

"Look I am on my way straight there", Morgan said. "We will sort this out today. Okay?"

"Okay", came back the tearful reply.

Chapter Twelve

Morgan looked at Sinead in disbelief as she stood there crying. Her arms were wrapped around her chest as if she was trying to give herself a comforting hug. She had been crying hard all night and she looked it. Her face was tired and drawn, her eyes red and swollen. Her whole persona was very fragile. Morgan's gaze went to her mother standing beside her; his expression asked if all he had heard was really true? Did someone really break into the back garden and threaten both her and the children? Pauline, who had also started to look equally haggard, said nothing. She simply closed her eyes and gently nodded. Her expression said that she couldn't believe it either but it was true.

Morgan sat down on the edge of the settee speechless. What the hell was happening? This was madness. He couldn't believe it. It was like a scene from a bad movie. He knew Rob or at least he thought he did and he could not have imagined that Rob would have left his family in such a predicament. What was he thinking of getting involved with these thugs? The answer was simple. The stupid foolish man had not been thinking beyond his own immediate problems.

"What am I going to do?" Sinead sobbed and put a hand up over her face in an attempt to hide her tears.

What was she asking him for? What choice did she have? But what option did anyone have in this situation? As far as he was concerned this was a no brainer. She had to get the professionals involved and sooner rather than later. They should have been called immediately when there might have been a chance to catch the guy.

"You have to tell the Gardaí Sinead. You have no other choice".

"I can't," she said slamming her hand down on the kitchen table.

"I don't understand why you can't. You have to", Morgan implored, reaching out a hand to her, but she shrugged it off.

"No, I can't. I won't", she said firmly turning her back on both Morgan and her mother, walking over to the lounge window and staring out of it.

"And what are you going to do now then?" Morgan demanded to know. Sinead had to do something. It couldn't be just left to go away. This guy, whoever he was, wasn't going to just walk away and never come back. But Morgan got no answer from her. Sinead had gone into what seemed like some sort of catatonic state. She was so engrossed in her sadness that she didn't hear his words. She just stood there at the window. The stress and worry for her children's safety were driving her beyond normal reason. This was the stuff of gangster movies in America, not a quiet leafy Dublin suburb. Nobody should have to deal with this. And Sinead wasn't dealing with it. It was her mother who finally spoke for her.

"This man from last night, he wants the drugs that Rob was holding. If we give them to him, then he will leave us alone."

"It is that simple is it?" Morgan asked. "A man sneaks into your garden and threatens your daughter. He is probably the very same man that killed your son-in-law. And you're going to let that just go? Are you?"

"What choice do we have?" Pauline asked. "This man has threatened my daughter and her children. Their safety is more important than getting any revenge or half-hearted justice for Rob".

"You have to tell the Gardaí. They can protect you...." Morgan said.

"No, we can't tell them. He said I couldn't or it would be worse", Sinead pleaded as she turned back to face Morgan and Pauline.

"How could this be worse?" Morgan demanded, his voice rising in frustration.

"Weren't you listening? He said he would hurt the children," Pauline cried.

Exasperated with the way the conversation was going, Morgan stood up and then threw his arms up in the air in annoyance. "So what do you want to do then?" he asked.

"Sinead needs your help," Pauline said softly.

"Help with what?" Morgan asked, not sure he liked where he imagined that this was going.

"We need to find the drugs that Rob was apparently holding and we need your help doing it. We don't know where to look or what to look for" Pauline said.

"And I do?" Morgan said incredulously.

"We didn't know if you would, but you have a better chance of finding them then we would", Pauline said looking forlornly over at Sinead who was standing motionless by the window. She was desperately frightened for her daughter. She had never thought that anything like this could happen to any of her children. This was unlike anything she had ever faced in her life and she felt completely lost and useless. All she knew was that despite her age, Sinead was still her little girl and had to be protected. And as her mother that was still her job.

No one said anything. There was a heavy stillness in the air. It weighed on them all. Morgan looked at Sinead, before giving Pauline a deflated look. He didn't know what to say. Part of him felt he had failed Rob's family yet again. And he wasn't going to let it happen a third time. "You should have called me sooner", he eventually said.

"Sinead didn't want to call anyone. It took me all night to convince her to agree to get in contact with you. This thug or whoever he was threatened her with hurting her children if she goes to the Gardaí. She has nowhere else to turn but to you." Pauline said it with the complete conviction that this was the only possible course of action to be taken.

"I don't know what you think that I can do. I wouldn't know where to start," Morgan stated. And in fairness he didn't. And why would he know? He had hardly seen Rob the last year while he had been living down in Wexford. On the few occasions that they had talked on the phone, Rob had seemed distant. Now Morgan realised that Rob had been keeping a secret.

"Please Morgan. You are supposed to be her friend", Pauline said, taking Morgan's hand in hers and rubbing it gently while she stared into his face.

Morgan looked into Pauline's eyes and saw the desperation in them. But in his opinion, what she was asking him to do was going to put both Sinead and her children's lives in even more danger. That's if such a thing was even possible. These were obviously not people to be messed with. They had already killed once and appeared to be getting more desperate as the days wore on. Morgan would risk it, as he could look after himself but not take responsibility for anyone else. The death of his fiancée Eimear had been proof enough of that. Sinead's mother wanted him to do his best for her, to help protect them from this new menace threatening to tear what was left of her family apart. He would help but not in the way that they wanted him to. He was convinced that going it alone without the help and support of the Gardaí was a wrong and dangerous strategy. So Morgan looked at Sinead's back as she continued to stare out of the window before staring straight into Pauline's eyes and said, "No."

"What do you mean, no? You cannot just abandon us", she let go of his hand immediately. Both Sinead and Pauline were taken aback by Morgan's answer. They were convinced that he would go along with their plans and his apparent refusal to help them in their hour of need stunned them both.

"I am not going to abandon anyone. I would never do that", Morgan said reaching out and gently touching her arm to reassure her. "But you have to look at this logically. What do we know? The Gardaí technical team or whatever they are called was all over the house after Rob was killed and they found nothing. A Garda task force are investigating the murder. They have nearly a lot of officers working on the case. So if they can't find it, I sure as hell will not be able to either".

"But..." Pauline said, trying to interrupt.

"But nothing... That is the reality of it and you both might as well start facing it now. Wherever Rob hid those drugs, it was not in your house. The Gardaí have searched everywhere, so where do you intend for me to look?"

"I don't know. I just thought that you might know. He was your friend after all", Sinead said. She spoke silently, more like a whisper. Morgan wasn't sure that he heard her properly at first.

"Fair enough he was", Morgan said. "But you were his wife, living with him day in and day out and you did not know either. He kept it from both of us. You just have to face it. We are not going to find those drugs."

"But we have to!" Sinead shouted, her jaw line tightening aggressively as she did.

"No," Morgan said determinedly. He knew that they had to be practical about this. "What we have to do is tell the Gardaí what has happened. They will put you and the children into some sort of protective custody or whatever the Gardaí call it. You will all be safe."

"That will destroy the children. They need stability now. We need to get them back into a normal routine. Back into school", Sinead stated.

"And what if we cannot find the drugs?" Morgan asked. "What then? Do you think that this man will simply walk away? No, he will come here to kill them."

"But you can stop him. You rescued that girl before from those kidnappers", Sinead interjected defiantly.

"That was a fluke", Morgan replied. "I just got lucky. And what if I can't? You are taking an awful risk, depending on me. I love those kids like my own and I would do anything for them and you Sinead. But you need more help now than I can give. You have to contact the Gardaí. They will know what to do."

Pauline had remained silent throughout the exchange, processing what Morgan had said. Could they really handle this on their own? The reality of the situation was sinking in. Morgan could see her think it over and knew that he had won her over. His way was the only realistic way. Pauline walked over behind her daughter and put her hands onto her shoulder, turning her around. "Sinead, love, we need to talk".

Chapter Thirteen

It was nearly one o'clock when two cars pulled up quickly against the kerb outside Sinead's mother's house. The passenger door of the lead car opened first and out stepped Sinead quickly followed by Morgan from the driver's side. He locked the car and they waited for the two detectives to join them on the path. The two detectives got out of their car and without saying a word, they all walked up together to the front door.

Unlike the following Gardaí, Morgan scanned the houses and gardens closest to them before he went in. Watching for trouble he then turned and studied the playing field across the road from the house. As the parkland was open with bushes only along the far wall, Morgan had an unobstructed view to the other side. There was nothing suspicious happening, only an old man out walking his dog.

Sinead's mother Pauline must have been watching out for them as she opened the hall door long before Sinead could get the key out of her bag. She must have been very anxious, since she had had no word about what was happening since Sinead and Morgan had left earlier that morning. Pauline was obviously glad to have her daughter back home safe but she looked very worried at the sight of the two detectives accompanying her. Neither Sinead nor Morgan said anything as they passed by her but the two Gardaí nodded polite greetings before the door closed behind them.

They were going to walk into the front room but Pauline stopped them saying that the kids were in there and indicated that they should go into the kitchen instead. Little Ian, Sinead and Rob's second youngest, was in there sitting alone at the table eating a bowl of cereal and drinking a glass of milk. He stopped reading the cartoon on the back of the cereal box and looked up when they walked in, milk dripping from the corner of his mouth.

"Eh..." he said, unsure of what was happening and who the strange people with Morgan and his mother were.

"Go on back up to the front room", Pauline said as she literally dragged him to his feet.

"But I don't want to go up there. Linda and Niamh are hogging the television," he moaned, looking to his mum for support. But she was in a world of her own.

"It's okay. I will tell them to share with you, okay?" Pauline replied, not really paying attention to him either, just trying to placate him enough so that he would go. Ian dragged his feet as he walked out of the room carrying his bowl, spilling milk as he went. Pauline followed him briefly before returning. Everybody was strangely silent until she returned, as if they were waiting for her, the matriarch of the family, before starting their discussion.

"Well what's happening?" Pauline asked upon her return. She closed the kitchen door quietly behind her and looked everyone up and down with the sort of stern expression, which only Irish mothers could pull off properly. Sinead said nothing, she had just sat down when she came in and now she had a distracted look on her face, like there was something else on her mind. It was strange Morgan thought, she was more animated, determined even when they were in the car on the way back, but now in the house, it was like she was off in a world of her own acting like a little girl again waiting to be told what to do. Nobody was saying anything. Apparently everyone was waiting for someone else to start first. Morgan broke the silence by relating to her mother what had happened in the Garda station over the last few hours.

"They showed Sinead mug shots of Murray's gang. Although she could not be positive, she thinks that one of them could be a man called Brian Johnson. He seems to be a right bastard if what the Gardaí say is true...."

"That's all well and good but what are they going to do about him?" Pauline interrupted, sounding very concerned.

Morgan looked at Sinead to see if she wanted to take up the story from there, but she just sat there fiddling nervously with a piece of crumpled up piece of tissue she had taken from her pocket.

"Well it seems that this Johnson is currently the chief suspect for the murder of both Rob and another man called Dave Murray", Morgan explained. "Johnson was part of Murray's gang and apparently it was some sort of an inter-gang fight for leadership or something like that."

Pauline looked sternly at the two detectives standing in the kitchen and demanded some answers. "Then why didn't you arrest him immediately after this Murray character was killed. Why let him walk around so he could kill Rob?"

Although there were two Gardaí of apparently equal rank, Callaghan had clearly decided in her own mind that she was the lead officer. "We did not have enough evidence to arrest him at the time. We questioned him but we had to let him go. We had no physical evidence against him at Murray's murder site and as you know we have precious little at Rob's, but we are working on it. We are looking into other lines of enquiry but we still feel that he is the chief suspect." As Callaghan spoke the last line, her gaze lingered on Morgan a second longer than it should have.

Pauline was still catching up on the day's earlier events and was full of questions, the same ones that both Morgan and Sinead had asked down in the station. "Well now that Sinead has identified him, why don't you arrest him now? He has murdered two people, probably more as you people don't seem to know what's going on".

Detective Callaghan ignored the insult. "He has gone into hiding, but as he gave you a definite timeframe for handing up the drugs, we believe that he has to come out of hiding again to collect the drugs before he tries to leave the jurisdiction. Don't worry we'll get him."

"The jurisdiction?"

"It means the country."

"But what until then?"

"We still strongly recommend that Sinead and the children move elsewhere, a hotel or in with other relatives. It would be just for a couple of days", Callaghan said.

"I am not going into hiding now or ever," Sinead said determinedly, speaking up for the first time. "The children have been upset too much already. What do I tell them? That they are being stalked by the same madman who just killed their father?"

"We can protect you better at another location. Somewhere far away that nobody knows about."

"The children know this house. They practically grew up here. They feel safe here. After everything that has happened, I will not take that away from them," Sinead said staring at Callaghan. "You will just have to protect us while we're here won't you?"

She looked away from the detectives, catching Morgan's eyes as she did so. He knew her, knew she was scared but she was holding things together for the sake of the children. And he knew then that he would do anything that he could to protect her. There was an awkward silence in the room. At this point Pauline walked over and put her arm around Sinead's shoulder and gave it a firm squeeze of support. Sinead turned and looked at her and smiled in gratitude, giving her mother a tight lingering hug as her tears welled up once more.

Little did everyone in the room know that before they had all left the station, Callaghan had had an argument with DI Higgins over providing Sinead and her family with 24 hour Garda protection. She had been taken aback when he had initially refused her request. When she had asked him why, he told her that he had new information which he would announce to the entire team later that day which ruled out the need for protection. Callaghan being Callaghan had insisted on knowing what it was right then and there. This seemed to only put her superiors back up but he did say that Johnson was no longer a threat. When she had asked him why, he had taken a swipe at her saying that they didn't have the man power to spare and what was the point when the only remaining possible threat was this John Morgan person himself, a man whom she herself had identified as a subject the previous day.

But Callaghan hadn't been convinced and pressed him further for a protection team to be put in place. He eventually caved in, but said that since she felt so strongly about it that she should co-ordinate the staffing rotas of the various teams required. She agreed and told him that she would take the first watch and carry out a security review of Sinead's mother's home. But convincing him turned out to be the easy part. Sinead didn't want them there either. She didn't want them hanging around and frightening her children. To break the impasse, Higgins then suggested to Callaghan that Sinead should leave the area and go somewhere else until all of this blew over. When the suggestion of moving was mentioned, Sinead relented and accepted a Garda presence on her doorstep as he lesser of two evils.

Once at the house, Callaghan felt that away from the tense atmosphere of the station, that she might have another attempt at convincing Sinead to leave the house. A little bit of woman-to-woman persuasion, she had thought. But no luck, Sinead was not for moving. She was going to make her stand here.

"Okay. We are just going to have a look around okay?" said Detective Callaghan. She gave Morgan a strange look before leaving the room. He didn't trust her or her motives and wondered what she was up to now?

The two Gardaí split up and looked over the house and gardens for anything suspicious that could have been secreted by Johnson and also to check for anything that might cause additional security issues. They were in no rush and took their time, checking each room carefully to make sure that each of the windows were closed and secure. The house was built back in the early seventies and at fifteen hundred square feet was fairly big especially compared to the size of the most recently built houses. It had four good sized bedrooms; the stairs were located in the middle of the house, which meant that you could circle the ground floor of the house internally, a feature the kids loved when they were playing chasing. Before this Pauline had been planning to downsize as she wasn't getting any younger and since it was only her living there now, it seemed like such a waste. Her plan was to sell up and buy another smaller more manageable place, spending the profit on a world cruise for herself and giving the rest to Sinead and the kids. A type of living inheritance she called it.

The two Gardaí had divided the house between them with Callaghan checking upstairs and her partner the downstairs rooms and out the back. She could find nothing of any interest upstairs. On the landing, she noticed a door in the ceiling leading up to the attic with a hook in it. Looking around for something to hook onto it, she found a homemade pole with a long screw coming out of it in the hot press, which seemed to do the trick. The attic door pulled down and a ladder slid down which she noisily climbed. Unfortunately upstairs provided little more of interest. The attic had a light fitted and had been floored but was largely empty except for a few boxes of Christmas decorations and black bags labelled clothes or sheets.

Downstairs, the other Garda wasn't finding anything of interest either. In the front room she had to step over toys spread out on the floor and disturb the children playing as they tried to distract themselves from the nightmare that they found themselves in. The children went silent when she entered the room and their eyes followed her as she checked the windows. The back garden had one large concrete shed, which was firmly locked. Because of insanely high bushes, neighbours didn't overlook the rear of the house. Around the side of the house, the scene of the previous night's attack, the side door was securely closed.

Pauline had had a break in a number of years ago. They had not stolen much, just some jewellery and a small amount of money but the break in had shaken her up a lot. It had made her feel vulnerable in her own house and it had taken her a long time to feel safe in the house after that. She had got a locksmith in to put new locks on the doors and windows and had an alarm system installed. The height of the rear garden wall had been increased on all sides where her neighbours' gardens met her property. Rob had hung a new taller side gate, with heavier hinges and a stout lock. Unfortunately, this had been left unlocked by a man delivering home heating oil a few days earlier.

The two female officers seemed reasonably happy with what they found. If all of the doors and windows were secured properly, it was as good if not better than the security of most houses. At night the monitored house alarm could be set so that only the sensors on the outside of the house were activated. When the Garda walked back into the kitchen, they found Morgan hugging Sinead. Her head was tucked under his chin and she was clinging onto him as if her life depended on it. They did not seem to be aware that the detectives were back in the room.

Pauline had gone outside to give Morgan and Sinead some space, but she was visible through the kitchen window hanging school uniforms onto the clothesline to dry.

"Ahem", Callaghan coughed into her hand to alert Morgan and Sinead of her presence, "Are we disturbing anything?"

Morgan and Sinead looked up. They both looked slightly embarrassed as they parted. Sinead went back to her seat, her eyes red from crying while Morgan stood over by the sink.

"DI Higgins has asked us to go over the security arrangements again with you before we leave," Callaghan said finding the cosy scene that they had disturbed very interesting. It seemed to confirm her initial doubts about the family friend.

She was getting closer.

She could feel it.

"We heard what he had to say the first time", Morgan said irritably, eager for them both to be gone.

"We just want to make sure that Sinead and the children are all safe that's all", replied the other Gardaí in a backhanded tone.

"Of course you do", he answered sarcastically.

"Do not leave the house or gardens without a detective being with you. We need you all to stay together as much as possible. A technician will be around later to put a wire trace on your phone. Until then do not answer any calls from a number you do not know."

"He could still get in here," Morgan stated.

"No, he cannot", replied Callaghan. "We have checked over the house. It's pretty secure. Somebody will be outside the house at all times. We will be on until four o'clock then another team will come on duty. Here is my card with my numbers," she said before handing a card to both of them. Sinead did not even look at hers, just left it on the table. "If you need us, we are just outside. Remember you are not alone."

"It is all too much," Sinead cried, covering her face with her hands.

"It will all be over in a few days. We will get him don't you worry about that. It will be all over very soon", Callaghan said.

"Worry? I buried my husband yesterday and now my children have been threatened. How could I not worry?" Sinead spat back at her.

The two detectives did not have an answer for that and awkwardly left the kitchen. A second later Morgan could hear the front door closing. He left the kitchen and walked into the front room, where he saw young Ian watching cartoons while his older sister Linda helped her younger sibling Niamh to draw pictures. Morgan pulled back the net curtain and looked out. He watched the detectives get into the front seats of their car but they did not drive off. Instead they just sat there watching and waiting.

Chapter Fourteen

Just as the two female Gardaí were beginning their security vigil outside Sinead's mother's house, another man was planning to take a well-deserved break from his. He was sitting behind a long row of thorny bushes, which bordered the open grass area directly across from where Rob O'Dwyer's widow was staying with her children. While the Gardaí were only starting their watch, he had already been there for hours, sitting cross-legged on the cold hard ground. He had remained motionless, only moving as his legs went dead.

In a moment of uncommon foresight and preparation, he had brought a thermos flask that he had found buried at the back of a bottom cupboard in his own mother's house. He had filled it with tea but it was all gone now and with the cold creeping into his bones he needed more. He was an ex drug user whose body and nerves had been destroyed by his long-term use. Only with the consistent and often violent intervention of his family had he cast off the need but he didn't escape the life completely as he owed a small fortune to Murray, the now murdered gang boss. Back then it was either work it off or end up dead. It didn't take much thinking to decide what to do given those options. While he could have used the present circumstances to escape the clutches of the gang, it was too late for him. Like any long-term prisoner he found himself institutionalised into the gang and its mentality. Like it or not, he found himself a lifer.

It was far too cold to be sitting there without something warm inside him. The cold was penetrating right into his body and his drug history didn't leave him with a big physique or body weight to help keep him warm. He did not want to be there at all, but Johnson had been very insistent. And even though he was scared of what the Gardaí might do to him if they found him watching the house, he was terrified of what Johnson would do if he failed to carry out his orders. He had heard rumours that Johnson had shot a number of other gangland figures in his time but that was commonplace nowadays. What really freaked the man out was when he had seen Johnson knife one competing drug dealer though the eye as a warning to others. It was a very gruesome wound, with blood spurting high up into the air. The dealer had screamed a scream like nothing he had ever heard before. Seeing it had made him sick to his stomach. It was about then that he had wanted to get out of the gang for good but he couldn't, as he owed them far too much and not just money.

Anthony Jones or Anto as he was more commonly known was never going anywhere in life. But in fairness to him, it wasn't really his fault. An alcoholic, chronically depressed, mother had tried to raise him, but failed miserably with no father in sight. That bastard had apparently fucked off back to Wales to his wife shortly after he was born abandoning him and his mother. Because he had been allowed to run wild and fall in with a bad crowd, Anto had failed school and due to a growing drug dependency lost every job he ever had after that. With no skills to fall back on, he was a prime target for gang lords. When he was younger Anto had done three years in Mountjoy prison for an attempted armed robbery, but even that was a joke. He had been coming down off drugs, getting desperate and looking for an easy score. He had tried to hold up an ordinary looking middle aged man by using an old hypodermic needle that he had used the previous day as the man came out of a bank with night lodgement bags, but he couldn't even do that right. In his drug-starved state, he hadn't realised that the man was collecting empty bags that had already been previously deposited and emptied by the bank staff. What was really unfortunate for Anto though, was that the man he was attempting to rob had about ten years' martial arts training and proceeded to kick him up and down the busy street. For the first time in his life Anto was delighted to see the Gardaí arrive to rescue him from his furious victim. While languishing in prison Anto ran into Murray and started doing errands for him. Once outside he just continued doing what the gang boss wanted. Whatever he wanted and whenever he wanted. Murray owned him.

As far as Anto was concerned, Murray's death should work out well for him, Johnson was distracted and everyone else had jumped ship, either gone into hiding or moved to other competing outfits. Anto would flee to Alicante in Spain with Johnson then simply disappear altogether. He thought that he might leave Johnson in Spain and make his way to Amsterdam for a fresh start as he had a sister there that would put him up for a while until he got on his feet. The mere idea of getting away from all of the shit in this country excited Anto and he wished that he could get on a plane right now and just go.

But there was still one big job to be done.

Since it was a good two hundred yards to the house, he had brought along the binoculars that Johnson had given him. From his vantage point, he had a clear view of the front of the house. He had seen Sinead and the big guy drive away in the classic Mercedes car a few hours earlier and had immediately called Johnson. Anto had been delighted and speculated that they were going to collect the drugs. Anto thought then that he could go home but Johnson had told him to wait and tell him when they came back. Recent developments didn't make Anto optimistic of a speedy conclusion though, as the old car had returned with a new Garda car in tow. They had all gone inside, but the Gardaí had reappeared shortly afterwards and took up position outside.

He had called Johnson from his new pre-paid mobile phone that the main man had bought yesterday. Johnson had insisted that he buy new phones just in case the Gardaí were listening in or tracing their whereabouts by their old mobile phone signals. Johnson had not allowed him to store his new number in the phone and with him not being good with numbers; it had taken Anto a long time to remember it. Even now typing it in, he was not sure it was the right number.

Hoping that he was calling the right person, it was answered so fast that Anto barely had time to hear the phone ring. Neither man said hello, neither wanting to give their identity away in case it wasn't the correct number. "They're back and they brought two fucking pigs with them", Anto said. There was silence on the other end as this news was digested.

"Did you see them carrying in any packages?" asked Johnson after a few seconds.

"Not that I could see".

"What are the Garda doing now?"

"They went into the house for a few minutes but now they are just sitting in the car outside".

"Is it a patrol car?"

"No, it's unmarked", stated Anto clearly.

Johnson thought about this for a few seconds. An unmarked car and plain clothes Gardaí, instead of finding his drugs the fucking bitch had done the exact opposite and gone and told the fucking pigs on him. They must already be looking for him, now they would only double their efforts.

"Were you seen?" Johnson asked.

"Not by the Garda. But a big family dog spotted me in the bushes and wouldn't stop fucking barking until it was dragged away by the old bollocks walking it."

"Good," Johnson said. The Gardaí were being sloppy. They really should have had the area searched before allowing them to stay in the house. This gave them an advantage and the element of surprise.

"With the pigs here, we have to find another way to get her to see sense. You should have just killed her last night", Anto declared.

"I was not ready last night. I will not rush into this and blow it all." Johnson said. "There is too much riding on this".

"But...."

"No buts. I will think of something else, but we are not leaving this country without those drugs even if I have to gut each one of her fucking kid's right in front of her."

Anto said nothing, just closed his eyes as he imagined Johnson killing those children. The mere thought of it was nearly making him physically sick.

"Ok. Let me know if anything else happens" Johnson continued.

"How long do I have to stay here?"

"As long as I fucking tell you to, that's how long. Make sure you call me as soon as anything happens", came the sharp reply before the phone went dead. As instructed after each call, Anto went into call register option on his phone and deleted the number dialled, so the Gardaí could not recover the number if he was stopped. Granted they could get the phone records from the service provider but that would take time and he wasn't about to make it easy for them.

Anto was far from happy with the way things were going. Why did he have to sit out here all fucking day? He decided to go to the petrol station up the road to get some hot food and if Johnson did not like it... well fuck him.

Anto crept along the inside of the bushes that bordered the side of the playing field across the road from the house. At the end, he had about twenty feet of open space to cover before he could get around the wall and back onto the road where he had parked his car. He checked the two Gardaí in the car with the binoculars.

Nothing.

They appeared to be just watching the immediate area in front of the house and the road, and not the surrounding area. Anto slipped the binoculars back into the shoulder bag he had brought with him. He did not run but walked straight out of the bushes across the open section, around the corner out of sight.

Chapter Fifteen

Later that day the assigned briefing room was a hive of activity. As the meeting had been hastily arranged, the various uniformed Garda and detectives were still arriving back from whatever tasks they had been given. Callaghan sat quietly at her desk at the top of the room, early for once, stiff and tired from sitting in the car for so long. As she did not get on particularly well with Detective Moore, the time had dragged and dragged. It had been a very slow day. They had very little to talk about and now she had the making of a good headache coming on. She could not wait to get home and have a shower and a glass of wine. As she sat there thinking of a big glass of Chardonnay straight from the fridge, she watched DI Higgins and another man she had never seen before. They were standing patiently at the top of the room waiting for everyone to take their places. The DI was leaning in towards the other man and speaking in hushed tones to the new man while seemingly doing his best to ignore her. After everyone had sat down, the DI called the meeting to order.

"Right everybody settle down. I have called our meeting early because there have been some dramatic developments since our briefing this morning. We have finally got the results back from the ballistics lab regarding the guns that killed both Dave Murray and Rob O'Dwyer. And it appears that they were both shot with different weapons."

"But I thought they were both shot with a Heckler & Koch 9mm?" asked one young Garda, slightly confused.

"They were, but according to ballistics, they were two different guns." There was an astonished murmur from the detectives as they contemplated this new evidence. Two linked murders using two separate guns. What were the chances?

"That seems more than a bit of a co-incidence," said Callaghan.

"Yes it does, but I have just been informed by the National Drugs Unit that a shipment of Heckler & Koch military hand-guns was stolen from a US army base in Germany a month ago. These guns were sold on the black market to a dealer in Holland and it is believed that a significant number of them made their way into the Republic in the last few weeks," Higgins informed them.

"And two of them were used in the killing of members of the one gang?" came the sceptical reply from someone in the room.

"It appears so", came the reply from DI Higgins.

"Okay," he continued swiftly. "Because of this new information, we are now treating this as two separate murder enquiries. I will lead one team and DI Russell will be joining us to head the other. I have been in touch with the Assistant Commissioner again and he has promised us more resources. However, due to the high level of unsolved murders that the bureau is currently dealing with, it will be a few days before this can be organised. So close co-operation between the two investigating teams is essential and therefore we will be having a group debriefing every evening here at five pm. Attendance is mandatory and I don't have to tell you how important it will be that everyone shares any information that they might have... okay, at this point, I'm going to hand you over to DI Behan," he said, gesturing to DI Behan to take centre stage. DI Higgins, who was a large brooding man himself, seemed small compared to the man now taking his place. DI Behan was a hand-some, highly groomed man, who looked like he was carved out of a large chunk of granite. He was wearing an immaculate suit, black, white shirt and blue tie, which hung perfectly on him, and a pair of expensive Italian leather shoes.

DI Behan gestured a silent hello to the men and women that made up the investigation team as DI Higgins introduced him properly. "DI Behan is being seconded to us from the National Drug's Unit. He is up to speed with where we are at the moment and will be giving us an overview on both the drug dealers and weapons that we will be dealing with. However, he has other information pertinent to the case."

"Hello everybody", said DI Behan with a heavy Cork accent. He clasped his hands together like a schoolteacher about to give a history class. "Ok, please pay attention as I will be giving you a lot of information and I will be passing around notes afterwards. First I am sure that you are all wondering about the guns. As DI Higgins pointed out, both of these guns appear to have come from a batch stolen in Germany from an American military base and distributed through various criminal gangs in Holland. They then came into Ireland in a container containing twenty-eight pallets of a well-known Dutch beer. We got wind of it and were following the load into the country but due to problems with some of the information supplied by our informant, the guns slipped through our fingers. Our understanding is that they were not going to a single dealer here. These guns by the way if you are not already aware are not some cheap Saturday night special but top of the range military handguns used by the US special forces. They are expensive and will not be bought by any run of the mill little fucker trying to make a name for himself. That should make tracking them down a bit easier".

DI Behan paused both to take a breath and to look around the room to see if the people assembled were still listening to him.

"Okay, moving on. First, a man matching the description of Brian Johnson was seen getting onto the Larne ferry in Northern Ireland leaving for Scotland this afternoon. I informed the Scottish Police about his impending arrival but by the time they got to the ferry he had slipped away". DI Behan gave an exasperated sigh before continuing. "He is probably in mainland Europe by this stage so I am in the process of getting a European arrest warrant issued for him. We should pick him up soon enough."

"With the main suspect out of the country, does that mean that the case is effectively closed?" asked Callaghan.

"No", answered DI Higgins, cutting in. "According to new information that you are about to hear, it appears that we have been going in the wrong direction with this case".

"We believe that we are dealing with a new gang headed by these two Polish men - Jan Krupski and Zygmunt Piasecki." The careful way he pronounced the two names sounded even stranger with DI Behan's Cork accent. As he spoke he stuck up two 12" x 12" colour photographs onto the board behind him. Pointing to the picture on the right, which showed a refined tall thin man, with a shaven head and wearing an expensive suit standing beside a car. "Firstly, we have Krupski, he is called the Wilk which apparently means the Wolf and he is both the leader and the brains of their operation. Then there is Piasecki, pictured here on the left...." This picture showed a different character all together. He was a mean looking heavy-set man, also shaven headed but wearing green army camouflage type clothes ".... who acts as his muscle.

They have a friendship that stretches back over ten years. They met while doing their obligatory one-year conscription service in the Polish Army and stayed on for a further three years. They served together in a tank regiment before moving to the quarter-masters branch. Although they were honourably discharged, there was a suspicion around the theft of a large amount of diesel and machine parts, but nothing could be proven. Back in civilian life they quickly moved into prostitution and protection and soon branched off into drug dealing, but were eventually caught when they tried to fence stolen weapons and served one year of a three-year prison sentence in Mokotow Prison in Warsaw. When they got out, Poland had become one of the European Accession states permitting greater movement of workers within the EU and they decided to start again over here."

Just then a mobile phone started to beep repeatedly and very loudly indicating a message had been received. As one, the room turned around to face Callaghan who was frantically trying to get her phone out of her jacket pocket to turn it off. "Sorry", she said to DI Behan. He just smiled at her before continuing.

"They came to Ireland nearly two years ago, however they did not appear on our radar until about six months ago. It turns out that their names were on both Interpol and Europol lists of suspects flagged as part of an investigation into a large shipment of stolen weapons. With a bit of digging, we soon learned that along with forming associations with a number of other fledgling and more established foreign national criminal gangs operating in the country, their names have been linked to a growing list of suspected crimes including the disappearance of a known dealer and intimidation of several others. However, despite this even up to about a month ago they had not seriously come to our attention. I suppose that they were doing a good job of keeping their heads down but surprise, surprise they have now decided to move into dealing. It seems that they realised that Murray's group was weakened by some of our recent successes against his gang and have decided to move against him by simply killing him and his lieutenants and moving into supplying the area using Murray's old distribution network."

"If they have made no attempts to deal drugs directly and if as you say they are keeping their heads down, why are you putting them under surveillance now?" came a question from the back. Callaghan turned to look but could not see who asked it.

"Good question. Piasecki was seen meeting with Johnson a number of times in early December. We were given new information that have tied these two groups together in a way not previously thought and their names have popped up on the periphery on a number of other investigations that we have made. All gangland related – dealing, extortion and money lending. Nothing concrete as yet but make no mistakes, these are very dangerous criminals. They are both trained soldiers and we believe that Piasecki is always armed. So do not approach them casually. In fact", he said, looking at DI Higgins, "I would suggest that in any attempt to arrest either man, that you have the Emergency Response Unit present."

The various young Gardaí in the room looked around at each other, realising the very real dangers they were facing in investigating these types of murders. For most of them this was only their first or second murder case and it was all still very exciting. Up to this point, when they were involved with murder suspects, any threat was always directed towards someone else, never at them. The criminals always tried to run and hide, never fight back. This time they were dealing with another level of criminal, more ready to shoot their way out than the average Irish one. Seeing that his warning had struck home, DI Behan was about to continue, but Higgins stepped in.

"As you are aware this changes everything", Higgins said. "After receiving this information we now believe that the Wolf killed both Murray and O'Dwyer. We are pretty sure that he killed Murray to gain control in the area and O'Dwyer for the drugs that he was holding for Murray".

"If he did kill them both, why did he shoot them with two separate guns?" Callaghan asked.

"I don't know yet," Behan stated.

"But what about the threats made on Rob O'Dwyer's widow and children?" asked Callaghan sceptically. She was not convinced by what she was being told. It just did not seem right to her. Maybe Higgins was right about the Murray murder but not about the O'Dwyer killing. That was a different killing for a different reason. She was sure of it.

DI Higgins answered, "We still believe that the threats were made by one of the remaining members of Murray's gang, but not as a follow up to the murder. According to DI Behan here, the remainder of Murray's gang are running scared. Getting these drugs back is important to them but getting away from here is even more so, so we believe that they will not come back and will stay in hiding abroad. I am therefore downgrading the protection offered to the O'Dwyer family from two armed detectives to one patrol car keeping an eye on the place."

"Isn't that a bit premature. We still don't know if these Krupski and Piasecki characters are definitely involved yet", Callaghan persisted.

"The NDU and DI Behan here seem sure of it", Higgins said abruptly.

"But we still don't know one way or another", she argued. The tension in the room increased, everybody in the room sensed it. They were witnessing a tug of war over the direction the case was going. It was between two unevenly matched opponents and there could be only one winner.

"Callaghan, our list of suspects has just increased greatly and we have to cover a lot of ground in the next few days. We have to do what we can with limited resources available to us," Higgins said, the irritation clear in his voice. "Both Krupski and Piasecki are currently under surveillance by the NDU but due to their lack of resources, we will have to take over from them".

"Are you going to tell Mrs O'Dwyer that you are taking the armed protection away from her?" Callaghan said as if she were scolding him.

"Yes, as it happens. I am going over to her mother's house to tell her the good news that the threat is over as soon as I am finished here. But have you considered the other possibility that if you are right that this Morgan person killed Rob O'Dwyer in collusion with Sinead O'Dwyer that this threat could have been fabricated ?"

"But...," Callaghan started to object.

"But nothing. We need to move on", Higgins said in a tone that told her not to push it further.

At this point, seeing that DI Higgins patience was wearing dangerously thin, DI Behan stepped in. "So where do we go from here? You will all need to check out the movements of these two men, Jan Krupski and Zygmunt Piasecki on the days that both Murray and O'Dwyer were killed. We will need to check their known phone records, bank accounts and find out what cars they own and have access to. And most importantly we still need to find the drugs, which we believe to be worth in the region of seven hundred and fifty thousand Euros. In the meantime, I am going to get a warrant to search Krupski's and Piasecki houses. This has the makings of a long drawn out investigation. So, as DI Higgins said earlier we have to be very thorough and share information on a daily basis. We have a lot of work to do, so let's get going."

As the detectives collected their new assignments, DI Higgins looked at their young faces. He was worried about what they might come up against in the next few days or weeks. Criminals today were not like the ones that he had to deal with when he was starting off. These men had ready access to guns and knives and no compunction about using them. Being confronted by a Garda would not faze them at all. "Killing one of us would probably just add to their image", he thought. He realised that he sounded very clichéd, but he had to drive home the point of being careful. "Remember that these men are very dangerous. They are military trained in both firearms and hand-to-hand combat. They are only in the country a short time and are already suspected of murdering two people. Be careful at all times".

Chapter Sixteen

Anto was squatting in the bushes in the field across the road from Sinead's mother's house and had had more than enough of hanging around in the cold. He did not think he had ever spent so much time on his own. It gave him time to think and he did not like that. After all, he had nothing nice to think about. He had ruined his life. There was absolutely no doubt about that. It had been dominated by self-destructive tendencies, which had led every social worker assigned to him, to eventually wash their hands of him.

So time to think wasn't any good to him. No good at all.

Anto had been spotted twice during the day coming and going from his makeshift hideout, but nobody had said anything to him. Because of the state of his ragged and dirty clothes, they had probably thought that he was a vagrant so they gave him a wide berth. By this stage, he was frozen solid with the cold and would have paid any amount of money for a line of coke and the chance to go for a few pints of cider down the local, but Johnson had insisted that he stay put.

Watching and waiting.

Anto hadn't had to wait long for his patience to be rewarded. There had been a lot of activity at the house in the first hour. First, the unmarked Garda car with the two plain-clothes female detectives in it was replaced with a regular marked Garda car. Then there was nothing for a few hours, then the big guy left. It wasn't long after that when the marked car started up and drove off. Just as he lost sight of the Garda car around the corner, he called Johnson to let him know. Johnson listened with intense interest and had asked a lot of questions about the scene. What they did? Who was there? Did they look like they were on to anything? Did he overhear them say anything? He tried to describe the events in more detail for his boss but he couldn't and since he was so far away, he could not hear anything being said either. It was like watching television with the sound off.

Johnson seemed annoyed that Anto could not give him any more detail. It was maddening for him not to know what was going on. But even if he only had an illusion of knowledge, it was better than nothing. The phone went silent for a few seconds before Johnson relented. "I'm coming over. It's about time that I give that bitch a reminder that I am not fucking around."

"Thank fuck," Anto said. "I have to get out of here, I am fucking freezing man".

"Shut up whining. This will all be over before anyone figures out what is happening. I am on my way over", Johnson said and hung up.

It had taken Morgan a lot longer than he had planned to get back to Pauline's house from the supermarket. He had gone to get the week's groceries for the house. Pauline had wanted to go but he had insisted. So under protest, she had given him a list as long as his arm. He didn't mind, he needed time to clear his head and think. He had reasoned that with the Garda protection outside the house everything would be all right without him for a while. After the supermarket, Morgan had found a late night men's outfitters shop and bought himself some fresh clothes and underwear before heading back.

It was dark as he drove up to the house, but he immediately noticed that the marked Garda car that had been parked outside the house earlier was gone. But why? Had something happened while he was gone? Morgan was very worried as he rang the doorbell. As agreed earlier, Pauline opened the curtain on the little glass panel beside the door and looked out to see who it was before she opened it.

She was looking concerned.

"What's happened? Where are the Gardaí?" asked Morgan.

"It's awful", Pauline answered. "No sooner had the Gardaí left than the house was attacked again".

"Jesus, what do you mean attacked?"

"A bag filled with dog shit was stuffed through the letterbox. Sinead's name and those of the kids were written on the side of it in marker", Pauline said, shutting her eyes to the memory of it all.

"Was anyone hurt?"

"No, we never saw anyone or heard anything, just the clatter of the letterbox flap. It was disgusting. Sinead was terrified when she found it".

"What happened to the protection team outside?" Morgan demanded.

"Sinead got a visit from the head detective telling us that the threat had receded and that they were therefore pulling the security from the front. He said not to worry and that everything was going to be alright".

"So the Gardaí just left and straight afterwards you got... shit... through the letterbox. That means that someone must have been watching the house?" Morgan figured. He walked over to the window and pulled the curtain slightly to one side before peering out. He couldn't see anything as the room lights reflected off the glass.

"There is someone watching the house?" Pauline asked worriedly.

"It doesn't seem that they are still there. Where is Sinead now?" Morgan asked.

"She is up in bed, she might be asleep though, she was upset and crying very hard so I gave her more of the sedative tablets that the doctor had prescribed", Pauline said.

Morgan looked at Pauline who seemed to be on her last legs herself. He put a comforting hand on her shoulder and asked, "How are you holding up?"

She tried to smile and put on a brave face. "I'll be fine. She needs you now." Nodding towards the stairs. "It's the first door on the left".

Morgan bounded up the stairs, tapping gently on the bedroom door before he opened it to find the curtains closed and Sinead lying in bed curled up in a ball, the covers pulled up tight under her chin. She seemed so small in the bed. The room was dark, he could not see properly but she appeared to be sleeping.

"Sinead..." he called out quietly.

A hand crept out from under the blanket and turned on the bedside light. She turned her head to face him. Her eyes were red and puffed.

"He was back," she said, barely whispering.

"I heard. Are the kids alright?" Morgan asked anxiously.

"Yes. None of them saw anything and I didn't tell them anything. But it was a warning," she said, "He is going to follow through with his threat and kill one of the children unless I do what he says."

"I don't understand why is the armed protection gone?" Morgan asked.

"The head detective called earlier, I can't remember his name?" Sinead hesitated.

"Higgins?"

"Yes, that's him. He phoned here shortly after you left and told me that they had new information that this Johnson character had left the country. He said that due to the reduction in my threat level that they had decided to remove the armed Gardaí from outside of the house. Although he said that he would alert the local station of the situation and ask them to keep an eye on the house as they patrol the area. What a bastard, eh?"

"Have you called to tell anyone from the Gardaí what happened?" Morgan asked. "This Johnson is obviously still a threat."

"No".

"Why not?" Morgan said exasperated.

"These are my children. They are my number one priority. I could not live with myself if I l let something happen to them. If this man wants the drugs, let's find them and give them to him. The Gardaí can sort it all out later."

"Look we talked about this earlier today. I care for you and the kids but I would not know where to even start looking. You have to be strong and tell the Gardaí what's after happening. Demand that they do something."

"No, no more Gardaí. They don't want to help and I can't risk them changing their minds again," she said very definitely. "Please Morgan, will you help me?"

After a long pause Morgan said with a heavy heart. "I am sorry, I can't do it. I told you that this is best left to the Gardaí and I still believe that".

"But I need you...," she begged.

"You don't need me, you need professionals."

"If you are scared, just say it," Sinead said. There was more than a hint of venom in her voice.

"I am not scared. I just haven't got the skills that you need," Morgan argued. He needed her to see reason but she didn't say anything else. Instead she started to cry again. Morgan reached out to comfort her but she pushed him away and shouted at him.

"Well if you're not going to help. You might as well get the hell out."

"Sinead I am sorry but....," Morgan started to say.

"Get out I said," Sinead screamed at him, grabbing at the night-stand for the first thing to come to her hand before flinging an empty mug at him. Morgan dodged it just in time and the mug smashed off the wardrobe behind him. "Get out!"

Morgan gave her one last long look at her lying there crying before walking dejectedly from the bedroom and down the stairs past her mother who concerned by the shouting was on her way up to see what was happening.

She went to ask Morgan what was going on but Morgan felt that he couldn't look her in the eye to tell her that he wasn't help-ing them so instead he just passed her by and walked quickly out of the front door. Once outside he stopped and took a deep breath, trying to regain his composure. The hall door closed heav-ily behind him. It gave a solid thud as it shut against the door jam. More solid than he had imagined it had previously. It had closed with a sense of finality. He imagined it to be a thud of failure.

Morgan slowly walked towards his car. Unlocking it, he sat in and started the engine but didn't drive away. Instead he just sat there staring at the dashboard. Sighing deeply he looked around but the streets were dark and empty. There were no passers-by, no neighbours walking their dogs but more importantly there was no Gardaí protection team watching over Sinead and her children. Looking over to the black space that was the park opposite, he knew that there could be anyone over there watching Sinead and the kids. Just waiting to attack them at the first opportunity. It shouldn't be up to him to protect them, he thought. He wasn't the best person for them in this situation. He didn't know anything about finding drugs. That surely must be the role of the Gardaí but they seemed to have taken themselves from the equation. Morgan's mind was racing but going nowhere fast. It kept coming back to the same conclusion. A conclusion that his head didn't want to reach but his heart kept pushing him towards. A promise is a promise.

Shaking his head despondently, he turned off the engine and climbed back out of the car. "I can't believe I am doing this."

He rang the doorbell. Sinead's mum opened the door slightly and glared at him from around it without saying anything.

"I am sorry for disturbing you but I need to talk to Sinead," Morgan asked.

"I don't think she wants to talk to you right now," said Pauline in a cutting way that only an Irish mother can manage.

"I know but I still need to talk to her," Morgan said meekly, trying to walk into the house but Pauline deliberately stood in the doorway blocking it.

"Well don't upset her any more than she already is," she ordered before opening the door fully so Morgan could enter.

Morgan walked up the stairs and knocked on the bedroom door. "Sinead, can I come in?"

"What are you doing back here?" Sinead asked angrily sitting up in the bed as he walked in.

"Look, I have been thinking about it and I will help you find the drugs," Morgan said.

"What?"

"I said that I will help you," he repeated.

Jumping up from the bed, Sinead wrapped her arms around him. "Oh thank you, thank you, thank you."

"Yes okay, okay," said Morgan as he tried too untangle himself from her arms. "But it's getting late so we should start tomorrow. Right now you need to rest".

Chapter Seventeen

Early the next morning, Morgan and Sinead were in the back sitting room of Pauline's house discussing how they were going to find the missing drugs. With no Garda protection team anymore, Morgan had stayed overnight in Pauline's home to give Sinead a sense of security. It had been a restless sleep and he had awoken early. His back sore from sleeping on the couch and unable to go back to sleep he had watched the television with the volume down really low until the family started moving around upstairs. Pauline came down first and made breakfast for them and the kids. She didn't make Sinead any as she wanted to leave her sleeping for as long as possible as she badly needed the rest. About ten, Pauline suggested that Morgan should bring Sinead up a cup of tea. Sinead had just woken up and was still in bed when he tapped gently on the door. She smiled as he walked in and she sat up in the bed, rubbing the sleep from her eyes. It was a woman's bedroom. It was painted a lilac colour with fitted mirror wardrobes all down one side. The bedside lockers had lace covering them and lamps with matching tassels sat on top. The bed itself was covered in fluffy decorative cushions and an Egyptian linen throw.

"Morning, sleepy", Morgan said cheerfully, putting the mug down on the bedside locker.

"Oh good morning, what time is it?" she asked as she struggled to settle the pillows behind her. She was still a bit groggy and yawned loudly as she stretched.

"It's ten o'clock", Morgan said.

"Already? I must have fallen into a deep sleep".

"You wouldn't have slept if you didn't need to," he said tenderly. "You've had a terrible few days".

"But it is all going to be better now", Sinead said happily. "You are going to get Johnson off our backs".

"Yes hopefully", he replied not sounding so confident.

"That's probably the reason why I slept so well last night", she said. "That and knowing that you were downstairs in case there was more trouble".

"Well I'm glad you slept well. Now drink your tea and let's get to work".

Sinead grinned from ear to ear and deliberately made a slurping noise from the cup. They both laughed.

"Enough, enough," Morgan protested as he sat down on the bed beside her. Sinead looked at him expectantly. "Ok, as I see it, we have two questions to answer. First what exactly are we looking for and second where are we going to look for it?" Morgan said taking charge.

"So first things first. What does that amount of cocaine look like? How big is it?" Morgan asked Sinead.

"I don't know", she answered shaking her head.

"Think carefully now. Did the detectives say anything about the drugs to you?"

"Say anything? They never shut up about them", Sinead said. "They kept on asking the same questions over and over again, each time in a different way. They were trying to trip me up. They got me so confused. I don't think they understood that I had just found my husband dead, murdered in my own home. I couldn't think of anything else. Drugs were the last things on my mind".

"I suppose it's their job," Morgan said. "They probably had to 'eliminate you from their enquiries' as they say."

"I don't care and don't you be sticking up for them," Sinead said angrily, remembering the questioning and how small and pathetic they had made her feel. She could recall the embarrassment of being quizzed repeatedly and realising how little she knew about her own husband and his movements.

Morgan did not say anything, he just shrugged noncommittally. "Look, can we get back to the topic at hand," Morgan asked Sinead. "Did they say anything about the size or description of the drugs?"

"Wait. Yes." Sinead said excitedly as if the penny had just dropped. "I think he said that it was probably a parcel about the same size as a small suitcase."

"A suitcase, like you would take on holidays?"

"Not a big one. A small one like you might bring onto a plane as hand luggage." Sinead held her hands out about eighteen inches away from each other and then turned them sideways about ten inches indicating a box like shape. She was very excited now, spurred on by the exhilaration that they were getting somewhere. She was smiling broadly for the first time in days. Her face was lit up and Morgan could not help but think how pretty she still looked, despite the tiredness and everything else. He had just caught a brief glimpse of the girl he knew nearly twenty years ago. He tried to stop himself but he couldn't help but wonder what would have happened to them both if she had married him instead of Rob? None of this shit anyway that's for sure, he thought.

"Okay. Now that we now know what we are looking for, we are getting somewhere," Morgan said encouragingly.

"So, where do we look?" Sinead asked.

"I am not sure yet," Morgan said. And he wasn't. The Gardaí had the benefit of background information, experience, resources and informants. All he had was his intuition and his stubbornness.

"Where did the Gardaí look?"

"Everywhere in the house", Sinead said very definitely, trying her best to help.

"Were they thorough?" Morgan asked. But it was a stupid question to ask, as he already knew the answer. The Dublin Crime Scene technicians were probably not as well equipped or as well funded as the American crime scene investigators that everyone was addicted to watching on television, but Morgan knew that they were no fools and could probably find three quarters of a million Euro's worth of cocaine if it was hidden in the house. He felt it was safe to assume that if they hadn't found it then it wasn't there to be found.

"They were there in our house for what seemed like hours searching around," Sinead said. "They pulled each room apart and went through every press and wardrobe. They were tapping on walls and floors. They checked in the shed, even going up in the attic taking up the insulation".

"Did they bring in a dog to search?"

"A dog?" Sinead asked confused.

"A sniffer dog, like you see at the airport".

"Oh, no. No dogs," she said shaking her head.

"And you never saw them taking anything out of the house?"

"No, but they brought me down to the station after an hour", she explained. "They could have taken out the Piano from the sitting room and I would not have seen them".

"Right..." Morgan said, thinking this through. "Okay, so we have to assume that the cocaine was not left in the house then, otherwise they would have found it. So where would Rob leave it? There cannot be that many places that he would feel safe to leave it. Look at it like this. He would have to go there regularly both to put it there and then to retrieve it, so he would need a reason to be there in the first place otherwise people would start getting suspicious. Wherever it is he would need a reasonably handy place to stash it, so nothing too elaborate. But it was a relatively big parcel to be hiding so he could not just stuff it under a mattress. And it would also have to be somewhere dry, especially at this time of year.

"That make sense," Sinead said following his train of thought. "So where does that leave us?"

"Right, so your house is out. He did not get on with your mother so this house is out. That only leaves the garage where he worked and maybe his parents' house? He goes up there a lot and they have two sheds if memory serves me right".

"You're right," Sinead said excitedly. "With his mother sick, he was up there every two or three days. He could easily have made an excuse to go outside for a few minutes. But wouldn't the Gardaí have already thought of all this and searched these places by now?"

"Probably, but we won't know till we check ourselves".

Sinead was silent, thinking over the possibilities.

"It does not sound too hopeful. Is there anywhere else?"

"It has just occurred to me," Morgan said. "Did Rob still have access to the old workshop he used to lease when he worked for himself?"

Sinead shrugged her shoulders. "God knows. I assume that the landlord has leased it out since."

"Maybe but maybe not. After we rule out the more obvious places, it's worth a look. Sure what harm can it do? Does he still have the keys for it?

"I don't know. He always kept a big bunch of spare keys in the car. I know that he had spare keys for both our parents' houses but I am not sure if there were any others on it. So maybe they're on there?"

"Are the keys still in the car?" Morgan asked.

"I think so..... I'm sure I saw them the other day in the glove box", Sinead said and with that she threw back the covers and got up. She was wearing a short mauve coloured nightdress, which stopped just above the knee. Morgan could not help but look. She still has nice legs, he thought. Morgan left the room so she could get dressed in private and waited downstairs for her. A minute later she appeared in a tight blue sweat suit with a pair of white runners.

She took the keys for the car from her handbag. "I'm coming with you".

"No, you're not."

"I have to. I am going stir crazy sitting here doing nothing," she pleaded.

"You have to stay here", Morgan insisted. "It's not safe out there".

"No", Sinead said firmly. "I am going. Rob was my husband. I need to do this".

Morgan grudgingly nodded okay and stood watching her as she went to tell her mother and the kids that she was slipping out for a short while. As Sinead hugged her mother, Morgan thought that she was the strongest, most resilient woman that he knew. She had gone through so much but was still standing, still fighting for her family. He was very proud of her. As he watched her, he felt the urge to take her into his arms and give her a hug.

Chapter Eighteen

Morgan drove his classic Mercedes faster than he really should have. It might have had a large 3.5 litre engine, which could still stand up for itself on a straight line, but it didn't handle nearly as well in tight slow moving traffic. The engine might have stood the test of time but unfortunately the suspension and the brakes were nearly forty years old and the handling and stopping power simply weren't up to it anymore. It was heavy and slow and Morgan found he was working very hard to keep the car pointing in the right direction. It was moments like this he wished he was still driving in his old Renault turbo diesel. While it would never have the same head turning class as the Mercedes, it did have lots of low end torque for acceleration and much better road handling. But after his earlier adventures Morgan assumed that what was left of the silver car was now rusting in a scrap yard and being picked over for spare parts.

But regardless of his vintage cars limitations, Morgan still broke most of the speed limits and a number of traffic lights until he reached the garage that Rob had worked in for the last year or two. It was a good-sized purpose built workshop with excellent road frontage located at the end of a row of modern red brick shops. The large sign that hung over the doorway said "Tony's Tyres" in large red lettering on a pure white background. A smaller sign standing on the side of the street said that they did all brands of tyres, fixed punctures and did four wheel electronic wheel alignments. Whatever that was. And judging by the number of cars parked outside, business was pretty good.

Morgan knew that Rob had hated working here. It had been very hard for him to go to work for someone else after having owned his own business. But when that business had failed, he had no choice but to find a regular job and it was all he could find.

Considering the state of the economy he was lucky to get even this. It wasn't that Rob hadn't liked the people he worked with. On the contrary, he got on very well with them. It was that he felt that his skills and talents as an experienced mechanic were being wasted, while he scraped a living fitting tyres and doing very limited mechanical repairs. Morgan imagined it something akin to an ex-Russian scientist coming over to live in Ireland only to end up working in McDonalds flipping burgers and cleaning up after drunken idiots with the IQ of a sponge.

Morgan parked the car in a spot marked, customer parking only, and turned off the engine. Turning to Sinead he said, "Well, are you ready?"

"No, I can't do this. I am too nervous," she said, picking anxiously at the nail polish on her fingernails.

"That is okay", Morgan said smiling and patted her leg reassuringly. He preferred doing things like this by himself anyway.

"What will you say to Tony?" she asked.

"Don't know yet. Something will come to me I'm sure".

As it turned out, Tony himself was not in and Morgan ended up talking to Dave who was looking after the place while Tony had slipped out to the bank. Morgan started to explain who he was, but Dave stopped him short, apparently recognising him from the cemetery. Morgan then proceeded to fill Dave with a bullshit line about Sinead going through Rob's personal belongings and not being able to find the engraved watch that she had bought him on their fifteenth wedding anniversary. She knew that he always used to forget it at work because he usually left it on the sink after washing his oily dirty hands. She had asked him to come down and see if he could find it. Morgan told Dave that the watch was of tremendous sentimental value to Sinead and she wanted it back.

"Sure, of course", Dave said, "Anything to help her. Isn't it terrible what happened? I'll show you where the staff room is."

Morgan nodded politely, wondering how exactly he could search the place properly with Dave hanging around when an irate customer walked in. She was complaining that one of the tyre fitters must have gotten oil on her tan leather seat as it had sure as hell had not been there before she had brought the car in. Dave excused himself and told Morgan and told him to check the sink in the canteen area himself before leading the woman back outside to the car park to assess the alleged damage.

The garage was built in a rectangular shape; it was wide but quite shallow. Not much deeper than the length of two cars. Unlike the garage that Morgan usually brought his car to, this one was clean and brightly lit. It composed of three car bays facing out onto the street, two of which had lifting ramps so the mechanics could walk under the customers' cars. A young lad was busily working under a green Ford Mondeo with a taxi sign on the roof, trying to fit a new back exhaust box and was not paying any attention to Morgan. Apart from a number of racks of new tyres, there were three large red toolboxes on castors, the type with numerous thin drawers and a computer terminal that presumably did the wheel alignment, there was nowhere to hide anything. As you stood with your back to the road, there was a small office on the right hand side with a toilet and an even smaller canteen area behind it. A quick glance told Morgan that there was nothing hidden there either. On the left hand side stood three piles of what looked like old worn tyres.

Morgan figured that his best bet was to go up the metal staircase that went up alongside the office to a large storage area above. Checking to make sure that Dave and the younger guy were still preoccupied, Morgan slipped quietly up the stairs. The storage area consisted of long rows of tyres and a large number of new exhausts hanging up on what looked like butcher's meat hooks. The workshop had, like most businesses, its own little dumping area. A place where one miscellaneous item was just flung on top of another, to make everywhere else appear that bit cleaner. At home it would be a specific drawer or a cupboard under the stairs but in Tony's Tyres this was clearly it. Morgan paused to find the best place to start before he began rifling through the jumble of boxes. Five minutes later he gave up. He had looked through every box big enough to hide the drugs, then he quickly searched through the tyres just to be sure that Rob hadn't hidden the drugs in a stack of tyres but it was no good.

They were not up here.

His search completed, Morgan managed to creep back down the stairs just before Dave reappeared; a rag and spray can in his hand.

"Well, did you find the watch?" Dave asked.

"No. No luck." Morgan replied feigning disappointment.

"Well I will keep an eye out for it and if I find it, sure I will get Tony to give Sinead a call."

"That would be great. Thanks", Morgan said as he made his escape.

"Give Sinead my best," Dave shouted after him.

"I will," said Morgan.

But instead of walking directly back to the car he slipped around the side of the building to where the rubbish was kept. He hoped that they might use a secure lockup to store other old parts or waste. But the rear of the garage backed directly onto a high wall separating the shops from a nearby housing estate. All Morgan found was a small skip on wheels with a green plastic flip open cover along with a pile of disused batteries and two drums of what he assumed was old used oil. There was no obvious lockup or shed to be seen. Just to be sure, Morgan flipped open the top of the skip to find it nearly completely empty. It must have only been emptied in the last day or two. Hope it wasn't in there, thought Morgan or there is going to be a lot of very high rats at the dump. He let the lid fall back down and returned to the car.

"Nothing there" he said to Sinead as he jumped back in.

"Where next?" she asked.

"Rob's old workshop", Morgan said as he gunned the engine.

Rob's old premises, from where he had operated his own garage business were only two minutes away from Tony's Tyres. It was situated at the rear of a large industrial unit which had been initially developed with generous government subsidies back in the nineteen sixties. It was typical industrial developments of its day, with its low wide flat buildings surrounded by large open areas. It housed low skilled, low-tech jobs, but jobs none the less and lots of them, just what the Irish economy needed back then. And now.

Unfortunately, it was not long before the company got into trouble and eventually with cheaper manufacturing costs in the Far East it had been forced to close in the late eighties. It had lain vacant for years and had eventually been broken up into over a dozen smaller units. Now it housed everything from a DIY store and a small gardening centre to a gym and a unit making toothpaste of all things. Rob's unit had been located off the main road, out of sight around the back of the main building. Which was far from ideal to run a garage in, but pretty good if you wanted to hide drugs.

Morgan was delighted to see that Rob's old unit was still unoccupied, as he pulled up outside the roller shutter door. There was a large sign nailed to the wall, informing prospective tenants that this unit was to let. Seeing it, Morgan remembered seeing a number of similar signs at the gate on the way in. It might be worth talking to the letting agent to see if Rob had been in contact with them about this or any other unit. Morgan turned off the engine and got out. This time, Sinead joined him. He made a brief reconnaissance of the area and was happy to find that they were completely alone. Trees around the exterior wall blocked the view of the surrounding houses. A place like this would be perfect to store drugs in, Morgan thought. There were no other units operating on this side of the building and it was deathly quiet. There was an old wreck of a car abandoned across from them on a wide expanse of unkempt grass; drunken kids had burnt it out, presumably. It was a Peugeot by the looks of it. Maybe Rob had left the car there when he moved out and it had been burnt out at some later date? The whole property, all fifteen or twenty acres of it, had seen better times and its days were well and truly numbered. Even in the current economic climate, property developers must be chomping at the bit to get their hands on this place, he thought. As they walked over to the single sheet metal door on the left of the main roller shutter, Sinead handed Morgan the large bunch of keys that she had brought with her.

"Any idea which key it is?" he said to her.

"I think it is the big black one with the yellow dot on it", she said staring at the bunch in Morgan's hand.

Morgan tried the key in the lock and amazingly it clicked open on the first try. But it must have been a while since anyone had been there. The hinges had gone so stiff that Morgan needed to put his shoulder to the door to open it. This made it very doubtful as to whether Rob had been using this place to stash the drugs. Frequent use would have made the door much easier to open.

"This isn't encouraging", Morgan said to Sinead, "but we are here now, so we might as well have a look".

They both stood in the dark doorway and looked inside. There were no windows and the main roller shutter door was still down, which left the unit in complete darkness except for the stream of light let in by the pedestrian door. Morgan reached his arm around to the left where he knew the light switch was and flicked it but nothing happened. He flicked it a few more times, up and down, for good measure but nothing. The electricity had obviously been disconnected by the landlord. Morgan went back to the car and opened the boot. He rummaged for a few seconds before putting his hand on a heavy duty rubberised torch. He pushed the on off button and nothing happened. Morgan rattled it a few times before banging the torch with his hand before it lit up.

"Miracle of miracles, it works", Morgan said out loud.

He walked up to the door and shone the light in before taking a tentative step inside, followed closely by Sinead. They were both very familiar with the layout of the industrial unit, having visited it many times over the years that Rob was running it. The doorway that they walked through led to a small reception area, which in turn led to both a small office and out to the workshop floor. Morgan spun the torch around checking each room. Apart from a thick layer of dust on the floor, there was nothing left, not even an old desk or chair. The shop floor where Rob had serviced the cars was no better. There was nothing but a small pile of rubbish in the middle of the floor that did not look like it had been disturbed in years. They spent five more fruitless minutes in the building before making their way back outside and locking up.

Deflated they walked back to the car. "Would he have hid it on some waste ground or one of the other vacant units?" Morgan asked as he once again looked out over the large patch of unkempt grass, which encircled the huge flat building.

"Well, if he did, we will never find it," said Sinead.

"No, I suppose not". Morgan answered dejectedly. But he did call the letting agent to enquire after the property or any others that Rob might have leased through them. But nothing. Another dead end.

"Where to next?" Sinead asked.

"You know where", Morgan stated.

"I do?"

Chapter Nineteen

It had to have been one of the most awkward moments of Morgan's life when he asked Rob's father if he could search the O'Dwyer family house for a parcel of drugs that his son might have hidden there. But in fairness to Mike O'Dwyer, he recovered very well from the question. Others would not have taken it so easily. He did not scream or yell or slam the door shut in Morgan's face.

Since his son's murder, Mike O'Dwyer had learnt more than he wanted to know about his son's dubious activities from the Gardaí. He had initially refused to believe what they were saying about Rob, believing that it was all a pack of lies. Mike had wanted to believe that it was all a case of mistaken identity and that his son's killer had mistaken him for someone else. But in the end the weight of evidence meant that he had no choice but to accept the bitter news. After his murder, it was like the Gardaí had twisted the knife even deeper. Now faced with this outlandish request, he simply nodded and stood back so that Morgan and Sinead could enter.

Once inside, Morgan asked Mike if Rob had ever left anything at the house? Had he spent a long time out in the shed or turned up at odd hours? To each question Morgan got a negative and almost apologetic answer. After that he did not hold out much hope of finding anything. It wasn't a big house and the search only took a few minutes. As before, they had reasoned that the drugs could not have been too well hidden, after all Rob needed reasonably ready access to them. Morgan searched the bottom of the house, the shed, under the stairs and the kitchen units, while both Mike and Sinead did the upstairs bedroom. Mike even checked the bedroom, which his wife Collette, was resting in.

But nothing.

Every time they came up blank in a room, Mike would apologise. Morgan was not sure what he was sorry for. Was it for not having the drugs or his son in general? Mike would probably spend the rest of his life apologising for his dead son and wondering what he could have done differently.

After only ten minutes, Mike despondently walked them towards the front door once again apologising that he could not have done more to help. He kept saying that he would do anything to help catch the murderers of his son. The three of them stood in the doorway and said their goodbyes. Sinead gave her father in law a long hug and a tender kiss on the cheek before she called out to Rob's mother upstairs that she was off and would be back to see her soon.

As they said their farewells, Morgan watched Mike closely. It did not take years of observing people to see that the older man wanted to say something, but every time Mike seemed about to open his mouth he would look at Sinead and immediately clam up. Morgan figured that whatever it was he wanted to say, it was not for her ears. Morgan and Sinead turned and walked back to the car. Morgan unlocked the passenger door of the classic Mercedes but did not open his door. Instead he told Sinead to get in and that he had to slip back to use the toilet and would be back in a minute.

Morgan returned to the house door but before he could ring the bell, Mike opened it and invited him in. He ushered Morgan into the front room and closed the door quietly behind them both. He looked very flustered. He kept rubbing his face and running his hands down along his sides with nervousness. Morgan knew that he was on the verge of spilling his guts about something but could not quite get started. All he needed was a little prodding and it would all come out. What did the old man know and why hadn't he shared it already?

"What is on your mind Mike?" Morgan asked, trying to encourage the man.

"I want to help you know. But he is…I mean, he was my son and I don't want to spoil his memory if I don't have to."

"It's okay. But I think that it's a bit late at this stage to be worried about your son's reputation. Under the circumstances, it is more important now to think about the living. Anyway it's only me Mike. So, what do you know?"

"He had a girl on the side for the past while".

"He what?" Morgan said, genuinely shocked. Rob had never said a thing to him about an affair. Surely he would have told him? But then again, he had hardly seen Rob over the last year. And if he had met, they had become so distant that he probably wouldn't have admitted it.

"Why didn't you say earlier?"

"I didn't want to tell you in front of Sinead. No matter what else she might have learned over the last few days, she must always think that he was a faithful husband. I know that deep down Rob still loved her. I didn't want to take that away from her. She has lost so much already."

"I understand. So who was she, this girl on the side?"

"I don't know her full name," Mike said. "But her first name was Helen. I think she worked at the bar with Rob. Do you know her?"

"Helen. Yes, I think I know her", Morgan answered, picturing the pretty blond waitress. "How do you know this? Did he tell you?"

"Yes...No, at least not at first," Mike said. "I overheard him on the phone to her one day. Of course, when I confronted him about it, he tried to deny it but I eventually got it out of him. He begged me not to tell Sinead and told me that he would finish it but I don't know if he ever did. I don't know anything anymore".

Morgan said nothing; instead he just let this new bit of information sink in, wondering how it would affect the search. He knew that he would have to find Helen and talk to her.

"I think he was embarrassed", Mike continued "He measured himself against you, you know and I think he felt that he always came up short. He said you were a good and decent man".

These words stung Morgan deeply. Rob thought that he was a good and decent man? A good and decent man would never have allowed something like this to happen to one of his best friends. He felt ashamed that he hadn't done more. That he hadn't done everything humanly possible to help Rob in his hour of need so that he hadn't felt obliged to turn towards the scum that had eventually brought his downfall.

"How long was he seeing her?" Morgan asked, still flabbergasted with this news.

"A few months I think. I am not too sure. Do you think that she could help?"

"I don't know," Morgan said. "I will just have to ask her that when I find her. Did you tell all of this to the Gardaí?"

"God, no", Mike answered shocked at the mere suggestion that he would share his son secret outside of the family circle.

"Okay", Morgan replied, unsure whether or not the old man's logic was correct. How could hiding this information help anyone now? Despite everything that he had learned in the past few days, Mike's loyalties were obviously still as strong as ever for his son.

"Don't tell Sinead", Mike pleaded. "Please, I could not look at her if she found out that I knew and never said anything".

"I won't," Morgan said. "But you know that these things have a habit of coming out".

"I know. I know", Rob's father nodded sadly in agreement. They walked back to the hall door and Morgan left Rob's family home for the second time that day.

Chapter Twenty

Garda Brian Collin's shift had officially finished nearly two hours ago. He had spent his entire day frantically running errands and manning phones for various different detectives. It was all mundane work but he knew that it had to be done. He was just glad to be a part of it. He would make his role in the whole investigation seem bigger than it was to his friends later that night in the bar. Having said that though, he would be delighted to be going home too and was already running late as he had to run a couple of errands on his way home. He had been literally half way out of the door when Detective Callaghan had caught up to him. He was asked, or rather told, that he had to stay back and finish all of the remaining surveillance tapes before he left. The last ones had finally arrived in from the road traffic cameras in the area. Callaghan told him that despite the overtime ban that the DI had promised to sign off on his overtime. Garda Collins had initially tried to protest, explaining that he had plans but they fell on deaf ears. He was told that it needed to be done and he was the man to do it. He had five minutes to make whatever calls he had to and then back to work.

So about two hours earlier Garda Collins had dejectedly sat down to watch even more grainy poor quality mini films. He had been working for nearly ten hours and it was with little effect that he tried to rub the tiredness from his sore bloodshot eyes. His back was stiff from sitting for so long. He stretched his arms up over his head and let out a long bored sigh and the bones in his shoulders cracked slightly. He took another gulp from his mug of nearly cold tea before letting his head rest once again in the raised palm of his right hand. Like yesterday, when he had spent six hours watching these tapes, Collins kept his finger on the video remote fast-forwarding the images on the screen. The people on the screen were moving at an unnaturally high speed, reminiscent of old black and white films. Occasionally Collins would stop and rewind certain scenes, studying them more closely if he thought that he seen something vaguely interesting.

But there never was.

Just more of the same black and white monotony.

The tapes of CCTV footage had been collected from a variety of sources located all around the murder scene. There had been cameras in the local shops, the bank and at the cash machine. Dublin County Council had cameras mounted on one of the major local road junctions, which was only two miles away. Sixteen cameras in all and he was covering a time four hours before and four hours after the murder looking for anything suspicious but primarily a high powered racing motorbike seen in the area around that time. When he finished he would have watched nearly one hundred and twenty hours of footage all squashed into about twenty hours. Collins had watched the equivalent of nearly one hundred hours of footage so far and he was goggle-eyed doing it. One or two of the camera systems were very modern and only recorded when there was something moving in the camera's line of sight, but most of them just kept on recording regardless of activity or not. Sometimes there was hour after hour of boring nothingness. These he got through quickly, thanks to the magic of the fast-forward button.

The previous day Collin's had been excited to get the opportunity to help. When the sergeant told the new shift detail that a Garda volunteer was needed for the next week to help the detectives investigating a murder he had practically leapt up from his seat, his arm high in the air. The other more experienced Gardaí in the room just laughed at his eagerness. He had smiled back more than a little self-consciously at his reaction and told them that he could not wait to tell his friends and family back home that he was part of a murder team, they would be so proud.

Collins had had no idea what he might be doing but was not too upset when he found out that he would be watching CCTV non-stop for the next few days. He had not been expecting to be involved in the questioning of suspects or anything like that. For now it was enough that he was in the middle of everything and could keep himself up to speed on how the case was going. The DI told him that by checking all of these tapes it could help them track the movements of the killer when he was staking out the house or getting ready to make his move. In reality they both knew that there was very little chance that he would find anything useful. But then again you never knew. In the few months that he had served as a qualified Garda, Collins had learnt that criminals could do the most stupid things sometimes.

So far Collins had not seen much to get excited about. The camera on the cash machine had picked up the machine being vandalised at eleven fifty on the night in question by a group of drunken teenagers, four boys and a girl. He had then picked them up on another camera across the street at the front of a row of shops, where one of the lads wrote graffiti on the shop front shutters while the other ones kicked them. A can of what looked like Dutch Gold lager was flung against a "No littering" sign by the girl as she went by. This security camera had no audio but if it did he could imagine hearing them as they shouted and roared drunken encouragement to each other. The sound would have carried further than normal in the chill air and must have woken everyone in the apartments above the shops. Although the quality of the black and white image was not great, he took down the details and description of the kids and made a mental note to ask the sergeant to let him investigate the vandalism after the murder squad was done with him. The set of cameras covering the major junction gave no better results. A few cars breaking the lights, one near miss between a late night bus turning right just as a car decided to overtake it. But the bus driver must have seen him at the last moment. The bus jerked back suddenly into its lane as the car zoomed by. Pity, Collins thought, a crash might have relieved his boredom.

Collins looked around the room. There were only two detectives left. The detective who had been researching the sale of motor bike tyres had given up on them and moved onto tracing the movements of the murdered man's satellite navigation device, trying to track any routes taken and stored locations. He had been on the phone all day. And then there was the tall cute female one that scared Collins a little bit. She was busy going through bank accounts. He couldn't help stealing glances at her from the corner of his eye. The soft light from her desk lamp lit her strong features. She looks gorgeous, Collins thought. I wonder if I should make a play for her when all this is over? But he doubted it. Apart from telling him that he had to work late, she barely registered his existence. Both detectives were concentrating on the computer screens in front of them and were not paying him the slightest bit of attention. The rest of the team were either out on some task or another or had gone home long ago. There was hardly any noise from the other sections in the station. It seemed that they were pretty much all alone in the building.

"That's it for me tonight guys", Detective Griffith said out loud. He yawned and stretched as he stood and slipped his jacket off the back of the chair and switched off the desk lamp.

Both remaining Gardaí looked up. "Goodnight", Collins said jealously, eager to be going as well. He was supposed to be going out to the cinema with that attractive foreign girl from the local newsagents later that night and needed to get home to get ready. Anything could happen afterwards if he played his cards right. No such luck now, he thought. Detective Callaghan did not say anything to Griffith, merely grunted something unintelligible before going back to work. Seconds later the door banged shut and there were only the two of them left. Collins put in the last tape into the antiquated cassette player and began to spool forward. He was about to give up, when he saw a motorbike fitting the very broad description that he had been given appear briefly on the screen. Could this be what he was looking for?

He looked at the clip again before looking over to Callaghan's desk and called her over. "Detective, I think I have found something. Could you have a look at it for me?"

"Sure", she said and dragged herself wearily from her chair. She walked over, leaned on the back of his chair and peered at the screen over his shoulder. Her head was only inches from his. All Collins could think off was how beautiful she smelt. Maybe working closely with her would not be a complete washout after all.

"Right", Garda Collins said, trying to sound confident. "This is from a traffic camera located on the junction close to the victim's house".

Detective Callaghan watched the screen passively as he played it forward at normal speed. The traffic lights on the screen were green so the bike did not have to stop. It just cruised through, left to right on the screen. It was a high-powered racing bike, so why was it going so slowly? Every biker she knew drove like a bat out of hell, so was this rider going slowly because he was trying not to draw attention to himself or was he just strangely cautious? The time, which was located on the top right hand corner of the screen said eleven thirty. Callaghan knew that the time made sense. At eleven thirty, there was plenty of time to park the motorbike, walk the short distance to the house, wait around and check everything was still all right then go inside and BAM, BAM.

Rob O'Dwyer is dead.

Then the killer jumps back onto the motorbike and is gone.

It was a tenuous leap to make that this bike and its rider could be a murder suspect but every lead must be followed.

"Play it again", she said. She wanted to be sure. This time just as the motorbike reached the centre of the screen, she said "okay, stop it there". On the screen there was what appeared to be a bright yellow sports bike, unfortunately the angle of the camera meant that the rear registration plate was not visible. The rider hunched over the petrol tank was a large man wearing black leather. There was no chance of seeing his face through the visor of the fully enclosed helmet.

"I can try to zoom in", Collins offered, clicking an option on a toolbar, but the more he tried to, the more blurred the picture went. So he brought it back to its normal size. "Sorry".

"The guys down at the tech lab might be able to get a clearer image on their equipment. Make sure they get this tape and the time sequence we need digitised," Callaghan volunteered. "You did well there. You could have blown the case wide open. In the meantime can you print me a colour copy of the screen?"

"Sure", Collins answered enthusiastically. A click of the mouse and moments later the still photo popped out of the high-resolution printer by the wall.

Callaghan retrieved the picture and stood staring at it. Was this their man? Could it be Morgan? The person on the bike was around the same build. The excitement grew in her and if she had her way she would have rushed down to Morgan's house immediately and dragged him out of bed for questioning. She took her mobile phone and looked at the time. It was almost eleven p.m. Was it too late to give the DI a call? Fuck it, she thought. This was her lead and it was too good an opportunity to miss.

"Hello sir, sorry for disturbing you sir, but something has come up that I don't think should wait".

Chapter Twenty-One

Morgan dropped Sinead back to her mother's house. He told her that he had to go back to his own mother's house for a short while, as there was something he needed to get and that he would be back in an hour or two. It was a feeble excuse and he knew by her expression that Sinead knew that something was up but she didn't say a word. She trusted him to look after her so she just left him to it.

He had thought that he had known Helen pretty well. Not as well, as it turned out, as Rob had known her but well enough none the less. Her name was Helen Roache. She was a twenty two year old business student from south Tipperary who worked weekends and holidays in the pub, first as a waitress then as a barmaid. When she first started, she had been a tall thin girl, very thin in fact, with her brown hair cut into a bob that did not suit her. Morgan remembered the first few weeks she worked at the bar. She had been so shy, not used to the fast paced and sexually charged atmosphere of a busy pub and nightclub. Watching her the first weekend, he had doubted that she would make it, but if you saw her now, you would not think that she was the same timid girl.

Helen had filled out, blossomed even over the three years since she had first started there. She had grown her hair long and started to flirt with everything that moved, she drank like a fish on her nights off and cursed like a docker when the occasion arose. She was nothing like Sinead, but that was probably the idea for Rob. While she was studying for her degree in economics, she lived in a small top floor flat in a converted Georgian house about a mile or so away from the club. Morgan knew this because he had dropped her home after work once or twice when it was raining.

Morgan did not have a telephone number for her so he could not contact her directly to find out where she was. As far as he knew she could be at any number of places, at home, at work or in college. But as it was only the start of January, he assumed she had no classes, but then again she could have been in the collage library doing a project. Or, worst case scenario, she had gone back down to her family home in the country for a few days. Morgan decided to cover the easiest option first, so he just dropped up to her flat. He rang the buzzer for flat eight but with no luck before knocking a few times on the heavy outside door but nobody answered. So he hung around outside just to make sure she had not popped out to the shops. But after twenty minutes, he was cold and giving up. He headed to the next easiest option, the pub to see if she was working.

It was his first time back to the pub in over a year. Some of the staff had started working there after he had left and he did not recognise him. Those who did recognise him came over and gave him their condolences. Morgan accepted them and promised that he would pass them on to Rob's widow but he was not really paying them any attention. He walked around the back towards the staff room where he found Helen on her own, drinking a mug of tea and reading a glossy gossip magazine. She looked up and initially smiled but the smile quickly faded when she saw the look on his face.

"Morgan, Hi....", she said.

"Hi Helen, could I have a word with you?" Morgan asked closing the staff room door behind him.

"Sure", she said. Morgan instantly felt that Helen knew why he was there. The guilt over the affair and the upset caused by Rob's death were clearly written all over her face. It was like she had been expecting a visit and that it was only a matter of time before someone got around to her. It was not if, but when.

Morgan sat down facing her across the table. He did not even have to ask her a question she just came straight out with it. "So you know?" she said immediately. She seemed relieved that she could talk about it.

"Yes", was his only reply and then it all came flooding out. Apparently it had been raining hard one night last March and she got a lift home from Rob. She had had a really bad day in work and things were not going well at college and when he had asked her how everything was with her, everything literally came pouring out. In one instant, she had torn down her emotional barrier and revealed all of her feelings, all of her pent up emotions, both good and bad. Rob and Helen had ended up sitting in the car talking till the sun came up. Nothing physical had happened at first, it was just talking, but that was when it had started to mean something to her. Then Rob started to give her a lift most nights that they were working together whether it was raining or not and they would spend the hours sitting in the car with the radio off, just talking quietly about themselves.

Helen paused to blow her running nose and wipe the gathering tears from her eyes. Morgan said nothing; he just sat there patiently waiting for her to continue. Composed, she said that she had asked Rob in a few times for coffee but he had reminded her that he was married and said that he had to get home anyway as he had work in the morning. She knew that it was only an excuse and she respected him even more because of it. But one night he did come in. And although she knew it was wrong, she could not help herself. He didn't want to just have sex with her like most of the men she knew. Instead he listened to her and made her feel special in a way that no one had in a long time. Cared for and loved. When she was with him she felt that all of her problems would go away, there was only him. Over the next few months, she said they had fallen deeply in love and he was going to leave his wife for her. He would move into her bedsit until they found somewhere better. It would be hard at first but as long as they were together they would find a way to make it work.

Morgan asked her if she knew anything about his murder. But she didn't. She had been back at her parents' home in County Tipperary over the New Year, as her sister was back from Australia, when it happened. The first she knew about his death was when she got back to Dublin. Nobody had called her to let her know, because nobody had known about her relationship with Rob. When she heard from one of the other girls who worked in the bar she had wanted to rush straight to the morgue to be by his side but what would she say when she got there? Let me in, I'm his mistress? The closest that she got to being with him after his death, was when she attended his funeral with some of the other bar staff but then she had had to stand twenty feet away from the man she so desperately loved.

She got angry when Morgan asked her about drugs. Had Rob ever left anything at her place? A bag or suitcase of some kind? No, she had answered, upset at the very thought of Rob having any dealings with people like that when he was with her. She would never have allowed him to get involved in anything like that. If he had, then she would have known about it.

"But would you have known?" Morgan pressed her. "After all he was having an affair with you and nobody else knew about that".

"Of course, there were a lot of lies. We had to, for the sake of his children", she replied sadly. "But we had no secrets between us". Helen said that he could search her place if he did not believe her. But he trusted her. Her face told him everything he needed to know.

Morgan left the pub's staffroom five minutes later, feeling very sorry for Helen. He had no doubt that she had loved Rob but because of the situation she could not mourn his death openly like any other loved one could. It wasn't her fault. She had simply fallen for the wrong person. And how many people had that happened to?

Chapter Twenty-Two

"How are you holding up?" Morgan asked Sinead when she came back downstairs after putting the children to bed.

"I really don't know", she replied, sitting down beside him burying her head into his chest. They had actually had quite a pleasant family night together. At least considering that they had a death sentence hanging over their heads.

Earlier that day Morgan had sat in his car outside the pub for nearly thirty minutes when he had finished questioning Helen. He had gone over and over everything that he knew about the murder, the drugs and the threat in his head. He played with time lines, suspects and his own theories until he had a splitting headache and couldn't think anymore. So he decided not to think about it any longer. He knew that they should be getting Garda help. He knew that they should be sharing all of their information with the detectives and not trying to solve this themselves, but they were doing just that. So it was up to him to get them out of this mess, but his well of ideas had run drier than the Sahara desert in the summer. Normally clever and imaginative, this was not like him, but he realised that he was completely lost. Not that he was giving up or anything, that wasn't like him either but he simply had no other ideas at the moment. He needed to relax and unwind. Then with a bit of luck, he might be inspired. He imagined himself sitting down with a nice cup of tea and then suddenly, WHAM! He would make the obvious connection and save the day. But until that moment of divine inspiration came he would just have to hold tight and stay the course.

So he had stopped at a local video store on the way back from the pub and picked up a few children's DVDs. He didn't know if they had seen them but they looked funny so they would have to do. Then he had dropped into the nearest supermarket and bought enough sweets, cakes and fizzy minerals to keep all of them up and hyperactive for weeks. He need not have worried, as the movies were a great success. Linda particularly loved them but they helped everyone, adult and child alike to forget the last few days even for a few hours.

Before they knew it, it was nearly eleven o'clock and well past their time for bed. So Sinead rounded them all up while Morgan and Pauline cleaned up the discarded pizza boxes and sweet wrappers, replaced the cushions strewn around the room by the kids and put the DVDs back in their boxes. Pauline had made herself a final cup of tea before heading off to bed herself.

Now, Morgan and Sinead sat on the couch, the television and lights off, the only light in the room from the dying embers of the fire. Neither of them said anything. They just sat there, Morgan with his arm around her shoulder and Sinead with her head on his chest. Her eyes closed. Feeling safe and secure for the first time in what felt like a lifetime.

They had been sitting like that for over thirty minutes when they found themselves looking at each other. Morgan never knew where that moment came from but he didn't stop her when she leaned over and took his head in her hands.

Her kiss was hesitant, tender and soft. Her lips lingered on his. Morgan could smell her. Could feel her breath on his lips. Taste her. He very nearly kissed her back but pulled away instead.

Coupled with the tension that they were all under, he might forgive himself a moment of human weakness but Rob had been one of his very best friends and here he was with his widow only days after he had watched him being buried. What type of friend would he be, if had kissed her? he thought. And what about his dead fiancée Eimear? He wasn't ready for this. It felt like he was cheating on both of them.

Sinead for her part looked upset that he had hadn't responded, "What's wrong?"

"I can't...," Morgan, stammered lost for words.

"Why not?"

"Rob was my friend. I can't be doing this".

"I know he was, but our marriage had been over for so long... You must have known that", Sinead replied

"Was it?" Morgan asked, the earlier revelation of Rob and Helen flashing through his mind. She had no idea.

"I have felt so alone for so long now".

"I am really sorry to hear that" Morgan empathised.

And he was.

Both Rob and Sinead were his friends and he only ever wanted the best for them both. He didn't blame her or think any less of her for trying to kiss him. God only knew what she was feeling and going through right now. She must feel very lonely and insecure. Physical human contact was probably exactly what she needed right now. But he wasn't the man to provide that for her.

"I want you so badly right now," she said quietly.

"And I you but we can't right now," Morgan said. "Maybe when this is all over? When I know that you and the children are safe and life regains some sort of normality, maybe then we can start something. But I can't now. The timing is not right. Everything that we will have would be based on something so horrible".

As he spoke, Sinead started to weep gently and Morgan leaned over to comfort her. She went to bed shortly afterwards while Morgan settled in on the couch, awash with mixed emotions.

Morgan had first learned about Rob's first tentative steps into the drug's world when he had brought Rob out for a mid-week pint about two years previously. They had gone out for their usual Tuesday night game of pool but Rob had said that he wasn't in the humour to play and wanted to talk instead so they went for what Morgan thought was going to be a nice quiet drink in the local pub. Rob had been uncharacteristically quiet as they sat down in a corner booth. Morgan could sense that he wanted to say something but it was as though he did not know where to start or perhaps was embarrassed to. Instinctively Morgan knew then that it was going to be a long night and having his own problems at the time, he was not sure he was in the mood for it.

The Rob that Morgan had known at school and had become friends with was now largely gone. He had been replaced with a man struggling under the burden of constantly trying to make ends meet. As he took his first mouthful of beer, Rob told Morgan that he had money problems. Although Morgan had loaned him over fifteen hundred euro last month to catch up on his mortgage payments. Lying there on the sofa in Pauline's house, Morgan could recall the conversation perfectly. It stuck in his mind because it was that night when everything between Rob, Sinead and himself changed forever.

"What do you mean, you need more money?" Morgan said shaking his head in disbelief.

"Work is very slow at the moment", Rob said. "I know that I can do some cash jobs but I need to get the last two upgrades to the diagnostic software from Autodata and that's bloody expensive".

"Can't you just borrow the diagnostics from the garage before you go home?"

"No, it's worth over five grand and it's kept locked up. I need to get my own one brought up to date".

"Okay. How much will that cost?" Morgan asked, a bit sceptical. Where was this going? Was he really expecting him to lend him the money for it? Because if he was, he was going to be very disappointed.

"About a thousand Euro, but I only need to pay half of that now and I can pay the rest myself over ten months".

"And you really need it?"

"Yes, I'm turning away work because I can't do it. I can't afford not to get it. I had to turn away three cash in hand jobs alone last week alone because I did not have the correct diagnostic upgrades. I had to give them to the garage instead".

Listening to him, it seemed to Morgan, that Rob was trying to convince both of them of the need for the extra money. But why? Was there something else in the background that he wasn't aware of?

"Have you talked to Sinead about this? Morgan asked him.

"No. She doesn't want to know," Rob said, shaking his head dejectedly. "She keeps getting at me about changing things in the house, wanting a new fancy kitchen and stuff that we don't need. She doesn't understand the pressure that I'm under".

There was a long awkward pause before Rob continued. But he seemed determined to let it all out. "The bills at home are just going through the roof. The electricity bill alone last month was two hundred euro. I can't get it through to her or the kids to turn off the bloody lights. And the washing machine, don't get me started on the fucking washing machine, it is constantly going."

"There are five of you in that house, remember?" Morgan said trying to be realistic about things. Rob wasn't listening though, he just sat there, wallowing in self-pity and contemplating what he thought was his miserable life as Morgan searched for some magical words to make it better.

Looking straight at his friend, Morgan said in as comforting a voice as he could manage "Maybe you just need to sit Sinead down and explain these things to her? I'm sure that she will understand. She has always supported you in everything and I'm sure that she will support you again. She loves you."

"I don't want to tell her I am broke again," Rob said. "Not this time. I look at her and I see her looking at me as if I'm such a failure. I do not want her to know I'm in trouble again". He looked at Morgan, his eyes pleading with him to understand his predicament and help.

"I am sorry," Morgan repeated. "But I can't loan you any money right now. Things are tight all round. Have you tried going to the bank?"

"Yes, of course I have. I was there today, but they said that I was overdrawn as it was and I also didn't have a good record of keeping up my payments".

"I'm sorry, but I cannot loan you any money right now, I have to pay for this trip over to Canada with Eimear, but maybe I can get you a few hundred euro next month if that will help? In the meantime, for what it's worth you can talk to me at anytime, you know that?"

Rob gave a deep resounding sigh as if he had known that this was going to be a long shot and it hadn't paid off. Just his damn luck as always, he had thought as he sat there staring into his pint, he never got a break.

"Yeah, I know," he said. "I'll get the money from somewhere. I will ask Smith if I can pick up a few extra nights on the doors." But Morgan did not think he sounded like he understood. What Rob said next had surprised him. Looking back it should have sent more alarm bells ringing than it did.

"If anything should ever happen to me," Rob said. "Will you look after them for me?"

"Who?" asked Morgan surprised, not sure he was hearing him right.

"Sinead and the kids of course".

"What the hell are you talking about?" Morgan asked.

"Would you look after them for me?" Rob persisted.

"Will you shut up? You are talking rubbish. Sure what is going to happen to you?"

"Just promise me..."

"I don't know what you are on about," Morgan said, "but okay, yes I promise that I will look after them for you. Happy now?"

"Much happier. Thanks. Thanks for everything".

"You'll be grand. It will all work out, you'll see", quickly draining his pint glass, Morgan said, trying to lighten the mood. "Come on I'll buy you another one, I'll even throw in a bag of crisps. How's that?"

After that, the conversation that night had changed back into its normal rhythm about girls, cars, fights on the door and inevitably back to girls again where it stayed for the remaining few hours. By twelve o'clock Rob was pretty hammered on a mixture of Guinness pints and Vodka and Red Bulls. Morgan who wasn't much of a drinker at the best of times had only had a few drinks and he had literally to carry Rob back home. He didn't mind though. It was obvious that Rob had needed a good night out. Maybe, tonight he had let off enough steam and everything would seem that bit easier after a good night's sleep. It usually did for Morgan anyway. But he knew as well as everyone that being trapped in debt is very hard to escape from. It might seem hopeless, especially if Rob didn't curb his spending habits. Morgan knew that Rob wasn't mentally strong enough to cope on his own with this kind of pressure. He was a good mechanic and a great dad, but wasn't suited to this type of stress. He just hoped everything would work out for his friend.

Luckily Rob didn't live far from the pub, but as it was uphill all the way, Morgan was out of breath by the time he got his friend home. Sinead must have been waiting up for Rob because he hadn't even got up the driveway before the front door was flung open, bathing them both in the bright light from the hall.

"Look at the state of him", Sinead said, crossing her arms while giving Morgan a look as if to say it was his entire fault. As if Morgan had dragged Rob out and forced the pints down his throat.

"Sorry, Sinead," Morgan said. "We got to talking and well one thing led to another".

"I expected better from you", Sinead said, shaking her head in disgust. "You had better bring him straight up to bed. I'll fucking kill him tomorrow".

Rob started to grunt and groan. He was slurring his words as he declared his undying love for his wife, as Morgan tried to carry him up the stairs.

"Shut up, you fucking eejit, before you wake the kids", Sinead said angrily, thumping him on the back of the head as he went past. Morgan was sweating hard by the time he got him up to bed.

He removed his shoes and jacket before dumping him fully dressed into the bed. Rob fell sound asleep and was already snoring loudly as Morgan shut the bedroom door and crept downstairs conscious of the children asleep in the other rooms. He went into the sitting room to find Sinead sitting with her head in her hands, looking very glum.

"He just needed a night out. He had a lot on his mind", Morgan said trying to apologise on his behalf.

"He will have a lot on his mind tomorrow when I get my hands on him", she promised.

Morgan remained silent. He did not know what to say to her. She had the look of a woman with a lot on her mind too. Maybe she could do with an opportunity to vent to someone as well, he thought.

"There always seems to be cars needing work yet we never have any money to do anything. The kitchen is falling apart and needs replacing and the washing machine is leaking." Sinead blurted out at last, twisting the corner of a cushion into contorted shapes.

"I'm sure he's doing his best," Morgan said.

"At the moment that's not good enough," Sinead stated. "I've taken extra cleaning jobs but there isn't much work going around at the moment because of all the foreigners who are doing it for next to nothing".

"Things will get better," Morgan said.

"I've heard that before. You know what, I just can't take it anymore", Sinead said shaking her head despondently.

"He loves you and the kids. You know that. He'd be lost without you".

"Well, at the moment I feel lost with him". At this point, she began crying fully. "It was not supposed to be like this. It's okay scrimping and saving when you're young and only starting out, but not now. We've been married nearly twenty years". Her voice was raised as her tears gave way to anger and frustration. Morgan did not say anything immediately, preferring to let her get it out of her system. He was not sure what to say anyway. She wiped her eyes, which looked red and sore from the crying. "Oh look at me. I'm sorry..."

"Look there is nothing to be sorry about", Morgan said cutting her short, "I'm your friend as well, you know".

"Oh, you have been so good to us this past while", she said trying to smile at him. "I don't know what we would have done without you."

"You are both my best friends. What type of friend would I be if I did not help you?"

Sinead had started to gently cry again but this time Morgan walked over to her and kneeling down beside her, he put his arms around her to comfort her. He rested his head on hers as she cried. Maybe it was the drink talking but she smelt so good. Normally so confident, she seemed so small and fragile and he wanted to protect her, to make whatever was upsetting her go away.

Chapter Twenty-Three

Morgan had stayed over in Pauline's house again the previous night but had slept badly. Although sleeping on the couch hadn't helped, it wasn't the real reason behind his staring at the ceiling most of the night. He couldn't help himself but he was getting more impatient and frustrated with every passing moment. Time was slipping away faster than they could afford and they were no closer to finding the drugs. He ended up restlessly prowling the downstairs of the house, his mind racing he was getting more and more convinced that searching for the drugs themselves was the wrong strategy. They should be going to the Gardaí before it got too late, not trying some foolhardy solo run of their own.

"This is all wrong. We can't find the drugs. We tried, we gave it our best shot but this is not working out. I think that you should call the Gardaí and tell them honestly what is happening. They will give you protection. They will have to", he said later that morning to Sinead.

"No, but I have had another idea. Why don't we just contact this Johnson bastard and tell him that we have searched every-where and we don't have the drugs?" Sinead asked imploringly.

She was really clutching at straws now, Morgan thought.

"I doubt he will believe us and anyway how can we just contact him? Unless he left his number on his business card the other night," Morgan said with a touch of sarcasm. But as soon as he said it, he wished that he could take it back. He did not mean to be sarcastic with Sinead. This was not her fault. She was only trying to do her best to cope under an extremely stressful situation. Right now, right this second, he felt completely deflated. This was a mess not of his making. He had tried to help her and his help had turned out next to useless. It was worse than useless in fact, since it had deflected them from doing the right thing. He had really wanted to help Sinead. After all he had not helped Rob as much as he could have. But all it did was get everybody's hopes up, including his.

"Could we get his number from the Gardaí?" Sinead suggested.

"The Gardaí? I doubt they have his number otherwise I am sure that they would have tried it themselves already", Morgan said. This time his voice was softer, the tone more gentle, more conciliatory. "And even if they did have, they certainly would not give it to us".

Sinead was right though. They had no drugs and they needed to communicate with Johnson as soon as possible to get him off both Sinead's and the children's trail. But they were all in the dark as to what was happening around them. Morgan felt like a solitary chess piece, a castle standing on his own forced into a corner protecting a vulnerable king, all the while being ignored while the real battle raged on the other side of the board. The other pieces representing the Gardaí and the dealers were making plans and positioning themselves for the next strike. While he, with the burden of trying to protect Sinead and the children, was effectively under house arrest and isolated from everyone else. Waiting around and watching the clock was not how he operated. He would rather take the fight to them.

Attack is the best form of defence after all.

He needed time to think. Morgan always prided himself on being able to think under pressure. His normal method was to start at the end, the conclusion and work his way backwards to where he was now. But he couldn't see this at all, no end and no middle, so maybe he needed to look at this differently.

"So, how did Rob communicate with them?" Sinead asked.

"Mobile phone I assume. Why?"

"Well, why can't we just use Rob's mobile to call them?" she asked.

"I don't see why not..." Morgan said.

"Yes, Yes", Sinead nearly screamed with relief. She lifted herself up out of the chair with excitement. She was smiling ear to ear, like a great weight had been lifted and was literally dancing foot to foot, but then she stopped dead as if she had run into a brick wall, her earlier enthusiasm having completely disappeared. "But the Gardaí, they looked everywhere for his mobile, but it had gone missing or the killer had taken it or something, I'm not sure. I'm sorry".

"Shit", Morgan said, he really thought they had it there. But wait a minute, maybe they still had.

"Rob, he was always big into his gadgets", Morgan said thinking out loud while wagging his finger like a schoolteacher dictating to his class. "He always had to get the next new phone, the new playstation or Xbox 360."

"Yes, the latest was his sat nav".

"Yes, but his phone, it was one of the flashy types that you could back up, wasn't it?"

"Well I know that he used to download the pictures of the kids from it. He didn't even need to link it to the computer, he could just sync it wirelessly and off it went".

"They have a function where he could backup all the numbers on the SIM card and I would say that he would have backed up his phone numbers on the computer as well".

Morgan felt pretty chuffed with himself but was a bit confused, as Sinead had not gone back to jumping with joy again.

"That's great, but the Gardaí took that as well," she said. "They said that they wanted to check his business records, emails, that sort of thing".

"Typical. That makes sense," Morgan said shaking his head despondently. He was getting nowhere. Okay, so Rob's new phone was gone and the laptop that he might have backed up the numbers on was sitting in a Garda station gathering dust somewhere. That was it – his new phone. What about his old one? He had only changed it last month and sure hadn't he been holding the drugs on and off for months now. Surely the same numbers would be on the old phone? Now it was Morgan's turn to jump for joy. "His old phone. What did he do with his old phones?"

"He usually gave them to one of the kids after he copied all the numbers over".

"Oh", Morgan said dejectedly.

"But I don't think he did this time," Sinead said. "The kids wanted their own new phones not his hand me downs".

"So since he wasn't giving the phone to one of the children, he might not have cleared the numbers from the old one," Morgan asked.

"I'm not sure. Maybe."

"Thank God, we needed something to go our way. Where is it?"

"I assume that it is back in the house," Sinead said.

"Fantastic, do you know where?"

"Yes, I am sure that I saw it the other day when I was cleaning. It was in the top drawer of his bedside locker".

Five minutes later, Morgan was in his car and on his way. The morning rush hour was finished and the traffic was light and it did not take long to get back to Rob and Sinead's house. He caught himself as he called it that. It wasn't Rob and Sinead's anymore. It was really just Sinead's now.

As he got out of the car, he surveyed the surrounding area. There was nobody on the pathway and there were no twitching curtains in the neighbouring houses. Nobody appeared to be watching. Ducking down under the blue and white striped Garda tape that was fluttering in the gentle breeze, Morgan went up the short driveway and let himself in with Sinead's spare key. The first thing that he noticed was how cold the house was after it had been vacant for a few days. Morgan had planned to just go straight upstairs to the main bedroom, open the drawer, and get the phone and leave.

But he could not.

He was inexplicably drawn towards the living room where Rob had been shot. The heavy curtains were still closed, leaving the room in darkness. Without walking in, Morgan reached around the corner, felt for the switch and turned on the main light. He looked apprehensively into the room and saw the couch. There was a dark black stain across one of the cushions that had soaked down onto the seat. There was also a black stain on the beige carpet where the pathologist must have laid Rob to carry out his preliminary examination. Saddened, Morgan turned away, not wanting to look anymore.

As he made his way upstairs, the staircase creaked in the empty house. When he reached the top, a big pile of clothes and sheets left in a heap on the floor beside the empty hot press blocked his way. The attic ladder had also been left down and Morgan was forced to squeeze by it on the narrow landing to get to the master bedroom. By the looks of it, the entire house had been searched thoroughly by people told to be careful but not really bothering to be. Through the open bedroom doors, Morgan could see that there were clothes in rough piles near the wardrobes in each of the rooms. Drawers had been emptied, clothes from the presses had been unceremoniously scattered across the floors. Every corner of the house had been searched in an effort to find the drugs and any other clues about the slaying. He got the impression that there must have been a hundred people, Gardaí, doctors, technicians, all strangers to the family, through the house in the last few days. He was probably not a mile off with his estimation. As for him, he couldn't count the number of times that he had been here before.

But it was different now.

Before it had always been full of life and laughter but it did not feel like a home anymore.

Now it was just four walls and a roof.

The master bedroom looked like the other rooms. It looked like a bomb had hit it. If the initial Garda search had not been enough, then Sinead's hurried collection of clothes the next day had only made it worse. When he opened the locker drawer, Morgan found the old phone in amongst a pile of discarded bills, old batteries, pens and a handful of stylish expensive sunglasses. Just as he had expected. The Gardaí had Rob's current mobile phone, his laptop and even his Sat Nav but didn't seem to be doing anything with them.

But Morgan would do something with this one.

He needed it to work.

He needed it badly. Morgan tried to turn the phone on, pressing down hard on the little button on top. No luck. The battery was completely dead. He rummaged through all of the drawers on both lockers looking for the charger but his bad luck was holding. He found two but they were for a Siemens and a Motorola, not Rob's Nokia. A dead phone was no good to him so he continued looking in the wardrobe nearest to him. But he came up short there as well.

Slightly deflated, as finding the phone dead had now turned the whole episode into an anti-climax, Morgan drove back towards Sinead's mother's house. He stopped off at a petrol station on the way, filling up the car with petrol and bought a cheap generic mobile phone car charger off a small rack on the counter. He sat in the car at the petrol pump and ripped the charger from its packaging. He went to plug it into the cigarette lighter and then realised that the car was so old that it didn't have one. Shit, he thought, he wasn't expecting to get caught like that. Not being a smoker he never noticed that there wasn't a cigarette lighter in the classic Mercedes.

Now he would have to wait until he got back to the house.

Ten minutes later he arrived back and walked into a mad house. Kids were running and screaming everywhere. The undeniable tensions of the last few days coupled with the fact that Sinead would not let them leave the house had eventually boiled over. Everybody was shouting at one another but nobody could hear anyone because of the racket. Morgan had to pull Linda and Ian, the youngest lad apart. They were wrestling with an old teddy bear, which he took off them and gave it back to little Niamh, who stood crying over to one side of the hall. Ian disgusted with this, ran upstairs shouting something unintelligible before slamming one of the bedroom doors so hard that the entire house practically shook.

"Ian, just stop it", Sinead yelled up at him, throwing her arms up in the air. "This is hard enough without you at each other's throats."

"Mam, she's after throwing my iPod against the wall", Ian emerged from the bedroom door and shouted down.

"But Mam, he…" Niamh went to counter protest.

"Ian, did she break it?" Sinead asked.

"No. Lucky for her", he answered giving his younger sister a vicious look.

"I just wanted to listen to it but he wouldn't let me", the little girl said, tears welling up in her eyes.

"I know honey. I know," Sinead said. "Why don't you go and watch some cartoons? I just need to talk to Uncle John for a few minutes. Alright?"

"Okay, mum", she replied sniffing loudly, her tears receding.

Morgan quickly told Sinead about finding the dead phone and the lack of a cigarette charger in his car before Ian reappeared out of the bedroom and stomped back down the stairs and into the kitchen.

"Let's go out and check the phone in my car. It will be more private", Sinead suggested to Morgan and grabbed her coat off the hook under the stairs, before shouting out to her mother that she would be back in a few minutes.

"Good idea", Morgan agreed. There were too many distractions here.

They went out and sat in Sinead's car, with Morgan in the driving seat. He turned on the engine so he could put the climate control on to keep them warm and plugged the phone in. He waited a few seconds and then turned the phone on. It came to life and the familiar Nokia jingle sounded. All good so far, Morgan thought. Then he came back down to earth as the phone asked for a security code. Typical. Morgan shook his head. Nothing was going his way today. The factory code was set at four zero's. If Rob had not changed it, then it was all he had to key in. He looked at the phone for a second, his thumb hovering over the phone before pressing the keypad four times hoping that Rob had not changed the factory setting.

Zero, zero, zero, zero.

The phone beeped and incorrect code flashed onto the screen before going back to the code entry option. Morgan did not try again. He knew that he had a maximum of three tries and then the phone would lock up completely. He would then need an eight digit unblocking code to reactivate the access code.

"That's it but now I need the code, any ideas?" Morgan asked Sinead.

"His phone code, oh, that's easy. He always used our wedding day, the thirteenth of December. He used that code for everything including the house alarm."

They leaned towards each other into the middle of the car. They were practically sitting shoulder to shoulder, so they could both see the little screen on the phone. Morgan was so close to Sinead that he could smell her sweet perfume, it was overpowering. Being so close to her in the confined space of the car made it all feel quite intimate. He glanced at her quickly before returning his attention to the phone, keying the security code into the phone. One, Three, One and Two. The phone beeped and a welcoming message saying 'Hello Sexy' came up on the screen. They couldn't help but laugh.

They both sat watching the phone as Morgan scrolled down through the names. But there was no sign of any Dave Murray or Brian Johnson. There was a Dave without a surname listed but Sinead recognised his number as that of a panel beater that Rob used from time to time. They quickly scanned through the listed names without anything obvious popping up. Occasionally there was a thumbnail photograph attached to the phone record but none of the images matched those that the Gardaí had shown them.

"Nothing", Sinead said disappointed.

"Well what did we expect? The number to be listed under "D" for drug dealer?"

"Would have been helpful, yes", she said cracking a rare smile, lightening the mood. Morgan looked deep into her eyes, deeper than he should have and could not help but grin. He went into the phone menu and looked up contacts, then settings and then the memory in use option. It said that there were two hundred and thirty nine phone numbers listed. Hmm, this was going to take some time, he thought.

"Okay, back to the beginning. Rob would have needed to contact this Johnson or Murray or whoever. Their number is in this phone somewhere. We are going to go through this list number by number and eliminate the numbers we know and we will simply call the other numbers".

"Sounds like a good plan," Sinead said.

"Okay, let's start with the "A's". The first one was for an Adam Winters. "Adam Winters, who is he?" Morgan asked.

"Oh, he is the artist that did that lovely painting of Dun Laoghaire Harbour at sunset that hangs in the dining room".

"The one I wanted to buy at the exhibition but you beat me to it?"

"Yes, that one," Sinead said. "We actually met the artist when we went to collect it from the gallery. He gave me his number and I promised to buy another one from him but we've never had the money to splash out like that again".

"It was a nice painting", Morgan said, moving onto the next name on the list - Alan Brown, Alan Gordon, Albert Rice and so on. Some of the names he recognised himself, the others Sinead knew. They were mostly either relatives or people that Rob knew in the motor trade. A lot of the names had thumbprint pictures attached to them which was very useful in helping to identify the numbers listed. Morgan got to the letter "G" before they reached a name neither of them recognised. George Guichard. Who was he? Was he the man they were looking for? They noted his name on a piece of paper Sinead found in the glove compartment and kept on scrolling through the list. Morgan involuntarily paused on Helen's name, Rob's secret mistress, when it came up but moved on quickly before Sinead would start wondering why. They found three more unidentified names by the time they reached the last name on the phone list, a "W" for the Waterford Marina Hotel. Sinead looked mildly embarrassed to inform him that this was the hotel where Rob had taken her last year for her birthday for what turned out to be a very dirty weekend. Morgan smiled back, cheekily saying "lucky guy". They looked at each other and Morgan thought he saw a hunger in her eyes and he didn't think it was for food.

"Right, we have four names," Sinead said reading from her list. "George Guichard, Gary Breen, Matthew Lucas and somebody called Noel O'Hara. What now?"

"We call them. What else?" Morgan scrolled back down to the "G" section to start with the first on the list. He reached George Guichard. He opened his own phone and after turning off his own number sending option, dialled the number that he read from Rob's mobile. Apart from the fact that there was probably no credit on the phone, he did not want to ring it from Rob's as the person would see Rob's name pop up and after all they hoped that one of the people they were calling had actually murdered Rob. It was a strange wish to make, but it was the one they found themselves hoping for. The phone rang six times before it went straight to message minder. Morgan left a brief message but not wanting to give anything away, neither stated his name nor what it was about. There was no need to alert the person any more than he needed to. "Hiya George, It's me. Call me back will you" and hung up.

He then called Gary Breen. It was answered straight away. Morgan tried to play it cagey but he needn't have bothered. Gary was very forthcoming with information. It turned out that he had printed leaflets and put them onto cars around the neighbourhood for Rob's boss in an attempt to bring in some extra business. He must not have heard about Rob's death as he asked if Morgan needed any leaflets printed and sounded very disappointed when Morgan said he didn't. Morgan hung up and struck Gary's name off the list. One out of two so far and potentially two more to go, but the other two numbers turned out to be dead ends.

One was the number of a local chiropodist of all things. The other was an old man that Rob had apparently promised to adapt a car for handicap driving for the man's sister. Morgan sighed dejectedly; unless George turned out to be their man and was obliging enough to call back, today's work had amounted to nothing but another gigantic waste of time. He flicked through the phone one more time; he noticed that the last contact name was actually only an asterisk symbol. He went into the details and there was a number attached to the name. When he had checked a few minutes ago, he had assumed that the phone had rubbed off something in his pocket and had stored a nonsensical name with no number attached to it. After all it had happened to him many times if he did not put the keypad lock on. It never occurred to him to check it. But there was a proper number linked to the asterisk.

"I have found another number," Morgan said, twisting his hand around so that Sinead could see the number.

"You might as well call it. What have we got to lose?"

He nodded agreement and with a little trepidation pushed the button with the little green phone on it. The phone gave three rings and Morgan thought that it was going to ring out when a man with a deep Dublin accent answered it. "Yeah?"

"Hi, who is this?" Morgan said, trying to sound cheery, like a telesales person about to launch into a pre-arranged sales pitch about potential savings in long distance phone calls. He watched Sinead fidgeting nervously in the seat beside him.

"Who the fuck is this?" came back the gruff reply.

"I am calling on behalf of Rob O'Dwyer," Morgan said tentatively.

There was silence on the other end, but the phone was not hung up. "Who is this?" said the voice suspiciously.

"I am calling on behalf of Rob O'Dwyer," Morgan repeated.

"No, you're not," said the voice emphatically.

"Why wouldn't I be?"

"He's dead". There was silence again. "Who are you?"

"I am actually calling on behalf of his widow, Sinead".

"Are you a fucking pig?"

"No. I am a friend of the family".

There was a short pause before the voice asked, "Well, friend of the family, have you got a name?"

"Morgan".

"So Morgan what do you want?" the voice asked.

"I want to know if you are the man that...eh... came late to the wake the other night?" he asked speculatively, not wanting to give the game away too quickly.

"And what if I was?" the voice sneered.

Morgan took this to mean that he had been there. "So it was you then?"

No answer.

Was it him? There was no point in beating around the bush, he might as well come out and say what they needed to say.

"Look, we have searched everywhere we can think of but we can't find the drugs".

"Not my problem".

So that was all the confirmation that they needed. It was him after all. It had to be Johnson.

"We cannot find them, okay," Morgan said, trying to appeal to him.

"No, it is not okay. You tell that bitch that her stupid fucking husband had stuff that belongs to me. And I want it back."

Morgan looked at Sinead and could see the sheer dread in her expression. "She has already lost her husband, she's been through enough. Just leave her alone".

"I'm a reasonable man. I gave her plenty of time to find them. Time you're wasting by phoning me. Her husband's debt still has to be paid. One way or another".

"You're not listening. We can't find them, alright!" Morgan shouted exasperated by the man's refusal to see reason.

"You keep saying that, but that's no fucking good to me. I just want my stuff back."

"And I keep telling you that we have searched everywhere and can't find them".

"Well then you had better find someone who can, if I am not wrong, you only have till midnight tomorrow. I either get my stuff or I get my money's worth".

"You can threaten all you want, it won't help us find the drugs any quicker," Morgan said.

"You say that but just imagine me in a dark room with that little girl or even better the oldest one, she looks a bit of alright doesn't she?"

"Shut the fuck up you bastard. If you lay a hand..."

"I'll do more than lay a hand on her, now how's that for motivating you? You have until tomorrow night," he said laughing before hanging up.

Morgan sat staring at the phone wondering what he could do now. As he sat there a dog barked in the distance, its snarl sending a shiver running down his spine.

Chapter Twenty-Four

Last night the DI had felt that Garda Callaghan's information could wait until the morning. He had been out for an anniversary meal with his wife and Callaghan's enthusiasm about the inconclusive still picture did not translate well over the phone. So begrudgingly she had waited until the morning to show him her big find.

That morning, while drinking a hot steaming cup of coffee, the DI studied the picture for a few minutes, not making any noises good or bad. It was a pretty clear photograph but it didn't tell them much. The picture did not show the registration number plate. The bike did not have any markings or colours, nor did the rider's leathers or helmet stand out in any way. There was no distinguishing flashing, colours or style to help identify either. But both the timing and the direction the bike was travelling in were about right and the lead couldn't be ignored. Callaghan realised that her belief that the rider was Morgan did stretch things, but he was a big guy so she figured that it was possible. But was he as big as the man in the picture? The DI was even more impressed when Callaghan told him that Morgan had applied for a motorbike licence but had never applied for the test and allowed the provisional licence to lapse.

"But he has never owned a motorbike according to our records?" the DI asked.

"No, but it means that he can ride one," Callaghan said. "And it was not one of those old type licences where you just ticked the box on the application form and got it automatically. This was just over two years ago, he had to actually sit a test or drive a test or whatever you have to do."

"So, why would you apply to get a licence unless you are going to get a bike?" the DI said out loud.

"That's what I thought," said Callaghan smiling. Now he was on her wavelength.

"Why didn't you tell me this last night?"

"You told me to, ahem, 'wait till the morning,'" she answered, trying to be diplomatic.

"You're right, I did. Sorry about that".

"Well?"

"Why don't you go and find your Mr. Morgan and ask him some questions?"

Morgan was not happy to see Garda Callaghan at Pauline's hall door when he opened it. He openly grumbled, making no attempt to mask his hostility.

"I thought that I would find you here", Callaghan quipped. "You never seem to be far away from this family".

"I have to remain here as you lot saw fit to remove the security from the house. So what do you want?" Morgan asked belligerently. He had no time for any of the Gardaí at the moment. They had let them all down.

"Morgan, could I have a few minutes of your time please?" asked Callaghan asked with false politeness as she smiled menacingly at him. Morgan did not smile back.

"What's happened now?"

"Some new information has come to light and we just want to ask you a few questions".

"I am very busy", Morgan said in an exasperated tone.

"Doing what? Anyway it won't take long", said Callaghan determinedly.

"Okay then. Come into the kitchen." He led her down the corridor, ignoring Sinead's eyes burning a hole into the side of his head as she watched from the sitting room as they walked past and closed the door behind them.

"What's this all about?"

"You told us that you did not own a motorbike", Callaghan stated.

"Yes that's right. I don't", Morgan confirmed.

"Yet only a few years ago you applied for a provisional licence for one. Why is that?"

"I was planning to get one at the time."

"You were planning to get one?"

"Yes, I was," Morgan answered. "Some of the lads that I used to work with on the door had them and were always going on about how great they were. I thought that I would get one but it turned out that I did not have enough money to get the one I wanted, so I ended up getting nothing. Look, what is this about?"

When he mentioned money the female detective gave him a knowing look. "I would like you to look at a picture taken on the night that Rob was murdered", she said as she pulled a glossy ten by twelve picture from the envelope she was carrying. "Do you recognise this motor bike or its rider?"

Morgan stared long and hard at the picture, studying the bike and its rider. It was a black racing bike. It had no discernible markings on it and the angle of the shot was not great. And not knowing motor bikes that well, he had no idea what type it was. The rider was also dressed all in black, black leathers with a black helmet. Morgan came to the same conclusion that the Gardaí had earlier. There was no way of telling who the rider was from this picture.

"No.... no, I don't know who that is".

But he did not immediately hand the picture back. He just kept staring at it. There was something about the rider. He couldn't put his finger on it, it was just that it reminded him of someone he knew. It wasn't the bike or the rider's clothing but was the way that the rider was sitting on the seat, it did not seem right. He was sitting slightly to one side even though the bike appeared to be going in a straight line. He had seen someone ride in that style before. Could it really be...?

"Are you sure that you have never seen this bike before?" asked Callaghan, "Take your time".

"No." Morgan replied less sure of himself.

"If you ask me, it looks like you on the back of that bike," said Callaghan accusingly, pointing at the picture.

"Fuck off", Morgan snapped at her. "I thought I told you never to come near me again."

"This is a murder investigation, Morgan, and I will ask any questions that I feel are necessary," Callaghan replied taking a step closer to him.

Closing in on him.

"You did not ask a question. You made a statement. There is a subtle difference. You should look up the definitions in a dictionary", he quickly spat back at her.

"Okay, okay. Morgan have you seen this bike before?"

"No. Never", he said determinedly, staring straight at her. Daring her to keep this line of questioning going.

But Callaghan decided that there was nothing more to be gained from continuing this now. His back was up and would just answer negatively whatever the question. But despite his denials she was even now more convinced that it was Morgan on that bike. She would go back and convince DI Higgins to apply for an arrest warrant. As far as she was concerned, this investigation was nearly over.

Once the Garda had left, Sinead came out into the hall to see what Callaghan had wanted but Morgan wasn't listening to her, his mind was elsewhere. He was thinking about the photograph.

He felt like he knew the rider. But he just was not sure. It was just a feeling. But it did not make sense. Why would that person want to kill Rob? What could he gain from it? Morgan knew that he had to find out.

"But why would Smith do something like this? He really liked Rob. Why would he kill him?" Sinead asked questioningly. She looked very shocked at hearing Morgan's suspicions.

Morgan hardly believed it himself, but the more he thought about it, the more it felt right. His gut told him he was right and Morgan always went with his gut. But could he do such a thing? Could he really have killed Rob? But what for? Money, drugs? Things must be very bad for him if he had decided that murder and robbery were the only solutions.

Morgan knew that Smith's business had been suffering badly in the last three years or so since new legislation came in regulating all the private security firms in the country. Obeying regulations never bothered Smith before, but the threat of prosecution and big fines for the publicans to whom he supplied bouncers, made them adhere to the letter of the new laws.

A number of night clubs around the country had already been made an example of and fined in a way to show that the government was serious in tightening up an unregulated industry littered with ex IRA and INLA members running protection rackets. To operate legally, Smith now had to get a tax clearance certificate, something very difficult for somebody registered as unemployed and running his business in the black economy. Another problem for him was that each of his door staff now had to pay tax on his income. The reduction in trade brought about by the recession also meant that publicans dramatically cut the number of door staff on their doors or the hours that they worked. This had a disastrous effect on Smith's income and that wasn't something that he liked at all. Smith was, now how could you say it? Tighter than a County Cavan shopkeeper. Morgan remembered Rob joking that Smith would wake up in the middle of the night just to make sure that he did not lose any sleep. It was an in-house joke about Smith between the doormen that when they worked an extra fifteen or twenty minutes after the normal shift, he would charge out the full time but only pay the normal. It doesn't sound much but when you think that he could have fifty lads working for him over a weekend, it meant that he was pocketing tens of thousands of euro over the years. It reminded him of a record shop that Morgan where they had been stiffing him on the five cent's change every time he bought a CD for years. One of these days, he was going in there to demand a free CD just to get his money's worth.

But having said all that Morgan really liked Smith on a personal level. He was this big lovable rogue, who like Rob was always getting himself involved in crazy get rich schemes that invariably backfired on him. But unlike Rob, he had cash flow to keep him going. And despite whatever was going on, he was always smiling and offering a welcoming handshake that would dislocate your shoulder whenever he met you.

However Smith was not a man to be taken lightly. He'd trained both as a body builder and a boxer for years. He was a formidable fighter and had in fact competed well at national level in mixed combat style bouts in the past. When you were working for him though, you could always trust him to back you up in a fight. And he was vicious if he heard that another door crew was coming around sniffing at one of his doors trying to take it away from him. Smith just looked after number one; everything he did was focused at making him more money. There were times when Morgan was glad Smith was on his side, but that was only when it suited Smith. Could he really have done it? Could Smith have murdered Rob? Knowing Smith like he did, if the profit was right, Morgan had no doubt that he could.

"Money. He did it for money. What else?"

"We are going to need more proof than that if you're going to tackle him," Sinead said.

"You're right of course".

"So what are we going to do about it", she exclaimed. "Come on, don't keep me waiting Morgan, tell me".

"There is only one person that Smith trusts with his money and I know where to find him!"

It was nearly lunchtime and DI Behan from the National Drugs Unit watched from behind the one way security glass overlooking the reception area of the district Garda station as both the Wolf and Piasecki left the building. The Wolf slammed the double doors open as he stormed out, a wide grin on his face. DI Behan had spent the last four hours secretly observing and listening to the two foreign nationals, as they were being interrogated about their activities since arriving in the country.

The two Polish gangsters had been put in adjoining rooms and DI Russell had spent his time watching the two on separate video links from the interrogation room. The interviews themselves had gone pretty much as had been expected. The detectives supported by the Emergency Response Unit had raided the men's houses very early in the morning and brought them both down to the station for questioning. DI Behan had been asked to sit in during the interviews but refused the request saying that he needed to maintain a certain level of anonymity, which could not be compromised. It would give him more flexibility to do his job properly. So instead of directly questioning the men, he waited until they had been arrested and then led the search of the two men's properties using the search warrants that he had obtained late the previous evening.

As expected, both men said nothing on arrival at the station, initially claiming that they did not even speak English. Behan knew that they spoke better English than most of the lads that he grew up with in Cork and that this was just a standard delaying tactic.

And it had worked.

The Gardaí couldn't interview the men for nearly two hours until two Polish translators turned up and the interrogation could start properly.

But the arrival of the linguists did not help matters much. The Wolf sat in the interview room very calm and composed. He had the confidence of a man who had nothing to fear, because he knew that they had nothing on him. Hard, cold and supremely confident, the Wolf made Russell sick to his stomach. None of them stood a chance against men like this. The Wolf would smile as the policemen asked their questions and only answered tak (yes) or zaden (no), nothing more than one word answers. The Gardaí in turn would ask him the same questions over and over again, changing the phrases subtly or the order in which they asked them but it didn't matter. The Wolf never tripped himself up as he had plenty of time to think of an answer while the translator relayed the question. He was just playing with them. If he was back in Poland, they would be beating him now, but here in Ireland there would be no such methods. Questions he did not want to answer he would say "nikt nie odbiera" which apparently meant "no answer".

He did this a lot.

But he seemed like an old fashioned movie stool pigeon compared to Piasecki, who spoke even less. It was like he had taken a vow of silence upon entering a monastery. He just sat there in the interrogation room and stared at the camera monitoring him, refusing to answer any and all questions put to him by either the detective or the translator. He didn't even speak to confirm his name. Eventually the young detective interviewing him gave up and passed the voluntary mute over to his superior to have a try. But the older man had fared no better. He tried to suggest that the Wolf was in the other room; telling everything there was to tell and that unless he talked, that he would be serving all of the jail time. Piasecki broke into laughter when he heard this feeble attempt to trick him into talking before eventually collecting himself and going back to staring vacantly at the small blinking red light on the security camera mounted high up on the wall.

Higgins then called Behan into his office looking for his advice on how to deal with the men, complaining to him about their lack of progress and wondering what they should do next. But Russell did not tell them anything more than they already knew. That the two men would not talk and would certainly not give any information about the other and that to pursue that particular line would only end up wasting time and effort. Unfortunately the other reason for arresting the men in question was to remove them from their houses so that they could be searched. Regrettably the search of the houses revealed nothing useful, no caches of drugs or guns. Certainly there was nothing to tie either of them into the murders of either Dave Murray or Rob O'Dwyer. And as they had now had no direct or technical forensic evidence against them for either murder, the Gardaí had no reason to hold them.

While disappointed, the murder squad felt that it had probably been worth it. This would have rattled the criminals somewhat and it would make them keep their heads down for the next few weeks until things blew over. It was not the preferred option, that would be a conviction and a long prison sentence but it would have to do, at least for the moment anyway.

Recognising their hopeless position, DI Higgins reluctantly agreed with DI Russell. Like him, he hated to see their main suspects simply walk out of the door, free men.

It made DI Higgins angry.

Men like this shouldn't be able to walk out when they all knew that they were involved so deeply in the drugs trade. But they had to let them go. Without anything solid against them, they had no choice but to. But it didn't mean that they had to like it. The Gardaí still had one slim hope that either of the two Polish men's finger prints and DNA samples might turn up somewhere during the investigation. Higgins decided to leave them waiting a bit longer in the interrogation rooms until the forensics had a chance to run their fingerprints through the computer. Having been questioned in connection with a serious crime, the two Polish men's fingerprints would now be entered onto the Automated Fingerprint Identification System being rolled out nationally. Eventually after three long hours, the report from the lab came back a blank as well. As neither man's finger prints had been found at either murder scene and there were no outstanding international arrest warrants on them, so it was at four o'clock that evening that the Gardaí reluctantly let them go.

As he watched them leave, DI Behan was desperately trying to figure out a way to get these men off the streets. But he could not come up with any. He was actually about to walk out of the station and go home, when Callaghan opened the door at the end of the corridor and strode towards him. She was clutching a large pile of files to her chest. From her demeanour it was obvious that she was not in a good mood. She looked stern and her features were a little drawn but he kept staring at her all the same. He always loved watching good looking women, especially those with a fiery streak. Her hair was down from its usual ponytail and she looked particularly beautiful.

As she came up alongside him, he turned to face her properly but kept leaning on the handrail with one arm.

"So, how's it going?" he asked smiling like a Cheshire cat.

She stopped and eyed him up and down before answering. "Okay". What did he want?

"Having a tough day?"

"I've had better", she acknowledged.

"That's the breaks. Don't worry, we all have bad days when the bad guys seem to get away but don't worry we'll get them in time".

"I know all of that. I have been doing this job long enough now to know and appreciate the poor success rates that we have, but it doesn't get any easier when the criminals are practically laughing in your face", Callaghan replied, not in the mood to be patronised. She got the feeling that there was more to what he said but she was tired, it had been a long tiring and frustrating day and she couldn't figure where they were going to go from here.

"Look", DI Russell said, standing upright and opening his hands out "I have read your report and your ideas with regard to this Morgan character. Maybe you're right, maybe he planned it or maybe his murder of O'Dwyer was an opportunistic one."

"I think he should still be a suspect", she said, delighted that someone was agreeing with her, regardless of his intentions.

"Look, here is my card", he said, passing her a card from his shirt breast pocket. "If you have any more ideas or leads, why don't you run them by me before you go to the DI with them", he offered smiling. "I might be able to help you with your presentation".

"That would be great. I would appreciate your advice", she said, not able to stop herself smiling back at him. With her free hand, she flicked her hair over to one side, revealing a long slender neck. "Thank you, I will do that".

"Well, I better be off. These bad guys won't arrest themselves, you know".

"Yes, of course, me too", she said before walking off through another set of doors at the other end of the corridor. Behan took a second watching her walk away before leaving the station through the front doors.

Chapter Twenty-Five

As Morgan marched through the double doors of the bank, he was still not sure how he was going to handle this. But despite all of his lingering doubts about practically everything to do with the events of the last few days, he was positive that he was right about Smith's involvement in all of this. It just felt right. It seemed so obvious now that he was nearly embarrassed about not realising it sooner. Less than an hour earlier, the decision had been made to confront Smith. But he knew that it was going to be next to impossible to get Smith to talk to him voluntarily without some evidence somehow to convince him that he already knew his entire goings on. So Morgan had to get confirmation of his suspicions before he made his next move. Always a man of action and with little time to ponder any other alternatives, he had simply left the house to find the proof that he needed.

And that was why he was here now.

Morgan just wished that he did not have to do it the hard way. If he had more time, he would simply have followed the Bank's loan manager Brian Fitzpatrick home that evening and confronted him there, well away from prying eyes and security guards. Instead he was being forced to face the man openly in his place of work. Morgan had read somewhere that you should always plan for the worst but hope for the best. If he had had more time, Morgan knew that he could have planned his approach carefully, right down to the very last detail, to do his utmost to limit the risks involved. He would have done a reconnaissance of the bank to see how many staff the branch had, where Fitzpatrick's office was located and what the security in the building was like. But Morgan had no time to spare for such niceties. The deadline for the retrieval of the drugs was looming ever closer and it weighed on him no less than if it had been a time bomb counting down to zero.

Five, four, three, two, one. Which wire would he cut?

So he found himself effectively winging it and hoping for the best. You never knew, maybe Fitzpatrick would open up to him willingly. Stranger things had happened surely.

As he walked in from the bright winter afternoon sun, it took a couple of seconds for Morgan's eyes to adjust to the comparative darkness of the interior of the bank. Customers pushed past him as he stood there taking in his surroundings. The busy branch was laid out in a rather outdated style. It looked like it had had a major remodelling back in the late eighties, but apart from the odd coat of paint had been largely forgotten since. As Morgan went in through the glass double doors, there were two cash machines in the hallway before he entered the bank proper. Both of which were 'out of service' according to the piece of paper sellotaped over their screens, forcing any prospective customers to go inside and queue. Inside there were small private glass walled offices lining the left hand wall. All of them seemed empty. Most stood with their doors open. Cluttered desks and filing cabinets appeared to be the norm. These glorified cubicles were separated from the comings and goings of the branch customers by a long counter scattered with deposit slips and leaflets on the various investment opportunities available. Where the counter ended, a number of large potted plants, which Morgan suspected were fake, helped delineate the area.

It was ten minutes to two o'clock and the bank was pretty busy. A long line of customers of all ages and sizes formed a semi orderly queue, helped along by red coloured ropes hanging loosely on silver uprights, snaking them towards the counters at the other end. People shuffled impatiently as they waited their turn. Although you could not see any one person shouting or purposefully making noise, there was a loud collective din in the bank. A dull electronic voice directed those customers at the head of the queue to the next free teller.

Counter number one please.

Counter number four please.

One woman had her hands full pushing a buggy full of shopping bags while trying to quieten two young boys as they chased each other through the waiting crowd, bumping into everything as they went. Most of the other customers seemed to take the opportunity to fiddle with their mobile phones to pass the time, hoping that nobody in front of them wanted to do anything too awkward to slow the tellers down.

The one piece of preparation Morgan had made prior to his arrival was to phone ahead, just to make sure that Fitzpatrick was working that day. With his luck the way it was going lately, the man he was looking for would have been away on holidays or off sick or something. Anywhere except where Morgan needed him to be. He had asked to speak to Mister Brian Fitzpatrick, the Loans Manager and was delighted when he was informed that he was in but he had hung up while the receptionist had tried to redirect his call. There had not been time to make an official appointment and anyway Morgan did not want to alert Fitzpatrick to his arrival. More than likely Fitzpatrick wouldn't have read anything into it, but Morgan wasn't taking any chances.

Once inside Morgan surveyed the layout looking for a security guard. There was none to be seen, which was a relief. He was not afraid of the semi-retired security guards normally seen on duty in banks tackling him, but he was worried that he might be interrupted by one of them before he got the information that he needed. With none there to worry him, he then focused on each person in the queue to identify any possible threats. There did not appear to be any obvious off duty Garda or gangster lurking in the line, just ordinary people going about their business.

Trying not to draw too much attention to himself and as casually as he could Morgan looked up towards the ceiling and noted the number and direction of the security cameras. As expected, the bank was bristling with security cameras, seven in all that he could see. At least one of them had caught him as he had walked in the door, but there was nothing that he could do about that. Once again, maybe if he had had more time. But he hadn't and it was time to just get on with it.

It was then that Morgan saw Fitzpatrick coming out a side door behind the teller's counter. Brian Fitzpatrick was quite tall, about five foot ten, had an athletic build and weighed a fit one hundred and eighty pounds. He was in a suit and tie but was not wearing the jacket and strode across the floor with the self-important confidence of somebody who thinks that nothing or nobody can touch him. Morgan watched him as he walked out of the side door and along the inside of the ropes back towards what Morgan assumed was his office. As he neared, Morgan took this as his cue and headed over towards him. At the right moment Fitzpatrick looked up and Morgan who was forcing himself to smile caught his eye. Fitzpatrick stopped and recognising him, stood facing him.

Fitzpatrick had become Smith's private banker a few years before. For the princely sum of €2,500, he managed to set Smith up with a fake bank account in the name of Eamonn Brett. He said that with all the new regulations brought in by the Criminal Assets Bureau to curb money laundering, that it was no easy task, but that's only if you believed what Fitzpatrick had said was true. He may just have been trying to make himself seem more important. Either way, this untraceable account allowed Smith to deposit cash from his various businesses and not declares it, saving him considerable money in taxes and charges. Fitzpatrick had also advised him on a few dodgy investment opportunities along the way. These were so dodgy that Morgan, as a trained accountant, would not have touched them with a barge pole. Morgan knew that if anyone knew about the inner workings of Smith's financial situation, it would be Fitzpatrick.

"Oh hi, Morgan isn't it? You used to work in the club didn't you. How are you? Fitzpatrick greeted him confidently, sticking his hand out to shake Morgan's.

"You have a good memory. I am grand, thanks", Morgan replied politely.

"I heard what happened to that other doorman. I would have gone to the funeral but I couldn't get away from work", he said slightly embarrassed. "We are short staffed as it is." He continued by way of an explanation.

"I understand. I'll pass on your condolences to his wife and children", Morgan said through gritted teeth. If you had anything to do with his death, I will make you pay, he thought forcing himself to smile. It looked more like a strained grin, which was good enough under the circumstances.

"So what can I do for you?" Fitzpatrick said rubbing his hands together. Recession or no recession, here was another idiot coming to beg him for money.

"I need a loan," Morgan said. "And I was wondering if you could help me".

"Okay", Fitzpatrick answered smugly. Oblivious to what was going to happen to him. "Well why don't you make an appointment and come in to see me later on in the week?"

"Could we do it now? I am kind of a bit stuck for time. Would you have a few minutes free? I hate to bother you as you seem so busy", said Morgan trying to act like he was desperate. He did not have to act too hard. He was just desperate for a different reason than he was letting on.

Smith thought for a second before looking at his watch. "Yeah okay. I have a few minutes free. Come on into the office", He smiled like a spider inviting a fat fly into his web before entering the second of the glass walled offices. Morgan followed him and closed the door behind them.

The office was only about ten foot by ten foot. It was cramped but quite tastefully decorated. A leather-topped desk positioned slightly over to one side dominated the small room. The walls were all of glass but the dividing walls to the offices on both sides had the blinds closed. Against the right hand wall stood in tall grey metal filing cabinets. The Venetian blind on the front glass wall facing out to the queuing customers was open. As Morgan walked in he had closed the door behind him, shutting out most of the noise of the bank. Now he twisted the shiny round knob on the glass frame to close the integrated blinds. Fitzpatrick, who walked around the desk to sit down on the high backed swivel chair behind it, only noticed that Morgan had closed them after he sat down. He looked quizzically up at Morgan, who stood there staring down at him from the far side of the desk.

"What are you doing?" Fitzpatrick asked unsure of what was going on.

"I need to ask you some questions," Morgan said seriously, his tone changing from the desperate potential bank customer from a few moments earlier to the determined individual that he really was.

"About a loan?"

"No. Not about a loan. About Smith's finances."

"What do you mean? About Smith's finances? You must know that I can't talk to you about anybody else's accounts."

Morgan stepped closer to the desk before sitting down on one of the two chairs provided for customers. He did this all without breaking eye contact. Who was the spider and who was the fly now?

"I need to know if Smith is in trouble with money with the bank or other creditors. Or if he has recently deposited a large amount of money into that dodgy account you gave him," Morgan demanded.

"I don't know what you're talking about," Fitzpatrick answered, fidgeting nervously with his tie.

"Yes, you do and I don't have time for a long protracted conversation with you. I need to know if Smith has recently come into a lot of money and I need to know now".

Fitzpatrick broke eye contact and looked around nervously as he tried to figure out what was happening. "I told you I don't know what you mean. Yes, John Smith is a valued customer here and no I cannot tell you anything about his accounts and now I think it's time for you to leave." At this point Fitzpatrick stood up and trying to assert himself, gestured towards the door.

But Morgan had other ideas. "Sit down" he ordered. He didn't raise his voice or change his tone. He said it almost quietly but with such conviction that it caused the banker to sit back down as if he was a child scolded by an angry parent. At no time did Morgan stop looking directly into his target's eyes. Morgan had watched Fitzpatrick come and go from the pub over the years. From their many fleeting conversations, he had learned that Fitzpatrick had done well for himself in the banking world. Starting out as a teller, he had completed all his bank exams and had risen to the position of Senior Loans Manager. It seemed he was well respected within the branch and was being groomed for a manager's position in one of the smaller branches when one became available.

But Fitzpatrick always had an eye for the girls, something that getting married the previous year had done little to curb. He would splash out hundreds of Euro every weekend on expensive champagne and take limousines to Dublin city centre's trendiest clubs, all just to impress the women and the group of lackeys that hung on his every word. But he did not have it all his own way. On one occasion Morgan had had to drag one disgruntled boyfriend off him, but not before the man had given Fitzpatrick a black eye, a burst lip and a broken tooth. It would have been much worse if Morgan had not turned up. Normally, you might have expected someone who had received such a beating to press charges against the assailant but Fitzpatrick did not want to. He did not want to draw attention to his philandering any more than he had to. His new wife, Cathy, Morgan thought her name was, seemed to be a shy girl who did not like to go out much. This suited Smith to a tee, as this did not interfere with his extra-curricular activities. But it was on one of the rare occasions that Cathy had been out with him that Morgan learnt that she had money and that it was her family that had paid for their wedding and put up the large deposit on their new house. Morgan remembered standing there at the door as Cathy proudly told him about their new four bed house and all the furniture that she was planning to get for it. She was nest building. If she only knew what Fitzpatrick had been up to? Maybe she ought to?

"So are you still banging everything that moves?" Morgan asked coyly.

"What do you mean?" Fitzpatrick answered, unsure where this was going. Standing back up again, he stood looking down at Morgan staring up at him from his seat. He did not know whether to sit down or stay standing up. He begrudgingly sat down, hands on the arm rests ready to spring back up. He was like a human yo-yo. Up down and up again.

"You remember that girl, the brunette with the nice tits whose boyfriend nearly beat the shit out of you?

"I don't know what you mean?" Fitzpatrick answered, starting to sweat.

"You don't. Or what about the blonde one that I caught giving you a blow job out on the fire exit a few weeks after that? You know the one with the short cropped hair?"

"That was all a long time ago, I don't remember", Fitzpatrick answered cautiously.

"You don't remember? But I do, I know all about you. But does your lovely new wife know?" Morgan smiled as he saw the colour drain from Fitzpatrick's face.

"What the fuck do you mean? Of course she doesn't know," he said angrily, his face becoming flushed. He was starting to sweat profusely.

"Ah, so you do remember after all. Maybe I should tell her? Let her know what you have been up to on your nights out".

"Look, what do you want?" Fitzpatrick asked.

"I told you want I want," Morgan said. "And I want to know now".

Fitzpatrick leaned over and practically whispered "I can't tell you about a customer's accounts. I would get fired".

"I don't care," said Morgan as casually as he could.

"Well I do. Why do you want to know anyway?"

"That does not concern you," Morgan said.

"Smith is not going to be happy when I tell him about this", Fitzpatrick said threateningly, thinking that he could still turn this around and wriggle out of it.

"Don't you worry about it, I will tell him about it myself later when I see him".

Fitzpatrick went quiet again as he weighed up his options. Judging by his expression, Morgan figured that he had decided that he was in a busy work environment and Morgan wouldn't dare start a fuss there in front of everybody. Chancing his arm he decided to reassert himself.

"Look it's time for you to go or I will have to call the Gardaí", Fitzpatrick said as he leaned forward and put his hand on the telephone but before he lifted the receiver, Morgan slammed his hand down on top of it pinning it to the phone and squeezed. Hard. He leaned forward across the table so his face was only about twelve inches from the banker's and spoke softly.

"No you are not. So put that phone back down."

Fitzpatrick was scared but did not try to remove his hand. Morgan knew that he was going to have to do this the hard way. Nothing was going easily this week. Fitzpatrick was a physically big guy in good shape, younger and almost as big and muscled as Morgan himself but it was muscle born out of a gym, not from sweat and toil like Morgan's. Fitzpatrick's muscles were really just for show and lacked inner strength. That was the difference between them.

Or at least that was what Morgan now hoped.

Morgan suddenly grabbed Fitzpatrick by the throat and attempted to drag him over the desk. Fitzpatrick brought both hands up to the one at his neck and managed to prise himself free. He fell backwards sending the chair crashing noisily into the small set of shelves behind him causing the items on it scattering everywhere.

Morgan dashed around the desk to grab Fitzpatrick, bunching the loan manager's expensive shirt in his fists before twisting him up and around and sending him crashing backwards onto the floor. Fitzpatrick tried desperately to crawl away but Morgan dived on him, rolled him over onto his stomach and twisted Fitzpatrick's right arm high behind his back while burying his right knee deep into the banker's back with as much force as possible.

"Now tell me about Smith", he said leaning right down so his mouth was nearly at Fitzpatrick's ear. Fitzpatrick struggled, kicking out aggressively as he tried to get Morgan off him, but to no avail. Morgan simply pulled his arm higher, practically making the man touch the back of his head with his own hand. Fitzpatrick cried out in pain.

"You will never get away with this," Fitzpatrick gasped in agony.

"You have me figured wrong. I am not trying to get away with anything. You either tell me everything I need to know or you can tell it to the Gardaí. You know that it will all come out and you will end up in jail and your precious career will be finished". Morgan pressed his knee harder down into Fitzpatrick's back "You tell me everything that I need to know and I will just walk away. You will never see me again." Morgan looked around at the wrecked and dishevelled office. "I am sure that you will be able to talk your way out of this. Either way you are going to tell me what I need to know."

He waited for a second for Fitzpatrick to make up his mind and was just about to snap Fitzpatrick's arm when he surrendered with the inevitable, "Okay, okay, I'll talk".

Morgan slowly got off him and pulled the broken man to his feet and dumped him back into his chair. Fitzpatrick said nothing initially; he just sat there, rubbing his aching shoulder. From the expression on his face, Morgan thought he was going to cry.

"Well?"

"Smith isn't doing too great. He bought two apartments two years ago on interest only mortgages just before the bubble burst and hasn't been able to rent one of them yet. That coupled with a high level of personal debt means that he is teetering on the edge of bankruptcy". Fitzpatrick paused to wipe his nose, which was running furiously. "He's already missed a couple of payments on one property and made none on the other and now he has turned up on an Irish Credit Bureau high risk list. About a month or six weeks ago, he came in here looking for a re-mortgage to consolidate his debts. I had no choice but to refuse him as the applications all have to go to head office now for approval. It was out of my hands, I explained to him that we were going to have to foreclose on the mortgage soon if he did not start making payments immediately. I could not do anything for him. He went crazy, threatening this and that..." Fitzpatrick stopped again to look at

Morgan, who just gave him a look as if to say continue, 'why are you stopping'? But the banker seemed reluctant to continue.

There was a soft knock on the door. "Are you alright in there, Mister Fitzpatrick?" came a woman's worried voice from outside.

Morgan snapped Fitzpatrick a dirty look.

"Yes.... I'm fine. Thank you Maureen", was his nervous stuttering reply. Morgan listened intently and heard her feet as she padded off. He knew that she wasn't going far, to find reinforcements more than likely, Morgan thought.

Morgan turned back to face Fitzpatrick and demanded "What next? I know by the look on your face that something else has happened? What?"

"He came back to me about two weeks ago and said that something had come up and he now had a plan to get himself out of trouble."

"How?"

"He did not say".

"How?" Morgan said grabbing him roughly by the shirt collar again.

"I honestly don't know. But he asked me to put off the bank for a few more weeks. I did what I could for him", Fitzpatrick said begging Morgan to believe him. From the pitiful look on his face, Morgan knew that he was telling the truth. The man was too scared not to tell him, he was in enough trouble as it was and he knew it. It was all he was going to get. It was time to go.

"If you tell Smith or anyone about our little conversation today then I will be forced to tell this bank about the account you set up and your lovely wife about your little indiscretions. Your life will be ruined." And with that he patted Fitzpatrick on the cheek in an almost friendly manner. He turned and walked towards the door without looking back. He left Fitzpatrick looking more than a bit dishevelled in his plush chair. Fitzpatrick was just glad that he had survived his encounter.

Two young male members of staff were hurriedly approaching the office with concerned looks on their faces just as Morgan opened the door and marched confidently out. The long line of queuing people turned to stare at him, dying to know what had just happened in there. The few standing closest to the little office strained to look over his shoulder into the office before he closed the door behind him. Morgan walked past the two men who gave each other a questioning look as he passed them by. Should they

stop him? He in turn gave them a look that said 'go on try it' as he
went by. Sensibly, they did not do anything. They saw the look in
Morgan's eyes and let him pass. As he walked around the end ropes
and back by the queuing customers, Morgan looked at them and
said loudly making sure that everyone could hear.

"It's ridiculous what this bank wants you to go through just to
get a loan, it's like trying to get blood from a stone".

And with that he strode out of the door and back into the winter sunlight.

Chapter Twenty-Six

Sinead looked up from the glossy magazine she was flicking through as Morgan walked back in through the living room door. "Well how did it go?" she asked concerned, putting the magazine to one side.

"It went as well as could be expected", Morgan said thoughtfully, taking off his jacket and flinging himself down heavily onto the couch. There was no one else home and after the last few days of the children noisily occupying every last corner of the house, the house felt empty. "Where are your mother and the children?

"She has brought them out shopping for more groceries. The kids have decided that they want normal food and don't like any of that strange stuff that you bought yesterday. But that's not important, did he confirm what you thought?" Sinead asked anxiously. She had been sitting waiting anxiously for the last few hours and was not in the humour to have to drag the information out of him. Morgan however was still shell shocked from learning that a man whom he had considered not just an employer, but a friend, could have done this to another one of his best friends. It was one thing for a stranger but to kill someone you cared about, that was hard for anyone to deal with but it was still possible. It was quite another thing when it was someone you knew who had done the killing. That cut deeper to the bone, right into your very soul.

"I think so," Morgan said. "Smith is in money troubles but apparently he recently told Fitzgerald that he would be able to get himself out of it in the next few weeks. It could be a coincidence, but I don't believe in coincidences."

"Well there you go, between the picture that you were shown by the Gardaí and this news, it proves that it must have been Smith all along", Sinead said but did not seem nearly as shocked by the conclusion as Morgan had been earlier.

"I hate to say it but it does feel right", he conceded and looked at her. "Right then, let's call the Gardaí and tell them".

"No," Sinead practically shouted at him and grabbed him by the arm. "We can't involve them yet. We need to get the drugs back from Smith and give them to this Johnson character first. Then we can tell them".

"But he killed Rob. Your husband, remember? We have to tell the Gardaí", Morgan said incredulously.

Her voice softened and she moved over and sat beside him, twisting her body around to face him. "And we will tell them, but Rob got himself killed. We didn't cause it but we are caught up in it now. But this is not about him anymore. This is about me and my children".

"Look, I want to help, more than anything", he said, "But I think that we should call the Gardaí about what we have learned".

"No Gardaí, not yet. I want this bastard away from us first. I want to feel that my children are safe again", she said her voice rising again before leaning over and burying her head in his chest. Giving in, Morgan folded his big arms around her and hugged her tightly.

"I suppose that we now know who has the drugs so we could just tell Johnson where they are. That would probably be enough to get him off your back", he said. He was trying to comfort Sinead by suggesting that that would be enough, but was unconvinced by his own words as they left his mouth.

Morgan took out his mobile phone and called Johnson. It was answered after two rings.

"Yeah," came the gruff voice on the other end. Morgan could hear a television on loud in the background.

"It's Morgan again".

"That was quick. You have my stuff?" Johnson asked, sitting up straight in his chair, putting down the can of beer that he had been drinking and lowering the volume of the television.

"No, but I know where your fucking drugs are, if that's what you mean", Morgan replied in a hostile tone.

At the other end of the phone line, Johnson nearly cried out with relief, but hid it well. It was as though he had just had a death sentence commuted. Finally, something was going his way. "Yes, of course that's what I mean. Where are they?" came back the equally aggressive reply.

"Do you know a John Smith?"

"Yeah, I know him". And Johnson did know him. He knew him pretty well in fact. Nearly two years previously, Johnson had sent two young lads into one of Smith's clubs to sell some drugs. They had been quickly spotted and thrown out, by Smith himself no less. He had given the two young lads a few slaps and had taken the gear away from them, telling the two frightened whelps that he would destroy it himself. Both Murray and Johnson had always thought that he kept it and sold it in the club himself. A few weeks later they had sent another two men along to teach Smith a lesson, but he had got the better of both of them and ended up putting one of them in hospital for nearly six weeks. At that point they decided, pride aside that they would give the clubs and bars that Smith ran, a miss for a while. Johnson was now faced with a dilemma. He was delighted that his drugs had been located but did not fancy trying to get the drugs back directly from Smith. The last thing he needed was to get his legs broken. It would make slipping away to Spain more than a little awkward. Anyway, with every guard in Ireland looking for him, he could not be seen out.

"Well he has them", said Morgan conclusively.

"So, what's that to do with me?"

"What do you mean?" Morgan said. "What's that got to do with you? They're your drugs. I found them. Now you go get them and stay the hell away from Sinead and her children."

"That's not our arrangement..."

"None of this was our arrangement, you forced it on us", Morgan snapped back.

"Ooh, it's us now is it? You did not take long to slip into a dead man's shoes. He's barely cold in the ground", Johnson said, laughing out loud.

Caught off guard, Morgan was not sure what to reply to that, he had thought exactly the same thing as the words had come out of his mouth. "You know where your drugs are".

"I don't see it like that. Our arrangement was for you to get my stuff back and I still don't have my drugs. According to you, Smith has them. What good is that to me? How do I get them back?" Johnson knew that this was the wrong approach. He was allowing Morgan to get the upper hand, forcing him to reason with him. But there could be no reasoning. There was too much at stake. He needed to let this Morgan bastard know who was in charge.

"Well how do I get them back?" Morgan said, putting it back up to him.

"I don't give a flying fuck how you do it but if you don't by twelve o'clock tonight, I'm going to fuck up those kids, you know, the ones you seem to want to play daddy to". That was better, Johnson thought. Now I have the upper hand again.

"If you hurt those kids...", Morgan said venomously.

"What? What will you do? You'll come find me? Hunt me down? Ha, half of the fucking pigs in this city are looking for me and can't find me. What are you going to do? I know people that will fucking tear you apart", Johnson spit back at him.

"You fucking coward. Can't do it yourself?" Morgan said contemptuously.

"I would but you're not worth the time. But the kids, now they are..."

"I doubt anybody will back you up threatening little kids," Morgan stated. "They'll do to you what they do to those paedophiles in prison. They will segregate you and lock you up for twenty-three hours every day but the other inmates will still fuck you up just as quick if they get you. But that is nothing compared to what I'll do if I ever get my hands on you."

"Oh, I am scared", Johnson tried to say mockingly but some of the confidence had gone out of his voice.

"You should be". Morgan said calmly and evenly. There was a sense of unwavering determination to his voice. When this was over, he and Johnson had unfinished business.

A lot of it.

"Don't worry big man, you'll get your chance, but only after you deliver my drugs, intact and on time. If you're five minutes late then the deal is off and I'll come looking for you and the brats. You say that there will be no one around to back me up after I hurt those kids? Maybe, maybe not. But by then it will be too late to help them". And with that Johnson hung up. Morgan stared silently at the screen before putting the phone down. It was no good; they would have to go to the Gardaí now.

They had no choice.

"No Morgan", Sinead insisted, angrily jumping up out of her chair once again, standing up against him, her chest practically touching his. "I told you before, no police".

"But Sinead, we have no choice in the matter."

He caught himself, there was that we again, Morgan thought. All the mentions of we and us, he had slipped into the role quicker than was right. What was he really doing here? Was he imagining a future together? Johnson was right. Rob was not even cold in his grave and he could not get her out of his mind.

"Yes, we do. We go and get them ourselves", Sinead said. Was she doing the same as him? Feeling the same? Rob was gone. They were in this together. When this was over, where would they be?

"We are pretty sure that it was Smith who killed Rob and then took the drugs," Morgan said. "We have to tell the Gardaí. Smith has to go to jail and not just for the drugs, after all, Rob needs justice as well".

"We talked about that," Sinead said. "I know what you're saying, but right now, before anybody else is involved, I want the threat to my children removed. Then I'll worry about Rob, but not until then."

"Fine," Morgan said. "If Smith has the drugs and we are still not one hundred percent sure that he does, he is not going to hand them over without a fight. And I am not sure if I fancy going up against him on my own."

"You can do it," Sinead said with conviction.

"Well, I wish I had your confidence. I know Smith longer than you and I am not so sure," Morgan quickly replied.

"I know you will find a way", she implored, touching his arm gently which sent a shiver running through his body.

"Obviously, Johnson is not too eager to go up against Smith either," Morgan said. "That is why he is still insisting on us getting them back before tonight".

"I don't care about Johnson. I need you to do this for us"; Sinead said putting particular emphasis on us? "I am not bringing those Garda bastards in on this now." She looked up into his eyes, tears forming in hers. "They abandoned us earlier when they took away the protection. I'm not letting them do that again or try to get us involved in some sort of set up to trap him like you see them do on the television".

"Look nothing like that is going to happen, Sinead," Morgan said earnestly. "I won't let them do that to you."

"I don't trust them. We have to do these ourselves", she said, running her hand softly along his face. Morgan just stared down at her. She looked so vulnerable. He could not believe the words that were coming out of his mouth.

"Okay", he said, "but how?"

Chapter Twenty-Seven

The Wolf was still extremely angry when he marched back inside his house and headed straight for the kitchen. He opened a cupboard and took a bottle of Vodka from it, opened it and drank straight from the neck. Piasecki stood in the hall doorway watching him closely. The Wolf had been silent all the way back in the car. Only now in the privacy of his own house, did he let down his composure.

"Who the fuck do they think they fucking with?" he spat, his rage making him nearly incoherent. "Fucking police. If this was back in Poland, I would have him fucking shot". He took another big gulp of neat Vodka. He nearly gagged at the rough taste of the Boru Irish Vodka, which was much rougher then the Extra Zytnia Vodka that he had been practically brought up on.

"Tak," was all Piasecki said.

The Wolf took another slug. "How did they know about Murray? We were very careful. Who talked? When I find out who talked I am going to torture them until they beg for death? Who is this O'Dwyer character that they are saying we killed?"

"He was small time," Piasecki said. "They said that he was shot with the same type of gun that we used on Murray".

"I don't waste my time on nobodies. Who do they think they are dealing with?" The Wolf ranted.

Piasecki shrugged his shoulders but remained silent. He knew that the Wolf would not appreciate anyone interrupting him when he was in one of his rages.

"Go and talk to our contacts and find out what the fuck is happening," The Wolf said. "I want to know where Johnson is right now and I want him dead. Find him and make him pay. Gnój."

"I will start asking around", Piasecki answered, anxious to get away from The Wolf when he was in this type of mood.

"Yes, yes and do it now. I want that bastard Johnson out of the way tonight", The Wolf roared, "He must be eliminated before we take over the Dublin network. Time is against us, old friend".

It was about half four in the afternoon and already nearly dark when Morgan reluctantly made his third phone call to Johnson. "Okay. I'll get you your drugs from Smith", said a beaten Morgan into the phone as he paced along the path in Sinead's mother's back garden. He was shivering as it was cold out and he had forgotten to put his jacket back on. Every time he turned around to face the house, he could see Sinead staring out of the sitting room window watching him. He would look away quickly, not wanting to let her distract him.

"Good. Glad to see you've come to your senses." Johnson was smiling at the other end like a Cheshire cat. It looked like he was going to come out a winner in this after all.

"But I need a gun, if I am going to get them back", Morgan said quietly, not wanting any nosey neighbours to overhear. He had pulled his hair out earlier thinking about how he was going to tackle Smith and despite his every instinct telling him otherwise, he knew he had no choice. Smith was too hard, too self-contained to just admit his involvement. He needed something to threaten Smith into confessing. Something that Smith couldn't ignore, something that would make him sit up and pay attention. Morgan didn't like guns. In fact he would go as far as to say that he hated them. But he couldn't think of anything else. He had thought that he could just bring along a knife but he didn't feel very confident challenging Smith with only six inches of kitchen appliance to back him up. No, as much as he hated the idea it had to be a gun. As he had worked on pub doors for years, Morgan figured that he knew enough dodgy people to get a gun for himself but he didn't have the time, energy or money to go searching for one. Getting one from Johnson was the simplest option. Let him do some of the work for a change.

"What the fuck do you take me for? I'm not giving you a fucking gun". Johnson said in disbelief. What was Morgan thinking? That he would just hand over a gun so that he could turn it on him?

"You will, if you want your drugs back. It is the only way".

"Fuck you, get them back yourself".

"What do you think is going to happen?" Morgan asked. "That I am going to walk up to Smith and ask him politely to give me the drugs back and he is simply going to hand them over, without a fight? I need a gun."

"I am not giving you a gun. No fucking way."

Neither man spoke and the phone line was silent. Morgan imagined Johnson thinking hard on the other end of the phone weighing up the pros and cons. Johnson needed the drugs back, more than anything but couldn't get them himself. Morgan knew he had no choice but to accede to his demands. He just had to keep pushing him.

"Well in that case," Morgan said. "You get them back yourself." Once again there was an awkward heavy silence, which went on for so long, Morgan thought that Johnson had hung up.

Johnson sat with the phone on his lap contemplating Morgan's demand. There was no way he was going to give him a gun. The first thing Morgan would do, would be to turn it against him. He would be signing his own death warrant. But then again, Morgan was right. He would need something if he were to go up against an animal like Smith and win.

No gun, no drugs, that's what he had said.

But what if, Johnson thought, a smile creeping slowly across his face, what if he gave Morgan a gun with blanks in it? It would look normal to someone who was not used to guns and he would not have time to go and fire it to check if it worked properly or not. He would use it to threaten Smith, get the drugs back then meet Johnson to hand them over. Then if Morgan tried to use the gun against him, Johnson would just laugh in his face, knowing that the bullets were blanks. It could work. But where would he get blanks? A gun and real bullets were no problem in Dublin today, but blanks? This was going to cost him...

"You still there?" Morgan asked

"Okay. Okay", came back the terse reply. "I will call you back in fifteen minutes," Johnson hung up and with only a brief pause started making phone calls.

Less than ten minutes later Morgan's mobile phone rang. It was Johnson again. "Right. In one hour, walk to the shops down the road from the house and wait there for another call to give you the rest of the directions. And remember you will be watched. If the cops turn up or you try anything stupid, the deal is off."

"Okay," Morgan said a bit disappointed. He had been hoping that there wasn't going to be an awkward contrived drop off or meeting. There was simply no time for that. But what did he really expect?

"Call me when you have my stuff and then I will be out of your hair for good," Johnson said.

"Not a moment too soon". Morgan said.

"Remember, if I don't hear from you by twelve. I'm going to come looking for all of you."

"Well, you know where we are," Morgan answered as a challenge.

"Don't be so fucking cocky you little shit," Johnson said. "If I don't get my things by midnight, I will have nothing to lose by killing those wonderful sweet little children and making that slut wife of Rob's watch. You got me?"

"Fuck you".

"No, fuck you. Midnight or else." Johnson spat back down the phone before hanging up and flinging it onto the couch.

Chapter Twenty-Eight

Sinead gave Morgan one final hug before he left the house. She stood watching from the doorstep, her arms wrapped around herself, trying to ward off the bitter cold, until he disappeared out of sight. They had spent the last hour pretty much in complete silence. Just sitting there staring into the fire, neither of them able to talk about what was about to happen. Morgan had decided that he would go and collect the gun, walk back to the house and then go directly up to Smith's. He would not come back inside the house before he collected the car. The tension would have been too great and he needed time to get his head together before what was possibly going to be a life changing experience for him.

If he was right and Smith had the drugs, he was effectively going to rob a murdering drug dealer before handing them over to another murdering drug dealer in the dead of night. Morgan would spend the rest of his life looking over his shoulder for someone who decided to even the score. If he was wrong, he was going to threaten his innocent employer at gunpoint and lose his job forever. It was a small industry and when news of that got around, Morgan would never work as a doorman again. Not that that really bothered him. He was more worried about having to face Smith's wrath sometime in the future. Morgan sighed deeply. How on God's green earth did he get himself into this situation?

Morgan turned right as he walked out of the gates and up towards the shops. He had his hands shoved deep into his coat pockets, trying to keep himself warm. His breath was clearly visible in the streetlight. It took only about five minutes for him to reach the row of shops. All six shops were located on the other side of the road. There were two newsagents, one of which had a large brightly lit front advertising a delicatessen and specials on cans of beer and bottles of wine. It was considerably larger than the other, more old-fashioned version. They were separated by a citizen's advice centre, which was now closed. A Chinese takeaway, a fish and chip shop and a Laundromat made up the rest of the shopping area. There was a large wire mesh gate at each end of the shops allowing rear access, presumably for deliveries. Both gates were currently shut. There was some parking outside the shops for customers, but the whole street was clogged with cars as their drivers just abandoned them before nipping into the shops, to get whatever last minute things they needed.

Morgan decided to wait across the road to get a better view of the whole street and watch the passers-by. That way he could see who was coming and would be able to spot anybody acting suspiciously. Looking anxiously at his watch for the tenth time in about five minutes, Morgan realised how tense he was and made a deliberate effort to relax, by closing his eyes and taking five deep breaths. Morgan stood waiting for nearly ten minutes and was starting to get concerned when the phone rang. He did not recognise the number.

"Hello?"

"This Morgan?" came the rough Dublin accent. But it was not Johnson's. Was it someone who worked for him?

Morgan looked up and down the street to see if he could spot anyone using a mobile but there was no one. "Yeah".

"Go to the delivery area at the rear of the shops. There is a blue plastic bag on the rear step of the Citizen's Advice shop. In it, you will find what you are looking for."

"How do I know it's working?"

But the caller did not wait to answer. He simply hung up. Morgan put the phone back in his pocket and headed to the side gate. Although the gate was closed, it was not locked and Morgan pushed it open just enough to slip through. There were no lights and the entrance was in pitch darkness. Morgan stood at the entrance as his eyes tried to adjust to the dark. He could make out large wheelie bins, stacks of pallets and a car. He did not like the thoughts of the alley. It was perfect for a trap. There could be ten guys waiting around the corner, ready to beat his brains in and he wouldn't know it until they were right on top of him. Morgan cursed himself for not coming down here earlier to check the place out, but what could he have done? Until a few minutes ago, he could have been going anywhere. He made his way carefully and slowly around the back of the shops, listening intently for any clue of an ambush. He wondered how he was going to find anything around there in the dark but mercifully, the shops all seemed to have lights on over their back doors.

The Citizens Advice Bureau was the third shop on this end. And as promised, a blue plastic bag sat on the rear step. With a quick look around to make sure that nobody was looking, Morgan did not pick it up straight away but opened it carefully as if it was booby-trapped. A compact black handgun was lying in the bottom. Snatching it up, Morgan stuffed it into his pocket and headed quickly back out onto the street. Glancing furtively each way, he quickly walked back to Pauline's, got into his old Mercedes and drove off.

Chapter Twenty-Nine

Morgan drove into the West Dublin housing estate where Smith lived. It was a massive sprawling complex of the type that had sprang up all over the greater Dublin area and surrounding commuter belt over the last seven or eight years. As was the trend, it had a mixture of houses, duplexes and apartments that were developed in blocks so that they could be sold off in chunks to aid the already wealthy developer's cash flow. Smith's house was at the back facing a half constructed block of apartments that been abandoned when the housing market and economy collapsed. It was like the construction site version of the Mary Celeste.

When Smith had first moved into his four bedroom house, Morgan used to go there a lot, either to collect the wages for the other door crews but being good with his hands he was always getting caught to help to put together furniture or do other jobs around the house. But after one of the neighbours had made a complaint to the Gardaí accusing Smith of suspected drug dealing from the house, Smith was forced to stop all his doormen showing up there. Morgan used to joke about it, thinking that it was just some nosey neighbour with too much time on their hands, but it seems that they couldn't have been more right, even if their timing had been a little off.

Morgan cruised slowly past the house. Smith's Range Rover was parked across his gates pointing back towards the main road. He was home. By parking the big 4x4 like this, it had left the street very narrow as the builder had left a number of stacks of concrete blocks directly opposite Smiths house, up alongside the hoarding of the building site.

Turning around at the turning circle at the end, Morgan looked for somewhere to leave the car. But parking was a problem. Morgan found himself parking in the section of car spaces the small green right back up at the top of the road. He was extra careful as he slid the wide classic Mercedes into the tight space designed for more modern and slender cars. He got out of his car, slipping the handgun from the glove compartment and into his jacket pocket.

Morgan walked up to Smith's gates and looked up at the house, which was set slightly higher than the road with a sense of dread. Smith's house was gorgeous. It seemed from the front that it was just a typical two story, three bedroom house, but the architect had been very clever. The roof design was quite square, allowing the architect to completely convert the attic space into a fourth bedroom, a large en-suite bedroom which Smith had converted into an office with a gym area. There was a time in his life that Morgan had been jealous of Smiths house. He knew that Eimear his deceased fiancée would have loved it. The size and its status. While he still liked it, he would have wanted to pick it up and move the house out into the countryside where he was more settled now. But things like houses didn't bother him anymore, not since his Eimear had died. Now he was happy down in Bayswater in the little house owned by his Aunt.

Standing there at the gates Morgan swallowed hard. He wasn't looking forward to this, not one little bit. But it had to be done. As he thought about Rob, shot to death as he sat watching television, Morgan's inner strength returned. In his pocket he grasped the gun handle tighter and with a shrug of his shoulders, started up the steep drive.

He rang the doorbell, which gave a sophisticated chime instead of a ringing sound. After four or five rings, his former employer eventually answered the door, bathing the front porch in light and looking very surprised to see him.

"Hiya, what's up?" Smith said yawning, his voice sounding groggy as if he had just woken up from a nap. Smith was wearing a tracksuit and Morgan assumed that he had been exercising earlier before falling asleep on the couch.

"I need to talk to you", Morgan answered pushing past him, marching straight into the kitchen at the end of the hall.

"Okay....", Smith replied, closing the door, sounding somewhat unsure of what was happening. He followed Morgan into the kitchen giving him a curious look. "Do you want some tea or coffee?" he asked as he switched on the kettle. Morgan didn't reply, he just stood there facing him squarely, his shoulders as broad as they could be but with his hands still in his pockets. Holding the gun.

"Well, what's all this about"? Smith asked.

"How are you holding up?" Morgan enquired. "Rob's murder must have had an effect on you?"

"It's awful sad what happened to him, but I'm fine. I'd be more worried about you. You were friends with him. I wasn't that close to him".

"Apparently you spent a lot of time with him towards the end," Morgan said. "You were quite friendly from what I have heard".

"Yes, he did some work for me on the Range Rover," Smith replied as he took mugs down from the press. "There was a problem with the fuel pump and the main dealer where I bought it said that it wasn't covered by the warranty and they wanted too much money to fix it".

"That's not what I heard," Morgan said.

"Why, what did you hear?" Smith's voice had developed an annoyed tone. "What's really on your mind?"

"I know you killed Rob", Morgan stated bluntly, cutting straight to the point.

"I did what?" Smith said incredulously, "I never killed anyone".

The kettle boiled loudly before clicking off. The two men just stood there staring at each other, as they tried to size up one another.

"You heard me," Morgan said. "You murdered Rob. You shot him dead as he sat in a chair in his house".

"You think that I killed Rob?"

"Oh, I don't think that you did. I know you did", Morgan stated with absolute conviction.

Smith laughed out loud. "You're fucking mad", he said before turning his back to Morgan once again and poured the boiling water into two mugs he had taken off a mug tree on the countertop. There was a tense silence in the room as Smith took the teabags out of the press. You could have cut the tension in the room with a blunt knife.

"This morning, I had a visit from one of the detectives investigating the murder".

"Oh yeah, what did they want?" Smith asked. Morgan could see his shoulders tense up.

"I was shown a picture of a motorcyclist taken at a junction near Rob's house about the time of his murder".

"So fucking what? There could have been dozens of motor-bikes going through that junction. What does that prove? Maybe they thought you did it? Did you ever think of that?"

"You're right, it proves nothing really and there must be thou-sands of motorbikes in the city, but not the person on the saddle. The rider couldn't have been anyone else. He was sitting on the saddle in that strange way that you do. There can't be too many of riders like that around. Is that dodgy hip of yours still giving you problems?"

"My hip, no that is all cleared up. I had an operation last year", Smith answered sarcastically. "I was shown that same picture myself. The Gardaí questioned me about it as well today. I don't know anything about the motorbike in that picture, so fuck off and get out of my house".

Ignoring Smith's instruction, Morgan continued, "You know, seeing that picture got me thinking. So I started asking around and it turns out your business is struggling. But apparently you've just come into some money. Maybe this money came from a load of stolen drugs that you could sell back to the dealer or a rival gang?"

There was strained silence in the kitchen.

"I don't hear you denying it now", Morgan stated somewhat insulted that it seemed like Smith wasn't taking him seriously and still had his back to him.

Smith turned around to face him, "You still don't take sugar right?"

"What the fuck, are you doing? Stop making fucking tea and tell me you didn't kill Rob for the drugs".

"I can't do that. I did kill him", Smith smiled confidently. "So what are you going to do now?"

Morgan's heart thumped loudly in his chest. He spat out, "I don't care about you. I just want the drugs back. I have to give them to Murray's gang to get them off Sinead's back or he will kill her and her children".

"And what makes you think, I am going to just hand you over the coke?"

"This is why I think that you are going to go along", Morgan said, slipping the handgun out of his pocket and pointing it directly at Smith. Smith looked down at the black handgun before looking directly into Morgan's eyes. You could see him weighing up his options. It was like watching a rattlesnake getting ready to strike.

"Put that down before you hurt yourself. I've had harder men than you threaten me. You're not going to shoot me, you don't have the guts", Smith declared confidently.

"Who says I don't?"

"I do," Smith said. "I've known you for over five years and I know that you won't pull that trigger. You have too much of a sense of right and wrong. You were always too easy going when you were working for me on the doors. I kept telling you to hit first and ask questions later but you always preferred to talk them out first. You're weak".

"Don't bet on it. I'm not doing this for me. I am doing this for Rob and Sinead. What's left of Murray's gang is threatening their family. They need those drugs back and I will do anything I can to help them".

"If you were going to shoot me, you would have done it as I opened the door". Now Smith's tone of voice was mocking as if he was scolding a naughty child for disturbing him watching a football match. "Now, I'm not going to telling you anything so fuck off out of my house, before I take that gun from you and use it to beat you to a pulp".

And with that Smith casually placed the cup of tea on the counter beside Morgan spilling some of it out onto the expensive marble top. Morgan involuntarily looked down, following the hand movement. With Morgan momentarily distracted, Smith took the opportunity that he had manufactured and sprang forward. He grabbed Morgan by the wrist holding the gun with his left hand while driving the palm of his huge right hand hard up into Morgan's face, instantly breaking his nose and sending his head snapping backwards. Morgan collapsed onto the floor, banging his head on the countertop behind him as he went down. The gun clattered noisily onto the tiled floor.

"That was too fucking easy", Smith laughed standing over Morgan, as he lay curled up in pain on the kitchen floor.

Morgan wiped the blood gushing from his nose and across his face. He could taste it as he looked up dazed and confused at the man standing over him. He couldn't believe what had just happened. This wasn't the plan. He was the one supposed to be dishing out the justice, not to mention the pain, not receiving it.

"Don't you ever come into my house and threaten me with a gun you little prick", Smith sneered, giving Morgan a powerful kick in the side of his chest for good measure, before picking up the gun. Morgan slid backwards on the floor and groaned loudly, rocking himself gently to and fro as he tried to cope with the pain in his ribs. Smith grinned devilishly at the prone man. He was in charge now and this upstart was going to pay for threatening him, in his own house of all places. How fucking dare he!

Lying there Morgan knew that he was in real trouble. He knew Smith's methods. He had seen him in action often enough. He quickly began to visualise what was going to happen. Smith would probably tie him up and force him into the back of the 4x4. It would be nothing to him to bring Morgan up the mountains where he would kill him and bury him in a shallow grave. But Morgan wasn't about to allow that to happen. He would never give up, he never did, but he needed to take back the initiative.

And soon.

His mind began to formulate a plan. But he couldn't do anything lying there so first he needed to be up on his feet. So dragging himself up onto his feet, he stood upright, using the kitchen units to drag himself painfully up so that he could face Smith. And Smith, overconfident as usual, let him. Sure, what could Morgan do now when he had lost both the initiative and the gun? Morgan leaned both arms onto the counter to help balance himself before directly looking at Smith.

"Sit down on that chair so I can think of what I am going to do with you", Smith said, nodding toward the kitchen table and chairs. Morgan took the mug of tea off the counter in one hand, took a large mouthful of it, wincing, as it was so hot and went to sit down. As he pulled one of the chairs out, he spun around and flung the contents of his cup directly into Smiths face. The big man roared in pain, the hot tea temporarily blinding him. He brought the heels of his hands up to his face to rub the hot liquid from his eyes, but he hadn't dropped the gun as Morgan had hoped.

With nothing else left to do, Morgan threw himself at Smith in an effort to wrestle the gun away from him. But Smith reacted more quickly than Morgan thought possible under the circumstances. Sensing his movement rather than seeing it, Smith with one swipe of his huge arm into the side of Morgan's head, sent Morgan tumbling onto the floor once more. Smith followed up with a well-placed kick from his size 12 boots, which caught Morgan across the side of his chest again, flipping him over. The air rushed out of Morgan's lungs and he could feel at least two of his ribs break. Gasping in agony, he crossed his arms over his body in an attempt both to ease the pain and protect himself from more blows.

But none came.

Glancing tentatively upwards he saw that Smith was standing over him, still rubbing his burnt eyes, unable to focus clearly.

"Ah you bastard, I am going to fucking kill you", Smith screamed, practically bouncing around the kitchen in unbridled frustration. "Arrgghh", he roared in anger as he continued to rub his eyes, trying in vain to soothe the deep burning sensation.

Once more, Morgan lay sprawled out on the tiles of the kitchen floor. But this time he was at the other end of the kitchen looking out into the hall towards the closed front door. Fight or flight?. Morgan had tried fight with no success, now his survival instinct kicked in. Being heavily outmatched, overpowered and in pain Morgan did the only thing that came to mind. He had no other choice. He had attempted to force Smith's hand and lost. If he stayed he was a dead man . He got up and ran towards the front door; his broken ribs grinding against each other as he ran. When he got to the door, he flung it open so hard it that it left a door handle shaped dent in the plasterboard wall behind it.

In his desperate hurry to escape and trying to cope with the agonising pain in his stomach and ribs, Morgan stumbled out of the front door, falling heavily on to the ground and rolled unceremoniously down the short steep drive. His momentum sent him crashing with a resounding thud into the side of Smith's jeep parked across the bottom of the driveway. Morgan groaned loudly as he slowly hauled himself back up onto his feet, leaning on the 4 x 4's bonnet for support.

Every bone in his body seemed to ache.

They screamed for him to stop and rest.

But he couldn't. Fight or flight and he chose flight. He had to keep going.

Looking back towards the doorway, Morgan saw Smith appear from the kitchen and make his way up the hall towards the front of the house. He was still trying to rub his eyes clear with one hand while attempting to point the gun with the other.

Morgan started to stumble up the road towards his car but had only gone two short steps before a shot rang out. The bullet hit the white painted ornamental concrete ball on the gate pillar of the neighbour's house and ricocheted against the wall, forcing

Morgan to dive to the ground behind the small garden wall. The loud report of the gun shattered the frosty stillness of the night air. Morgan weighed his alternatives quickly as he lay on the cold ground. The partially incapacitated Smith was only seconds away from being in a position to get a clear shot.

Morgan couldn't go towards his car as he had very little cover in that direction and the opposite way was a dead end with eight foot high builders hoarding topped with barbed wire blocking off any possible escape route. Morgan quickly looked around him, where could he go? At that point he noticed the concrete blocks stacked in steel bound bundles across from Smiths house. The way that they were stacked created a type of staircase up to the top of the builder's hoarding. And if he went that way he could use Smith's Land Rover as cover to get over there. Morgan instinctively knew it was his only chance.

With a quick glance towards the brightly lit hall door and the big man standing in profile there, Morgan was running bent over double, around the Range Rover and across the narrow road, scrambling up the blocks. Every step he ran he expected a bullet to tear into him and mortally wound him. And when he reached the top of the stack, the shot finally rang out. But like the first one it missed and instead of pulverising his soft flesh, it sent chips of stone and masonry flying up into the air, hitting Morgan's shoulder. Another piece rebounded off the side of Morgan's head but he had no time to stop and congratulate himself on his lucky escape. Without looking he flung himself blindly, head first over the barbed wire and into the dimly lit building site beyond.

Flying through the air Morgan mercifully just missed hitting an old battered white digger and bounced and rolled down the high mound of sodden sand beside it. He came to a stop in a large rain filled puddle just a few feet away, soaking his legs in the process but at least he hadn't landed on anything that could have hurt him.

Or possibly killed him.

If he had landed a few feet to the left, he would have broken his neck on the digger.

A few feet to the right, he wouldn't have had the benefit of the mound of sand and he would have hit the hard ground and probably seriously hurt himself.

Morgan closed his eyes and lay motionless for a couple of seconds and regained his breath. He knew that things were bad. He had been disarmed and was now being chased by the very man he had gone to confront. A man that Morgan knew would kill him if he caught up with him. Smith had killed at least once before for profit and would have no compunction about doing so again when his very freedom was at stake.

Morgan stood up and looked around. He was standing in an area about fifteen feet wide that circled the outside wall of the half completed apartment block. The ground was rough and uneven. There was rubble and bits of scaffolding strewn everywhere. Security lights placed high on the outside hoarding every twenty feet created areas of bright light and competing dark shadows. It seemed like the shell of the building was nearly complete and Morgan found himself looking at a large section of blank wall surrounded by a high mesh of scaffolding. It's web like appearance covered most of the outer building and made the structure look like the home of some large predatory spider ready to snatch and slowly consume anyone that dared enter. But some one hundred feet to his left, Morgan could see a dark square in a blank section of the facade, which he assumed was an open entranceway.

With no other way in sight, Morgan ran towards the doorway, stumbling in water filled holes and over abandoned rubble to get there. Once he was inside the empty doorway, he turned to look back the way he had just come. Panting hard and with the painful combination of his broken nose and his cracked ribs, Morgan's head was now spinning and the exertion had made him feel dizzy and light-headed. He closed his eyes for a moment and tried to concentrate on calming his breathing but stars danced vividly inside his eyelids and he felt physically sick. Morgan opened his eyes just in time to see a large dark form land on the ground with a loud thud where he himself had been only a few seconds previously. Shit! he thought, Smith was still coming after him.

The apartment complex was in a large rectangular shape, made up of two separate three storey H-shaped buildings, surrounding what was one day supposed to be an ornate garden. Each of the buildings had three levels of thirty, two bedroom apartments, each comprising of six rooms. None of the apartments had external front doors. Their front doors were all off a central corridor, which also held the cleaner's storage areas, lift shafts and emergency stairwells. When you took the number of rooms in the apartments, taken along with the two storage areas per level, it meant that there were a total of one hundred and eighty six possible hiding places. Give or take

Morgan only needed one of them.

Morgan ran deeper into the building, which was lit with bare bulbs hanging down on their wires from the ceiling at irregular intervals. But they were a low wattage and too far apart to give out any proper light. Instead they only turned the interior from black to a light grey colour. Once inside the doorway Morgan found himself in a partially completed foyer with three passages running off in different directions. Unsure which way would be best, he started down the corridor to his right, back in the general direction that he had just come from. As a precaution in case there were any holes in the unfinished ground floor, Morgan kept to the edges, feeling along the unpainted wall as he did so. Despite trying to be careful he promptly fell over a pile of rubbish and debris piled neatly to one side, cutting his hand badly on some protruding metal as he reached out to stop his fall. Stifling a cry of pain, Morgan picked himself up and stumbled on, holding his hand tightly in an attempt to stop the bleeding.

As he stumbled along, Morgan passed by a series of dark entranceways on both sides. Doorways to unfinished apartments he presumed. It crossed his mind that he could hide in one of them until Smith had passed by but it was too soon to think of hiding anywhere yet. He still needed to put some more distance between himself and his hunter. In the badly lit corridor, going from dark to light was becoming very disorientating. Morgan's aching head started spinning and his back and forehead were drenched in sweat. The empty building was eerily quiet; hollow like you would imagine an ancient Egyptian tomb to be. Morgan tried to move silently but every noise, every footstep he made seemed to be magnified tenfold by the unfinished building. It echoed down the empty halls and into each of the vacant rooms, drawing Smith unerringly towards him. Morgan was afraid and there was no use in denying it. He had never been in a situation as perilous as this before. But he wasn't about to let it get the better of him. Even though he was fleeing, he still had his wits about him enough to keep an eye out for something, anything that would swing the advantage back to him. He never quit and wasn't about to start now.

After about twenty seconds, he came up to his first junction in the long corridor. Facing a blank wall, he was left with a fresh dilemma.

Should he go left or right?

Which way would lead him to safety?

And which to a dead end and his doom?

With hardly any visibility and no obvious difference between the two options, Morgan turned right. His worst fears were realised when he rounded another corner and immediately came to a dead end. But all was not lost. There were two rooms at the end, one on each side of the passageway. The doorway on the left opened up to a square room about eight feet by eight feet. It had a sunken floor two foot deep into the foundations and there was no obvious ceiling. Morgan strained his neck looking up to see the stars shining brightly in the gap in the concrete roof high above. He assumed that this would eventually be a lift shaft. But that information didn't do him any good now. The shaft was completely empty, with bare flat smooth walls and no place to hide there.

Turning around and going into the doorway on the opposite side of the passageway, he entered a room a bit bigger than the other one as it was about twelve feet square. However this time there was no sunken floor. Like the previous lift shaft, he could see the clear stars twinkling high above him. But unlike the seemingly smooth and barren lift shaft, Morgan could just about make out the shadow of a small mezzanine floor about twelve feet above him. Morgan assumed that if the building was ever going to finished that this was going to be a stairwell. It was then that Morgan noticed a ladder propped up in the shadows in the corner allowing temporary access to the next level up. Looking back nervously over his shoulder, he knew he had no choice. There was no going back now.

With his broken ribs, Morgan struggled to get himself up the twelve rungs to the top. He kept glancing over his shoulder as he went, his broken ribs making the task incredibly painful. Once up at the top and covered in sweat, Morgan paused again to catch his breath, his aching chest heaving painfully with the exertion. He could not help himself but vomited onto the dusty ground.

"Morgan, I am going to fucking rip your heart out when I get my hands on you... do you hear me Morgan?" screamed Smith like some sort of half demented animal from somewhere on the main floor below. His loud, deep, threatening voice carried like a shock wave throughout the hollow mass concrete building. The echo created by the different sized rooms and the still silent cold night air made Smith's ranting seem even more menacing. Morgan shivered involuntarily, struggled back to his feet and kept on going into the near dark.

As on the floor below Morgan passed more empty rooms as he stumbled blindly along the second level corridor for what seemed like ages. He left an obvious trail in the heavy dust as he went. This passageway ran back in the direction of the downstairs foyer. Far up ahead there was a window high on the end wall. The bright moonlight tried to use it to sneak into the hallway but its high angle limited its effect. Underneath the window there was complete darkness ahead indicating that he was almost coming to another end. There did not seem any good place to hide and he certainly couldn't reach up to the window to escape.

He was trapped!

Unlike Morgan, Smith was making no effort to move quietly and Morgan could hear him crash into each room as he searched for his prey. He knew that Smith was too close for him to get away from now. And with no other place to go, no other corridor to slink down or stairs to climb to safety, Morgan's opportunity for running had passed.

Now it was time for another strategy to be tried.

Morgan knew he needed to take Smith down, here and now, to get justice for Rob's and more importantly for Sinead's sake. So once again that night, he needed a plan for dealing with Smith and hopefully this time, his plan would actually work. He tried to calm his mind, to think rationally and assess the dire situation that he now found himself in. But first he had to fight the fuzziness and the throbbing pain in his head, to concentrate on it to make it go away. Morgan wasn't deluding himself. He knew that he had no chance against Smith in a straight fight. And to make matters worse, Smith now had his gun and after years of martial arts training, he had a serious skills advantage over him.

But everything wasn't lost yet, Morgan thought, trying to remain positive and confident. So, Smith might be the better fighter but he wasn't the sharpest of guys. He could be out thought and that was what Morgan had to do.

Nevertheless Morgan was afraid. He knew that it didn't make him any less of a man to admit it but it didn't help him either. But he wasn't going to buckle under his fear either or just sit down and wait till Smith caught up with him. No, he was going to use his fear. Let his fear sharpen his mind. Knowing that he couldn't beat Smith head on, Morgan knew that somehow he would have to take him down fast and hard. And keep him down.

But how?

As he shuffled along the last few steps of the darkened corridor, Morgan kicked something metal with his foot, sending it clattering along the floor and thumping off the retaining wall. The clanging noise magnified tenfold, echoing down the empty still corridor. Cursing under his breath, he bent down and picked up what appeared to be a crowbar dropped by one of the builders. Weighing it in his hand and feeling the balance, he thought, perfect.

With his heart pounding, Morgan backed up a little bit and waited just inside the last of the doorways on the right hand side. Twisting back around the doorway, he held the crowbar tightly in both hands over his head, like a woodsman would hold an axe as he chopped down a tree. As he waited silently for Smith to appear around the corner, he tried to regulate his racing breath, which he thought was so noisy it must be leading Smith directly to him. It was only another ten seconds or so before Morgan heard the big man coming. Smith had changed his tack as Smith sensing his victim ahead of him, treaded more carefully but his quiet and deliberate movements were still audible. The big man's early noisy searching had been replaced by quiet stalking. Morgan's mouth was bone dry as he took a deep breath and waited, his arms already starting to ache with the weight of the iron bar.

Despite the cold, Morgan was sweating profusely and his clothes were stuck to him. Not only that but his fear and dread were making him feel nauseous. But he wasn't going to let it get the better of him. That wouldn't have been like him at all. He closed his eyes and shook his head to clear it. The problem he now faced was his timing and when exactly he should strike the devastating blow. If he swung too early, Smith would be too far away when he pounced and the crowbar would cut harmlessly through the night air. Too late and he would come face to face with Smith, losing his opportunity hopefully to break the arm that was holding the gun. It reminded him of a similar situation he was in six months ago when he went up against two German neo-Nazi thugs. It had ended then with mixed results. Hopefully this time around, it would go better.

Morgan strained his ears, listening to the very darkness enveloping him. He could just make out the quiet steps of Smith's feet as he came closer. The big man was obviously wary of a trap. From the low scrapping noise he was making, Morgan guessed that Smith was only about six feet away from the doorway. So he took a deep breath and despite the blood freezing in his veins in near terror, he tightened his grip on the crowbar and sprung out. He twisted his body out from the cover of the darkened doorway while simultaneously swinging the heavy bar with all his might towards where he hoped Smith's gun arm would be. It connected with a loud satisfying crack into Smiths upper right arm.

Caught completely by surprise, Smith screamed in agony and dropped the gun. But to Morgan's horror, he reacted quickly to the strike, much quicker than Morgan would have given him credit for. Like lightning Smith reached out with his good left hand and took a firm hold of Morgan's coat. He wrenched him forward, before trying to head butt him again. Luckily though for Morgan, Smith's aim was bad and instead of connecting with his already broken nose, it ended up connecting with the edge of his forehead. The strike made Morgan's head snap backwards. The sheer force of the blow was enough to send him reeling backwards towards the corridor wall.

Unlike earlier though, he didn't fall. But before he could recover fully, Smith followed through with his attack . Smith punched Morgan in the head twice, albeit with his weaker left hand. Two short fast jabs that left Morgan dizzy and his legs weak. The two men started to trade blows, first Morgan, then Smith, then Morgan again. But Smith kept on Morgan relentlessly, pressing against him with his massive frame while still using his left hand. His last few blows sent Morgan reeling back into the darkened room in which he had lain in ambush only a few moments earlier. Slamming into the wall behind him, Morgan coughed violently and droplets of blood spotted the dusty floor. Defeated and with the wind knocked out of him, Morgan slumped exhausted to the hard cold floor.

But Smith hadn't had the fight go all his own way either as was evident by the grunting and groaning coming from him. Smith stumbled back out into the corridor and over to where he thought he had dropped the gun and after a little bit of searching around bent down and picked it up. He was so battered by this time that he scraped it along the ground as he picked it up. Turning stiffly he trudged back into the room, his right arm hanging down uselessly by his side. It must be broken, Morgan thought delighted. But his sense of accomplishment was very short lived as he found Smith once again standing triumphantly over him, pointing the gun in the general direction of his head. Smith was clearly not as fit as he once had been and he was panting hard from the physical exertion of the last thirty seconds.

"I got you now you little shit, no getting away from me now," Smith gasped, bent over, his hands on his knees for support. "And you're going to pay for what you did tonight".

As Smith talked, Morgan looked around at the dimly lit room was he found himself in. He realised that it could very well be the room that he was going to die in. It was a poorly lit grey concrete room, which appeared to be missing its back wall. Where Morgan expected to see another non-descript wall, instead he found that it had a dark chasm. From his vantage point, it appeared to be for an unfinished emergency stair well. Morgan imagined that this must have been for a fire escape but hadn't had the metal stairs fitted yet. It was like the one that he had climbed up to with the ladder at the other end of the building. A poorly constructed wooden balustrade barred the exposed gap. By the look of it, a carpenter with a very bad hangover had put it together first thing on a Monday morning. It didn't look like it was up too much. In the dim light there was what looked like a large yellow sign with a white border saying 'Beware of Fall' in large white lettering on the wall beside the gulf.

Morgan took one look at it and instantly knew that this was his only chance. He went to stand up, sliding his body up the dirty wall behind him for support, but a more cautious Smith was having none of it.

"And where the fuck do you think that you're going?" Smith demanded as he took a step closer to him.

Morgan looked him straight in the eye. "If you're going to kill me, if it's alright with you, I want to be standing up like a man, not lying down like a dog", he spat back at his ex-employer with forced venom.

"No fucking way. None of your tricks. I am not falling for that again so sit the fuck down before I shoot you in the fucking stomach. I heard that hurts like fucking hell. That will be a nice hard fucking death for you. What did you think, that you could beat me" Smith said waving the gun casually around in the air. "Well think again, you little prick. Nobody beats me".

As far as Smith was concerned, the insolence of Morgan was unbelievable. He paced around the empty room shaking his head and waving the gun as he talked. He knew that he was in total control of the situation. But somewhat optimistically Morgan still thought that he could turn things around. But now he found himself in a physically awkward position. He was neither standing nor sitting but kind of half crouching with his back to a wall facing Smith who in turn had his back to the empty stairwell.

This was Morgan's moment.

It was going to be the only chance he was going to get.

He knew that time was running out and that Smith would stop gloating any second now and shoot him in the stomach or head or wherever. Either way Morgan knew he was a goner. Smith wouldn't leave him alive. He couldn't. "If I am going to die then I am going to go out with a bang, not a whimper", Morgan thought. So he tried to gather what was left of his depleted inner strength. Taking a deep breath, he pushed himself up and out with all of his might. He ignored the throbbing ache in his head and the searing pain in his ribs and rugby tackled Smith.

Morgan covered the short distance and drove his broad shoulder into Smith's stomach while shoving the killer's good arm that was holding the gun high up into the air in one motion. Smith had thought that he had Morgan at his mercy and was caught completely off guard by the attack. He dropped the handgun once again. It went clattering onto the floor before sliding off into a dark corner. Driving home his attack, Morgan wrapped his arms around Smith's waist and pushed up against him hard, partially lifting the bigger man off the floor. Morgan's fingers locking tightly behind Smith's back, his tired leg muscles straining with the effort as he drove the big man backwards towards the poorly protected ledge.

In an attempt to make Morgan break his iron grip and force him down onto the cold floor, Smith's good arm came down repeatedly onto Morgan's exposed back in a hammering motion. But it was too little, too late. Morgan was pushing forwards as strongly as if he was twenty years old again and in the middle of a rugby scrum. Smith was completely knocked off balance by the sudden attack and no matter how hard he struggled was forced to stumble backwards. They crashed into the wooden barricade and the combined weight of the two big men proved too much for the poorly made safety barrier to bear. It cracked loudly in the empty building before splitting in half. In an effort to balance himself, Smith put one foot deliberately behind him but to his horror, he found his foot falling into empty space, dragging him backwards with it. If Morgan had been looking up, he would have seen Smith's face go from surprise to shock to sheer panic in the space of a millisecond.

Smith, realising that he was going to fall, let go of Morgan and his arms began to flail around hopelessly trying to grab onto something. Anything to stop himself from falling.

But it was no good.

He was already going backwards much too fast to save himself. To stop himself sharing the other man's fate, Morgan let him go and let his own body fall to the floor with a heavy thump. Morgan landed hard, grunting in pain and raising a small plume of dust from the building site floor. His momentum nearly carried him over the ledge after Smith. At the very last second, as both his head and shoulders went over the edge and he got the sensation of falling, he mercifully grabbed an upright belonging to the now broken barrier just in time to stop himself from falling forward headlong into the dark concrete pit below.

Smith wasn't so lucky though. He had gone over backwards into the dark dimly lit space. His descent was violently ended as his body was skewered by a section of half disassembled scaffolding which had been left sticking up from the ground floor below by the departing builders. Smith screamed out in agony as the two inch diameter metal pole pierced his body through his lower chest, smashing out the front of his body just under his sternum, his massive bulk acting against him now, as his weight and momentum helped drive him further down on to the pole. Morgan could just about see the combination of clothes, skin and thick bright red blood on the top of the pole as it had ripped mercilessly through Smiths body. He finally stopped sliding on the pipe and hung there motionless halfway down its length, a set of fat circular connections fitted to the pole, which allowed other poles to be connected to it, stopping his descent. Smith was a pathetic sight as his arms and legs were hanging limply backwards toward the dusty floor only six or so feet below him. Hanging there, he looked like a torn discarded rag doll.

Above him Morgan lay collapsed on the cold concrete floor, looking down at Smith below. It was an overwhelming sight, seeing his former friend like that. He winced at the terrible scene before him. Smith's broken body hung in mid-air impaled on a blood caked pole.

Morgan was completely exhausted from the struggle, every muscle in his body aching from the effort of the last ten minutes. Looking at Smith, the thought that that could easily have been him so he silently thanked God, Allah or whoever it was who had just saved him from certain death. Closing his eyes, Morgan rolled over onto his back and stared at the concrete slab that formed the ceiling of the floor above him. From there he imagined that he could see all of the way up to the roof but he couldn't be sure. It could have been his eyes playing tricks on him. He closed his weary eyes and after all his battling, the cold hard concrete under him felt soft and comfortable. As he lay there, unable to move for what seemed like hours but was probably only ten seconds he heard a faint moan from behind him. He didn't register at first but then as it grew louder, he realised what it was.

Somehow Smith was still alive.

Morgan opened his eyes and immediately twisted his body around to face the open shaft, closing his eyes once again to help block out the pain the movement caused his aching body and looked down towards Smith's hanging body. Unbelievably Smith had started to come around and was staring in horror and disbelief at the pole sticking up through his body.

Chapter Thirty

"Help me", Smith croaked softly to no one in particular before looking up to see Morgan's head appearing from the ledge above him, watching him intently.

"Help me", Smith half whispered again. But Morgan said nothing, just continued to stare in dismay at him. Smith had the most wretched pain etched across his face. A face full of wordless grief. Morgan almost felt sorry for him. Almost. Morgan wasn't squeamish but the sight of Smith hanging there nearly caused him to vomit again. He gulped in large amounts of air and closed his eyes as he concentrated on not getting sick. Lying there he could feel his blood pounding in his head as the feeling in his stomach and throat subsided.

"Help me", Smith pleaded louder this time, still hanging there, still impaled on the upright scaffolding. He had one arm underneath him, trying to support his massive frame in an attempt to stop himself from sliding further down. The other arm was outstretched towards Morgan, desperately appealing for him to save him.

Pleading.

Begging.

If Morgan was going to let him slide down all of the way, Smith had another six bone scraping, skin wrenching feet to go before he reached the end of the length of scaffolding to the cold concrete floor just below him.

"Fuck you, you did this to yourself you murdering bastard", Morgan spat out at him. Under different circumstances Morgan wouldn't let another human being suffer needlessly but this time he suppressed his natural urge to help. This wasn't another human being after all, this was the animal that had murdered one of his best friends and caused his friend's family to be terrorised. There were three young innocent children who had never done any wrong who had been given a death sentence because of this man's greed. Morgan would let him slide, but judging from the thick pool of blood pooling on the wooden boards lying haphazardly on the ground below, he'd probably be dead long before he reached it.

"Please, I'm begging you", there was unbelievable agony in Smith's cracked voice. The words came out in a series of hacking coughs along with a thin trickle of blood. "I'll give you anything that you want".

"You'll give me anything I want now, eh? I want my friend back you fucking prick. Can you give me that?" Morgan raged back. But there was no answer from the impaled man. "Well, why did you do it?"

"I already told you.... I needed the money. I had buyers lined up to take the lot for a good price. Some Polish lads....and...." Smith hissed but he couldn't finish the sentence as his body slipped down the pipe another couple of inches. He moved in a jerky fashion as he slid over the welded notches on the pole which ripped his ghastly wounds even more. The rate of blood loss increased as he slid down. It could be seen running down the pipe underneath Smith in a thicker darker stream. Morgan thought that even if he wanted to help him, there was very little that he could do for him on his own. Smith was not long for this world. And the world wouldn't miss him. There were enough vile, selfish and dangerous men still left to see it ruined for the rest of humanity. Killing Smith wasn't part of the plan although it did give some justice to Rob, but what about the threat to the children. Smith's death wouldn't help them.

In fact it probably made their situation worse.

Morgan realised that he couldn't let him die without getting the location of the drugs first. Was the threat to the kids real or was all that a lie as well?

"You intended to sell the drugs to some Polish drug dealers and what?" Morgan called down. He found it hard to watch Smith like this, but he forced himself to.

"Sinead...," Smith said faintly.

"Sinead what?"

"She was part of the deal too...", Smith's voice was now very weak and laboured.

"What the fuck do you mean? She was part of what deal? Are you trying to say that Sinead helped you?" Morgan roared in disbelief. His facial expression was full of sudden rage at the very insinuation. How could he say such things? Even now with his last few breaths, he was creating trouble for other people. Even now, he couldn't be honest.

"How the fuck do you think I got into the house... so late at night without... without making a sound or running into one of the kids?" Smith whispered. The words were barely audible through the pain. He paused again, collecting what was left of his strength. "She left the back door open for me".

Smith gasped, trying to hold the pipe steady with his good hand as it stuck through him. Morgan didn't say anything, just looked down at him in total disbelief. Sinead had been in on this the whole time? Smith was lying. He had to be. She couldn't have been, how could she have done this and then lied to him and everyone else for so long? And she had lied so convincingly as well.

"You're lying", Morgan responded determinedly. It was more of a question than a statement.

"It was her idea. She wanted to get rid of Rob", Smith stopped talking to gather his strength "She wanted to get out of the marriage...to start somewhere else....half of the money was hers," he paused yet again and gritted his teeth. ".... She was desperate".

Smith closed his eyes and drifted off again. Morgan just couldn't believe it, that Sinead had conspired to kill Rob. That she had played him all this time. But why would Smith lie? Why now of all times? Surely he couldn't be calculating at this moment, mere minutes away from death?

"Please help me," Smith cried softly, sounding scared like a hurt frightened child. His eyes were wide open. He didn't have long left and he looked alone, vulnerable and very scared. He never thought that a moment like this would come.

That he was invincible.

Untouchable.

But the moment had come. Morgan didn't have any time to waste, he would get the truth from Sinead later, but there were other issues to be dealt with first. Smith didn't say anything else. He had closed his eyes and seemed to slip into unconsciousness.

"Smith, Smith wake up!" Morgan shouted, trying to get him to wake up, but it was no good.

Morgan realised that he needed to get down to him immediately.

The only staircase down that he knew of was the ladder that they had come up earlier and that was on the other end of the development. It would take ages to get down that way and he might get lost in the poorly lit building site. Smith would probably be dead long before he could get to him going that way.

If he was ever going to get anything out of him again, he was going to have to climb down to Smith. Morgan looked around frantically for something to help him climb down, but there was nothing. He would have to lower himself down. There was no other way. As he looked around, he saw the gun lying in one corner of the small room, the faint light reflecting off its silver metal casing. Unable to muster the energy to stand, Morgan crawled over to it and snatched it up, sticking it awkwardly in the back of his jeans like he had seen so many bad guys do in movies.

Turning around, he edged his battered body closer to the edge before letting his legs slip off. Morgan cried out as the hard concrete came into contact with his aching ribs. The hard sharp corner of the concrete ledge dug into his stomach as his legs dangled in open space below him. He had done this countless times as a child, when climbing over neighbours walls or into the local factories to steal wood for Halloween, but that was a long time ago and he didn't remember it hurting as much as this. The edge scraped along his chest as he slid down, bunching his shirt up around his neck. He sucked in and held his breath as he tried to deal with the pain searing through his chest. The tired muscles in his shoulders ached as they tried to support him. Eventually he was left hanging on by his fingertips, his arms outstretched, his body just dangling there.

He was still about eight feet from the ground.

Now or never, Morgan thought to himself and let go.

He landed hard, collapsing with a loud painful grunt into a heap on the concrete ground beside the scaffolding.

Morgan dragged himself to his feet and stood in a pool of blood beside Smith, looking at the mess that was before him. Smith's body was at Morgan's head height as it hung precariously on the solid pole. Smith looked half his normal impressive size. There was no spark left in him. He was like a puppet that had his strings cut. Smith might still be alive, but only just. His body was broken, beyond repair. Morgan turned Smith's head sideways and put his ear to his open mouth and listened carefully for any signs of life. Smith was still breathing but it was very faint, very weak. In an attempt to wake him, Morgan gently shook Smiths shoulders, careful not to move his body too much, in case he would tear the wound even further.

Morgan softly whispered in his ear. "Smith, Smith, can you hear me?"

Nothing.

"Smith, Can you hear me?"

Smith's eyes fluttered open and he stared vacantly at Morgan, barely registering his existence. He didn't have long now.

"Okay, I am going to help you. I'll phone for an ambulance for you", Morgan said in a reassuring voice, "but first you have to tell me where the drugs are?"

It was about then, that Morgan registered the distant wail of sirens. He turned his head towards the sound to be sure that he heard right. The neighbours must have called the Gardaí, he thought. By the sounds of the sirens, it wouldn't be long before they got here and found them. Decision time.

"Please...."

"Where are the drugs?" Morgan demanded.

"The house...," came the faint reply, nearly inaudible reply.

"Where in the house?"

But this time, there was no reply. "Smith, where in the house?"

Still nothing.

Smith had slipped deeper into unconsciousness either through loss of blood, shock or through the pain. Either way, he was saying nothing else.

Probably forever.

No loss. The world would be a better place if he died.

If he survived he would only incriminate Sinead and she had to be protected. If not for herself anymore, then for the sake of her children. They couldn't cope with losing both parents.

The sirens were growing louder now; they couldn't be more than a minute away. He didn't have long. He was hurt but that would have to wait. Morgan took another second to look at Smith and ran for the nearest exit. He had to get the drugs out of the house before the Gardaí arrived.

Chapter Thirty-One

Badly shaken by the night's unexpected revelations, Morgan collapsed in exhaustion at the bottom corner of the ground floor corridor of the half built apartment block. Lying there collecting his breath, he used the time to try and figure out exactly what he was going to do next. His mind was racing at a hundred miles an hour and unless he took charge, it was likely to crash and burn at the first corner it came to. To say the least his initial plan was, quite literally, not going to plan. His original plan, which had seemed so straight forward, was to threaten Smith into giving him back the stolen drugs and then in turn, hand them over to the other gang to stop them threatening Sinead. But he also knew that if he managed to get the drugs from him, Smith would come after him and that he would have to be dealt with. Morgan foolishly had thought that he could simply tell the Gardaí about Smith. That they could then go and arrest him and that by morning all this would have gone away.

But now he had been involved in the death of someone. It wasn't the first time and like the events of last summer, Morgan kept saying to himself that it was in self-defence. But that wouldn't help him, as he lay awake at night. But if he was honest with himself, what had he really expected to happen? That Smith would just hand over the drugs and have his life ruined without fighting back? Deep down he had to have known that Smith would fight back. But knowing that about him had he subconsciously wanted him to? Smith's death now changed everything.

Up until this point Morgan could have walked away from it all. He wouldn't have liked himself for it, but he still could have done it. That wasn't possible now. The only way to make something from all of this would be to find the drugs and give them back. But that was just a start, what would he do then? And what about

Sinead? He still couldn't believe Smith's accusations about her. What if they were true? It changed everything. He was so confused.

Forcing himself to concentrate and to regulate his breathing, Morgan reasoned that the only thing to do was to salvage what was left of his plan – getting the drugs back. Deciding on this, he felt much better. His mind was now distracted with the job at hand and he no longer thought of the image of Smith's broken body impaled on scaffolding. If nothing else Morgan was a practical man. He would have to go into Smith's house and search it and this time he wouldn't have the luxury of time or freedom of movement. Simply getting into the house now wouldn't be easy either. At the very least probably every neighbour in the estate would be standing outside on the street now eagerly watching events as they unfolded. Soon there would be a growing army of Gardaí, followed by technicians and reporters. It was going to be quite a challenge but he still had to do it.

Reinvigorated, a determined Morgan ran as best as he could down the dimly lit corridors, around the pile of rubble on the floor that he had tripped over earlier and out of the apartment block. As he ran he clutched his side in an attempt to try to give some support to his bruised and cracked ribs. He ran as fast as he could but as he reached the entrance that he had come in, he realised that he was already too late. When he cleared the building foyer, blue flashing lights were visible over the hoarding and unintelligible raised voices could be heard shouting commands. The Gardaí were already here. He'd have to find another way back to the house.

Morgan thought quickly.

If he couldn't get in the front of the house, then he would try the back. He imagined that the Gardaí would make an initial search of the house and finding no one there, would then move off and try to locate them in the building site. Hopefully they would leave the house temporarily unguarded or at the most someone on the front door. So if he could find a way into the back of the house he still had a chance.

Moving away from the blue lights, Morgan made his way as best he could towards the bottom corner of the building site. He passed discarded piles of timber, rubble and an abandoned Port-a-loo on the way. There he had his first bit of luck that night as the hoarding didn't go straight down into the corner of the estate but actually crossed the bottom of the road and was attached to the last house on Smith-s side of the street. It meant that Morgan didn't need to climb over the hoarding and cross a now busy street leaving himself completely vulnerable. He could get past the watchful eyes of the Gardaí and neighbours without being seen.

As he moved, Morgan knew that when he arrived at the back of Smith's house he would probably have to create some sort of diversion. He didn't have any idea what he could do but he decided to worry about it later. He was simply going to have to make this up as he went along.

The builder's hoarding butted straight up against the pebble dashed sidewall of the last house on the block. Now it became the garden wall that separated the residents from the abandoned building site. This area wasn't a complete mess like the other sections of the building site and its grounds. Instead it was largely completed. It had a path and grass up to a tree line about thirty feet to his left hand side, it just appeared to need some final landscaping before it was completely finished. But to Morgan's benefit and delight the height of the garden walls dropped to only six feet high, from the ten foot high hoarding surrounding the site. The pebble dashed wall continued on for about two hundred feet, before it apparently became hoarding again.

Moving stealthily along the garden end wall, Morgan came to the boundary between the house and the house backing on to it. He wasn't going to be lucky enough that there was a back lane and that he would be able to just walk up the lane straight to the back gate in Smith's garden and let himself in. After he found the section with the dividing wall, he gave one last look around and with some difficulty scrambled up, leaving multiple scuffmarks on the clean wall.

Smith's house was sixth from the end and with each garden about twenty five feet wide, Morgan knew that he had over one hundred and twenty feet to go before his destination. Although there were no lights on in the back gardens, Morgan knew that he was very exposed crouched where he was and needed to move immediately. As he saw it, he had two choices. He could either make a highly visible and risky run along the top of wall to Smith's back garden or drop into this neighbour's garden and make his way there, climbing over each wall in turn. He decided that there wasn't any time to lose; he would have to make a dash for it along the wall.

Morgan began well, but went too fast and started to wobble wildly after he passed the second house, his body seesawing on the wall in a desperate attempt to keep upright. Luckily, the next garden had a wooden shed placed up against the back wall. With his arm outstretched, Morgan just about grabbed onto the roof of it before he fell. Any further and he would have ended up in someone's garden. Crouching down behind the shed, he caught his breath and attempted to steady his nerves. He took the opportunity to scan the neighbour's back windows and gardens for any movement but all were quiet.

Nobody had seen him.

Morgan took a deep breath and set off again. But this time at a more reasonable pace to make sure he wouldn't fall.

Just as he reached the sixth back garden, a light from his left hand side came on and then a small dog barked loudly as a neighbour let the family dog out. Morgan dashed the last few feet before he literally flung himself off the back wall and landed into one of the many high bushes at the back end of Smith's garden. Wincing from the fall, Morgan sucked in a deep breath through gritted teeth until the pain in his ribs slowly subsided.

The back of the garden was completely black in stark contrast to the area near the house, which was awash with bright light from an outside security light placed high on the rear of the house between the upper windows. The Gardaí must have turned on the rear lights when they started their search. But they hadn't ventured out into the back due to the presence of Smith's two German Shepard dogs, Jessie and Cassie who were barking loudly and doing their best to chew their way through the back patio doors to get inside.

Morgan knelt in the shadows created by the bushes and studied both Smith's house and the houses to either side looking for any signs of life. Apart from the two dogs, there was nothing immediately apparent. This wasn't surprising at all as the excitement was out the front on the street. Morgan felt highly encouraged though. He had the element of surprise as he was sure that nobody was expecting anyone to try and sneak in the back door. As he knelt there, a surreal thought crossed his mind. It wasn't every day that you lay in your ex-boss' back garden, having just killed him and plotted to break into his house. Being careful that he wasn't walking himself into a trap, he sat motionless for almost two minutes before he spotted some movement. Morgan watched a uniformed Garda lazily check the upper rooms. At one point the Garda looked out of one of the upstairs back windows and Morgan thought that he must have seen him, but no. He turned around and walked away oblivious to the presence of the very man that they were looking for. Morgan breathed a sigh of relief, counting himself lucky. The young Garda probably wouldn't have been able to see clearly looking out into the dark through a window from a brightly lit room.

As he examined the back of the semi-detached house, it occurred to him that something was different about the house. He couldn't put a finger on it, it might be just a feeling and he was probably wrong. After all he wasn't looking at the house in a normal frame of mind or maybe it was just seeing things from a different angle. It could have been the garden that seemed different but Morgan just couldn't figure out what.

Holding his damaged ribs, Morgan started to edge himself slowly up along the side of the garden wall towards the house. There were various bushes along the edge, which gave him some level of cover. One of them was particularly thorny and scratched his hand badly as he held it back from his face. As he crawled along, Morgan wasn't worried about making any noise and alerting any Gardaí. The excited barking of the two dogs was loud enough to mask the noise of a small army on a forced march, never mind his creeping up a garden.

The shrubs and bushes lining the sides stopped about ten feet from the raised decking area that spread out from the double French doors at the rear of the house. The deck area basked in the bright light mounted high over the doorway. It was open plan decking, about twelve inches higher than the badly kept lawn and had no railing separating it from the garden. It was going to be very hard to get to the doors, as there was no cover at all, not even a table and chairs to hide behind. The only thing on the decking was a large dog's kennel against the wall, to the left of the French doors, diagonally across from him. The dogs themselves still hadn't noticed him, as they were too preoccupied barking at the intruders in their house. With no opportunity to search the house, Morgan felt at a loss as to what to do next. Nothing had gone right tonight and now the Gardaí were firmly camped inside the house. It was hopeless, there was no realistic way that he was going to get into the house, get the drugs and get out again without anyone seeing him. He was about to turn around and sneak back away but instead he kept staring at the house. Something was definitely wrong? He just couldn't put a finger on it.

Then it occurred to him. The dog's kennel was sitting higher than he remembered it. It was like it was propped up on a few bricks but from where he was lying he couldn't see any dark patches underneath it as matching wood had been fitted to surround the exposed base. This was very strange as Morgan had collected the large kennel from the pet shop himself in a van that he borrowed from a friend he had laid it directly onto the decking area. If it needed to be moved or raised up for some reason, surely Smith would have asked him to do? Granted it had been well over a year since he had been up at the house but Smith always got him to do anything that he needed around the property. So why was it now nearly a foot higher?

Why would Smith have done that?

Morgan's face was filled with concentration as his inner cogs turned. Could Smith have hidden the drugs under the dog's kennel? It was a pretty good place to hide them after all. Anybody searching the house would keep well away from the two big guard dogs, yet it would be easily accessible for him. Morgan thought that since he had come this far and apparently was not going any further, that it was worth a look.

As the doghouse was over the other side of the decking area, Morgan lay on his stomach and crawled along the bottom edge of the decking, using it for cover to get across to the other side of the garden. He did his best to keep low, but he had visions of his bottom being stuck up in the air, with a big neon sign saying "Look everybody, I'm here!" as he crawled along.

One dog, Jessie, the older of the two German Shepard's turned and saw Morgan crawling by, but continued to bark a bit more at the house before recognising him. She bounded over wagging her tail and started licking him across the face regardless of his attempts to push her away. It wasn't long before Cassie left her post at the window and joined her. They both acted like they hadn't seen him in years, tails wagging, licking his face and nuzzling him like their lives depended on it. One dog momentarily disappeared before reappearing with a ragged rabbit shaped chew toy dangling from its mouth wanting to play a game of tug of war. But Morgan didn't have time to play. He knew that he would have to act quickly as the Garda searching the house might come to investigate the sudden deafening silence. Pushing the eager dogs away, he crawled along the edge of the deck until he was beside the kennel. Thankfully there was nobody around, so he crept up to the doghouse and taking a deep breath, he stuck his head in over the lip. He couldn't see anything so he reached his hand in and tried to feel inside but his arm wasn't long enough to do it properly. There was only one way he was going to do this.

Checking that the coast was clear, he squeezed into the narrow entrance of the dog kennel and attempted to turn around. He found it very hard as both dogs were trying to get in along with him. "Cassie, Jessie, get out", Morgan hissed, pushing them back out. They grudgingly left him alone, letting out the odd bark to remind him that they were there as they lay waiting patiently for him outside. Morgan began to feel around the wooden bottom of the kennel, wary of any dubious presents that the dogs might have left him. Three boards near the entrance were loose and came up far too easily. Reaching into the dark hole, he felt a large rectangular parcel wrapped in heavy plastic. Bingo. It had to be the drugs. There was nothing else that Smith would go to the trouble to hide. The package fitted very tightly into the compartment and hampered by the lack of space inside the kennel Morgan struggled to get it out before eventually freeing it.

Time to go.

Morgan carefully looked out of the doghouse, checking that there was nobody looking out the French doors. Nobody was there, but from where he was lying he couldn't see the other windows properly. He couldn't be sure if anybody was peering out one of the upper windows, but he would have to take a chance. Seeing him move, the dogs came over to him, pushing up against him looking for a pet and a tickle. They weren't helping him slip away quietly.

"Get out of it," he said, doing his best to push them gently away.

Morgan made his way cautiously back down the garden, cursing the dogs as they shadowed him on the grass. They began barking again as he scaled the wall as quickly as he could, before dropping over the far side into the rear neighbour's garden. Checking that nobody had seen him, he quickly walked up the side of the house before opening the side gate and simply walking out onto the next street. Turning right, he headed back towards the main road. He ignored his car as the Gardaí were everywhere and had probably had roadblocks up near the estate entrance.

Where it was on the next street, it was safe and out of the way, nobody should find it and connect it to him. Morgan could get out of the estate by using a pedestrian entrance about five hundred feet up the road. So, reaching into his pocket, he pulled out his phone and called the person that his future was inextricably linked to.

"Sinead"

"Yes. How did it go?"

He wasn't going into that now. "I need you to collect me."

"Why, what's happened?" she asked, sounding very concerned

"Do you know the shops up near Smith's? The ones up near the roundabout".

"Yeah?" She answered confused.

"Collect me there in fifteen minutes. And park over by the recycling bins on the left hand side. And be careful not to be followed," Morgan said before hanging up, not giving her a chance to argue.

Chapter Thirty-Two

Morgan knelt down in the middle of a number of large bushes and surveyed the car park in front of him. There were two businesses still open, a late night newsagents that sold alcohol and a chip shop. Even at this hour, both had a steady flow of people through their doors. The chip shop had the usual gang of noisy teenage kids hanging out along the wall outside, shouting and cursing as they joked amongst themselves. Outside the newsagents there was a dog tied up to a drainpipe, wagging its tail and playfully barking at everyone passing by.

Morgan had been hiding there for the last ten minutes and had taken the opportunity to properly go through the parcel of drugs. Of course, he had seen what cocaine looked like in numerous films and television programmes but he had never seen what three quarters of a million euros worth looked like up close. The heavy carryall had Scubapro Dry Bag branded on its side. A good choice thought Morgan. The last thing any dealer would want is for his product to get damp. He didn't know what a gram of coke was going for these days but when he was working as a doorman, he heard that it was worth about €60 per gram. There were twelve blocks of what felt like a kilogram each. If each block was worth sixty thousand Euros, which meant that the whole bag was worth seven hundred and twenty thousand. The Gardaí had said that they had information that Rob had been holding seven hundred and fifty thousand euro worth of coke, so assuming his maths was right, where was the other half a kilo or thirty thousand worth gone? Had Smith taken it? Used it himself maybe? Or used it as proof that he had a larger consignment so he could sell it? He would probably never know the answers to these questions.

Zipping the bag back up, Morgan went back to watching the cars coming to the shops. Over the next few minutes, he studied each car to make sure there were no unmarked Garda cars cruising around on the lookout for any suspects in the death of Smith. There was a constant stream of cars driving in and out of the car park, but by now Morgan had stopped watching the centre entrance, ignoring all of them and instead was staring at the car now parked in the shadows close to him. Sinead was inside it waiting for him. Her cars lights were turned off but the engine was still running, probably so that the occupant could keep the heating on. The engine fumes from the exhaust were clearly visible in the cold night air. Morgan watched her and surveyed the car park for another five minutes to make sure that she hadn't been followed before slipping out of his cover and approaching the car from the rear.

Morgan opened the car door and sat in heavily, placing the heavy parcel containing the drugs awkwardly at his feet. Without looking at Sinead, he simply said, "Drive". Sinead was about to say something, but upon seeing his dark expression she thought better of it. She turned on the headlights, gunned the engine and took off out of the car park. Her nerves coupled with Morgan's surprising attitude made her drive much too fast until the routine of driving helped calm her down.

The drive back to her mother's was very tense. Sinead kept looking at him from the corner of her eye, eager to ask what had happened. What had Morgan gone through in the last couple of hours to put him in this mood? She was very proud of him after all, as she assumed that he had managed to do what the team of detectives had failed to do, and he should be elated. But the longer Morgan kept his silence, the more worried she got. Morgan simply sat in the front seat and stared forward out of the window. For his part, he was barely containing his rage, he wanted to scream, to lash out at her, but now wasn't the time. Now he simply had to get away from Smith's house and the building site. God knows how much time he had until the Gardaí realised his connection and arrived to pick him up. He needed space to clear his head and plan out his next move. Too much was depending on what happened in the next few hours.

Fifteen minutes later they pulled up outside Pauline's house. Still silent, Morgan got out and walked straight up to the porch and waited impatiently for her to catch up and unlock the hall door. Inside he went straight into the kitchen. Although it was still early, the house was in darkness; Pauline and the children seemed to be in bed. Sinead followed Morgan into the kitchen; but she barely had time to turn on the light before Morgan could no longer contain his rage. He dropped the package containing the drugs heavily onto the kitchen table and grabbed her roughly by the left wrist, swinging her around so that she was pressed up against him, face to face. Her arm was twisted up behind her back as he held her, and this time there was nothing romantic about it.

"You're hurting me," Sinead complained, trying to pull away from him. She sounded like she was going to start to cry.

Morgan stared directly into her eyes before saying "I don't care. I know you had Rob killed", he spat with venom in his voice through gritted teeth.

"What do you mean, I had Rob killed?" she shook her head and trembled in reply.

"Don't fucking lie to me, I know you had him killed", his voice rose as the bottled anger and emotion spilled out.

"Who told you that?" She sounded shocked.

"Smith did, just before he died. You had Rob killed and you have been jerking me around since, you fucking bitch".

"Smith's dead? How? What exactly did he say?" Sinead said angrily, trying unsuccessfully to twist herself out of Morgan's grasp.

"He fell and anyway what does it matter, 'what exactly did he say'? You had your own husband murdered so you could get your hands on some fucking drugs". Morgan tightened his grip on her arm, pulling it higher up her back, hurting her a bit more.

"It wasn't like that," she pleaded, struggling to free herself. But the more she struggled, the tighter and more painful his hold on her got.

"So you admit it then?" Morgan proclaimed excitedly.

"Yes... I do, but it wasn't like you're making out".

"Then what was it like?" Morgan snarled.

"Let me go, please", Sinead begged.

Morgan looked at her, contempt in his eyes. Let her go? He wanted to wring her bloody neck. But as his anger had subsided slightly with her admission, he let her arm go anyway and walked away from her, placing his hands on the draining board and staring out of the kitchen window. He looked at the face staring back at him in the reflection in the window. He looked battered, bruised and tired, but all he felt was beaten. Not just physically but mentally as well. The fight had gone out of him. It was all too much to deal with. Sinead stood behind him, tears in her eyes, rubbing her shoulder where he had twisted it.

"It wasn't supposed to be like this," she pleaded desperately. "I just wanted the money from the drugs. Nobody was supposed to get hurt, especially not Rob. That was never the plan. But then Smith shot him. I didn't know what to say or do. No matter what I did, I would end up in jail. Smith shouted at me when I tried to call him, he kept saying that he had to kill him as Rob would only find out it was us and get Murray and his gang after us. That we wouldn't last ten minutes if it got out we stole them. I didn't know what to do then. I had got myself in so deep that I couldn't get out. I was frightened."

"But you went along with it. You could have stopped all of this it if you really wanted to. You should have told the Gardaí", Morgan answered turning around to face her, hate in his eyes.

Sinead said nothing, just stood there, her arms folded staring back at him. But as Morgan looked at her, he realised that she wasn't staring at him, she was staring back in time. A few weeks, a few months, God only knew.

Or cared.

He knew that he certainly didn't.

"He was your husband, my friend." Morgan paused for emphasis. "You knew what could happen and you just went along with it?" he continued incredulously.

"I didn't think it would come to this," Sinead answered, nearly whispering. "Smith was going to arrange to sell the drugs to his buyer for a hundred grand. He was going to give me half".

"Yeah right. What did you think would happen? How stupid could anyone be? Did you really think that Smith would give you half of the money that he got for selling the drugs? That the gang you stole it from would simply walk away. Come on and grow up. You had my friend murdered. How could you be so fucking naïve?" Morgan waved his hands up in the air, frustrated by her lame pathetic excuses.

"Don't talk to me about him being your friend. You ignored him when he asked you for help," her words stung as she uttered them, her answer catching him off guard.

Morgan looked at her and shook his head. "That doesn't take away from the fact that you had him killed".

"I never intended to have him killed, but all of my life he has let me down. He was always letting me down, right from the first time we fucking met. I just couldn't take it anymore"; Sinead spat back at him, slamming the palm of her hand on the kitchen table. Now there was venom in her words, her blood was up. "He was a stupid idiot, always going from one stupid get rich plan to another. Never achieving anything. Losing more money than we could put together. We were always in debt. And then he went and got himself involved in drugs. I begged him to stop when he told me. But oh no, he wouldn't. He was the big hard man".

"He was no hard man, he loved you and the kids," Morgan said firmly.

"You weren't there", Sinead screamed, the anger in her voice burning like a furnace. "You didn't feel the humiliation of going to court over those stolen cars. Or having to go to the social welfare officer to beg for money to pay for food for the kids. I went so often we knew each other on a first name basis. Not to mention having to go down on bended knee to get loans from my mother or from his mother or you for that matter, just to make ends meet."

"Fair enough, but you have always had problems, so why now? Why go to such lengths after all of these years?" Morgan demanded, begging her for an answer. He needed to understand what had driven her to set off this train wreck of consequences.

"I found out that he had been cheating on me with some little slut that he worked with in the bar, apparently he was planning to leave me and the kids for her and I couldn't take it any longer. He had let me down so many times." And for what was probably the hundredth time in the last two weeks, Sinead put her head into her hands and started to cry. Maybe these were the first genuine tears of remorse or maybe just tears of relief that it was all out in the open, Morgan didn't know and he still wasn't sure if he cared. But he let her continue. So that was what it was really over, Rob's affair.

"Then why not just leave him? Kick him out or something? You didn't have to start all of this mess", Morgan snapped angrily.

Sinead gave him a look like he had ten heads. "And what, be broke again? Struggle on again? The same shit that I have put up with him nearly all my life. I am nearly forty years of age and I am dirt poor. I have nothing, mostly because of him. I could have gone to college and made something of myself except he got me pregnant and kept me that way." The tone of her voice changing from pleading to angry as the frustration that she felt in her life bubbled over. How long had she felt this way?

Neither spoke for a few minutes. Morgan tried to absorb everything that was being said. Finally Sinead broke the silence. "The affair wasn't the only reason," she said, looking directly at him. Morgan didn't say anything just let her continue.

Sinead tried to compose herself, her voice becoming softer. "Rob hardly looked at me anymore. We hadn't had sex in over a year. I wanted to meet someone else. Smith was coming around a lot a few months ago, getting Rob to do jobs for him. Work on his jeep. He would mess and flirt with me when he was here. He made me feel that I was still attractive to men. That I was still desirable, Rob hadn't made me feel that way in years. I needed to be free to find someone and feel loved again."

"You didn't have to get him killed," Morgan repeated. "So why shouldn't I just go the Gardaí now and tell them that you and Smith conspired to kill Rob to get the drugs that he was hiding?"

"You can't, please! Who will look after the children?" She pleaded.

"You should have thought about that sooner, shouldn't you?" he snapped. "Anyway, your mother can."

"She's too old. They will take the kids off her, split them up and put them into care. Especially Linda. Who is going to foster a teenager with Down syndrome? She wouldn't last five minutes without us looking after her. Don't do that, after everything that has happened". Sinead started to sob again. Hands up to her face, trying to stifle the tears. She suddenly looked up, defiance in her eyes. "Anyway, you can't go to the Gardaí either, you killed Smith. They will lock you up just as quickly".

She was right of course. He could try and plead self-defence with them but they would ask why he hadn't gone straight to them as soon as he knew about Smith, about why he had brought a gun to the house with him, if not to kill Smith? Why he had run afterwards? He had no answer for the last one. But he wasn't going to allow Sinead to turn this around on him and let her slip out of her part in this. Justice had to be done, maybe all around.

"I'll take my chances", Morgan said.

There was a tense silence, as they stood in the kitchen, the stark bright light, making the room seem very cold and impersonal. Morgan looked at the black parcel sitting on the edge of the table.

"What about the threats from Murray's gang. You probably lied about that too?" he said to Sinead.

"They were real. They really want their drugs back. They think that I still have them".

Morgan thought quickly. If Sinead had arranged all this, she hadn't figured on what was left of Murray's gang fighting over the scraps with her. And he was sure that Murray using her kids as leverage wasn't part of her plan either. He still had to help them, if not for their mother's sake any more, then because of Rob. He owed him that.

At this point, the kitchen door creaked slowly open and Sinead's mum peeked her head around the door, before opening it fully.

"Is everything ok?"

Chapter Thirty-Three

It was over an hour since the initial call had come in across the main Garda call centre desk, reporting that there were gunshots fired in an affluent housing development in the south west of the city. As protocol demanded in such circumstances, the Emergency Response Unit, the ERU, were immediately called out to support the local Garda units. As the shooting had occurred in a different Garda district, Callaghan wasn't immediately informed. But when she read about it on the internal email bulletin through the PULSE system, she learned that the address of the incident was that of John Smith, former employer of both John Morgan and Rob O'Dwyer. It might be a coincidence, after all Smith led an interesting and varied life and could easily have fallen foul of some other group of people, but Callaghan would have put money on it all being connected with her case. But how exactly? With nothing else pressing on her desk, Callaghan had immediately taken it upon herself to go out and have a look at what was happening first hand.

When she got there, she found that the lead Garda on the scene was DI Connick. While she had never worked directly with him, she knew him to be a capable and well respected member of the force. When she arrived he was busily coordinating the search of the half completed apartment block opposite Smith's house. Not to mention the other hundred things that needed to be done in such circumstances. The fire brigade had forced the hoarding surrounding the building site open to allow proper access. They were currently in there assisting an ambulance crew in removing Smith's body from the elevator shaft.

Judging by the sheer number of Garda on the scene, it seemed that Connick had called in as many local patrol units as he could muster and they were trying to seal off the surrounding area while the ERU team finished their search of the building site and the houses immediately around it. The residents in all of the nearby homes had been removed as a precaution while the searches had gone on. Connick's team of detectives were interviewing potential witnesses and liaising with the various emergency units.

It was unusual for Callaghan to be at a scene and not be directly involved in it. As she stood there watching as everybody running around, she knew it seemed like chaos to the casual onlooker, but there was an order about it. The Gardaí were busy, efficient and effective. She knew that Connick would have prioritised the long list of things to be taken care of. Secure the scene, search for any perpetrators and then locate and attend to any victims, gather evidence and interview witnesses. It was a long list but an experienced officer like Connick would always have his mind on proper procedure and securing of evidence for any later trial. But what Callaghan did notice was how little noise there was. While there were a lot of blue strobe lights rhythmically flashing, none of the vehicles had their sirens on. There was no shouting from any of the personnel on the ground, they were just going about their duties in a calm professional manner. There was also a growing group of onlookers who were talking quietly amongst themselves being held back by two uniformed Gardaí. It was actually so quiet Callaghan could hear herself think.

Detective Callaghan marvelled at the wide variety of uniforms milling around from standard Garda, to ERU, crime scene analysis, ambulance crews and Fire & Rescue personnel involved. Callaghan approached one of the Gardaí on sentry duty to get directions to the various scenes. She was told to follow the lights by the young Garda as he struggled to contain a number of reporters eager to get a better vantage point in which to take some pictures.

"Do they have any leads yet?" she asked him quietly before leaving.

"I am not sure of the details", he replied, trying to keep his voice low so that no one else would over hear, "but as far as I know the victim was seen with a gun chasing another large man into the building site over there, where he fell to his death. They haven't found the other man yet but they are still looking. Apparently, it's pretty horrible the way he died as he was skewered on some sort of pipe. Perhaps you had better get in touch with the DI yourself."

"Of course, good luck with that lot", Callaghan said, gesturing towards the reporters.

Callaghan first went in to check the goings on in the building site but couldn't get to see anything with all of the activity around. So she went over to Smith's house instead. She knew where she was going as she had interviewed him there only a few days previously. The kitchen was closed off as it was being photographed prior to the crime scene technicians moving in, so she took a slow walk around the house for a few minutes instead. There was nothing remarkable about the house except that she noticed how expensively it had been decorated. While her unofficial search had been brief there were no obvious signs of any activity in the house apart from the kitchen and the hallway. No rooms had been aggressively searched or torn apart by fighting. Whatever had happened, it seemed that it had stayed downstairs. Although, when she spoke to Connick she would recommend that this house be thoroughly searched for the missing drugs. It was a long shot but just in case.

Callaghan paused at one of the rear upstairs windows to look out at the dogs barking furiously at the Garda photographer through the downstairs patio doors. There is another branch of the state going to turn up for them, animal control, she thought before heading back downstairs and out of the door. Once outside, she went to find Connick to tell him about the possible link but he seemed to have disappeared. Instead Callaghan walked back to her car, but did not get in. Instead she stood at the driver's door, rattling her car keys and looking around the hectic crime scene, unsure of what to do next. A sharp breeze came up, making her shiver. She wrapped her long heavy coat tighter around herself. This had to have been the work of Morgan, she thought. She felt it in her bones.

As DI Connick wasn't around Callaghan decided to call DI Higgins to update him on the events and her suspicions. But she only got his message minder so she left a message for him to call her back. Damn it, she thought, where was he? This new development needs to be followed up immediately. She thought about going to talk to DI Connick, but then thought otherwise. It was then that she took what her mother always jokingly called an executive decision and decided to go find Morgan herself.

So half an hour after she arrived, Callaghan got into her car and gunned the engine but she found it slow getting out to the road junction as she manoeuvred around the myriad of Garda and

Emergency vehicles, not seeing Morgan's old Mercedes hidden behind a parked fire engine as she passed by. Callaghan pulled into the middle of the roadway out of the housing estate and indicated to turn right towards Morgan's family house but then changed her mind and drove off in the other direction towards the house of Sinead O'Dwyer's mother. If Morgan was going to be anywhere, he was going to be there.

Chapter Thirty-Four

"Will the both of you keep your voices down?" Sinead's mother ordered as she barged in through the kitchen door. "You must have woken the whole neighbourhood with your shouting, not to mention the children upstairs. They are scared enough as it is".

"Sorry, Pauline", Morgan answered, half under his breath before turning back away. Out of force of habit he walked over to the kitchen counter and turned on the kettle and took mugs down from one of the presses.

But Pauline continued scolding them. "It's all the neighbours will be talking about tomorrow, more trouble with this family".

Both Sinead and Morgan looked at each other but they said nothing, wondering exactly what she had overheard. "What happened to you?" Pauline asked, seeing the bruises on Morgan's face and the dirt on his clothes.

"Nothing, I'm alright," he answered, trying to shrug off the question.

"No, you're not".

"I said I'm fine, okay," Morgan said sharply, hoping that Pauline would realise that he did not want to talk and go back to bed. He still had to talk to Sinead.

But Pauline wasn't buying it and she gave him a knowing look that all Irish mothers quickly master. A concerned one that could easily see through his protests. "I know you're not, so don't try to kid me."

"Here, let me make the tea. You always make it too strong", Pauline said before unceremoniously pushing Morgan away from the counter. "You could tarmac the road with your tea".

Morgan went and joined Sinead over at the kitchen table. She was just sitting there staring at the floor and smoking a cigarette.

An awkward silence enveloped the room. The only sound was the kettle as it came to a boil and the rattle of mugs and spoons.

Pauline made the tea before sitting down with them. Nobody said anything for a few minutes. They just sat there and sipped their tea quietly. It was a strange surreal silence. Forcing himself to keep calm Morgan used the silence to try and piece together everything that had happened in the last twenty four hours. Then out of nowhere something dawned on him. If Pauline had heard everything as she had claimed, why wasn't she full of questions? Why wasn't she grilling her daughter? If it had been him and he had found out that his daughter had been accused of stealing half a million euro worth of drugs and getting her husband killed in the process, then he would have more than a few questions for her. He'd be screaming the house down looking for answers. That was unless of course, she already had those answers.

He stared at Pauline in disbelief as she sat there quietly, as if she did not have a care in the world, prompting her to say, "What?"

"You knew about this didn't you?" he questioned.

There was a long pause as she decided on her answer. "Yes I did," she admitted looking slightly embarrassed.

"You knew?" Morgan repeated in disbelief. Now he had heard everything. His mind was spinning with this latest revelation.

"Only since yesterday. I felt that there was more to it all than Sinead was letting on. I sat her down and would not let her go until she told me everything. It took a while but I finally got it out of her", Pauline replied, looking rather sternly at her daughter, who was trying to make herself seem smaller.

"So why didn't you say anything?"

"Do you think I like being told that my daughter is involved in the murder of her husband?" Pauline responded.

"Well, I don't know what to think anymore", Morgan answered shaking his head in disbelief. "This just keeps getting better. Don't you think her actions were abhorrent or does anybody in this family believe in right or wrong?"

"Of course I do. She told me everything yesterday, after you left. But it still hasn't sunk in with me properly yet".

"And..." he asked curiously.

"And what?" Pauline said. "What do you expect me to do? Did you expect me to pick up a phone, call the police and see my daughter being carted off to jail? Do you really think that I want to see my grandchildren put into care? Well do you?"

"Of course not but she is involved up to her neck in Rob's murder. And what about Rob? He'll never see his kids again. She took that away from him. Does that not bother you?" Morgan retorted. Pauline wasn't going to get away with reasoning like that. It didn't wash with him. What Sinead did was wrong. It was black and white. There were no grey areas. And anyway, grey areas didn't come into murder. Plain and simple.

"Rob was a lovely guy. But he was a loser, I always knew it but she wouldn't listen to me. You knew Sinead when she was young. She could have had anyone, but she got saddled with him instead. I have seen her waste her life because of him."

"Did he deserve to die?" Morgan demanded.

"No. No, he didn't," Pauline conceded. "It was a horrible, horrible thing to be party to and she is going to have to live with that for the rest of her life. But I am not going to make this worse by sending my daughter to prison."

"And what if the children get hurt by this psycho that's threatening them now?"

"You are going to get his drugs back and he will go away. Then we can start rebuilding our lives", Pauline said confidently.

"Don't you understand that these people never go away?" Morgan said. "You are in their world now and unless they go to prison they will always be out there. Even then you might never be safe again".

"You give him what he wants," Pauline said. "Sinead hasn't been accused of any involvement in any part of this debacle. There is no reason for Johnson ever to come back. As soon as she can she is going to sell up and move down the country and start again."

"And play happy families? Is that what you want?"

"No it's not," Pauline said. "But I don't want to see Sinead spend the rest of her life in prison either. What effect do you think that would have on the kids? Knowing the truth would destroy what little chance they have left of coming out of this in one piece. Is that what you want?"

"How can you use that as an argument to defend her?" Morgan asked. "She was not thinking about the kids before she started all this."

"If I'm honest, I don't think she thought about anything before all this, except herself that is", Pauline gave her daughter a look of contempt. "But I am her mother and I have to do my best for her".

"Stop talking about me as if I wasn't in the room. I'm not some child you know", Sinead said angrily, standing up and slamming her cup down onto the table. She walked over to the kitchen window and stared out of it, arms folding across her chest like she was trying to hug herself. Morgan could see in the reflection of the glass that she was crying.

"Well, if you had been acting like a responsible adult, then you wouldn't be in this situation." Morgan replied. He looked across and back at both of them. "And what about the kids? Do they know?"

"Of course they don't. And they never will", Pauline replied in horror.

"Ok. So who else knows?" Morgan demanded. He needed to know who knew what if they were going to get through this.

"Nobody else...as far as we know", Pauline answered looking at Sinead, who gave a barely perceptible nod in agreement. It was just the people in this room.

People with a vested interest in keeping it like that.

"You know, I have done some dubious things in my life but I have always done them for the right reasons. Up till now I have always been able to look myself in the mirror and know that I have always done my best for people. By keeping this quiet, you are asking me to give this up", Morgan stated angrily. "How will I look at myself now?"

And with that, a heavy stony silence descended the room once again.

"So", Pauline asked, looking at the parcels on the table and trying to change the subject, "Are these the drugs? Is this what all the trouble is for?"

"Yes, that's them", Morgan replied coarsely.

"Was it hard to get them back?" Pauline asked, looking at his bruised and battered face.

"What do you think?" Morgan replied sarcastically. And with that he took the heavy gun out of his pocket and laid it on the table before relating the night's events to both of them. They both stared at the gun like it was a magnet. Their eyes were inexplicably drawn towards it. Neither commented on it, they remained silent but the expressions on their faces as Morgan described Smith's last few moments told it all. The horror of it was taking its toll more heavily on Pauline as reality dawned on her, the nightmare that her daughter and her hapless husband had dragged her family into.

Up until a week ago, they were a normal enough family, caught up in life and all its everyday problems like everyone else. School, work, money, new kitchens, old bathrooms, TV soaps, you name it. Now, they were a party to two deaths, a large drugs deal and probably looking at a lifetime of imprisonment. The three children would end up scattered throughout a social services system that would leave them shattered for life. A lot would depend on what happened in the next twelve hours. Pauline gave Sinead a disgusted look. How could her daughter do this to her family? She would never forgive her.

"Oh Jesus, Morgan. What are we going to do now?" Sinead said, openly crying.

"I don't know. I simply don't know".

And with that the doorbell rang.

Chapter Thirty-Five

Morgan, Sinead and Pauline stared at the inside of the white panelled kitchen door as if they all could look through both it and the hall door to see who was ringing the bell. Who could that be? Tonight of all nights, Morgan thought. He instinctively knew that it couldn't be something innocent, like a neighbour calling around, or a distant relative turning up late to offer the family their condolences on Rob's death. No, it had to be someone connected with either Rob's or Smith's death. Smith's probably, considering the timing. Each one of them involuntarily held their breath. Would the person calling give up and go away? The bell rang again, but this time the person rested their finger on the bell. They were not taking no for an answer.

DING DONG. DING DONG. DING DONG.

Morgan felt compelled to look down at the handgun lying prone on the table. Knowing he had to go to the door he reluctantly picked it up, felt the weight of it in his hand and stood up stiffly, groaning imperceptibly with the effort and walked to the kitchen door, opened it and looked out into the hall. He could see the shape of one person through the frosted glass hall door, possibly a woman by their stance.

But he couldn't be sure.

Nor could he know if there were more people out of his limited view.

"It's a woman and she appears to be on her own", Morgan called back in a hushed tone to the terrified women in the kitchen. That was a slight relief to them all. It was not Johnson arriving early to collect his drugs. Nor was there a posse of Garda coming to arrest him. Maybe it was just one of Pauline's friends who had come to visit after all. It had just gone nine thirty, a bit late but you never know. Either way, as it was Pauline's house, so it made more sense for her to answer it. He turned back to face the kitchen to see Pauline already on her feet creeping up behind him. She must have been thinking along the same lines.

"I had better get that. This is still my house", she said.

"Be careful. Keep the security chain on the door. Whoever it is get rid of them. Don't worry, I will be right here, keeping an eye on you." Morgan said firmly, trying to sound confident. Pauline just nodded and walked up the hall. But just in case it did turn out to be some half deranged drug dealer masquerading in a woman's silhouette, Morgan was going to cover her. He tightened his grip on the butt of the gun and held it around the half closed kitchen door pointing it menacingly towards the hall door, ready to come to Pauline's rescue if she needed it. Sinead crowded in behind, trying to look around Morgan to see what was happening.

Pauline reached out tentatively to touch the door handle but despite his earlier warning, she opened the hall door without first putting the chain on. Morgan hissed a warning to her but it was too late. She opened the door enough for him to see who was standing there.

It was Detective Callaghan.

Pauline nervously asked her what she wanted but Morgan could not quite make out Callaghan's answer as a car with a loud exhaust drove by at exactly the wrong moment. But Pauline obviously did not like what was said as she attempted to close the door over but the detective wasn't having any of it and shoved her foot in the gap preventing her from closing it fully. Pauline looked around to indicate to Morgan that she needed help but as soon as he left the cover of the kitchen door, Callaghan had burst the door opened and stood facing him. They both paused, looking each other up and down. Morgan stood there in his filthy clothes, his face bloodied, bruised and starting to swell and looking as guilty as hell. Callaghan in turn looked like the fox had caught not just the hen, but also the whole damn henhouse napping. He quickly held the gun down to his side and behind his leg so she could not see it.

"John Morgan, I've been looking for you," Callaghan said firmly, striding past Pauline into the house. She looked very determined.

Confident.

Victorious.

She had her man.

Nature designed us with a fight or flight mechanism. Earlier he had initially run when faced with Smith. Making a break for it again, crossed Morgan's mind for a split second. But where would he go? He could not live in hiding for the rest of his life. No, this time it was fight. Just not with his hands.

"Well looks like you found me", he forced himself to say in a casual manner, backing slightly into the kitchen so he could conceal the gun better.

"I want to ask you a few questions", Callaghan stated.

"Fine", he replied, trying to remain nonchalant but his shoulders dropped a small bit. "Why don't we all go into the living room"?

Morgan passed the gun backwards to Sinead, who was standing behind him still in the kitchen. She in turn hid the gun in one of the drawers of the big dresser underneath a pile of ornate lace napkins that were only brought out on special occasions. He then led the way and sat in one of the big deep armchairs. This time he groaned out loud as he sat down. His whole body ached as it slumped into the soft chair. The three women followed him in and sat down. Sinead and Pauline on the couch, Callaghan on the second armchair. Sinead was crying and held her mother's hand for support.

"Looks like you had a rough night", said Callaghan knowingly as she sat on the edge of her seat facing Morgan. That was an understatement. He looked like he had gone ten rounds with Mike Tyson. She had absolutely no doubt that he had been to Smith's that night and fought with him. And Smith had ended up dead. Now all she had to do was to get him to admit it and tell her why. It shouldn't be hard, he was no match for her, she thought. This would be a great opportunity to advance her career. In an American TV cop show parlance, she was about to bust this case wide open and that made her feel good.

"I've had worse", Morgan said, leaning more onto his left hand side trying to make himself more comfortable. It wasn't working.

"Have you?"

"Yes, but the night's not over yet. Unfortunately it's my experience no matter how bad things are, they can always get worse", Morgan said with a wry smile. He was trying to drag out the idle chitchat for as long as possible. It gave him more time to think. More time to get his story straight and plan his next move. He was wondering however, why they were all sitting there, pretending to be polite. Why hadn't she called for backup? Why wasn't he already in handcuffs face down on the floor with a knee in his back? What was her game?

"Want to tell me what has happened so far?" Callaghan said watching the women's reactions closely. Sinead was obviously in a panic and doing her best to hold it together, while her mother sat beside her, holding her hand tightly, trying to give her daughter strength and support while looking very composed.

Morgan in turn looked at the two other women in the room before replying. "I got mugged".

"Mugged? A big guy like you?" Callaghan knew he was lying but she played along. "Seems unlikely. Did you report it?"

"No I didn't get a chance yet. I hadn't decided if I was going to at all. It was embarrassing. That's why I don't want it spread around. Professional pride, you understand."

"It's a bit of a coincidence then that you're ex-boss Smith was found dead earlier tonight after apparently falling on some scaffolding in a building site across from his house. A man matching your description was apparently seen in the area. And then you turn up like you have been in a train wreck. Can you explain that?"

"No. I can't. Smith's dead you say? That's terrible news," Morgan said unconvincingly feigning sympathy.

"Don't play fucking games with me", Callaghan suddenly spat back at him, as she was already tired of the game. "Look at the state of you. There must be more than enough physical evidence on you to tie you to Smith. And we will surely also be able to tie you to the scene and then you will be charged with his murder".

Morgan was worried. It was not that he could not stand up to her questioning. If he wanted to he could have kept quiet about tonight until his deathbed, it was just that he did not have time to be dealing with this right now. He still needed to make that all-important phone call to Johnson and arrange to give him back his drugs before the deadline ran out at midnight. Morgan ran through his options. And as he did not really have any, it did not take long. Bar somehow knocking Callaghan out and slipping off into the darkness to make the drop, there was only one other way to get her on his side. And that would be no small order. It was time to take a calculated risk.

"Okay. You want to know what happened?" he said watching the other women's faces for their permission to tell her. Both women looked horrified at him as if he was about to betray them.

Was he about to sell them out to protect himself? You could have cut the tension with a knife.

"Yes, I do", Callaghan said triumphantly, thinking that she had broken Morgan down. That didn't take long.

And with that Morgan recounted everything that had happened over the last forty-eight hours since Sinead had first reported the threat. He covered everything from searching the different possible hiding places for the drugs, going to Rob's place of employment, his old industrial unit, the photo of the biker and up to the part about going to the bank to confront Fitzpatrick. He included everything. Well, everything except Robs affair with Helen. Occasionally as he spoke, he would turn to look at Sinead or Pauline as their names were mentioned, to watch the horrified expressions on their faces. From time to time Callaghan occasionally interrupted him to ask a question, or to get clarification about something he had said.

"You say that you have been in regular contact with Johnson and that you are planning to meet him tonight," Callaghan said. "Yet my sources tell me that he has already fled the country. How does that tally?"

"Well, your sources are either wrong or lying. I have his number in my phone and I have to meet him by twelve midnight tonight to hand over the drugs or he will harm Sinead and the children," Morgan answered. "And just remember that we wouldn't be in this position if you and your boss had listened to us when we came looking for help. Your collective inaction has forced us to go down this road."

But Callaghan wasn't listening to him as she was thinking about the ramifications of this new information. So Rob was holding the drugs after all. Smith who was broke and needed the drugs to sell had killed him. But there was more, a lot more. What had happened to Smith for a start? "You have certainly been through a lot but none of what you have said entitles you or anyone else to take the law into your own hands. But let's hear the rest, so go on".

Morgan continued to tell Callaghan the events of the night. He told her as much as he could, including what had happened up at Smith's. Well nearly everything. He left out Sinead's sordid involvement in it all. He did not know why he did not come out and just tell Callaghan that part. It would have been so easy. He could have just stood up, point at Sinead and shout, "She did it! She planned to steal from her husband. She was instrumental in his death". After all she deserved everything that she got, but Pauline had been right. If Sinead were put into prison, the children would be put into care. And he could not let that happen. Especially Linda. He couldn't see her being put into a special home. It would be tantamount to killing her. Whatever else he had done in his chequered past, Rob had loved those children and he would hate to see them end up separated in some home.

Morgan knew that he was taking a calculated risk cherry picking the information that he was telling Callaghan. Most of it could incriminate him and result in him being asked some very difficult questions but as far as he knew Smith was the only other person who knew of Sinead's involvement and he was pretty sure that he wasn't going to be telling anybody. Not without holding a séance to communicate with him anyway.

Morgan also left out the part with the gun. Callaghan probably knew about the gun because of the gunshots up at Smith's but she didn't know it was his. It could easily have been Smith's gun, lost in the honeycomb of the apartment block. If Callaghan had known he still had it, he was sure that she would have demanded him to hand it over immediately. It was evidence after all but he could not let her take it from him. He would need it later tonight when he did the exchange. That was, if there was to be a later tonight. He still had to talk Callaghan into letting him go, to complete the handover. But this bit seemed to be the easy part as Callaghan got very excited when Morgan told her what Smith had intended to do with the stolen drugs. She was practically bouncing in the big soft chair with excitement. This was getting better and better as far as she was concerned.

"Let me get this straight. You say that Smith stole the drugs from O'Dwyer and intended to sell them to a new Polish gang that has recently moved into the area. Were they the gang that killed Murray?"

"I don't know for sure," Morgan said. "That's what he said but I don't know who they are or anything else about them. We started arguing and fighting and that's when he brought out a gun. At that point I just tried to get out of there. He chased me through the building site before he fell. I tried to save him but I couldn't lift his body off the pole. I know that I should have called the Gardaí immediately but I panicked. Well there you have it".

This information clearly struck a cord with her, but she did not comment on it further. This could be an opportunity for him.

Now, that the questioning phase had ended, Callaghan stood up and held out her arm indicating that he should follow her, "Ok. Come on, I think we need to finish this down at the station".

Morgan looked at her closely. She had always come across as a right ambitious bitch. He imagined that she would do anything to further her career. To climb up that male dominated ladder. He hoped that she would play to type. He had only one shot at this.

"Not yet. Let's make a deal," he said.

Callaghan looked at him sceptically. "What sort of deal? You have nothing to offer me. Now come on. Let's go".

"Look. You have me", Morgan said, putting his hands in the air as if surrendering. "You might or might not get me on manslaughter charges for Smiths death. But if you let me go ahead with the drop tonight, you can arrange to capture a major drug importer that has evaded everyone else. Not only that, you'll catch him in the act of extortion and in possession of a significant amount of drugs. You might even get to prove a connection with this new Polish crew and stop them before they even get started. Now think of all those lovely Garda brownie points you will get. You can't lose."

"Yeah right. As soon as I let you go, you will skip out on me. No chance, you're coming with me." But Callaghan did not say it with any conviction. Morgan knew that she could still be convinced. He just needed to push her that little bit further. Give her some assurances to calm her nerves. But she was almost there.

"You still have me to arrest but I can't go anywhere with you now. I can't leave Rob's children high and dry. He was my friend and I made a promise to him. I won't do it. It's not in me", he said with as much sincerity as he could muster.

"Please, you have to let him finish this. For my children's sake", Sinead interrupted. She stood pleading.

Callaghan looked at her then back at Morgan. "I must be mad to be even considering this. Tell me where you're planning to meet him and we'll go there and arrest him ourselves. You can stay at the station under arrest until it is all over. Then we decide what to do with you."

"No. I need to be there. He won't go through with it unless he sees me. I need to follow this through to the end. I want to see the look on his face as you lead him away. After all I have been through, I have to be there. I've earned it," Morgan answered determinedly.

"Well I don't trust you", Callaghan replied staring at him. And who could blame her, he thought. I wouldn't under the circumstances.

He felt that he was losing her; she was just not going along with this. But she had to. He had no other choice. He knew that he just had to keep working on her. "Look at this another way. I am the bronze prize in all this. If you play your cards right, you can get silver and gold. And you don't look like a woman who would settle for second best."

Callaghan sat silently for a few seconds as she thought. The entire room held its breath as they waited for her response. All their futures would depend on what her answer would be. Callaghan looked around the room at everybody in turn. Morgan, Sinead and Pauline. She saw the anxious desperate faces staring back at her.

"Okay," she said. "I don't believe that I am doing this. What is your plan?"

"I am going to contact Johnson and tell him to meet me at Rob's grave at twelve midnight." Morgan looked at his watch. It was just gone nine thirty. "That gives you over two hours to get ready. Set some sort of trap for them".

"I don't know if that gives me enough time." Callaghan said, biting her bottom lip uncharacteristically. First she would have to get DI Higgins approval for the operation and then there would be a lot to organise.

"Well it's all you have. I am meeting him at twelve. Now if you will all excuse me, I have a telephone call to make and then I am going to have a very hot shower."

Chapter Thirty-Six

Callaghan knew that if she made this exchange work, if she could handle it just right, that she would get an immediate promotion to full detective. But if she couldn't, then it would almost certainly be a serious blot on her career, maybe even the end of it. It was an all or nothing decision. What would she do? There was no doubt about it. Do it. She was ambitious and this would catapult her upwards. Failure was never an option for her. Nervously excited, she paced the room as Morgan made his phone call to Johnson.

After a loud and often heated discussion, the two men had agreed to meet at exactly midnight at Rob's graveside in Deansgrange Cemetery. A bit morbid, Callaghan had thought when Morgan had suggested it, but he had been adamant that that was the location. He wanted to do the exchange over Rob's grave. It seemed a bit melodramatic but who was she to complain? It had to end where it had all began. With the death of his friend.

The more Callaghan thought about it, the more she was impressed with how much Morgan had discovered in the last few days. He had tracked down his friend's killer, found the consignment of drugs, all things that her team had failed to do. And to top it all, now he was in a position to ensnare a dangerous criminal that was on the run. Not bad, not bad at all. Morgan was right, if this went down well, she would have led the way to solving at least one murder, foil a drug's deal and arresting the last remaining members of one of the more dangerous gangs in the city. And even though it had been handed to her, she could take all of the credit for it.

Once the meeting had been arranged, Callaghan left the living room and went into the privacy of the kitchen to make her own phone call. She tried to call DI Higgins again, but like earlier the call went straight to his voicemail. She left him another message, more urgent this time, to call her as soon as possible. Then she contacted the station to see if anyone knew where he was but she came up a blank there as well. That was strange she thought, Higgins had never been out of contact like this before. This put her in a very difficult position. She had taken a huge risk by giving Morgan the go ahead to meet Johnson. Something she hadn't the authority to do. But time had been against her and she had taken a chance, hoping to get approval from Higgins afterwards but now she couldn't reach him, she was in trouble. She had broken the command chain and she desperately needed to restore it to remain credible.

With no other real option, Callaghan took the business card from her pocket and looked at it carefully as she weighed up her options. If she rang this number she would be betraying the trust of the DI, circumventing him. But surely it wasn't her fault if he couldn't be reached? But much as she tried to convince herself, it was with some trepidation that she called the number on the card.

"Hi, is that DI Behan?" she asked enquiringly.

"Who is this?" came the somewhat out of breath reply. She got the impression that she was disturbing something. Was he out running?

"This is Callaghan. I am on the Murray and O'Dwyer murder investigation team. We spoke today and you gave me your card".

"Oh yes. Callaghan. What can I do for you?" he asked enthusiastically.

"Well, you said that I could call you if I needed any advice. Well, something has happened. Something big and I need a senior officer's opinion."

"Right. Hold on there a minute will you. I need to go somewhere more private".

Callaghan could hear him mumble something in the background and then a door closing.

"Okay, I'm back. What did you want my advice on?"

And with that she gave him a brief overview of what Morgan had told her, overstated her role just enough to make it sound plausible.

"And where are you now?" Behan enquired.

"I am still at Rob O'Dwyer's mother-in-law's house".

Why was she telling him this? he thought. Why not just arrest Morgan and get it over with. What else was there? "Why are you telling me this?"

Callaghan paused before continuing.

"I was thinking...I was thinking that we could use Morgan as bait. Let him meet Johnson as arranged and set up a sting opera-tion at the cemetery. We could arrest both him, Johnson and retrieve the drugs all in one go. Morgan is getting ready to make the drop now. But I need a senior officer's support to call in the ERU team and to sanction the operation".

"That's some ambitious plan. You are certainly risking a lot. There is a lot that could go wrong with it. What has DI Higgins said about it?"

"That's it you see. I have not told him yet. I tried to get him a few times with no luck".

"Ehm...."

"What?"

"Nothing, I was just thinking there for a second", and with that there was further silence on the end of the phone.

"It's okay. You have done the right thing," said Behan finally. "I will be able to get the Emergency Response Unit in place at the cemetery before the deal goes down. We'll get your dealers and you'll be the hero of the day".

"Oh thank you," Callaghan said, the relief in her voice was pal-pable.

"Okay. Meet me back at Harcourt Street Garda station in one hour and we will go through your plan. Where exactly in the cemetery are they meeting?"

"It is in Deansgrange Cemetery. It is a grave near the cemetery wall in the St. Mary's section of the cemetery. They are meeting there at midnight".

"St. Mary's section at midnight. That's great," said DI Behan. "But I advise you to keep trying to get your hands on Higgins".

"What about the DI? What do I tell him?" asked Callaghan.

"You must not tell him that you have had any contact with Morgan tonight. DI Higgins will insist upon you arresting him immediately. Just tell him, that you received a tip off from a woman about the drop off later on. She would not give her name. You did not recognise her voice either in case he asks. You tried to contact him and when you couldn't reach him you rang me instead."

"Why would someone give me a tip-off?"

"If you are like me back when I was starting out, you gave your Garda business card with your number on it to everyone you met," said Behan. "Somebody you gave it to must have had a sense of civic duty and called it."

"I'm not sure. He won't believe that".

"Keep to your story and he will have no choice but to believe it."

Callaghan made a noise meaning that she was still not convinced. Behan being gifted with this opportunity, was not going to let her back out now.

"Look, leave another message on his mobile voicemail asking him to call you urgently," he said. "But dial straight into his voicemail. It will look like you tried to contact him and for some reason, maybe bad reception, the call went straight to his message minder. Later I will try him as well and explain what is happening. I will put forward your story and back your plan."

"Okay. That sounds good. Talk to you in one hour".

Detective Callaghan hung up the phone looking worried. She was not sure what she was doing. Whatever way she looked at it, not arresting Morgan or calling the DI as soon as she had information on the drugs drop was going to seriously affect her career. But she felt more relaxed and assured of herself after talking to Behan. She just hoped that, if all this went down as she wanted it to, its success would overshadow her own deceit.

In his apartment overlooking the heart of the trendy and highly sought after area of Ballsbridge in South Dublin, DI Behan ran over the conversation with the young detective Garda once again in his head, to make sure that the idea he had midway through their conversation was plausible. He was sure that it was more than just plausible. It was inspired. He checked his watch. It read nine forty-five.

Just over two hours until midnight.

Two hours to put it all together.

So there were a few calls he had to make.

Chapter Thirty-Seven

The Shadowman stared at his mobile phone. The time monitor on the screen told him that the completed call had lasted less than three minutes, but they were three important minutes. The caller hadn't been one of his normal contacts or informants. In fact they were only calling him inadvertently. It just proved that you had to put yourself out there for people to contact you. He would have to buy the caller a drink except that would probably prompt more questions than he could answer. So they would have to go unrewarded. This didn't seem fair as the information supplied was worth its weight in gold.

He couldn't believe the intelligence that he had just received. It seemed that all of the uncertainty that had started with the gangland killing of Murray two weeks ago was coming to a head. Tonight. And in a matter of hours in fact. If he was going to do anything to influence matters, he would have to do it quickly. But what? He was still trying to come to terms with its various implications. It seemed to put most of the players in this charade in the same place at the same time. That was a good thing. The bad part of it was that the Gardaí would be there as well. If they arrested the various conspirators alive then that would be a bad thing. Things would unravel quickly and his position would be compromised.

If he did nothing, he had no doubt that Johnson would be arrested, questioned and broken. The weak willed bastard would open up and reveal the workings of the whole operation in return for some sort of immunity. His confessions would destroy what was left of the Irish operation before he had a chance to rebuild it. He should have killed him the first moment he saw him coming out of the bookies. If everyone ended up getting arrested, the missing drugs would surely be confiscated as well, although that would be the least of his problems. He needed a plan. Something to get the key characters killed rather than arrested. To get rid of any witnesses, to break the chain of evidence, he needed to put something in the mix to ensure a bloody conclusion. As he sat there thinking, a wry smile crossed his face. His plan quickly began to formulate. It was all going to be too easy, he thought.

First he had a couple of calls to make, the first one being the easiest. It was to Johnson, confirming the time and place of the rendezvous. Johnson had been very surprised that he knew about the drop so shortly after it had been arranged. With smug satisfaction, the Shadowman told him that it was his job to know these things, which was the main reason never to try and double cross him. Although he had no way of knowing it was true, Johnson told him that Morgan had a gun and was planning on ambushing him. Johnson was to come armed and finish him off. He should bring that fucking idiot sidekick of his along with him as backup to make sure he got the job done. But remember, that the offer of exile to Spain did not include him, so the best thing to do would be to kill him as well and make it look like the two men killed each other. That should confuse things for the Gardaí on the ground for a while.

The next call he made was a much more difficult one. It was to the Wolf himself. He had discovered his mobile number a few months earlier through the surveillance he had put on him. It had taken a while and cost him a lot in time, effort and money to come up with it. Once he had acquired it he had stored it in his mobile phone as the number of the local Four Star Pizza branch, thinking it might come in handy to have it close at hand.

And how right he was.

Unsurprisingly the telephone conversation went badly at first. The Wolf was deeply suspicious about how this stranger had managed to get his number. The Shadowman started off trying to be vague about his identity but quickly realised that this approach was not working. He then switched to being belligerent and aggressive, which resulted in both men trying to shout each other down.

At this point in the conversation, the Shadowman challenged the Wolf to meet him later that night at O'Dwyer's grave in Deansgrange cemetery. They would sort out the rivalry between the competing gangs once and for all. To antagonise him into making the response that he wanted he kept calling the Wolf a Nieślubny (bastard) and a Tchórz (coward), saying that he was too scared to turn up to face him. The Wolf was suitably incensed by these insults and throwing away all of his usual caution, promised to be there at midnight and to kill everyone in sight for these insults. Who the fuck did the caller think he was? If the Wolf ever found out who he was, he would make it a point to reserve some quiet time for just the two of them where he would teach him the meaning of respect. Feigning anger, the Shadowman hung up his mobile a very happy man. It was all going perfectly to plan. With any luck they would slaughter each other before the Emergency Response Unit even got there. If not, he was sure that the Polish gang boss would refuse to go to prison. He would stand and fight. With any luck there would be no survivors.

Including Morgan.

The Shadowman was going to make a final call to his former drug dealing boss and mentor with an update but decided to leave it until the next day when he knew he would be able to give him good news.

But there was a lot to be done before then.

Chapter Thirty-Eight

DI Behan hung up his call to Callaghan and immediately placed a call to the Harcourt Street Garda station, located in the heart of Dublin City. This was the operational base in Dublin of the Emergency Response Unit, the Irish version of America's SWAT team. Behan reasoned that Morgan meeting up with a well-known dangerous criminal like Johnson wasn't a matter that could be handled by the local unarmed Gardaí. This was a meeting that could potentially turn bloody and he needed properly equipped Gardaí on the scene. Once connected to the switchboard, he gave his name and rank and asked to speak to the ERU Detective Inspector on Duty.

After a few moments delay, he was put through to DI Kennedy, a detective inspector of long standing who was nearing retirement age. Callaghan had had a lot of dealings with him over the past few years. In Behan's opinion he was a cornerstone of the Garda ERU team, he was always ready to do his duty, fearless in speaking up in defence of his men and critical of anything that hampered his team's effectiveness. He had initially joined the Garda straight from leaving the Irish Army and was one of the first members of the force to be transferred to the newly formed Special Detective Unit back in 1978. This special unit was renamed the Emergency Response Unit in 1987. Over the years, DI Kennedy had been instrumental in getting funding increases for proper training both at home and abroad. Regardless of modern protocols and procedures, he was old school.

Shoot first and ask questions later.

Which was probably a condition of his early army training and the effect on him of his stint in the Lebanon back in the seventies, this gung-ho and uncompromising attitude had kept a Garda of his years and experience at the relatively low rank of DI. Behan gave Kennedy a brief overview and history of the operation to date, the meeting that was to take place and the value of the consignment of drugs being exchanged. His details then became a little sketchy. Something that he knew Kennedy hated. He always wanted as much information as possible. He hated the unknown. It was risky and led to people getting hurt. Behan knew that Morgan was meeting Johnson but how many men Johnson would have with him he didn't know. He also didn't know if there was going to be anybody else at the drop off.

But he was sure that at least one of the gangs attending tonight would contain a man wanted in connection with a recent murder.

Behan then gave the time and location. DI Kennedy took some notes and promised to put a call into the Detective Chief Superintendent for approval. He would then put a plan together and call a briefing for eleven pm in ERU headquarters. Thanking him for his time and quick response, Behan hung up satisfied that Callaghan's gamble was getting the support that it required.

His next telephone call was to DI Higgins, who it turns out was out with his wife celebrating their twenty-fifth wedding anniversary. The DI was understandably very annoyed when he got this call. What did he mean that Detective Callaghan had received a case-breaking tip-off and not informed him? What message? He never got a message. Callaghan had said that she tried to get through to him but only got his message minder, Behan said. She had left messages for him to call her urgently. Failing to reach you, she had then called him, as a senior Garda for advice. Behan could imagine the DI sitting there in some fancy restaurant, incandescent with rage and smiled to himself. Ignoring the DI's rant, he informed him that there was to be an impromptu briefing at the Harcourt Street Garda station at eleven pm to put a tactical plan into place. If he could attend, it would be appreciated.

Behan found, he had some empathy with Callaghan, as she was going behind her superiors back, supporting her own agenda, like he had done so many times himself. It wasn't easy rising to the rank of Detective Inspector. You ended up burning a lot of people as you climbed up the official ladder. God knows he had. And he would use anyone that he could to forward his career. No one was exempt. No one.

Chapter Thirty-Nine

While this series of phone calls was taking place, Morgan stood in the shower, his head leaning against the tiled wall in front of him. His eyes were closed and he was letting the piping hot water cascade over his shoulders and down onto his back. All of his body ached, every muscle, every tendon. The hot water was finding every cut and graze on his body, momentarily sending stinging pain shooting along every nerve ending. He felt completely exhausted and he wasn't sure he would be up to it later. The hot water was relaxing his tense muscles to such an extent that if he did not have to do the handover tonight, he would have gladly crawled into his bed and refused to come out for a month.

But unlike his tired body, Morgan's mind would not relax. It was still operating at a hundred miles an hour. Thinking. Scheming. Worrying. Reliving the fight with Smith over and over again. What he did and what he should have done. Should he have gone there at all? Should he have gone behind Sinead's back and simply told the Gardaí? Should he have waited for the Gardaí at the building site? Given himself up right there and then? It would only be over the course of the coming days that he would get these answers. In the meantime, the tension was killing him and it was not over yet. Not by a long shot.

It had all become too much for him and Morgan didn't realise it at first, maybe it was because of the water pouring down from the shower head but he found himself crying. They were gentle tears at first which crept out from the corners of his eyes growing into a torrent from deep inside of him. The salty tears were streaming down his face only to be washed away by the showers moments later. His body convulsed as the anguish of events of the last few hours rushed out of him. While he tried to control his crying, he simply couldn't. All he could see were images of Smiths body impaled on a metal pole. As the water washed down his body, he kept thinking about Smith as he lay dying impaled on a scaffolding pole. He shook his head in despair. He had never thought it would come to anything like this. These were memories that would haunt him until the day he died. As he sobbed uncontrollably, his knees gave way and he sank to bottom of the shower with his head in his hands where he stayed unable to get up, water crashing down on him till he could cry no longer.

Twenty minutes later after he had regained some semblance of self-control, he dressed himself and tried to figure out what exactly he was going to do next. He was also trying to figure out the huge implications of admitting to a member of the Gardaí his part in Smith's death. And a Garda who didn't like him, no less. It had been a risky strategy to take but he had to take it if he was going to get the chance to finish what he started. He was not sure why he was even going through with it now. After all, Sinead certainly did not deserve his help. After what she told him, she deserved everything but his help. She was at best a naïve fool and a user, at worst a murderer. She had made a fool of him and made him complicit in events that he would have normally run a mile from. But maybe it was the obligation to Rob's memory or the promise that he had made to look after his family if something happened that kept him here. Right or wrong he was in too deep and he wanted to see the thing through to the bitter end.

He was not a quitter, never had been and never would be.

But he could not get over what an idiot he had been. Maybe it could have been the momentum of the situation, the tight time limit hanging over them all but he realised now that he had rushed to Smith's house without thinking things fully through. A confrontation had been inevitable. He should have known that and he wished that he had been more prepared for it when it had come. Smith hadn't needed to die. And now because of his actions, he was in an even bigger mess than to begin with.

He looked at his watch. It said ten forty. He had an hour and twenty minutes till his rendezvous with Johnson and he had to come up with a plan quickly. Morgan tried to get his mind away from the events earlier in the night for a few minutes at least and try to come up with some sort of plan for later but he found it too hard to concentrate. A few days ago, he had a pretty carefree life. No particular stress at all. But now was not the time to dwell on things he had no power over. He still had a job to do, a handover to complete. Come on think properly, he railed at himself. But it was no good. His attention span was gone.

He realised that he needed a plan not just for getting the drugs back, but also for keeping himself out of prison for his part in Smith's death. But while he felt he could recover the drugs he knew deep down that he was only kidding himself about keeping his involvement with Smiths death quiet. He had probably left a lot of evidence at the scene that would make all of his efforts wasted.

Despite his earlier admission to Callaghan, he had decided that he was simply going to deny any and all involvement in Smiths death. As far as his confession to Callaghan was concerned, he would simply deny he ever said anything. He didn't do it. He didn't even know that Smith was dead till Callaghan approached him. He knew that both Sinead and Pauline would back him up in his denial and provide him with an alibi. But Callaghan was right, there was probably plenty of physical evidence on both Smith and himself to tie him to Smith's house that night. But what if there wasn't? By Callaghan letting him shower and then putting on some of Sinead's father's clothes that were, according to Pauline, still left in a few black bags up in the attic, he hoped that Callaghan had made a huge mistake.

Earlier that night, he had asked Pauline for two favours. First he had given her the keys to his car and asked her to collect it from Smith's housing estate as soon as possible. She should be all right to collect it and drive it back to her house, as the attention of the Gardaí would be focused on the cemetery. He then told Pauline to dispose of his old clothes in the fire as soon as Callaghan left. He did not know if it would be any good changing his clothes but he hoped that along with showering it would remove all trace evidence connecting him to the Smiths death that night.

Maybe even Callaghan would play along with it to save the embarrassment of having to admit to letting this evidence be destroyed. But he did not think destroying the clothes that he had been wearing could hurt. Either way he prayed that before the night was over something might turn up to get him off the hook.

"Come on now Morgan. Think, think," Morgan said out loud this time, while shaking his head as if he was trying to shake the awful memories away and re-focus on the here and now.

First, he had to be practical. So he found himself thinking back to Rob's funeral four days previously. As his own father was buried in Deansgrange, he was pretty familiar with the cemetery's set up. But he had never been there at night before so he went over in his head the location of Rob's grave in the cemetery. What was the best way in? How far into the cemetery, was the grave? What cover was there for him? Satisfied he had a reasonable mental image of the location, he now turned his intention to Johnson himself.

Having never met Johnson, Morgan had no idea what he looked like. From the sound of his voice though, he pictured a large overweight man with the typical bald head. Morgan's prejudices and stereotyping imagined him wearing a tracksuit and adorned with lots of gold. Not that he was dismissing Johnson as some weak stereotypical character, but he wasn't afraid of him either. He wasn't afraid of any man enough to stop himself from doing what needed to be done. His actions earlier that night and on previous occasions were proof of that. But it would serve no purpose to underestimate Johnson either.

Judging by their many telephone conversations, Johnson sounded like a right hard bastard or at least he talked a good game. Their most recent telephone conversation, some twenty minutes previously had been brief. When Morgan confirmed that he had the drugs, the rendezvous time and location, a delighted Johnson had held off threatening him this time. He probably did not want to scare Morgan away at the last moment or was just happy to be getting his drugs back. Either way Morgan would find out soon enough. He would have to leave soon if he wanted to get there early.

What worried Morgan most about the impending rendezvous was that Johnson might bring other men with him for backup. He had no way of knowing if he would or not, but he had to assume that he would. Morgan also had to suspect that Johnson would come armed. So he had to be careful and that was where the gun came in. He knew that Callaghan was going to organise armed Gardaí to swoop after the drop-off but he needed to make sure Johnson was caught and questioned. That was the main reason that Morgan had allowed Callaghan in on his plans, to have her arrest Johnson. If he was to have any chance of escaping a prison sentence, he needed Johnson to confess to the harassment of Sinead and her family, which would in turn somewhat justify his own actions over the last few days.

But what was Callaghan's motivation in this? He was stunned when she agreed to go along with the handover. Why was she taking such a chance with him? Why didn't she just arrest him? Put him in handcuffs, read him his rights and lead him away like they do on the television. She had her own game but Morgan didn't have time to worry about her, as he wasn't comfortable with his plan yet. It was far too rough, far too many unknowns. Even for one of his.

Morgan figured that he would turn up at the cemetery at least a half hour early and scout out his planned hiding space properly. He would leave the drugs in an obvious place at the graveside, high enough so that it could be seen from a distance. Morgan hoped that this would act as a lure to Johnson and anyone that he brought with him out into the open. He in turn would hide at a distance until he was sure that Johnson hadn't set a trap for him, Morgan would pounce on Johnson and hold him until the posse in the form of Callaghan and the other Gardaí turned up to lead him away. It sounded so simple. But so had his plan to confront Smith and look how that turned out.

Satisfied that he now had the bare bones of a workable plan, Morgan turned the temperature gauge on the shower up another notch. Little did he know, that events elsewhere had passed him by, making his plans pointless.

Chapter Forty

The Garda had a long tradition dating back to the foundation of the State, which saw the majority of them armed only with batons and more recently pepper spray. While detectives of the Special Detective Unit were currently armed, it was the new specialist sub-division of the SDU that Behan knew he needed to call in for an operation like this. The Emergency Response Unit was a secretive unit comprising nearly fifty highly trained men and women to provide tactical back up for frontline Garda.

DI Behan was always more than a little impressed by the Emergency Response Unit's briefing room every time he visited it. The room was of ultra-modern design and fitted out with state of the art equipment, all in stark contrast to the spare room that the Murray and O'Dwyer murder investigation was currently working out of. Just to get access was no mean feat, as security for the select team, was extremely tight Missions were organised here that would affect criminal gangs and paramilitary organisations all over the country. These subversives would give their eye-teeth to know what was going on in there or to carry out revenge attacks after an operation. Entry inside their unit was a privilege, not a right.

As he made his way through the normal Garda station, Behan by-passed the large administration section in the floors above it, by using the private secure lift set aside for discrete movement of ERU staff. All in all, Behan had to come through three sets of locked and guarded barriers. At each door, his Garda ID was checked by an armed member of the force, before being scanned in. According to DI Kennedy, who always seemed to enjoy showing off about the security in place in the building, panic buttons were located at every doorway, that once pressed would lockdown the entire building, preventing anyone getting any deeper into the building if there was a breach in security. The walls were shielded to prevent eavesdropping with equipment currently being used by criminal gangs. What was said in this room, stayed in this room, he would say proudly.

Inside the briefing room each officer had his own powerful computer. Where Behan was used to looking at an old blackboard, peppered with thumbtack pinholes, here there was an array of big flat screen televisions hung on the walls linked to the computers. Everything seemed so shiny and high tech compared to what he was used to. To improve the teams efficiency it even had its own dedicated in-house crime scene technical unit on standby twenty-four hours a day to support them. They had immediate and direct access to the most modern state of the art finger print matching, called AFIS and facial recognition systems which used biometric technologies from photographs and video recordings. Resources that other divisions of the force could have only dreamt about.

Unknown to even senior Gardaí outside of the unit, they also had a direct link to the more senior government departments in the State including a special direct link to the planning offices in each county, giving them real time access to the plans for every building and public area in the country. It gave them everything that they needed to enable them to make quick and tactical deci-sions. Seeing the look on Behan's face as he looked around the room, Kennedy took the opportunity to brag about how these computers were not directly linked to the main Gardaí central computer but instead linked through heavily protected sub servers located in a secure building a mile away. Security firewall after fire-wall after firewall made hacking a near impossibility.

The unit on duty were already assembled by the time Behan arrived. Normally the entire unit was composed of forty Gardaí and eight sergeants and the DI commanding them. They were then broken up into four smaller groups of ten Gardaí and two ser-geants, working in twelve-hour shifts. However due to operating constraints caused by them permanently placing a number of members on secondment in the troubled hotspots of Limerick city, they were currently operating smaller units. Number three unit was currently operating with only six men and one sergeant. Each man on the team was extensively trained abroad in a special-ist school, the core content of which was firearms training. DI Kennedy judged that a single team would be more than enough to arrest one or two gang members and the one member of the public whom they expected to be dealing with.

After brief introductions, DI Kennedy began in a very business like manner.

"Okay, I have been informed that in approximately fifty minutes a number of men will be meeting a member of the public to take possession of a substantial amount of cocaine. So that does not give us much time to prepare."

With that he pressed a few buttons on his laptop and the screens on the wall behind him lit up with schematics of the cemetery and pictures of the main suspects. DI Behan gave the room a brief biopic of the two men on the screen, including Morgan's run in with the German Neo-Nazis the previous year before handing back over to DI Kennedy for the tactical part of the briefing.

"Right then," Kennedy said, pointing to a large multi coloured map. "This is Deansgrange Cemetery. Each coloured area denotes a different burial plot. We are looking for St. Mary's, denoted here in green. Morgan and Johnson's group are making contact at a particular grave in this area. It is the grave of Rob O'Dwyer, who was murdered only a few days ago by one of the gang members. We are not sure exactly where the grave is situated yet but are trying to find that out". Pointing to the screen, he continued, "My plan is to split you into three sets of two men. Each set will approach the target area from a different direction, effectively boxing all our suspects in the middle."

Murmurs of approval echoed through the room. It all made sense to them. It seemed like nothing that they hadn't done and trained for before.

"Six men will go in over the wall along the main road here. They will then split up. The first two-man team will proceed straight up along this path and turn right into the designated area. The second team will go over the wall further down the road near the funeral gate, then go north along the wall and turn left at the top approaching the St. Mary's area from the other side. The last team will scale the back wall here at this park area and approach from the north."

Pausing so that each man could run through the approach Kennedy said. "Now remember that DI Behan here will operate as scene commander. This is his operation. Because of the time constraints we will have no time to do anything but the most basic of reconnaissance. We will be going in largely blind so everybody must be on their toes, maintain radio contact and keep an eye out for each other."

The team collectively shrugged off the danger with an air of indifference. They always operated in difficult and risky situations under the leadership of an outside officer. But it was Kennedy's plans that they followed and his plans always worked, he always thought of everything so they were not concerned.

"The Garda helicopter will also be despatched but I have requested that it keeps its search light off and remain at a height where it will not be heard until called for. When called upon, it will use its large light to illuminate the area and help with the arrests or searches as necessary."

"It is still a pretty large area for us to cover," said the Unit's sergeant thinking out loud as he looked at the map on the screen.

"It is. In the event of any of the suspects fleeing and managing to avoid detection in the target area, I have asked that the dog unit from Kilmainham Garda Station also be in attendance to help in conducting a search. Any questions?" asked DI Kennedy.

"How are we going to get the dogs in? Lift them over the wall?" laughed one of the Gardaí. The rest of the unit joined in. DI Behan looked at them. Confident, relaxed, assured of their abilities and those of their commanders.

"Very funny," said the DI, waving his hands up and down to get them to settle down. "We are currently trying to get somebody from the council out of their beds or off a barstool or wherever they are, to get keys for the main gates".

This of course caused more laughter. The room got quite boisterous as the adrenalin started to pump and the men joked crudely amongst themselves.

"Okay, settle down. All the main roads around the cemetery will be sealed off to stop passers by getting caught up in any potential gunfight in case things go badly wrong. And finally as it is the nature of these men to carry firearms and that there is a probability that fire could be exchanged when we move in, two ambulances will also be on standby on a side street in case they are required. Any further questions?" Kennedy asked but nobody said anything. They had their mission and there was a lot of work to do and very little time to do it. They were ready to go.

"Okay, as time is of the essence," finished Kennedy. "Sergeant Logan will select two of you to go straight to the cemetery and make a preliminary check on the area. Keep a low profile and there is to be no contact until the rest of the team arrives. Right, let's go."

Chapter Forty-One

Deansgrange Cemetery is one of the oldest cemeteries still in use in Dublin city. It is located in the more affluent south side of the city and was opened initially back in 1865. At thirty-five acres it is also one of the largest in the country. It is comprised of four-teen different plots named after various saints along with the large original cemetery development broken into another four sections designated north, south, west and south west. These older larger rambling tree covered sections surround the original gate lodge, encompassing the Catholic and Protestant chapels. While the older parts are not as accessible, the new plots have been designed in long narrow rows stretching out until they reach the wider access roads which wind through the plots designed to allow hearses greater access.

Morgan had once read that it was the last resting place of over one hundred and sixty five thousand souls and still counting. It had received the remains of many famous men and women over the years and more recently one deeply flawed friend. His father who died when Morgan was much younger was also buried there. But not near Rob. His father was further up behind the trees, in one of the slightly older sections called St. Brigid's.

It was a well-known location for Dubliners as most people liv-ing on the south side of the city had an older relative or some member of their family buried there. Morgan knew the place well. Not only was his father buried there, but also both sets of grand-parents. Morgan's father had committed suicide nearly ten years previously after a business deal had gone wrong and he had lost his business, a business that he had taken all of his working life to build. Morgan, his sister and their mother had all come here reli-giously for years afterwards. Although both his and his sister's visits had petered out to a single visit on their father's birthday, their numerous earlier visits had meant that Morgan had learnt the layout very well.

A knowledge born of sadness, but that he was going to make the most of now.

The cemetery layout was roughly that of a large square, sloping gently upwards away from the main road. A tall wall surrounded it, ten feet high with a two-foot high metal fence with six inch spikes on top of it. There are three entrances, all of which are located along the same stretch of road. The first is the original main gate, which leads up a short but wide central avenue, passing by the original caretaker's home and offices, up to two small churches, one Catholic, the other Church of Ireland, before melting into the various plots that make up the vast cemetery.

The second gate, located approximately half way along the outer wall was a high pedestrian turnstile gate that only revolved one way so that visitors or grieving relatives could get out if accidentally locked in late at night. Metal bars were extended at head height to stop people re-entering this way. It was a simple yet effective security method.

The third and last gate at the far end of the main road was an additional double gate put in mid-way through the last century to make access easier for hearses in the expanding cemetery. It was unimaginatively called the "funeral gate".

With his car parked in the street behind Smith's place, Morgan had to borrow Sinead's ten-year-old Renault Scenic to get to the drop off point. It had taken him longer to get to the cemetery than expected as the underpowered engine struggled to move the large MPV's body. He parked the family car across the road from the pedestrian entrance mid-way along the boundary wall, turned off his lights and looked around to see if there were any watchers. The streetlights and the bright moon that night made it easy to see in both directions, but the long straight road seemed completely deserted. There was no sign of either Johnson or the Garda yet but as it was only half past eleven Morgan still had plenty of time before the twelve midnight deadline. So just to be sure, Morgan sat there for another five minutes. Watching and waiting to make sure another car did not pull up and off-load passengers before exiting his car.

Finally deciding that it was safe to leave the car, he got out and hung the heavy bag containing the drugs over his shoulder, put the gun deep into his jacket pocket and crossed the road. With one final scan of his surroundings, Morgan grabbed hold of the bars of the turnstile and not without some pain and discomfort climbed up using them like a ladder, dragging the heavy bag up with him. He reached the top, paused to catch his breath and swung his leg and the bag over and climbed back down.

Morgan walked along the path directly in front of him, clutching his aching ribs as he went towards the rear of the cemetery and Rob's grave. The left side of the path was a wooded area and was one of the oldest sections of the cemetery. It went all of the way back southwards towards the main gate. In the bright moonlight, Morgan could see the white headstones between the trees and the occasional low square shaped mausoleum. His parents had joked with both him and his sister, when they were younger that there were all sorts of ghosts, mummies and zombies wandering around in there, waiting to get them if they should wander in. Things like that stayed with you. Now, Morgan's nerves were so on edge that he would not have been too surprised to see a ghost float out in front of him. It had scared him then and it was more than a bit creepy now. Even at this hour birds fluttered eerily through the trees, kept awake in the moonlight, Morgan thought.

He hoped.

On his right hand side, the cemetery design was more of an open plan. He could see row after row, section after section, of headstones disappearing into the darkness for nearly as far as the eye could see. They were of every size and shape. Most were single family plots but some were large multiple graves reserved for members of the clergy or in one case a plot for men who had fallen in the Easter Rising of 1916. There were crosses, both traditional and Celtic pointing up into the sky and a large number of statues carved in the shapes of saints. Their changing shadows kept tricking Morgan into thinking that they were people standing there.

He walked for another few minutes before turning right towards St. Mary's plot and found Rob's grave immediately. He stopped about twenty metres from it and crouched down. He took his time to look around and check for any watchers but he was sure he was alone.

Alone with the dead.

Morgan continued cautiously over to Rob's grave. The grave itself stood out from the others around it as it was still piled high with flowers and wreaths. The large yellow flowered DAD wreath took pride of place at the front, its flowers starting to die. Despite the risk of staying out in the open for too long, Morgan took a moment to himself and stood solemnly beside Rob's grave, exhausted he leant on the neighbouring grave's marble headstone for support. The cold in the stone ran through his hand and up his arm. But he did not take his hand away. He didn't want to let go because seeing Rob's grave made him feel numb inside but touching the cold stone was like a challenge to him. To hold on no matter how cold it went. To do what had to be done, no matter how far he had to go.

"You certainly left an awful mess behind you," Morgan said to the pile of wreath covered earth.

"I need you to look after them for me..." he imagined Rob replying.

"I am doing my best," Morgan replied. But Rob did not answer. And he never would.

After another look around, Morgan placed the bag containing the drugs onto the top of the cold headstone where it would be most noticeable and stepped back on to the narrow path. Now where exactly to lay his trap?

He surveyed his surroundings. Right where he thought it was, about seventy-five metres away to the north, there was a squat workman's compound. From where Morgan was standing, he could just make out the top of the JCB above its surrounding wall which itself was obscured by large bushes and shrubs. There also seemed to be some sort of single story building, which he assumed housed tool sheds and a canteen for the men. Morgan figured that if he could get onto the roof of the shed, he would have a clear view of anyone approaching the grave. Much better than hiding behind a headstone a few meters away.

As he stood there, it suddenly occurred to him that Johnson or one of his flunkies could be watching him right now. Fearful of giving his plan away to any observers, he ran, bent over towards the shed where he found the gate locked by a heavy metal chain. The gate looked as if it had been hit by the JCB a number of times and as a result did not close properly. The chain secured the gate but there was enough of a gap to allow him to squeeze through and into a small courtyard behind.

Once inside, Morgan's luck appeared to be changing for the better as he noticed a ladder propped up against the building behind an overflowing skip. The cemetery maintenance staff must have been having problems with the water tank on the roof because even from the ground Morgan could see that somebody had put a sheet of timber over it and weighed it down with four concrete blocks. The ladder had been left against the wall, instead of locked up in a tool shed. Morgan climbed the ladder and crawled onto the roof and lay beside the water tank, hiding in its shadow.

Between the bright moonlit sky and his vantage point on top of the shed, Morgan had an excellent view. Apart from the occasional high shrub or tree, he could see all around him quite well. The rows of graves disappeared in straight lines going off into the distance with the interconnecting pathways criss-crossing like a concrete mesh. He could see all the way to the far wall and the houses beyond it. He was happy that Johnson would not be able to sneak up on him without him noticing. Once settled Morgan took the handgun out of his pocket, checked that the safety was off and laid it down on the roof close to his hand.

It wasn't long lying there before Morgan was freezing cold. The thin layer of frost that had covered the shed roof was starting to form over him as well. He was glad that he had worn extra layers of clothing including two pairs of socks and three heavy tops but it still wasn't enough. The cold air was penetrating the layers and causing his tired muscles to cramp. The longer he lay there the colder and more uncomfortable he was getting. He knew that he would be in trouble if he had to lie there much longer.

The eerie quiet of the cemetery was shattered by Morgan's mobile phone beeping loudly in his pocket, indicating that he had received a text message. "Fuck," he cursed as he noisily scrambled to get it out to shut it off before it told everyone within a mile exactly where he was. He fumbled it out of his pocket and hit the middle button. The noise cut short, he held his breath and looked around him to see if anybody had heard it and was running toward him. But luckily he could not hear or see any movement. So with some annoyance he read the message. It was from Callaghan's number and was short and to the point. "On way" it read. The text seemed so casual like a friend telling him that they were running late and would see him in the pub soon. Not on their way with armed policemen to help him catch a drug dealer. Nevertheless he breathed a sigh of relief. Good, maybe this will be over soon as the tension was killing him.

Before returning the phone to his pocket, he turned it to silent, just in case Callaghan tried to call or text him again at just the wrong moment. Although he was not sure what he was doing, Morgan checked over the gun one last time and laid it delicately onto the roof beside him. Its heavy weight felt very reassuring. Morgan checked the time on the luminous hands on his watch. They read eleven forty-five. Fifteen minutes to go till all hell was going to break loose.

The phrase 'time flies' did not apply to his situation Time seemed to stand still and Morgan was freezing cold and very uncomfortable waiting for it to pick up the pace. As he lay there watching the various paths leading up to Rob's grave, he couldn't help but notice the lights on in the back of the houses over the other side of the cemetery. Morgan imagined himself sitting there in a nice warm house cosying up in front of a blazing fire, watching television. It was a pleasant distraction and took his mind off the cramp he was getting in his right leg.

The cold made it hard to focus but as Morgan lay there getting colder and colder a depressing thought occurred to him. He had not needed to find the actual drugs themselves. All he ever needed to do was lure Johnson out in the open, with the promise of his drugs and get him arrested. He realised that the last few days had been a complete and total waste of time. The revelation made him squirm. A few days ago he had been faced with a family in crisis and had reacted accordingly. He had been left with no time to think. Only react. He knew in his heart that he had done the right thing at the right time for Sinead and the kids. But all he could do now was settle in and wait to see what happened next.

Chapter Forty-Two

Detective Inspector Behan walked out of the secure private elevator and down the small flight of stairs to the foyer of the Harcourt Street Garda station. He passed through the body scanners just as both DI Higgins and Garda Callaghan arrived at the main door, each from separate directions. DI Higgins was clearly angry at being left out of the loop earlier. As they met at the doors, he gave Callaghan a cutting look but said nothing to her as each opened one of the double doors and walked in together. All three Gardaí now stood facing each other. There was no public office in this Garda station but at this time of the night there were very few people around. The foyer was large and empty, the stillness seemed to echo around them with a hollow dull tone. There was tension in the air and an uneasy pause before the DI broke the silence.

"Can somebody please tell me what the hell is going on?" DI Higgins demanded looking from Behan to Callaghan and back again, barely keeping his composure. Despite the expensive suit that he was still wearing since rushing from the restaurant, he looked ragged and harassed, as though he had just got out of bed and rushed over there. "I have just heard about the death of Smith and then I hear that you are both planning a midnight raid on a cemetery of all places".

Behan fought back an inappropriate smile. He remembered when he was a young Garda starting out. He had had a real ball breaker of a detective sergeant as his superior. The detective sergeant had worked him the harder than all of the other young Gardaí. He would always belittle him in front of others, but Behan had shown him. He had surpassed all the recruits in his year. While DI Higgins seemed a much more level headed and pragmatic superior, Behan had an automatic reaction to get one over on anyone of a higher rank than him. He supposed he was just hardwired that way.

"As I explained on the phone earlier," Behan said. "Callaghan here received an anonymous telephone call earlier tonight informing her of an impending meeting between Morgan and Johnson. She was told that Morgan has found the drugs and is going to hand them over to Johnson".

"Are you telling me that all of our main suspects will be in one place tonight? Not only that, but they will have the missing drugs?" asked Higgins incredulously, "I should have been informed immediately".

"I tried to contact you. I left two messages on your phone to call me urgently. When I couldn't get you, I called the next senior officer assigned to the case. I can't see how you could say that I acted inappropriately," Callaghan said in her defence. She resisted the urge to look at Behan as she spoke.

"You should have tried to send me a message through the station switchboard or something. You knew that I was going out to dinner with my wife tonight," Higgins snapped, patently unhappy with her unsuccessful attempts. While he had received the call from DI Behan, it was only afterwards that he had accessed his voicemails and found the two unanswered messages from Callaghan. But Higgins was at a loss to figure out why he hadn't heard the phone ring in the first place. His phone had been on. It was always on. He never turned it off, not even when he had attended the births of his two children.

"I understand that you are upset, but remember that time was short and we had to do something. Callaghan deserves a pat on the back as this operation is only going ahead because of information supplied by her," Behan said defending her. "You have the makings of a great detective here, you should be very proud of her."

"Of course I am," Higgins replied through gritted teeth. "And what are the plans to arrest them?" he directed at Callaghan.

"Eh...." said Callaghan, unsure of what to say.

"I have organised the ERU to assist in the arrest...they are preparing to move out now", said Behan stepping in to support her once again.

"The briefing...?" Higgins asked, looking at his watch.

"Over. Sorry. You are both too late, I am afraid. We had very limited time to put this together and could not wait any longer," said DI Behan.

"Well, now that I am here, I will assume command of the operation," DI Higgins said a little bit too abruptly. He had nothing against DI Behan but the last thing he wanted was for Callaghan to steal the plaudits for a major bust on one of his cases after she had seemed to side step him so easily. From now on he wanted to limit her involvement in the operation as much as possible. She seemed to be playing at something, but what?

"But sir..." Callaghan began to object, this was her lead after all but before she could make her case she was interrupted when DI Kennedy came down the stairs followed noisily by the rest of the ERU team. The ERU team looked impressive. They had dropped the more casual branded baseball caps and t-shirts and instead wore their tactical outfits. The outfits were hi-tech full bullet proof suits and looked similar to black army uniforms complete with bullet proof vests, leg and arm protectors, helmets and side arms. DI Behan considered himself a man of the world, hardened by years of working as a Garda but he had to admit that these men looked very impressive. DI Higgins on seeing Kennedy arrive on the scene then decided that he should assume authority with the head of the ERU instead. A man whom he had known for years.

"Ah George," DI Higgins said, walking towards him, hand outstretched. The rest of the ERU unit filed past them noisily out of the front doors towards the waiting vehicles.

"Mick, it's been a long time since I've seen you. How are you?" DI Kennedy said warmly as he shook his hand. Callaghan threw her eyes up to heaven. The two men obviously knew each other very well, considering their similarity in age and rank, they probably joined the force at the same time and had become lifelong friends.

"Grand. Look George sorry I was late but where are we with this thing?" Higgins asked.

"I would have thought you would know. They are your officers after all".

"I am still catching up on developments," Higgins stammered awkwardly, too embarrassed to admit his lack of up to date knowledge of developments.

"Well, on information received from DI Behan and Garda Callaghan here, we are assisting them in apprehending members of a dangerous gang which we assume will be armed. They will be in the middle of a drugs hand over. In the middle of a cemetery, no less. DI Behan here is taking command as scene officer."

"Well I am here now and as senior ranking officer, I will take command"

"It does not work like that and you know that as well as I do," Kennedy said. He saw Behan moving over to join them, but he gave him a barely perceptible shake of his head to get him to stay where he was. He would deal with the DI's hurt ego.

"As DI heading up these murder operations, I insist that I take command", Higgins asserted.

"Mike, what's this? Do you want me to quote guidelines for you? DI Behan here has tactical responsibility. A senior ranking officer cannot assume primacy solely on the basis of rank or territorial responsibility, without being fully briefed and in knowledge of all the facts. Mike, Mike..." Kennedy said, opening his hands in a conciliatory fashion. "You are obviously not up to speed on either the background or the current action plan. And I don't have time to bring you up to speed. No offence, but I cannot risk my men being put into unnecessary risk by letting you lead them."

"But George...," Higgins started to say, but was cut off when DI Behan, who was listening intently, inadvertently coughed, the noise echoing around the empty area.

"I am sorry but this is Behan's show. Look, I have not got time to argue policy with you right now. In approximately..." said Kennedy as he paused to check his watch "... twenty five minutes, I have some armed men to arrest so if you will excuse me."

And with that he walked away from Higgins, leaving him fuming with his fists clenched in the foyer. Both Behan and Callaghan who had been listening took the opportunity to escape the DI's wrath and followed Kennedy out. As they walked down the few outside steps they saw the car belonging to the advance ERU team disappear out of the main gate, turn left and drive out of sight.

Chapter Forty-Three

At exactly eleven forty two, a large black 2001 left hand drive Audi A8 with tinted windows and chromed alloy wheels drove up quietly to the southern corner of the cemetery wall and stopped. Three bulky men in their early to mid-twenties all dressed in black hopped out. Standing close to the high cemetery wall they expertly checked each direction for any sign that they were being watched. The road was empty but there was noise coming from a popular bar at a busy crossroads about one hundred metres to their right. The lights were on but despite the smoking ban, there were no smokers desperate enough to brave the cold outside to get their nicotine fix. They gave another quick check in both directions. Nothing moved.

Their car pulled away from the kerb, its driver did a quick u-turn and sped back the way it had come, its brake lights flashing momentarily as it rounded the corner and headed up the hill towards Foxrock church. It stopped less than a mile away in one of the small exclusive leafy side streets, where it was out of the way yet still within close range of the men, ready to collect them quickly when their business was finished.

For a few seconds, the men were completely alone on the street. Once the three men were sure that their arrival had not been noticed, they climbed up onto a conveniently located post box and from there scaled the cemetery wall and railings. They dropped silently onto the ground on the other side and stayed in the shadows while they checked the area was clear. Once down, each man took out a black balaclava from their pockets. Once on, the balaclava's completely obscuring their faces. Now only their hard eyes were visible.

"Jesteśmy Wśrodku, we're in," Piasecki spoke briefly into his phone, updating the driver of the car. Nodding to his two accomplices that they were ready to proceed, each of them checked their handguns one last time, metal clicks clearly audible in the cold night, before heading off quickly through the bushes towards their objective. The Wolf had chosen these men himself. They were good men in a situation like this, fit, strong and very capable. Each of them had military training of some degree. One had even been in the Polish Special Forces, the elite GROM. The GROM unit had been specially trained in anti-terrorist tactics specifically to kill not capture. Skills that they were going to put into practice now. They were more than confident in their ability to deal with the expected opposition. It was going to be easy. In, collect the drugs, get out and leave no witnesses. If everything went according to plan, they should be done by midnight and back in their car by five past.

Twenty-three minutes.

Easy.

They could have done it in less than ten if needed.

The driver of the car nodded to himself, satisfied that everything was going to plan. He hung up and sat patiently, playing with a piece of red ribbon, knotting it then loosening it, then knotting it again as he waited for more news. He left the engine running so that the climate control would keep the car comfortably warm. Piasecki and the other men would be cold as they crept through a cemetery but it didn't mean that he would have to be.

He had time to calm down after the earlier phone call. He still didn't know who had called him, but by virtue of what he had said, the caller obviously had inside knowledge of the current system and it was for that reason that he was still there. Piasecki had said it was a trap and The Wolf had to agree with him but he still felt compelled to attend. His ego and sense of pride demanded it but if there was going to be a trap, he was the one going to spring it.

The caller, whoever he turned out to be was going to be sorry.

Less than five minutes after the arrival of the Polish gang members to the southern corner of the cemetery, a nearly new and very powerful black Volvo XC90 pulled up to the Northern corner. The custom built vehicle had a greatly enhanced engine, suspension and braking system and like the Polish gang's Audi, its windows also were tinted. It pulled up stopping less than half a mile away from where the Polish men lay hidden in the shadows of the cemetery wall.

The big car parked on the grass verge behind a mature elm tree in front of the house adjoining the cemetery wall. The house was the first in a row of nice pleasant houses, which were recessed back from the normally busy street. Parking there meant the car could not be seen by anybody looking down the road and also offered reasonable cover from any passers-by. The two man advance team from the Emergency Response Unit were normally armed and wore body armour, but as they had been told to keep as low a profile as possible, they had left their body armour, helmets and machine guns in the boot of the car. One of the men climbed up on top of the front wall of the house allowing him to peer over the higher cemetery wall. He snapped around and dropped back onto the ground when the porch light suddenly came on, bathing the front of the house and the unmarked Garda car in bright light. Both men's hands automatically went to their handguns on their waists as they looked expectantly at the hall door, waiting for somebody to come out to investigate their presence. But nobody came, nor did any of the curtains move. Nothing. There were two cars in the driveway so somebody must have been home but at this late hour they were probably sleeping.

"Must be only a movement sensor," said one of the men quietly to his companion.

"Huh," grunted the other in agreement, before slowly creeping back up onto the wall. By moving slowly, this time the cheap domestic sensor failed to spot him. It seemed that it only noticed bold obvious manoeuvres. He reached up tentatively to look over the wall just to make sure that there was nobody on the other side. With no sign of anybody hiding amongst the headstones, he checked the rough layout map that he had been given at the briefing, and made a more detailed inspection of the surrounding area with his small but powerful military issue binoculars.

His partner, still on the ground, kept a lookout while peering around the corner of the cemetery wall and checked the long main road for any movement using his own pair of high-powered binoculars. The cold night seemed to be keeping everybody in doors and it was still too early for the pubs to begin discharging their patrons. But he kept watching intently for any activity. Occasionally a car would cruise past but they were well hidden in the corner. From either vantage point, neither man could see anything out of the ordinary. But each knew from years of experience, that that meant nothing. Nevertheless, they reported that there was no activity to DI Kennedy and the rest of the unit making its way in a five car convey, some ten minutes behind them. Local unarmed Garda units were starting to close the roads around them sealing off the area. A discrete call had been made to the local bar, telling the landlord to keep everyone inside until they got the all clear. For the next thirty minutes, the smoking ban didn't apply to that small part of Ireland.

While all of this was happening at the front of the cemetery, Johnson and Anto were already walking cautiously through the rear of the cemetery, their guns at the ready. They were approaching Rob O'Dwyer's grave from the west, having climbed over a section of the wall at a public green space that was hidden by trees in the adjoining housing estate. By walking along the small gap between the back of the headstones and the wall they could then cautiously follow the old wall until they neared the right section. It took a lot longer than heading straight across the various paths to the grave but Johnson knew that, with the bright moonlight they would be too exposed and anybody watching would see them coming, so he decided to keep beside the high wall as they went, trying to stay hidden in its shadow until the last possible moment.

A bird fluttered between the trees lining the wall, startling the already tense Anto so badly that he pointed his handgun shakily into the air and nearly shot at it. Johnson wouldn't have been surprised if he had pissed himself.

"Will you fucking calm down," Johnson scowled at him, just as a dog in a neighbouring garden started to howl. Anto would wake the dead he was making so much noise, Johnson thought.

"I fucking hate cemeteries," came the nervous reply. Johnson just shook his head. Idiot, the sooner he was finished with this guy the better.

Johnson did not trust Morgan as far as he could throw him and although he was sure that it would just be him waiting on them with the drugs, he was taking no chances. He fully expected Morgan to try something on the graveside as Morgan wasn't the type to lie down. Their heated telephone conversations were clear evidence of that. He would fight. And fight hard but as Johnson clutched the sawn off shotgun in his hands, he knew that he was ready for him. He was more worried about Anto who was stumbling along anxiously behind him, muttering something to himself about it being bad luck being there. Anto's already frail nerves and disposition were getting the better of him as he walked through the cemetery and he was jumping at every shadow. Johnson would not have brought him but he believed in safety in numbers. Two against one were better odds, even if one of them was a snivelling wreck and would probably shoot himself if anything happened.

After nearly ten minutes of walking, Johnson stopped and dropped down to one knee, grabbing hold of Anto's thin coat and dragging him down beside him. A signpost ten feet away read "St. Mary's" and pointed straight ahead. Johnson had never been there before but from Morgan's directions, he guessed that they were not far away now, maybe only a hundred and fifty feet. Johnson carefully scanned the area in front of him for any sign of Morgan. But it was hard to see anything from this height. The headstones blocked his view and created strange shadows everywhere. Johnson imagined that you could hide a small army in here and no one would ever find it. Unwilling to expose himself unnecessarily he told Anto to stay where he was and crept forward to have a better look. He kept going until he had reached a tall bin located beside a group of tall manicured shrubs. Still unable to see anything, he climbed up on top of the bin conscious of every scraping noise that he made and using the shrubs as cover, surveyed the plot in front of him. Johnson could not see anybody or anything out of the ordinary and with the exception of workers sheds over to his right, he had a relatively clear view of St. Mary's and the surrounding plots. He couldn't see anyone but from his vantage point he could just about make out what looked like a bag perched on top of a headstone over to his left. That must be it, he thought. But where was Morgan? He got back down and made his way back over to Anto.

"The grave is just ahead," Johnson whispered. "I can't see that bastard Morgan but he has to be out there somewhere and I want to catch him between us so I need you to go about four rows over to the right and head down about six rows before going back left. You understand that?"

"Yes," Anto stammered nervously. "Four rows over, six down then back up."

"Good. Now go," Johnson ordered. He had been fine up to this point but now he was getting nervous. Where was Morgan and what was he up to?

Anto headed off looking very apprehensively. Why did they have to split up? He didn't want to be out here on his own. He looked back over his shoulder at Johnson for some support but Johnson just waved angrily at him to get on with it.

Chapter Forty-Four

If it was possible, Morgan had started to get even more uncomfortable lying down on the hard roof. The American secret service didn't need to use waterboarding as a torture technique to get information out of suspected terrorists. Just make them lie on freezing cold roof at night in an Irish cemetery in January and they would be singing like canaries before long, he thought.

Looking around, Morgan could see the clear sheen of frost that had formed on nearly every flat surface surrounding him. The marble headstones seemed to glimmer in the moonlight. It was quite a beautiful sight. Morgan knew that if he had kept moving he would have been warm enough. But he was stuck lying there in one spot and the unrelenting cold that had entered his body was taking its toll. Both his face and hands had gone numb and the temperature was still dropping.

Morgan was forced to shift his position regularly now as his battered tendons and joints stiffened and the cold got into his already torn and aching muscles. He wished that he could sit up straight and stretch out his arms and legs properly but was afraid any significant movement would give his position away. He hadn't long to wait but he was cold and the clothes he had borrowed had been more for summer than winter and although he had doubled up on layers they were definitely not designed for midnight excursions to a cemetery. He had decided not to wear gloves as the only ones in the house that fitted him were very bulky and he found that he couldn't hold the gun comfortably. Standing in Pauline's warm hall it had seemed the right idea at the time, but now he realised that he should have taken them regardless. The only consolation he felt was in the knowledge that his own blood and sweat stained clothes were burning nicely in Pauline's fire grate by now. Right then, he envied them.

Morgan checked his watch for the umpteenth time. It read eleven forty eight pm; two minutes since he last checked it and ten minutes give or take until Johnson should arrive. Morgan's body screamed at the thought of lying in this position for another ten minutes, but it was too good a vantage point to give up now. He found that he was staring at the distant grave so hard that his vision was becoming blurred. He tried to rub the exhaustion out of his eyes but it had little effect. In fact if anything they felt more swollen.

The next few minutes passed slowly. Nobody approached the grave.

There was nothing moving out there except the wind.

To keep his mind occupied, Morgan tried to figure out which direction the breeze was coming from. But he quickly gave up, as the gusts seemed to be coming from every direction.

Morgan had not received a text message from Detective Callaghan telling him that she had arrived and had brought the cavalry and he was starting to get concerned. What could be keeping them? he thought. He was going to send her a message when he sensed rather than saw the two men approaching from his left hand side. They were walking softly, keeping close to the cemetery wall as they came. At a larger cross road, wide enough to accommodate a car, they stopped and dropped to their knees as they checked the area in front of them, whispering to each other. One of them was large and bulky, while the other was shorter and much thinner. Morgan had no doubt that the bigger of the two was Johnson.

He watched them split up as they attempted to circle and trap what they must have believed to be an unsuspecting Morgan in a pincer movement at the graveside. The larger man crept quietly towards Rob's grave, still keeping to the shadows along the wall. And although Morgan could not see him clearly, he seemed to be holding a rifle or a shogun of some sort in his right hand. The other man came towards him and then turned sharply right to walk parallel to the workers sheds. As the man passed below him, Morgan could clearly see that he was holding a handgun down by his side. Obviously, regardless of whether he handed over the drugs or not, they never intended to let him walk out of here.

So that's the way they want to play, Morgan thought. Now more than ever, he was glad he had brought the gun with him. He could play that game as well. But he still inadvertently looked at his watch again. Where the hell was Callaghan and the cavalry? He was starting to get worried. Well, he was not going to let Johnson and his buddy get away now. If Callaghan was not here in five minutes, he would have to capture the men himself. It wouldn't be the first time that he had put himself in a situation like this. And the way his life seemed to be turning out lately, it wouldn't be his last.

Being as quiet as he could, Morgan picked up his gun and pushed himself backwards until he was at the edge of the roof. He winced at the slight grating noise made by the buttons on his coat as he climbed down the ladder and slipped back out of the locked gate. After lying down for so long, he found it painful to walk properly and his hands were so cold that he could barely hold the gun never mind aim and fire it. He peered around the building's corner and saw the back of the thin man disappearing between the headstones and set off quietly after him, gun in hand. His hunters had now become his prey. But Morgan was focusing so intently on the movements of the thin man in front of him, that he missed seeing the three other men standing in the trees in the old section of the cemetery watching intently every move they made.

The advance ERU member observing from the far wall wasn't sure if he was actually seeing someone moving through the forest of the headstones at first. Although his observational training and surveillance experience gave him an added advantage over Morgan, he like everyone else that night was confused by the moving shadows caused by the wind in the trees and the occasional cloud passing under the bright winter moon. It took a few seconds longer than normal for his brain to register that the shifting shadow far over to his right peripheral vision, was actually that of someone creeping around, until he managed to catch them squarely in his binoculars. He then watched the subject slowly advance until he stopped and stood hidden from view beside a large white statue of an angel located only twenty feet from the target graveside.

"They're here," he whispered anxiously down to his colleague on the ground.

"How many?" the other man asked, looking up at him.

"I can only see one at the moment," he answered, sweeping the area again. "But where there is one there is always more".

"Okay, I'll call Kennedy and let him know".

The call to his superior turned out to be a very brief and frustrating one. The armed Garda had been informed that the rest of the unit had become held up in a traffic jam on the one way street that Harcourt Garda station was located which had been caused by a car jumping the traffic lights and getting hit by a train on the LUAS light rail system. This left the LUAS tram blocking the only exit from the street. They eventually decided to turn around and go back up the road against the traffic to find another way and were on the move again but still fifteen minutes out. The orders to the men in the cemetery were to hold steady where they currently were and wait for them to arrive.

"Fuck it," said the disappointed Garda on the wall, fearful that their targets might make their getaways before they had a chance to move in on them. He hated the thought of that.

Morgan's plan was incredibly simple. His plans always were. He would catch up to the thin man, grab him from behind and disarm him - a move that he was well practiced in working as a doorman. The only difference was this man was holding a gun. But that didn't bother Morgan. It had to be done. Then using him as a shield, Morgan would surprise and confront Johnson. Then using his gun he would detain both drug dealers until the Gardaí arrived. He would then hand both of the men and the god-forsaken drugs over to them.

Sinead and the kids would be safe.

Job done.

Go home.

Simple.

Ignoring the swarm of butterflies in his stomach, Morgan slipped around the corner of the workmen's shed and was careful to walk on the narrow grass verge along the edge of the path so that his boots did not make any noise. He was bent over double as he tracked the thin man; never letting himself get directly behind him, but preferring instead to use the headstones as cover and to follow him at a slight angle as the thin man was very nervous and looked furtively around him as he slowly made his way to the drop off point. Despite this Morgan found it relatively easy to follow him as the thin man was looking at his surroundings but he wasn't paying attention. Morgan recognised his body language. The thin man walked slowly as if he didn't want to be the first to get to the grave. Morgan assumption was correct. "Let Johnson get his fucking drugs", the thin man had reasoned long ago, "the graveside was where it was all going to happen and he didn't want to be there at all".

When he had to, Morgan would cut across the rows by walking on the marble edges of the graves to the other side. He found it more difficult than he thought to follow the thin man and watch where he was stepping at the same time. Occasionally, he would have to duck behind a headstone when the thin man looked nervously in his direction, but other than that he made quick progress. Morgan caught up to the man when he was less than thirty feet away from Rob's grave. From his current hiding place, Morgan could not see Johnson but judging from the noise, the larger man was already there, rooting through the bag that Morgan had left on the grave. Morgan edged closer and winced as he could hear small stones crunching noisily under his feet as he went.

"Is that them?" the thin man asked out loud as he moved forward more quickly now, eager to look at the drugs and throwing all caution to the wind in the process. Morgan inched closer and got a much clearer view of the scene. The large man, which presumably was Johnson, was directly in front of him. He was kneeling on the ground with his back to both Morgan and his thin accomplice as he went through the contents of the heavy black bag. Morgan knew that this was his opportunity; Johnson was distracted and the thin man was so focused on him that Morgan could have driven an army tank up behind him and he would not have heard him. Morgan would never get a chance like this again.

Morgan gripped the gun in his hand one last time to give himself some last minute reassurance and standing up straight marched directly and purposefully towards the thin man, until the last ten feet where he gave up all pretence of stealth and ran. He had completely forgotten about his aching body, the freezing cold, his numb face and hands and just ran. After days of playing cat and mouse, the man who had started this whole fucking mess was in his sights. Anger rose in Morgan's blood with every step he took.

At the very last minute, the thin man must have heard him and began to turn around, but it was too late for him to do anything. Morgan was already on top of him. He slammed into him, grabbing him violently around the throat from behind with his arm, while jamming the gun into the side of his head. Anto tried to break free by twisting his body but Morgan just pulled backwards and squeezed his arm tighter, lifting him fractionally of the ground and shutting off the thin man's air supply. The man dropped his own gun onto the ground and grabbed frantically at Morgan's arm with both his hands but to no avail, Morgan had just too good a grip on him. His muffled screams alerted Johnson who was, up to this point, still engrossed in counting the number of small parcels making up the missing drug consignment.

Hearing the commotion behind him, Johnson dropped the packets and whirled around, picking up his shotgun and pointing it menacingly at Morgan sheltering behind the terrified thin man.

"Drop your gun and put your hands up!," Morgan roared aggressively, pointing the gun at him.

Johnson looked hesitantly at him for a second, the barrel of the gun dropping slightly before he surprised Morgan by smiling broadly.

"Glad you stayed around as I would have hated to have missed you. I have been looking forward to meeting you face to face," Johnson sneered confidently.

"Put the gun down and put your hands up," Morgan repeated.

"Not a fucking chance".

"Do it now or I will blow his bloody head off," Morgan threatened, his eyes wild with a mixture of anger and determination as he turned the gun back onto the thin man and jamming it hard into the side of his head. For his part the thin man, who was standing limply in Morgan's clutches was utterly defeated and started snivelling and mumbling incoherently. He vainly tried to pull his head away from the gun as if every extra millimetre away from the barrel could save him.

"I don't think you would. Do it, see if I care. Go on, I dare you!" Johnson said.

"Johnson, please!" the thin man begged. "He's got a fucking gun to my fucking head".

But Johnson just laughed.

Chapter Forty-Five

The heavily armed Garda on the wall was following events as they unfolded. It was like a television soap opera playing out in front of him with the sound turned off. But this scene wasn't scripted and the men in front of them weren't about to start firing blanks from prop guns. From his vantage point on the wall, he could clearly see through his binoculars that one man was holding another one hostage while threatening the third with a handgun. He could see it happening but was too far away to hear what they were saying. But he could imagine that it was a very animated encounter because there was a lot of gesticulating going on. If this was supposed to be a deal going down, then it was going badly wrong for someone. He just didn't know who. As he watched from his vantage point, he relayed what was happening to his partner standing watch on the ground.

"It looks like a double cross. There seems to be some sort of standoff? What do we do?" he asked.

"Nothing. Kennedy said to hold tight till he gets here. So we hold tight."

"But it looks he's going to kill them. People are going to die unless we do something".

"So what, they're drug dealers. Let them kill each other," his partner replied callously, staring down the empty road.

"I know what you're saying but there are only three of them. We can take them easily."

"Hell yeah we could take them, but we were told not to move until the rest of the team turns up".

"Come on, where is your sense of adventure?" the officer on the wall said goading him.

"At home warm in bed".

"I tell you what, let's just go over the wall and take a closer look then. We won't do anything unless they open fire on each other".

There was a long pause as the second Garda considered the suggestion. "You're always getting me into trouble. Alright then, I am fed up standing here freezing my balls off like a fucking idiot but we are not moving too close. Right?"

"Agreed," said the officer on the wall before hopping down. Both men rushed to the back of the car and got their equipment out of the secure compartment in the boot. The first Garda grabbed his Remington 870 shotgun and threw a bandolier of shells over his shoulder. His partner took his weapon of choice, the Heckler & Koch MP7, grabbing two more forty round magazines and stuffing them into the pockets on his body armour. They checked that they had everything they needed before pulling their balaclavas on and secured their ballistics helmets.

With one impressive bound the first Garda was back up on the wall and after checking that the three men were still visible, swiftly climbed up and over the small railing at the top, before dropping soundlessly to the ground, followed closely by his partner. Little did either man know that if they had taken the time to look a hundred metres further beyond the stand-off and over slightly to the left they might have seen three shadowy figures moving quickly towards the feuding men.

Once on the far side of the wall, the policemen crept unseen through the cemetery to within a hundred feet of the stand-off between Morgan, Johnson and Anto. Because the cemetery was very quiet without the noise of traffic passing by and the gusts of wind that were blowing in their direction, it meant that they were able to hear the men clearly even at that distance.

And things were obviously coming to a head.

The Garda who had been on the ground checking the comings and goings on the road called DI Kennedy and told him of the developments. Needless to say the DI was furious that they had disobeyed him and gone over the wall without backup, but decided to wait until a less delicate moment before berating the men. The last thing he wanted to do was distract them when they were so close to armed criminals. He did let them know that he and the rest of the ERU team along with the investigating officers had just arrived and were moments away from scaling the walls themselves. They would be putting the plan into operation in minutes and they were to keep low and quiet until then. No firing unless they were fired upon first.

"Go ahead," Johnson, said smirking at an unimpressed Morgan. "Blow his fucking head off. It will save me doing it later. He's a useless prick anyway".

At this news Anto cursed both Morgan and Johnson and started to squirm violently in an effort to break free once again until Morgan told him to be still and squeezed his arm tighter around his neck cutting off his air, while still keeping his gun pointed squarely at Johnson. But Anto was only a distraction. Morgan had learned while working as a doorman that in any situation involving a group that there were always a few who really wanted to get stuck in and start swinging. There would be some who would join in but only if they had to and finally those who wanted absolutely nothing to do with any sort of aggression. Thankfully most groups were populated with those who didn't want to fight at all. Morgan instinctively knew when he first saw Anto creeping through the cemetery that he was one of the latter. The only reason he was struggling now was not to attack Morgan but to get away. To save his own pathetic skin.

The only person Morgan really had to contend with was Johnson.

"The Gardaí have been looking for you, you know. I told them that I was meeting you here. They are on their way right now and they are going to arrest you for drug dealing and extortion", Morgan said triumphantly, hanging onto the now limp Anto. "You are going to spend the rest of your miserable life in prison".

"The Gardaí aren't going to do shit. I am taking those drugs and walking out of here and you won't be able to stop me", Johnson replied unimpressed with Morgan's bravado.

"If you try to, I will shoot you. Don't for a second think I won't".

And Morgan meant it. He didn't like guns. Never had and probably never would, but he would use it if he had to. After all he had been through the last few days, he wasn't going to allow Johnson to escape now.

"You fucking idiot. You are not going to shoot anybody. That gun is loaded with blanks," Johnson laughed mockingly as he waved his own gun casually in the air. "If it wasn't do you think I would be just standing here?"

"That's bullshit", Morgan said dismissing the idea completely.

"You really think that I would give you a gun with real bullets in it and then have it used against me? What kind of fool do you think I am?" Johnson gloated. "You're a fucking idiot".

"I don't believe you. You're lying", Morgan said but with less conviction than he had a moment ago. Doubt crept across his mind, could it be loaded with blanks? While he hadn't fired the gun himself, Smith had shot at him earlier with it not once but twice. Then again he could not remember hearing a ricochet. Was there a ricochet? He could not be sure now and the more he thought about it, the more unsure he became. Could Johnson be telling the truth? If so, Morgan knew that he was in deep trouble.

"No I am not", Johnson laughed as he walked menacingly towards Morgan with shotgun raised at the ready, ready to blast them both. "And now I am going to kill you both".

As DI Kennedy was talking to the two Gardaí already inside the perimeter wall, three vehicles of the Garda convoy pulled up sharply outside beside the advance team's Volvo. The other ERU Volvo had already split away from the lead vehicle to position itself at the rear of the cemetery to hinder any possible escape by the suspected dealers. The rest of the team started donning their black body armour, helmets, radios and checking over their weapons one last time.

Now, it was up to DI Behan as Scene Officer to confirm tactics with DI Kennedy as to how best to arrest these men. DI Higgins and Callaghan listened eagerly. "Things have changed. We are late and the suspects are already at each other's throats. The advance team inside are telling us that this standoff between our suspects is about to end and that shooting will start any second. So we have to move fast. I need these men alive if I am to try and find the original source of these drugs and help unravel two murders", DI Behan said.

"What do you have in mind?" asked Kennedy.

"You need more men to close this area down quickly now that a fire fight is imminent. You have two men inside, plus two going around the back to move from that direction. That leaves you, plus six men and myself, DI Higgins and Callaghan here.

"That's right so far, but with all due respect Garda Callaghan is not experienced enough to be involved in an operation such as this," objected DI Kennedy.

"On the contrary sir, I have all my firearm's certificates," Callaghan appealed. She couldn't be left out now.

"There are only three men in there. If you ask me this is a great opportunity for her," volunteered DI Behan. "Garda Callaghan here needs the experience and with you and six of your men in there as well, she should be okay".

DI Kennedy looked at each face in turn before shaking his head "Okay, but it's against my better judgement, but she gets a vest and she stays at the back out of harm's way. No direct involvement in the arrest."

"No problem. As per your plan earlier, I need two men to travel further down the road and go over the fence there and come back at the target area from the left hand side. Your other two men will accompany us over the wall to help support the two men there already. Can you give me a radio so I can keep in touch."

"Here have mine, I'll get another one", Kennedy volunteered.

"Can you co-ordinate your men for me towards the targets? And send in the helicopter when it's here?" Behan asked Kennedy, looking up to the sky as if searching for inspiration.

"Of course", Kennedy replied already moving off.

"I need you to seal off the area and make sure that both the dog unit and ambulances are on standby. You got that?" Behan asked Higgins, more to give him something to do so he would not feel completely left out.

"Yes, of course", Higgins said grudgingly, before turning to walk away to make the calls.

"Okay, sounds as good as it gets. Let's move people," DI Kennedy shouted to his teams. The already busy hive of activity stepped up a gear. Thirty seconds later, as the four Gardaí were about scale the wall all hell broke loose inside.

Chapter Forty-Six

Johnson walked another step closer to Morgan, who while keeping a close grip on the petrified Anto kept his gun pointed squarely at the advancing mobster.

"Stay right where you are or I will shoot", Morgan ordered, shuffling his feet to get a better stance as he aimed directly at the advancing man's head.

"Shoot. See if I care," laughed Johnson, coming closer still, challenging Morgan to shoot.

Morgan knew that he was going to have to shoot; Johnson was giving him no other choice. He didn't want to kill Johnson, that wasn't why he was here. Johnson was no good to him dead. He had not wanted to see Smith die earlier either, but it had happened anyway. So instead of aiming for the man's head, he dropped the angle of his gun slightly and a bit to the left as he aimed for Johnson's shoulder instead. Morgan squeezed the trigger of the gun, which was stiffer than he thought it would be and was deafened by the loud report. A tiny wisp of smoke curled upwards in the cold night air but apart from that nothing else seemed to have happened. Johnson stood exactly where he was a second previously.

Completely unharmed.

Blanks!

The creepy smile on Johnson's face was replaced by a massive grin.

"I told you but you didn't believe me," taunted Johnson. "I also told you on the phone that I would fucking kill you and now I am going to and you'd better believe that".

Johnson brought his shotgun up higher, braced the stock against his shoulder and pointed it directly at Morgan. At this distance Johnson's shot would kill both Morgan and Anto. But

Morgan knew he had nowhere to run. There was nowhere to hide. Anto for his part started to whimper and pissed himself. A steady stream of urine flowed down his leg and formed a puddle around his feet. Believing he was just about to meet his maker, Morgan said a quick prayer but before Johnson could fire the fatal shot, killing them both, three men dressed all in black, wearing ski masks and pointing large handguns, came out of nowhere and surrounded them. They looked very professional and not the type to be messed with.

"Drop the weapons and put your hands up," shouted one of the men in very broken English. He sounded of eastern European extraction. He left no doubt as to who was in charge. He was. Follow his command or die.

Of the three men caught in the circle, Johnson looked the most surprised. He just stood there, looking around in shock at the men circling them.

"Who the fucking hell are you?" he asked.

"We are the men whose guns are loaded with real bullets. Now drop your weapons or we will kill you. You have three seconds to comply. I will not ask again," the man said threateningly in his foreign drawl.

Eastern European, no doubt about it, Morgan thought. Despite the accent, Morgan recognised the tone of a man who is used to getting his orders followed. He could not see the foreigner's face behind the mask but he could see his eyes. As Morgan looked into his cold hard eyes, he did not doubt that statement for one second. Morgan didn't like surrendering. It wasn't his style. But dying needlessly in a hail of bullets wasn't his style either. He might still end up dead but he didn't know what these guys were after so who knew which way this might pan out. Morgan took one last look at the three men in black and dropped his gun onto the ground, letting go of Anto as he did so. A second later Johnson reluctantly followed suit, flinging his sawn off shotgun over onto the grave to his left before taking a step back.

There was an uneasy tension. All three men stood there waiting to see what was going to happen next. Were these others just here to rob them or something else?

The man who had been giving the orders, indicated to one of his henchmen to check the bag to make sure the drugs were all there. The black clad man went over to it and picked it up, rummaging through it briefly and clearly satisfied nodded. The black clad leader then used his mobile to call his own boss wherever he was. He didn't announce himself, just briefly said, "Mamto, I have it". He nodded his head as he listened to the reply before snapping the mobile closed.

He then turned and raised his gun to shoulder height, aiming at Morgan, who involuntarily took a step back, when he noticed one of the Gardaí moving in closer between two headstones. The leader dropped his phone and started shouting "Policyjny, Policyjny, Policyjny".

Everything happened so fast after that. The three black clad men spun around and began firing in the direction of the hidden Garda ERU team as they attempted to creep closer. They in turn understandably ducked for cover as bullets peppered the marble headstones around them, keeping them pinned down. The noise from the guns as they fired was deafening. It shattered the otherwise still night air, sending all of the local birds flying from their midnight roosts. The Gardaí waited for a break in the shooting so they could return fire. Bullets were flying everywhere. In the distance, other figures could be clearly seen scaling the walls and dropping down.

The cavalry had finally arrived.

The three black clad hit men quickly formed a semi-circle and started to lay down a field of fire that kept the two advance ERU team members huddled behind the headstones. The hit men didn't seem particularly perturbed by the appearance of the Gardaí. They didn't run and they didn't panic, they just aimed and fired in quick succession. As they fired, they called over to each other in what Morgan recognised as Polish. The noise from Morgan's older smaller gun had been loud but it was nothing compared to the deafening din from the larger more modern guns being fired by the men dressed in black. Although the cold night air was probably magnifying it, it was a different level of noise altogether that shocked the senses of the three Irish men currently trying to press themselves into the cold ground as they sought to avoid getting shot. It was like being caught up in a war.

The arrival of more of the ERU team caused two of the black clad hit men to turn their focus slightly to the right as they sought to stop their advance before they got too close. This time however they weren't having it all of their own way. They were forced to duck down as the new Gardaí fired upon them with a mixture of their high-powered shotgun and assault rifles. Morgan could see that the hit men with only their handguns were outgunned. Morgan reckoned that they would have no choice but to either surrender or try to escape. That didn't mean however that he was out of danger yet. The men might kill them as potential witnesses before they tried to get away themselves or they might get caught up in the crossfire. Killed as collateral damage in the gunfight. It wouldn't matter how they were shot.

The result would be the same.

Shots continued to ring out all around them. Cutting through the air, ready to pulverise anything that they came into contact with. The effects of the shotgun were the most devastating; causing chunks of marble and stone to fly up into the air. The nearest hit man to Morgan, the group's leader turned around and faced Morgan as he reloaded his gun. Wisps of acrid smoke rose up from the hot barrel. Empty magazine clip out, full one in, cock it and ready again. Morgan and the gunmen caught each other's glances, but a ricochet off a nearby stone angel that buried itself in the ground exactly midway in the ground between them, caused both men to squeeze themselves lower.

From his position on the footpath, Morgan's head was at the same level as the marble grave surround, he couldn't really see much of what was happening, although he could tell by the noise alone, that the Gardaí were closing in. Morgan figured that the Polish men would have to make a break for it soon as their ammunition must be running short. While the ERU team had a large supply of ammunition to fall back on, the Polish men didn't. They had only planned to ambush a small drug deal, so they would probably have only an extra clip at most each. Not nearly enough to get involved in this type of concentrated fire fight. Though for the moment it seemed to be a stalemate.

The skinny Irish gang member who had accompanied Johnson was lying to Morgan's right. He was using the mound of fresh earth, covering Rob's grave as protection. He was clearly terrified, shaking and sobbing that he didn't want to die. Johnson himself was lying approximately ten feet in front of Morgan. Unlike his accomplice, he was not panicking but was clearly anxious to make his escape.

With the black clad foreigners occupied, Johnson crawled to where he had flung his gun earlier and with a last quick glance towards the black clad men he jumped up and bolted away towards the trees. Taking his old bosses lead, Anto was up onto his feet and chasing after him. Morgan watched as Johnson disappeared into the night, he hesitated another second before sucking in a deep breath and sprinted after them. At the last minute one of the black clad men spun around to shoot him as he passed by, but Morgan ducked down and rammed his shoulder with all of his weight into the man's chest, sending him spinning around and collapsing heavily onto the ground with a grunt.

Before the man could get up, Morgan was gone, weaving frantically between the headstones in an attempt to give himself some cover. He knew that by running, he was risking a bullet in the back, but he was not going to let Johnson get away. Not after all he had been through. Seeing what had happened to his buddy, one of the other black clad men eventually turned to fire wildly after the three of them as they disappeared through the cemetery. But their luck held as each man zigzagged along the narrow pathways and made good their escape.

Morgan, Johnson and Anto ran as fast as they could away from the gunfight behind them, directly towards the trees of the old part of the cemetery. Morgan ran across paths, graves, flowers and shiny marble surrounds, slipping and sliding on the frost covered stone. All earlier efforts not to walk directly on graves as a sign of respect were completely forgotten in his effort to escape. Twice Morgan lost his footing and went crashing hard into a headstone, aggravating the injuries that he had sustained earlier in the night. The first time he went crashing down he smacked his chin violently off the ground sending a terrible vibration up through his head. The second time, he split his head open on an ornate flowerpot. As he struggled back up onto his feet, Morgan could feel a trickle of blood running down the side of his head. In a lot of pain and discomfort, he continued on, leaving the sound of gunfire behind him.

The third team of the Emergency Response Unit had managed to scale the rear wall and eventually come up behind the three black clad men. As they were forced to turn their attention to the men behind them, this gave the original two Gardaí a chance to break from cover. The ERU officer who had been the very first one over the wall, fired a long burst from his MP7 and managed to hit one of the black clad men square in the chest, sending him flying backwards into the air and sprawling onto the ground. Dead. The other two men seeing this started to retreat towards the cover of the workmen's sheds, leaving the heavy bag of drugs lying forgotten on the ground behind them. The cause of all this terrible mess, the reason that three men had died now lay forgotten and abandoned, useless and pointless now in the greater scheme of things. The two remaining Polish hitmen just made it inside the gate of the workman's shed before the various teams started linking up.

It was about then that DI Behan, Callaghan and the final two members of the ERU team scaled the front wall and came running up to the periphery of the fire fight, firing short bursts as they ran. They scouted the main road down to the workmen's shed. Cutting through the old ash trees they came directly to the rear of the shed, facing the broken gate. The hitmen were now well and truly outnumbered and out manoeuvred. Flashes of bright red tinted light lit up each of the members of the team as they fired their semiautomatic weapons. The two heavily armed ERU members quickly joined forces with their colleagues to lay down a withering suppressive fire.

Inside the compound, the two Polish men lay on the ground, sheltered underneath the parked JCB, firing back every chance they got as bullets peppered the ground around them. It was obvious that they had no intention of giving up easily. But Behan could not have cared less about them. He knew that the ERU team would eventually sort them out. As they had made their way down through the trees to come up behind the shed, he had caught a fleeting glimpse of Morgan slipping into the trees over to his left just a few seconds previously. Morgan could not be allowed to escape. Callaghan's career depended on it.

"Stay here and stay down for goodness sake," he said to Callaghan as she lay hidden behind a headstone beside him. He ran off, bent over, toward the tree line in hot pursuit of Morgan.

Callaghan watched him disappear into the night as bullets ricocheted off a large headstone only a few feet from where she lay. She found the sustained gunfire incredibly noisy and disorientating. Momentarily scared, she tried to make herself even smaller.

"You are not leaving me here while you are off getting all the glory", she thought to herself, overcoming her fear before making a decision to follow Behan. Callaghan drew her gun from her holster and taking a quick glance towards the shed decided to run after Behan, ducking as another bullet whizzed past her, this time only inches from her head.

"Shit," she said out loud and kept going.

Chapter Forty-Seven

Despite his exhaustion and his increasing number of injuries, Morgan was considerably fitter than Johnson and Anto and it was showing. He didn't smoke, rarely drank alcohol, and had trained regularly most of his life. Despite the injury to his leg he sustained at the light house, he was fitter and leaner than he had been in a long time. In contrast, the furthest Johnson and Anto had run in the last few years was from the car to the pub if it had been raining. Their head start meant that they had made it across St Mary's plot but they had only managed to get twenty feet into the trees in the northern section of the older cemetery when Morgan caught up with them.

Crashing through the trees, Morgan literally ran past Anto pushing him roughly out of the way as he made a beeline straight for Johnson. The bigger man was just ahead of him, lumbering along out of breath and struggling over the rough uneven ground. Getting within touching distance, Morgan dived on top of him, catching the drug dealer around the shoulders and dragging him unceremoniously down onto the cold ground. Johnson dropped the shotgun, it fell behind an old faded and lob sided headstone. Johnson tried to grab hold of it but it was just out of his reach. Even without his gun, the thug wasn't about to give up easily. He viciously kicked and lashed out in an attempt to escape. And despite the strong hold that Morgan had on him, Johnson somehow managed to twist his body around so that the two men were facing each other, trading clumsily thrown punches in equal measure. But Morgan wasn't feeling any of them, he knew he was being punched but that was all. His blood was up and adrenaline was coursing through his veins, blocking all of his other senses. Johnson could have hit him with a baseball bat and it wouldn't have made any difference.

After what felt like an age, both men were grunting and groaning with the sheer effort of the fight. Morgan knew that on any normal day, he would have taken Johnson easily. But today wasn't a normal day. He had been beaten, bruised and had nearly been shot God knows how many times. He was in a lot of pain, completely exhausted and frozen stiff but his anger was keeping him going. He wouldn't give up.

Not now.

Not ever.

At one point, one of Johnson's punches caught Morgan in the throat. The blow made him gag involuntarily and it had enough force in it to make Morgan release his grip just slightly. Johnson took the chance offered to him and twisted and rolled, driving his knee painfully into Morgan's stomach but he could still only manage to drag himself a few feet before Morgan had got a hand to him again. Johnson kicked out, his size eleven boot connecting squarely with Morgan's head sending him into a daze. Even now as he lay gasping for air, with Johnson desperately kicking out at him, Morgan recovered a little and began to crawl up Johnson's body. They exchanged more heavy blows before Morgan's strength and endurance began to pay off and he got the upper hand and started punching Johnson repeatedly in the face.

But just as he was getting the better of Johnson, Anto, forgetting about Johnson's earlier wish to see him dead, came out of the trees, screaming and shouting like some sort of madman before flinging himself on top of Morgan knocking him off Johnson. Johnson took the opportunity to drag himself to his feet and stumble off, stooping to retrieve his gun as he went.

Morgan and Anto rolled around on the ground, arms and legs flailing. Anto fought like a man possessed and by now Morgan's strength was flagging badly. Suddenly the Garda helicopter's "night sun" searchlight lit up the night sky like turning night into day. It was an eerie and unnatural light. Not only did it illuminate the area around the workmen's shed and the continuing gunfight but it also basked both Morgan and Anto in light as they fought on the ground. The sudden bright light distracted Anto just enough for Morgan to land a punch that must have broken his jaw. Anto fell off Morgan, screaming in agony and clutching his face.

Morgan scrambled unceremoniously to his feet and set off after Johnson, who was disappearing back into the darkness through the trees towards the south east corner of the cemetery.

Morgan left this section of tree-covered graves, crossed a narrow path and entered another wooded area. This must have been one of the oldest sections of the cemetery because it included a number of tiny mausoleums. In the dark, it looked like somebody had come along and abandoned a truckload of small grey garden sheds in a forest. Chasing Johnson was hard going, as the ground was very rough; constantly undulating. Unlike the newer sections, where the graves were clearly delineated in neat rows and columns, here in the trees the graves were placed randomly with no apparent rhyme or reason. None had marble borders of any description, just headstones jutting awkwardly out of the ground. As it was very dark in amongst the dense old trees, these haphazardly placed grave markers coupled with exposed bare roots and vines nearly tripped him several times.

In the distance, the loud reports of gunshots became more and more faint. In the back of his mind, Morgan realised that the gunfight must be over. The men in black trapped and cornered at the shed were either dead or captured. Relieved from covering the gunfight, the Garda helicopter banked right and began a slow crawl over towards the old section of the cemetery. It was probably under orders to act as a beacon to the Gardaí chasing them on the ground. The helicopter must have been still flying at a great height as Morgan neither felt any wind from the rotor blades nor heard its loud engine noise. Its searchlight illuminated the trees and caused thousands of new confusing shadows to form on the ground. His head was pounding and it was very hard to see anything properly as everything kept changing.

Light to dark and back to light again.

But then as suddenly as it had arrived the helicopter left. Veering sharply to the right before manoeuvring itself back over the work shed's for some reason. Maybe the men in black had managed to escape?

Now the only light was from the bright moonlight as it broke through where the trees were thinnest, but it was patchy at best. By now Morgan had completely lost sight of Johnson but ran on regardless. He continued in a straight line, hoping that Johnson had not veered off in any direction. Otherwise he could run right by him and never know. A large building suddenly appeared out of the trees in front of him. It had a short stocky spire and must have been one of the two churches on the site. It was the protestant chapel if he remembered correctly.

Morgan stopped running and leant against the chapel wall and tried to catch his breath, which was very laboured. He felt like vomiting but managed to suppress the urge. He figured that the Gardaí would soon start to search the rest of the cemetery for them. He hoped that they would not be too late. Johnson could not be allowed to escape. But the cemetery was such a big place and like a labyrinth in the dark. The chances of Morgan finding him were getting slimmer every second he stood there. But which way should he go? The question was which way would Johnson go? Left would bring him back to the wall and the road and right towards the more modern section of the cemetery. Morgan decided that Johnson would want to get out of here as soon as possible so he made off in the direction of the road. Setting off towards the wall Morgan hoped that he would catch him soon as he had developed a stitch and knew that he would vomit soon if he did not stop. But dogged determination drove him on. Johnson was not going to get away.

As Morgan rounded the back corner of the church, he could see the wall of the cemetery with its little railing on top about sixty feet in front of him. The street lights poking up above the wall, illuminated the top rail. Johnson was nowhere to be seen. 'Shit', he thought, 'he has made it over the wall already. He got away. Well not for long, I'm coming for you. Wherever you are. I am coming for you'.

An exhausted Morgan set off towards the wall but out of nowhere the barrel of a shotgun was put across his throat and pulled him back viciously, choking him and making him gag. Instinctively, from years both on the door and the rugby pitch, he dropped to his knees and twisted his body to the left. Johnson was caught by the sudden move, yelled out in surprise and fell over Morgan's shoulder, clutching onto his jacket as he went. This caused both men to fall. But instead of hitting the ground they started rolling down a steep embankment that led to a crypt door beneath the back of the church. They landed unceremoniously in a pile at the bottom on the hard concrete, both winded and grunting in pain. The gun clattered down beside them.

Just lying there.

Waiting to be picked up.

Morgan was the first to recover. But he ignored it, he sucked in the pain from his aching ribs and crawled over to where Johnson lay dazed, grunting with the effort as he rolled him over onto his back.

"I have you now, you bastard," Morgan spat at him triumphantly.

Johnson looked up at him, his battered and bruised face looking worse because of the blood pouring from a deep gash on his head from an edging stone.

"Fuck you," Johnson replied, hatred burning fiercely in his eyes. He was hurt but the fight had not gone out of him yet.

"Not this time".

Johnson suddenly reared up at Morgan and both men found themselves rolling around on the ground, each struggling to get the better of the other. But they were proving equally matched in size and strength. Morgan was fitter but Johnson fought dirtier. As Morgan rolled on top, he moved to try and get higher up on Johnson's body. Johnson gave him a vicious sucker punch to the kidneys, knocking all of the air out of his lungs. Groaning loudly, Morgan slipped off Johnson and curled into a ball by his side. Johnson saw that this was probably going to be his only opportunity and scrambled over to where the shotgun was lying on the steeply sloped path. He had difficulty bending over to pick it up, missing it twice before his hand grasped the handle. He turned and walked back and stood over Morgan. Johnson drove the butt of the shotgun viciously on to Morgan's temple. The blow stunned him, causing Morgan's head to spin and his vision to blur.

"I said fuck you, you little prick," Johnson gloated before raising the gun to fire.

"Armed Gardaí. Put your weapon down," ordered a strong authoritative female voice from behind them. Johnson froze and stood as still as a statue, initially unsure as to what to do. He smiled and gave the dazed and confused Morgan one last look before spinning around and firing in one fluid motion. Garda Callaghan, who was standing midway down the sloping path, took both barrels in the upper chest and neck. The bullet-proof jacket that she was wearing took most of the shot. But some of the shotguns five hundred and eighty five pellets in each casing pulverised her upper right shoulder, splattering blood everywhere. Callaghan was literally flung off her feet and into the air, before crashing heavily onto the ground, cracking the back of her head on a pile of rocks, her right leg twitching uncontrollably. Her borrowed handgun clattering unfired onto the black tarmac beside her.

Johnson limped painfully towards her to make sure she wasn't getting up again. He stopped midway up the slope as he saw someone coming out of the bushes. But he didn't react in a manner to suggest that he was afraid of the person, just startled by their presence.

"You?" Johnson said in wonder. From where he lay Morgan couldn't see the man. His head was still reeling from being hit with the shotgun but he still could hear what was going on.

"What are you doing here?" Johnson asked surprised to see the man, here of all places. But then again, why should he be surprised? The Shadowman was always at least two steps ahead of him and everyone else. So why wouldn't he be here at the centre of things now that things were coming to a climax. He imagined that the man must have contacts high up in the Gardaí to have the quality of information that he always seemed to possess.

"Are you here to help me get out? Cause if you are, you nearly left it too fucking late," Johnson said indicating Callaghan's body lying sprawled out on the ground. "Come on let's get out of here".

"I was here well before you all arrived", said the Shadowman but he didn't move.

"You were here? Well why didn't you do something? She could have arrested me!"

"I knew you could get the better of her. She was too inexperienced. Anyway, I wanted you to kill her..."

The Shadowman stepped further out from the shadows and shot Johnson once in the head with his Sig Sauer P226 9mm pistol. Johnson's body spun around several times and his gun flew up into the air before he crashed face first onto the ground in front of Morgan, never to get back up again. His open dead eyes staring terrifyingly back at Morgan.

Never to see anything again.

Expecting a bullet to smash through his head at any second, Morgan painfully raised himself up onto his elbows in an effort to survey the bloody scene better. He could see a man with a bullet-proof vest on walking menacingly towards him, his gun pointed at Morgan's head. Morgan saw a strange look in his eyes and he was convinced that he was going to shoot him, but just then members of the ERU team could be heard making their way around the small church. Before he knew it, he was alone again. The man who had just shot Johnson had gone, flinging the smoking gun at Morgan's feet as he left. Disappeared into the night. But any thoughts that Morgan might have had that the ERU team was coming to his aid, were instantly displaced when they arrested him and made the scene secure.

"Put your hands up in the air", two of the heavily armed Garda ordered Morgan as they pointed their automatic weapons at him. He was left in no doubt that if he made the slightest move that he would be shot. Sitting up, he slowly raised his tired arms in the air. One of the other Gardaí pushed him back and rolled him over onto his stomach and roughly cuffed his arms behind his back. He then rested his knee on his back, pinning him painfully to the ground. As he lay there he could hear the other men, moving over towards Johnson and Callaghan's bodies lying on the ground and checking them for any vital signs.

"Dead", the first ERU team member called out as he checked Johnson's non-existent pulse. That was bloody obvious even from here, thought Morgan.

"I've got a faint pulse here," shouted his partner excitedly as he checked Garda Callaghan's pulse. He pressed a button on his throat mike and radioed back to Kennedy. "We have an officer down. We have an officer down. I need to get an ambulance up here to the Church in the south east corner immediately."

The scene became quite surreal from this point. Morgan was left with a gun pressed into his back on the ground for what seemed like an hour but for what was in reality only a few minutes. He couldn't see much as he was facing the crypt door but could hear a tremendous amount of activity and noise around him. Men running this way and that, orders being shouted sirens wailing and the helicopter making another appearance, basking the scene in an eerie light. An ambulance arrived within thirty seconds suggesting to him that it had been on standby nearby, its blue strobe lights giving the dark cemetery a disco effect. The ambulance crew made Callaghan stable and put her on a trolley before loading her into the back. The ambulance then roared off into the night, its siren wailing loudly.

Eventually he was pulled upright and stood facing a distraught DI Higgins and two other senior Gardaí. The DI seemingly unable to speak nodded towards DI Behan, who stepped forward and knelt beside Morgan saying,

"John Morgan, I am arresting you for possession of a firearm. That should be enough to hold you till we charge you with more serious crimes. You do not have to say anything but anything that you do say may be used against you in a court of law."

"I did not shoot anyone, there was another man in the woods," Morgan said looking the DI dead in the eye, before turning his head and spitting out some blood.

"We have searched the cemetery thoroughly. There was no one over here but you".

"I am telling you that there was another man", stated Morgan angrily. "You know that I would not have been here in the first place if you had done your job properly".

But the senior Garda facing him appeared unrepentant and sig-nalled for the armed Gardaí holding Morgan to drag him up and take him away. But Morgan, weakened by his injuries, only man-aged to walk a few feet before he nearly fell over, only managing to continue the rest of the way with the support of the Garda. The officers from the ERU team called the second ambulance crew on the radio to come and check on him. Within minutes they arrived but Morgan waved them off. He was not in the humour to be poked and prodded. He really just wanted to go home and lie down but he knew that was not going to happen either.

However seeing his battered body complete with blood run-ning down the side of his head and obviously broken ribs, the ambulance crew insisted that they wanted to put him on a stretcher. But Morgan still refused. As weak as he was, he wanted to walk out of here tonight.

Upright and proud.

Not lying down.

Whatever happened from now, he knew that he could hold his head up high.

He was led slowly out of the cemetery in handcuffs by one of the ERU team, only to be faced by a tearful Sinead who had turned up, unable to wait at home not knowing the outcome any longer. She managed to get by the Garda blockade, past the grow-ing crowd of onlookers and the cavalcade of emergency vehicles with their flashing lights and held out her arms to him, wanting to hug him as he was led by, tearfully asking, "Oh my God, What has happened? Are you hurt?"

But he looked her dead in the eye, leaving her in no doubt about the contempt that he felt for her. He walked straight by her without saying a word towards the unmarked Garda car.

"Look after them for me", he heard Rob's voice say.
'I did', he thought. 'I did'.

Chapter Forty-Eight

It was sometime later that Morgan woke up in a bed. This felt very strange, as he did not remember falling asleep. Initially he was not even sure he was in a bed as he was still half asleep and his mind was hazy. It certainly wasn't his bed and it did not feel like it was his bedroom. Nor was he in his little house in the hotel grounds near the beach in County Wexford.

Thinking back, the last thing that he remembered was being in the ambulance as it bounced along the road. Morgan figured that he must be in hospital. Through half closed eyes, Morgan looked around the small room. It was painted in two green tones, dark green on the bottom half, light green on top half. It was a single room with a large exterior window and another smaller one looking out into the corridor however the blind was shut so he could not see anything. The room itself was plain and cheaply furnished. There was the bed he was lying in, a cheap bedside locker, a cheap chair and a wall mounted television that was turned off. Its remote lay on the top of the locker along with a beaker of water and a glass.

He had no idea what time it was or for how long he had been unconscious, although considering it was bright out, he had to assume that he had been out at least eight hours. What had happened during these missing hours?

His whole body ached. It felt like there was not a part of him without a bruise. He used to laugh at people who said that they had aches in parts of their bodies that they never knew existed but now he knew what they meant. He tentatively touched his face with his right hand. He could feel the bandages that had been put around his nose restricting his breathing and pulling a bit tighter than was comfortable.

From the bed Morgan could hear noises, an indistinct murmur of conversation, from outside the room and he strained his ears to hear what was being said but could not make it out. Too tired to concentrate and realising that he was very thirsty, Morgan struggled to sit up in the bed so he could reach the water on top of the locker. But it was only when he went to stretch over to the locker that he realised that he was handcuffed. The handcuff dangling from his left wrist was chaining him to the sturdy metal bed frame. This helped in no small way to focus his mind and he woke up immediately. Morgan pulled on the chain of the handcuff in a vain attempt to dislodge it from the frame of the bed, until his shackled wrist ached. "Shit", he moaned, before collapsing back onto the bed.

He lay in bed for what he thought was about twenty minutes, staring at the ceiling and going over what he remembered about that night before the door creaked slowly open and Sinead stuck her head in.

"What are you doing here?" Morgan croaked, his mouth was so dry, not having managed to reach the water.

"I had to see you," she answered nervously, closing the door softly behind her.

She looked tired.

"Why?" he asked sceptically.

"Because...."

"Because, why?"

"Oh, Morgan what are we going to do?" she asked frantically.

"Was I asleep long?" he asked. He had to catch up with events.

"The doctor told me that you got agitated in the back of the ambulance and that the crew had to sedate you", Sinead said apologetically, adding ".... for your own good."

"I don't remember that, but was I asleep long?"

"Yes, for nearly twelve hours. It is just after 1pm", Sinead said as she dragged the chair over to beside the bed and sat down, hanging her coat over the end of it. She tried to hold his hand but he moved it away as far as the handcuff would allow. It wasn't far but she got the message. Don't touch. Morgan watched her as she stared at the silver chain in shock. A single tear ran down her cheek.

"How is Callaghan?" he enquired, remembering her being shot and lying covered in blood on the sloping pathway.

"She' is in surgery now but although she was hurt pretty bad, they think she will be fine."

"Thank God".

Lying there, he realised that he shouldn't be too dismissive of Sinead. Whether he liked it or not, he still needed her. Not through any sense of love or devotion for himself or loyalty toward Rob but out of practicality and necessity. If he was to walk away from all of this, they needed to get their stories straight.

"Right," he said, more business like, "Everything happened exactly as it did. The murder, the threats, us searching for the drugs but we found the drugs at Rob's old lockup alright. We contacted the female detective...."

"Her name is Callaghan".

"I know what her name is. We contacted Callaghan to help us arrange a sting on Johnson. I did not go to Smiths...."

"But...," Sinead interrupted. But Morgan was determined to finish.

"Listen to me. I did not go to the bank or to Smith's and you had no part to play in your husband's murder. Okay?"

"Right," she agreed, sounding unconvinced.

Just then DI Higgins and DI Behan walked in accompanied by one of the heavily armed Gardaí. Other armed Gardaí wearing their body armour and helmets, with guns to the ready were clearly visible outside the door.

"What the fuck is she doing in here?" DI Higgins turned and demanded of the uniformed Gardaí. "I thought I ordered that he was to receive no visitors until I got here".

"I'm sorry sir, she must have gotten in when I went to the toilet," stammered the Gardaí apologetically.

"Idiot. I'll deal with you later," Higgins snapped back at him, before turning his attention on Sinead. "Since you're here, you might as well come with us down to the station to answer some questions". He turned back towards the negligent Garda once again. "Do you think that you could bring her down to the car or would that be too much responsibility?"

"No sir," the man replied meekly.

Sinead picked up her coat and patted Morgan on the arm before being led out of the room. She gave him one last glance over her shoulder before the door shut. Both of the senior detectives remained silent until she had left the room before starting to ask Morgan questions.

"What happened last night?" The DI demanded bluntly.

"I telephoned Garda Callaghan and told her what was happening. I told her that I had found the drugs and was meeting up with Johnson to exchange them at Rob's graveside. I asked her to meet me at the cemetery at midnight and to bring the cavalry. That was it, I figure you were late".

"Who were the three armed men that ambush you"?

"I don't know. I had never seen them before. They appeared out of nowhere.".

"What were they after?"

"The drugs. They went straight for them. Then you lot turned up and world war three started and I took the opportunity to escape".

"What were you getting in this exchange for the drugs?"

"Johnson promised to lay off of Sinead and her kids. You remember the threat that we told you lot about which you decided to ignore".

"Don't come all high and mighty with me. This is a serious matter. Now where did you find the drugs?"

"At Rob's old lockup, just inside the door. I literally fell over them when I went in. It's a pity none of you thought of looking there".

"We were following a definite line of enquiry. You should have left it up to us".

"Well I had to do something since you seemed so uninterested the day we asked you for help. Her children were in danger and you did nothing," Morgan spat at him. "You left me with no choice".

"Don't get smart with me you little shit. I have a close colleague undergoing an operation in an attempt to save her lifer", The DI spat through gritted teeth. "I have another member of the ERU team injured and I have three dead men still lying around Deansgrange Cemetery, waiting for the medical examiner to finish with them. And then I have you. Lying here, happy as Larry, pretending he has saved the whole fucking world. Well, let me take that grin off your face for you. You're in a lot of trouble and you'd better start talking".

"Don't start on me. If you had listened to us the other day, none of this would have happened. I am really sorry that Callaghan and the other policeman got injured but if you had gotten there on time, none of this would have happened. If you ask me the only people messing up here are you lot. So get the fuck off my back," Morgan retorted strongly, he did not want to lie down and let them walk all over him.

"I am not convinced about your version of events. There are a lot of unanswered questions. Why did you contact Garda Callaghan? Why not ring the station directly and speak to someone more senior?" the DI said.

"She gave me her card the day she was called up to Sinead's house. And unlike you we thought she cared about what was happening to the children."

"What else did you tell her?" the DI asked suspiciously. The story just didn't seem to add up. It didn't feel right to him. Morgan was lying, he was convinced of it. But he would get it out of the smug bastard yet.

"I told her the time and place of the handover that's all. If you don't believe me, why don't you ask her?" Morgan said with a sneer.

"Oh, don't you worry we will. We will be having a good chat about you as soon as she wakes up".

"You do that".

"Where were you earlier tonight, say around six, seven o'clock?" the DI enquired.

"I was at Sinead's mother's house desperately trying to come up with a plan to help save her kids from a group of desperate drug dealers. Why, where were you?"

"Well your old boss, Smith was involved in an altercation in the neighbourhood where he lived. He turned up dead in a building site shortly afterwards".

"What, Smith is dead?" Morgan mocked surprise. "How?"

"Yes, he was found impaled on some scaffolding. A very nasty way to go. Do you know anything about how he got there?"

"No, should I?"

"Do you own a gun or did you have a gun with you tonight?"

"No, I don't have a gun. I hate them," Morgan said.

"A gun was found at the cemetery, it is the same calibre and a likely match to bullet casings found at the scene."

"Good for you," Morgan said mockingly. "It must have been brought by Johnson. You'll have solved two crimes in one go. I'm sure that you will get extra brownie points with the Garda Commissioner for figuring it out".

"If gunshot residue is found on your clothes, it will tie you to the scene".

"There was gunfire everywhere around me tonight. There was so much noise and smoke I couldn't think or see. So I figure that my clothes, hair and everything else are covered in gun smoke. Don't you think?"

DI Higgins just stared at Morgan as he tried to understand him. They both knew that there was more to the night's events than Morgan was telling. But he wasn't worried. Forensics would tell him everything regardless of the bullshit that was coming out of Morgan's mouth right now.

"Well, the doctors say that you are in good enough shape to be moved, so we will be continuing this more formally down at the station", Higgins informed Morgan and nodded his head at DI Behan.

Behan, who had been standing quietly to one side, stepped forward. "John Morgan, I am arresting you under Section Thirty of the Offences against the State Act 1939 in relation to the shooting of a member of An Garda Siochana. You are not obliged to say anything unless you wish to do so, but whatever you say will be taken down in writing and may be given in evidence. Do you understand?"

But Morgan did not answer. He just stared back at the DI.

"Do you understand your rights as I have read them to you?" Behan asked.

But still Morgan remained silent.

"Alright, I will take that as a yes then", DI Behan said dismissively. He had no time for Morgan's games.

"I want to call my solicitor."

"You can down at the station. Right lads, take him away", Behan said indicating to the two armed Gardaí standing at the door.

They took the handcuffs off and handed Morgan a lime green hospital dressing gown and a pair of hospital slippers. "Here put these on," he was ordered gruffly.

"I am not wearing these. Where are my clothes?"

"They have been taken away for forensic analysis," answered DI Higgins, barely able to contain his rage.

Morgan painfully put on the gown and slippers before he was unceremoniously led out of the room. The hospital was a hive of activity but everyone fell into a hushed silence as he was led out.

Nurses, doctors, porters and patients, in fact everyone stopped to have a look at him as he was led past. As soon as he had passed, the conversation started up again, louder than ever. Who was he and what had he done? They asked.

Outside numerous reporters working on tip offs were waiting for Morgan to appear and the camera flashes blinded him. As he was marched out, he didn't try and hide his face. He had no reason to. He had done nothing wrong in the cemetery that night. Questions were hurled both at him and the arresting Gardaí but everyone remained silent as Morgan was put into the back of an unmarked car waiting at the main entrance. His car formed part of a cavalcade of cars that raced out of St. Vincent's Hospital towards Harcourt Street Garda station, lights flashing.

At the station the desk sergeant had logged Morgan's details and another Garda had taken his fingerprints and a swab from his mouth for DNA. He was then asked the same questions over and over again by a rotating team of senior detectives. His solicitor arrived less than an hour later and made them stop for a while so that he could get some rest and get a cup of tea before resuming. She was fantastic and fought them on every question that they asked.

With the approval of the Chief Superintendent, DI Higgins arranged a twenty-four hour extension on Morgan's detention to allow for further questioning. But although he was questioned over and over again, they could get no more out of him. DI Higgins was going to apply for more time but eventually at the behest of Morgan's solicitor, they let him go, as according to her they did not have enough direct physical evidence to hold him there any longer. It was three pm on Saturday afternoon when Morgan finally left the station on station bail. A file was being sent to the Director of Public Prosecutions and further charges were pending, according to the DI.

His solicitor drove him home to his mother's house, stopping off at a chemist on the way so that he could fill his prescription for a bottle of pain killers and pick up a bottle of Paddy whiskey to help wash them down with. Morgan took a good draught from both bottles and fell into bed shortly afterwards, completely unconscious.

Chapter Forty-Nine

It was two weeks later when Morgan pulled the curtain to one side and peered out of his second floor bedroom window, looking out at the dull January weather outside. There was no sign of life out as anyone with any sense was firmly camped beside their fires. The group of waiting reporters and photographers who had amassed outside the County Wexford house on his first day back had dwindled to just one, who sat forlornly in his car in the car park at the rear, eating sandwiches and drinking semi-cold tea from a flask. He was still one too many for Morgan's liking, but after another day even he had left, leaving Morgan to his thoughts.

Morgan had left the Dublin Garda station and collected his car from outside Pauline's house and returned to Wexford. Despite protestations from his mother and sister, he insisted on driving home himself. While he was delighted to get some peace and quiet, the drive home was slow and his injuries made it difficult to relax. The reporters had followed him and kept him under virtual house arrest for days, many of them the very same reporters who had branded him a hero after he had rescued the youngest members of the Muller family from Neo-Nazi kidnappers. But now they were here for other reasons. He was the villain not the hero. A target to be shot down from the lofty heights they had raised him to. He didn't care what they thought, nor mind initially that they were there as he wasn't up to much anyway but he quickly got sick of it. Despite the weather, he wanted to get out and go for a walk along the beach and get some fresh air but they made it impossible.

Morgan had nearly recovered from the injuries of that hectic Thursday night but his initial detention followed by the high level of press attention meant, that he was not able to go back to work either as a doorman nor as the hotels maintenance man and he was starting to get cabin fever. In fact over the past few days, the only time that he had been out of the house was go back up to Dublin to be interviewed again in the Harcourt Street Garda station. They had asked the same questions over and over until he did not know whether he was coming or going. But he stuck rigidly to his story despite their best efforts. The detectives would eventually give up only to call him back in for another day. His solicitor, a woman he had briefly dated before his engagement to Eimear was consistently brilliant in his defence. She was doing her best to keep the Garda at arm's length, constantly informing them of his heroic actions, glazing over his part in others. He would have been lost without her.

She had demanded that they turn up some actual physical evidence because as far as she could tell they had nothing against Morgan. Her client had to go out on a limb to resolve the threats against his friend's widow himself after a failure of duty on behalf of the Garda Siochana, a matter that she would be bringing to the attention of the Garda Ombudsman at the earliest opportunity. She laid out Morgan's case brilliantly, stating quite correctly that after Morgan found the missing drugs he then informed a member of the force of his actions and put himself in harm's way to set up a sting operation to help apprehend dangerous wanted criminals. He should be considered a hero, not a target of the investigation. So she had thrown down a gauntlet to the Gardaí, either charge Morgan or let him go. As far as they were concerned, this investigation was in its early days and was not over by a long chalk. He would be interviewed as many times as they felt it necessary. But his solicitor wasn't going to let it go at that and she had also written to the Garda Ombudsman requesting an internal investigation into the handling of the matter. In her opinion, the actions of the investigating officers had put her client and others at serious risk. Heads would role if she had her way.

The interviews were very tense occasions but things were eventually starting to go Morgan's way. The forensics on his borrowed clothes only showed his presence at the cemetery and nowhere else. His DNA however was all over Smith's house. But as a regular visitor that was easily explained away. His own tell-tale clothing that he had worn during the ordeal with Smith had been destroyed in the fireplace in Pauline's house and therefore couldn't be tested. The forensics from the building site were inconclusive, as apart from all the dust and rubble lying around, the Gardaí searching the site had clumsily disturbed the scene, tainting any evidence left around. So far so good, Morgan thought after yet another one of his meetings with his solicitor. He might yet just walk away from this. After the last interview, the Gardaí told him that they were going to send a file to the Director of Public Prosecutions, the DPP. But Morgan could see the look in their eyes, especially those of DI Higgins, that they were out for him regardless of what the DPP decided.

So far Sinead on the other hand was only summoned the once by the Gardaí to be questioned and Morgan's solicitor had sent someone from her office to represent her. Sinead's future lay in the balance as well, so apparently she kept rigidly to the story. She had attempted to contact Morgan on his mobile phone several times but he refused to answer it. He just let it ring out and deleted the messages left without listening to them. He wanted nothing more to do with her.

Not now.

Not ever.

The gunfight at the cemetery as the media had renamed it had reopened the debate on whether Gardaí should be armed or not. There had been a lot of negative controversy about the handling of the Garda operation at the cemetery, which had left three men dead and two Gardaí injured. Separate to an enquiry into the wider handling of the entire investigation as requested by Morgan's solicitor, The Garda Ombudsman had launched a separate inquiry into the circumstances surrounding the shooting of two Garda officers. As yet Morgan wasn't aware of any time frame for publishing their conclusions. As far as he was concerned, men had died simply because no one had listened.

The night of the gunfight, Callaghan had to have a three hour long emergency operation to repair the wound to her shoulder. Her family, friends and colleagues kept a round the clock vigil for her. Cards and flowers were poured into the intensive care unit from well-wishers. Even the President had publicly expressed her concern for Callaghan's well-being and recovery. DI Higgin's checked in hourly with the hospital to see if there had been any improvement, as they badly needed to get a statement from Callaghan. After days of waiting, a long time in an investigation like this, Callaghan finally stirred, waking for a few minutes before falling asleep again. She repeated this waking sleeping routine for a few hours before regaining a more normal sleep pattern.

Although her memory of the night was patchy which apparently was a common occurrence with people suffering from gunshot wounds, the first thing that she said under gentle questioning largely backed up Morgan's story.

The sole surviving Polish gang member had refused to talk and as far as Morgan was aware was still sitting silently in his prison cell, awaiting trial and presumably a long prison sentence followed by deportation. The thin man with Johnson had somehow managed to escape from the cemetery and was still on the run.

As he was largely house bound in those first few weeks, Morgan had a lot of time on his hands to think about that night. Despite learning a lot more about the night through the questions being asked at the interviews, he was still unsure about what exactly happened. Who were the Polish gunmen and where did they come from? How did they know about the drop off? The Gardaí still didn't know that for sure. DI Behan during the interviews was adamant that Morgan must have tipped them off. But that was ridiculous. He had never heard of them before that night. But it had occurred to him that someone had tipped these men off. Since it wasn't him, who?

Another question that nobody seemed able to answer was why Callaghan was allowed to be in the cemetery on her own considering her level of experience? She had apparently become separated from DI Behan during the gunfight and had stumbled onto Johnson and Morgan as they had fought it out.

But none of that was as confusing as what had happened to Johnson. Although he couldn't see properly as the blow to the head had stunned him, as far as Morgan could remember, Johnson was in no position to escape, so why had he been shot? And who had shot him? Had someone set out deliberately to kill him? And if so why weren't they themselves captured? God knows there were enough Gardaí present to arrest half of Dublin.

No, it was clear to Morgan that other forces were at play that night, forces whose motives weren't yet clear to him. But what did that mean for him in the future? Was this really over? He kept pondering the consequences but never reached a conclusion. So not having any control over these unknowns, he decided to just go with it. He wasn't the wallflower type and he would meet them head on, when and if anything ever happened.

So, unsure of what to do next, he spent his first few days confined to his house by the reporters and kept a low profile. Along with practising his guitar, he watched a lot of old movies and children's cartoons on television. His only visitors to his County Wexford retreat were members of the Muller family. They came over from the Hotel bringing him food and good conversation. On his last visit, Alfred Muller asked him to come over to the hotel on the following Friday as they were having a big band night to raise money for the local cancer support charity.

"You must come along, the whole family will be there", Alfred said.

"I will try," answered Morgan trying not to make a commitment.

"No, I won't accept that. I want your promise that you will come along. We all will be disappointed if you don't".

"Fine I will, I promise. Anything to shut you up", Morgan mocked. And I never break a promise.

Epilogue

The Shadowman stood in the comparative warmth of inter-view room number two in one of the six regional Garda headquarters and waited patiently for the phone to be answered. He didn't have to wait long. Which was good. He was due to give a lengthy statement about recent events to senior members of the force but he wasn't worried about giving his account of events. Although as anyone under investigation was entitled to, he hadn't even bothered bringing along any legal counsel. This investigation would amount to nothing. It was merely a distraction from his otherwise busy schedule. But he did find himself with a schedul-ing conflict.

For security purposes, all calls to his boss were always from a specific pre-paid phone at a specific time. He was not allowed to deviate from this. Such lapses in protocol had resulted in other associates getting beaten up or legs broken. Or worse. His Spanish based employer's rules were not for breaking. Therefore, he simply had to make this pre-arranged call. He couldn't avoid it. But he couldn't avoid this meeting either. So he had to make it quick before they came for him. After checking that the recording equipment in the corner was turned off, he checked that the door was closed tightly and rang the single pre-programmed number.

"Hello," came the voice from the much warmer climes in Spain.

"It's me", said the Shadowman depending on the person at the other end to recognise his voice and make any introduction unnecessary. Both men would be very careful to make sure that no names were mentioned. They used no words like guns, kill or drugs that might trigger any call interceptor or phone surveillance systems operating as part of the data retention directive. And con-sidering his present location, the Shadowman was particularly careful not be overheard saying anything incriminating.

The walls have ears after all.

"Well, is it done?"

"Yes. There are one or two potential loose ends but I am going to sort them out permanently very soon".

"Good. I was starting to wonder about whether you had the balls for this or not".

"Well, now you know", said the Shadowman defiantly. Any doubts about his ability should have been washed away for good.

"And my missing stock?"

"Unfortunately, I couldn't get that back. But your old colleagues are no longer with us and the competition that you were concerned about is firmly out of the picture".

"Good, good. I think that this is the perfect opportunity to start afresh. I want you to come and meet me in the UK, where we will discuss my expansion plans."

"Are you chasing a bigger distribution area?"

"Yes always, but I have decided that we are branching out into more diverse products", the man said like a businessman planning to introduce a new range of office furniture.

"Sounds interesting. Can you give me a clue?"

"Yes, people. You seem like a real people person so that's what we are doing; we are going into the people business. We are going to start importing them immediately," said the voice, laughing at his own joke.

"That's a hard business to break into", the Shadowman commented as he thought of the implications.

"It is, but I think you're up to it, however I am sending you a few skilled men to assist you".

"That would be useful". More than useful as the Shadowman thought of his competition in the human trafficking business.

"I hope that you are going to make this a year to remember for me".

"I will. Trust me nobody is ever going to forget this year".

"Good. Meet me in a week and we will go over the details," said his Spanish based employer before hanging up.

The Shadowman was both worried and excited at the same time about the possibilities presented to him. He patted his chest and felt the single hard metal cylindrical case containing the Bolivar cigar. He didn't normally smoke, but he did allow the odd celebratory puff on an expensive cigar. He found cigarettes and the whole idea of taking quick drags generally disgusting but loved to savour the flavour of a strong full-bodied cigar. But as he was savouring the possibility of opening the miniature case and smelling the rich texture, the door opened with a flourish and a uniformed Garda poked his head in.

"Oh, Sorry I didn't mean to disturb you DI Behan, but the Assistant Commissioner is waiting for you in the incident room".

"Right then, lead the way," he said smiling. The cigar would have to wait. But not for long.

To be continued...

Paperback
(10/2011 – 246 pages)

eBook
(02/2013 – ePub & Mobi-Kindle)

Available –
through your local bookstore or
online at www.publishedinireland.com

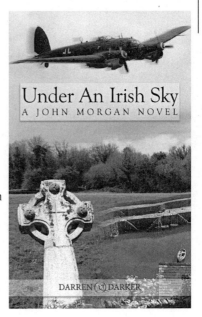

Under An Irish Sky
A JOHN MORGAN NOVEL

DARREN DARKER

It was November 1943 and a German Heinkel bomber limped over the Irish coastline. In high winds the pilots struggled valiantly to control the badly damaged plane but it was futile. Just as the plane crashed down onto Irish soil, a terrified Karl Muller looked back at the wooden box emblazoned with a swastika that was strapped down in the rear and wondered was it worth it?

John Morgan is an everyday Irish guy in his early thirties, who is has just lost his fiancée in a tragic accident. Unable to cope with her death, he leaves their Dublin house to stay in his aunt's holiday home in County Wexford to give himself the opportunity to re-build his life. In this idyllic seaside setting, not only does he find the peace that he is desperately seeking, he also finds new friends in the Muller's, the larger than life family who own the local hotel.

But one weekend all of their lives get turned upside down as Muller's past finally catches up with him in the most violent way possible. With the lives of Karl Muller's granddaughter and great grandson at risk from modern day neo-Nazi's they call on the only person that they trust to save them. But is Morgan already sixty years too late?

The first in a riveting new series of novels – Under An Irish Sky introduces John Morgan a new hero to thrill readers of all ages.

Designed, typeset, printed and bound in Ireland by

PubliBook Ireland
www.publibookireland.com